the Key to Time
Book One

R.M. SEIDLER

This is a work of fiction. Names, characters, places, and incidents are either the product of the author's imagination or are used fictitiously. Any resemblance to actual persons living or dead, business establishments, events, or locales is entirely coincidental.

The Key to Time

First edition: February 2017

ISBN: 978-0-9983624-0-3

ISBN (eBook): 978-0-9983624-1-0

To my grandmother for always believing in me...
...and to Helen, first chair cheerleader.

Contents

~the Oakley Grounds

Wild Woods

Polo / Game Field

the Timepiece

the Cliffs

Stables

waterfall

Learners Citidale

Oakley Main Hall

horse trail

SCHOOL BOUNDRY

to NEFS landings

~to the town of Oakdale~

N

W

E

S

CHAPTER ONE

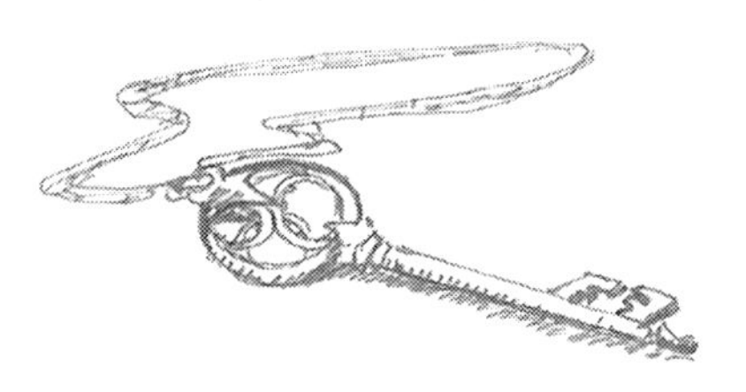

FOSTERS AND ORPHANS

Sharp knees pressed into Quincy's arms, stopping her from thrashing in the sheets of her bed. Before she could scream a second time, a pillow smothered her face suffocating her. Survival instinct kicked in and she fought against her attacker by throwing her weight to the right and forcing her and the assailant to the cold floor. The pillow fell away, allowing oxygen to her head, but the short-lived relief ended with a grimy hand covering her mouth.

"Scream again and I'll end you." Amanda hissed, the bully's breath hot against her skin. Quincy trembled in her grasp, but remained silent. "Tomorrow when you least expect it, I'll grab you and you'll never scream again. No one'll know and no one'll miss you."

"Don't make me come in there," an angry voiced called from outside the door.

None of the girls in the crammed bedroom moved until the hall monitor shuffled away from the door.

Quincy's body shook underneath the older girl's now even-tighter grasp. Amanda waited for Quincy to nod before releasing her. Quincy clenched her fists as Amanda leaned in close to her ear and whispered, "I'm not gonna have detention again because of your stupid nightmares and breaking the peace." She pointed a finger at Quincy's nose. "'Specially not from some No-Talent kid like you."

Quincy narrowed her eyes at the insult but said nothing as the older girl slinked off toward her own bed. If she had the same nightmares of falling into never-ending pits of darkness, a creepy man dressed in burgundy watching her descent with hooded eyes, then she'd never be so mean. Quincy slid under her blanket, covering her face as she tried to hide from the gaze of nineteen sets of resentful eyes. All twenty girls had already had detention this week, wasting two hours of their precious free time because of Quincy's night terrors. Her scream had brought the night watchman to the group home, opening an investigation into her well-being. After the unfortunate incident, Miss Heatherwood had decided that all the girls should be held accountable for Quincy's nightmares, probably hoping that peer pressure would work its magic.

It obviously hadn't worked.

Quincy waited until she heard quiet snores and deep breathing from the other girls, then pulled the covers away from her mouth. She closed her eyes and began to drift back to sleep herself.

She was walking down an empty street. It was a ghost town with the boarded street fronts, garbage strewn about, and the lone abandoned tricycle lying on its side in the middle of the road. She shivered, forcing herself to keep moving. The hairs on her neck stood straight up as the illusion of solitude disappeared by the quiet crunch of footsteps on the cobblestoned street behind her. A sinister laugh echoed in the street hurrying her along. Glancing to her side she searched out a sliver of uncovered glass in a shop window. The window reflected a man close behind her. She couldn't see his face, but she could distinguish his burgundy suit. She trembled at the sight of the familiar clothing.

He laughed mockingly at her, and with a burst of courage, she backed up into an empty doorway to face the man. But no one was there.

"Where are you hiding it, little girl?" a voice purred in her ear.

The grandfather clock in the hall struck six times, startling Quincy awake. She gasped and tried to slow her heavy breathing. She hadn't been asleep long, but there was no way she could go back to bed now. It wasn't worth risking a third nightmare. Instead, she tiptoed to her trunk at the end of her bed. She slowly opened the lid, wary of its squeaky hinges. She reached in for the rosewood box of intricately woven silver vines and leaves that she'd safely tucked between an unraveling brown sweater and her bath towel. She looked down and wished that she could turn the music dial at the bottom of the box. By closing her eyes she could almost see her parents dance to the tune late at night when she had been watching them instead of being asleep in bed.

The green velvet lining inside the music box housed a handful of memories, including a key on a silver chain. She looked at the faded daisy necklace that her younger sister, Emily, had made right before she'd died, as well as the dried rose from her and their father's funeral. She gently touched a flower from the necklace, and she was flooded with images, of their garden, and the tinkling of her sister's contagious giggles while they played hide and seek.

She pulled out the key by its chain and rubbed the cold metal between her fingers. The key's eye had been cut into different-sized jagged circles, like gears from some kind of mechanism. The key was—no, *is* her mother's. She wished she knew what it was for and why her mother had worn it every day. She'd even been wearing it when they had hospitalized her. Now, her mother, who had been so beautiful and vibrant in life, was stuck in the horrible place between living and dead. Even when she had opened her eyes two months after the accident, her mind had never awakened. Quincy was only planning to hold on to the key until her mother was finally well enough to ask for it back.

Quincy wiped her blurry eyes with the sleeve of her nightgown and closed the lid the music box. She placed it back inside the trunk, next to a worn sketchbook and broken pencils. She tiptoed to the window at the end of the room and sat down, grimacing at the cold that was seeping in through the glass but she huddled closer anyway, pressing her face against the window and peering outside at the street below. In the otherwise-deserted street, a stray cat hunted for its breakfast and the night watchman ambled his way home.

Finally, the tears that had threatened to materialize earlier—both for her mother and for her own circumstance—rolled down her cheeks, leaving watery streaks on the glass. Even after three years it still stung when Amanda used the belittling nickname she'd given Quincy, and she could hear it now, echoing in her ears. Amanda had dubbed her a "No-Talent"—a cruel term for a person whose Talent had not manifested by the age of ten—on Quincy's first day at the group house, and the bully hadn't let up on it since.

Quincy looked over her shoulder at her sleeping roommates, jealously burning through her. Jane could mimic any sound, Morgan could name every cooking ingredient in any food or drink she tasted, and Maggie could hum any music note in perfect pitch. Quincy would have liked to have that Talent, since music was not one of her strongest skills. But at this point she would have been happy with *any* Talent. Few people's Talents were discovered after fifteen. Quincy had been fifteen for over a month, and she was still Talentless.

She returned her gaze to the window, wishing that it hadn't been plastered shut so that she could jump out. In less than half an hour, this same sleepy street would be teeming with life and she could join them and disappear into the crowd. With the highest-class carriages pulled by well-tended horses and the refuse of the world all using the same street to enter Albany's city center, she would never stand out. No one would ever have to know that she didn't have a Talent.

A moving object high above in the corner of her vision, turned her attention to the brightening sky. She wiped her tears and smiled, despite her distress. In the distance, an eagle soared to its destination. The magnificent bird could easily transport eighteen people to any of the larger cities across the world. Quincy wondered if this particular eagle flew south toward New York City. She closed her eyes, remembering her first trip by eagle ten years ago. She hoped that she would experience another eagle ride one day.

She sighed and turned back to the gritty room, watching the girls in their slumber. Even after living at Miss Heatherwood's for so long, Quincy still wondered about her classmates' pasts. Not that it really mattered, because no matter who they were or where they had come from, they had all ended up at the same place: Miss Heatherwood's Home for Boys and Girls.

The youngest girl, Anna, whimpered quietly in her sleep. The tiny girl had only been at Miss Heatherwood's for six months, but at eight years old—the same age Emily had been when she'd died—Anna wasn't likely to be adopted. Just like the rest of them.

Anna sniffed, her eyes shut tightly, stuck in a nightmare of her own. Quincy wondered if the court counselor had told Anna the same thing that she had told Quincy when she first arrived at the group home. That nightmares were not unusual and would go away with time. The counselor had lied though. Night after night, Quincy never stopped having them.

Shivering, she reminded herself that the nightmares were simply a creation of her own mind. She looked out the window again and sucked in her breath. She saw a flash of red outside, and for a moment, it reminded her of the man in burgundy. Even when she was fully awake, the voice, which she presumed to be his, turned her stomach as if she'd eaten something sickly sweet.

Where are you hiding it? the voice suddenly whispered in her ear.

She whirled around but saw no one awake in the room. She rubbed the goose bumps on her arms as she remembered the dream man's favorite mantra.

I will find you. The predator always finds its prey.

The grandfather clock rang out the time. Six thirty, Quincy thought grimly to herself. She was thankful to leave her nightmare behind, but whether she wanted to or not, it was time to face the new day.

***

Half an hour later, after hearing the shrill warning whistle, all twenty girls stood next to their beds for inspection. Quincy looked down at her skirt and grimaced. She had grown during the summer and it needed to be taken out. She tried to smooth the particularly hideous blue-and-yellow plaid wool, but it refused to comply. Every time she sat down, the clothes seemed to stick in that same position as when she stood up. Mechanically, she followed the girl next to her out the door and down the stairs.

Quincy forced herself not to make eye contact with the school monitor, who the foster kids called "The Crone." The Crone rarely spoke more than a handful of words the most common one being *quiet*. Instead, out of habit, Quincy looked at the plaque nailed to the top of the staircase that read, *Children who are late... We simply will not tolerate*. Familiar with the consequence of watching while the others ate, or worse, a beating from the dreaded Death Strike, Quincy had not been late since her first week at Miss Heatherwoods.

The students shuffled down the stairs to the first floor of the three levels that made up the group house. Quincy touched the corner of the once-beautiful banister that had cracked and then been shoddily repaired two years ago. The building had been repurposed for wards of the state, but originally, it had been a chic boarding house in Albany's glory days. The wood paneling on the walls of the building must have been expensive ebony but now chunks of the decorative engravings inside the panels had fallen down, leaving gaps in the walls. Quincy walked into the musty dining room and took her place standing behind her place on the long bench in front of the girls table. Jane took her place on the opposite side of the bench, across from Quincy, and yawned. The clock in the foyer chimed the seven-o'clock hour and Quincy looked around to see if everyone had made it in time. Unfortunately, Thomas slid in just after the last clang.

Before Miss Heatherwood even walked into the room, her perfume permeated the air, reminding Quincy of a sterile hospital room. Her cheeks were smooth where there should have been laugh lines and she had wrinkles on her forehead from all her frowning. Her gray hair was pulled back into a high tight bun, and the pitch of her voice sent chills down Quincy's spine. Miss Heatherwood walked over to her seat in the center of the room and sat down. "Mr. Thomas. You are late."

Thomas gulped and backed away from his seat to the corner of the room.

"The rest of you, sit."

Everyone sat down and waited for the kitchen staff to serve while Thomas looked hungrily on.

"Never forget that food is power, children. Don't be late."

Miss Heatherwood took the first bite, indicating that the rest of them could begin to quietly slurp their morning mush. Quincy shared a grimace with another boy across the room as they ate the crunchy breakfast that hadn't been cooked enough. She searched for the one small piece of fresh fruit placed inside that fulfilled the state requirement of one serving per meal.

She looked around the dining room as she pushed her food around in her bowl. Her eyes passed over the timeworn portraits of six people who no one remembered, or could name, and she tried to catch a faint glimmer of sunlight through the moisture covering the old windows. Her gaze drifted towards the end of her table and she bit her lip as she stared into the cold eyes of Amanda. Feeling a stab of fear in her chest, Quincy mentally kicked herself for being scared. Amanda fed off of fear, smelling it like a bloodhound. How were you supposed to hide from a bully whose Talent meant she knew when you were scared? Amanda, whose Talent had revealed itself at seven year old, used it to her advantage to rule over the other kids. Amanda had few pleasures in her life, but bullying kids and reminding Quincy of her lack of Talent were her obvious favorites. She never let Quincy forget that there wasn't anything special about her. She was only another unwanted foster child lost in the system.

As Quincy focused on her breakfast again, a high-pitched squeal broke the eerily silent meal. Everyone froze and looked at the girl's table where at the unfortunate Anna had placed her feet on her bench and was rubbing her knee. She stared in confusion at Amanda sitting across from her. Anna's shoulders began to shake when she realized what she'd just done. Children were not allowed to utter a word during meal times except for a mumbled thank-you to the kitchen attendants handing out food.

Quincy bit her lip, watching Miss Heatherwood's reaction. The foster mistress had already reached behind her and pulled a whip, nicknamed 'the Death Strike,' off the wall. Standing up, Miss Heatherwood motioned the scared little girl toward her. Even though this was Anna's first punishment with the Death Strike, the small girl had seen it doled out enough times that she knew what was expected of her. Anna faced the rest of her foster siblings and bent down to touch her toes.

Miss Heatherwood's lips curled into something between a grimace and a demented smile. Quincy averted her eyes, not wanting to watch. She had been taught that it was wrong to hate anyone but she made a special exception for school's matron who took a sick pleasure in punishing children.

The whip whistled through the air and then landed on Anna's backside with a *crack*. Quincy squeezed her eyes shut as the sound came again and again. After the final whip, Anna limped back to her seat. She grimaced as she sat down, knowing well enough not to look at Amanda. Quincy's jaw tightened and she wished that she could make time go faster.

***

The clock noted their release to the main hall where they would all search today's chore list for their names. Quincy's heart quickened as a hand grabbed her collar and pulled her aside. Her nightmare still felt fresh, she half expected to meet her nightmare man.

"You're lucky you don't sit at my end of the table at breakfast." Amanda stated, looking over at Anna as the girl rubbed her backside. Bending down to Quincy's ear, she whispered, "That shoulda been you."

Quincy clenched her fists and ducked behind another kid. She looked up at the chore list labeled with today's date and groaned. It was August 15th, Amanda's sixteenth birthday, and because she wouldn't have any special recognition or treatment, the bully would be making all her foster siblings especially miserable.

"That's right. Run away," she hissed. "You can try and call for your mommy," Amanda's lips stuck out her bottom lip in a fake pout. "But it's too bad she can't hear you."

Quincy ground her teeth until she felt a sharp pain in her jaw. She needed to hold her tongue. She would only make herself a bigger target if she fought back.

"I dare you to try and hide. You know I'll just find you later," Amanda hissed in Quincy's general direction. Before she could say anything further, the Crone waved a dreaded yellow slip at Amanda's direction.

Amanda's face fell and skulked after the Crone. Quincy's shoulders sagged in relief. Thank goodness she was assigned to different chores than the school bully, and she would even get a short respite from that, given she had a private meeting with the court counselor today. She just had to stay invisible for the next few hours.

***

Quincy wasn't listening as she watched the counselor talk. Her mind was more interested in trying to decide whether or not she would have time left of her half-hour of free time to visit the stable today and enjoy what was left of the summer weather. She quickly crossed off that idea remembering that today was the stable master's day off. She liked Cigfran, and they'd become almost like friends over the past three years. It was always harder to get through the day when he was away.

"Miss Harris, are you even listening to me?"

Quincy's eyes refocused and she mechanically nodded.

The counselor sighed. "With these budget cuts, I only have ten minutes with you four times a year. We must make this time count."

Quincy continued to nod.

"Okay?"

When Quincy said nothing, the counselor frowned. "This is why you have difficulties making friends here. Your foster siblings construe your silence as snobbery. It's difficult enough that they're envious of your background. Most of these children here haven't even met their real parents, much less lived with them for as long as you did."

When Quincy remained silent, the woman grudgingly continued. "Meanwhile, the adults in your life—me for example—find it rude or think that you're scheming for trouble. Are you looking for trouble, Miss Quincy?"

"No, ma'am."

The court counselor gave her a satisfied smile. "Now let's take a peek at your file. You turned fifteen in July, it seems. Congratulations."

Quincy grimaced at the memory of her horrible birthday. Miss Heatherwood had refused to let her visit her mother at her care home.

"Good grades, little disciplinary action...Are you still having nightmares?"

Quincy nodded. The counselor looked up from the file and frowned.

"Yes, I'm still having nightmares," Quincy reluctantly confirmed.

"Has your Talent surfaced yet? Have you started speaking any new languages? Found that you have perfect pitch? Found a cure for the common cold?"

"Not that I know of," Quincy automatically answered as if she had been asked if she had any known allergies.

"Last time we spoke you were enjoying drawing. Any potential Talent there?"

Quincy had seen paintings made by individuals who had art as a Talent. The pictures felt alive, and the content incited deep emotion in everyone who stared at the scene. Her sketches certainly didn't fall under that category.

"They're not anything special," Quincy finally admitted. "But I am still enjoying it."

The court counselor tutted. "Oh well, not that it matters now. Have you chosen a discipline?"

"Education," she nonchalantly answered.

The counselor pursed her lips as if trying to hide her frustration.

"Sweetheart, I know that up until…the accident, you were preparing to attend Oakley Academy. I'm sorry, but you don't have the money to go. Besides, why would you want to go to a Talent school when you don't have a Talent?"

Quincy narrowed her eyes at the counselor.

"I mean that your Talent hasn't surfaced, and you know that you can't apply for a scholarship without one."

Quincy's throat tightened and her eyes burned. She was supposed to go to Oakley. Just as both of her parents had.

"So that brings us back to my question. Now that you are fifteen, what discipline are you going to choose?"

"Stable groom," she whispered. At this point, it felt like the lesser evil than her other options.

All fifteen-year-olds were sent to higher education or trade school, but Quincy, like her foster siblings, didn't have the luxury of choice. Living at Miss Heatherwood's meant that Quincy had four trades to pick from: a kitchen worker, a stable groom, classroom attendant, or a governess.

"Could I go to another trade school? Anywhere?"

"No, I'm sorry. The court has assigned you here. And you just don't have the money to board yourself elsewhere."

Quincy bit her lip in frustration. "But only half of my money is needed for my mother's health bills. Why can't the court give me the rest now? It's my family's money, isn't it?"

"No, it's being held for you until you turn eighteen."

"But—"

"No. That's how it's done. Now I'm writing you down for stable groom. You should take advantage of this beautiful day. Now off you go."

***

Quincy escaped the building and sighed in relief as she felt the sun on her face and breathed in the crisp air. Rarely did the sun shine through the seemingly permanent cloud of smog in the outskirts of Albany. She walked toward the fruitless berry bushes near the property's fence, but paused when she saw three of the other kids talking. She stood behind a tree and slid down to its base.

"Shh, I think I hear someone coming. What if it's Amanda?" Maggie hissed.

"It can't be Amanda. She's in an adoption meeting," Jane answered.

"Oh good. We don't need another excuse for her to freak out today,"

"I hate her birthday," a freckled boy named Daniel chimed in. "Can you believe that Miss Heatherwood scheduled an adoption meeting today of all days?"

"Now she's really going to be a bad mood," Maggie moaned.

"When was the last time someone got adopted from here anyway?" asked Daniel.

"Not since I've been here," Jane said. "And I've lived here for six years."

"Not one?"

"Nope. Meetings are rigged. You never meet with adults who would actually be interested in you. Once you're assigned to live here, you're stuck here."

Quincy frowned. Kids like Anna would be trapped at Miss Heatherwood's until they turned eighteen. But then, so would she if her mother never came out of her stupor. Quincy forced herself to remember the sunny day and walked away from where the others were huddled. She stopped when she found a comfortable spot next to a large sycamore tree. She curled against the trunk and closed her eyes, trying to take advantage of the last ten minutes of her free time.

A branch over her head rustled and she startled. She looked up at the branches and then around the base of the tree, but she didn't see anything out of the ordinary. She rubbed her arms to rid them of the goose bumps. Her stomach grumbled, her internal clock warning her that she had to head to the dining room soon or she'd be late.

So much for my afternoon break, she thought as she trudged back toward the house. She stopped mid-step when she heard Amanda's voice coming from an open window. Curiosity won against fear, and she listened to Amanda talking about who she was and the things that she liked to do. The would-be adoptive parents in the room responded occasionally, and asked her questions even less frequently.

Quincy grimaced. She felt momentarily guilty at the relief that she was spared these uncomfortable and useless meetings. Even though Quincy was a ward of the state, she wasn't an orphan. Quincy cringed when she overheard a yawn from one of the adults, and then quickly slid past the window and ran towards the dining hall.

***

That night after her shower, Quincy opened her trunk and pulled out her music box so she could grab a clean towel to dry her wet hair. As she patted at the roots, she couldn't help but admire Amanda's sleek blond hair, which Amanda usually forced another girl to brush.

"Whatcha looking at, No-Talent?"

Quincy ducked down and mumbled, "Nothing."

Amanda stood up and forced herself into Quincy's vision. She ran her fingers through her hair. "Admit it. You wish ya had strands of gold instead of that dirty brown hair. It's the truth isn't it?" Amanda loudly proclaimed.

Quincy shook her head, then thought better of it and nodded vigorously. Unfortunately, Amanda had seen the head shake before the nod and cracked her knuckles.

"No? Do you think you're better than me? No one would ever think that you're better than me anyways. 'Cept for your momma. Maybe you should ask her if you're prettier. Oh wait, she can't answer back."

An image erupted into Quincy's memory of her mom brushing her hair and saying that it reminded her of dark chocolate. She clenched her fists and felt her neck grow hot. Finally, she couldn't hold her tongue any longer. She jumped up and got in Amanda's face. "I don't care what today is, it doesn't give you the right to say that about my mom. And you know what, at least I still have a mother. Yours left you on the front steps without even saying good-bye. And you're still here aren't you?"

Scattered gasps sounded across the room. Unlike Quincy, Amanda had been left at Miss Heatherwood's as a small child. She had been even younger than Anna, who was now huddled in the back corner of the room. No student had ever been brainless enough to mention it. Except for Quincy.

Looking at Amanda's eyes, she immediately wished that she could re-wind time and take her words back. Screaming, Amanda grabbed the first thing in her path, the music box on Quincy's bed.

Before Quincy could utter a word in protest, Amanda grabbed the music box and began to take steps away, holding it up in the air.

"No, please don't. I'm really sorry," Quincy whimpered, reaching out for the box.

Amanda glared at Quincy and threw it, hard, against the ground. The box splintered into multiple pieces, and the bully stomped on the dried flowers that spilled out. The metal key bounced against the chipped tiles and slid across the room. Quincy watched in horror then looked up at Amanda whose stance showed she was ready for a fight.

"No!" Quincy screamed as she ran toward Amanda fists-first, but before she could throw a punch, someone grabbed her from behind.

The Crone yanked her back and now stood in-between the girls. "Enough. Do ya want Miss Heatherwood with Death Strike?"

All the girls immediately shook their heads.

"Then bed. Now!"

They quickly made their way back to their beds. After the monitor was convinced that the fight was over, she gave the destroyed box a sorrowful look and left the room. She didn't assign detention for anyone.

Quincy grabbed some of the pieces of the box and held them in her arms. Tears escaped from her eyes and slid down her cheeks. The rest of the girls began to quietly ready themselves for sleep, but she picked up the key from its chain within the pile of splinters and destroyed flowers, shoved it in her pocket, and ran out the door. She didn't care that she should have been getting ready for bed. She didn't care about breaking the rules and leaving the floor at night. None of it mattered.

All at once, Amanda had managed to ruin the one thing that proved Quincy had once been a part of a loving family.

She ran down the hallway and stopped before she reached the Crone's door. She bit her lip to stop from crying aloud. She tiptoed past and gingerly walked down the stairs, carefully avoiding the squeaky steps. She opened the front door and stepped into the muggy night where she crumbled to the grass and broke into sobs.

Five minutes later, she was trying to collect herself again when a gust of wind blew through her nightgown, making her shiver. She looked up to the sky and saw an animal fly into the tree above her as the clouds rolled in. Thunder rumbled in the distance and she hoped the storm would pass them by. She stood up, clutching the broken music box to her, and walked back toward the door, a raindrop hitting her head.

Apparently it would not.

She scanned the yard and caught something moving in the shadows. She wiped her eyes on the sleeve of her tattered nightgown. Whirling to the side to look again, she saw nothing but darkness. With a sinking feeling in her stomach, she grasped the broken shards tighter, her knuckles turning white. She began to shake as a shadowy form walked towards her. It was in the shape of a man who seemed to be wearing a long coat. Its hair pointed directions, and the smell of bleach permeated the air. She fought the urge to throw up. The shadow turned its head, and though it was featureless, it felt like it was looking directly at her.

Sweat pooled at her temples, her mind refusing to allow her feet to run away. Above her, a bird screeched, releasing her from her immobility and she jumped. The animal above swooped down toward her and slapped her in the face with its feathers. She gasped and ran back into the building and up the stairs to her bed. She placed the broken box back in her trunk and lay down. She turned onto her side and curled up into a tight ball. As thunder crashed over the roof, she fell fitfully asleep, holding on to her mother's key.

Chapter Two

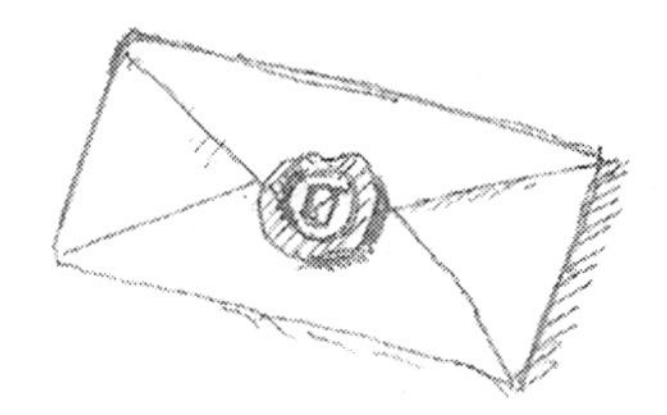

Keys and Their Locks

Quincy stared at her reflection on the window and rubbed her puffy eyes and throbbing head. She placed the key in one of her tattered shoes and slid them under the bed before cleaning up the mess on the floor and then herself.

During the first morning chore, Amanda found a student with curly hair to taunt, leaving Quincy in peace, even through lunch. When they were done eating, Quincy rushed upstairs to change into her afternoon chore clothes. She sighed as she rooted around in her trunk for appropriate stable garb, instead finding the metal music movement from the shattered music box. She sat on her bed and twisted the dial slowly. Nothing happened. She squeezed her eyes shut at the undeniable fact that it no longer worked. Never again would she hear its song, just like she would never again see her father or her younger sister. A tear slid down her cheek and landed on her hand.

A chime from the foyer startled her, forcing her internal clock back into action. Dismayed that she had lost track of time, she ran through the house, out the door, and across the small garden. She glimpsed the neighborhood stable over the hill as she went. The smell of horses reminded her of home. As a child, she'd loved horses more than anything. Growing up near a stable, she had learned to ride as soon as she could walk. It wasn't until the accident that she grew terrified of the powerful beasts. Only with the stable master's help and patience did she finally trust them again. For the most part.

"Of'en times it ain't the fault of the horse, but the one who 'olds the reigns," was the stable keeper's mantra as he gently forced her onto the back of a horse years ago.

Quincy's reverie ended at the stable door and she paused before going in. She stood on her tiptoes and peered through the window, hoping to slip in unnoticed by the stable master. One of the bored ponies looked over and Quincy put one finger to her mouth to shush the horse.

The crumbling neighborhood stable had seen better days. At one time it might have been red or maybe yellow, but it was difficult to tell with discolored, peeling paint. The rusty hinges on the doors creaked when opened. Cigfran always muttered to himself about the glory days of stables and horses long ago in another time and place. Sometimes he told Quincy stories about racing horses and a magnificent stable in a place where he had once lived, its walls decorated with broken shards of pottery and glass, and garnished with tiny silver tea spoons.

Quincy often wondered why the old stable hand had left his position working with such great horses to tend to one of the smallest stables in the Albany area. "It's important to know where you are needed," he'd mumble.

Placing one foot into the stable, Quincy prepared to sneak in behind the unsuspecting trainer and get started before he realized she hadn't been there on time. The one thing Cigfran had in common with Miss Heatherwood was that they both hated tardiness. She smiled in triumph as she got a little farther inside the stable. Until she stepped on a creaky floorboard...

"Ah hope that's ya, lassie." He shouted from the back of the stable. "Ya canna hide in this stable with those lov'ly dyin' floorboards an rusted hinges," Cigfran informed her with his odd accent. When they'd first met, Quincy asked him where he was from, but he brushed her off, simply replying that she wouldn't be able to find it on a map. Even though she was late, his familiar voice momentarily took her mind away from her abysmal week.

She faced him with a grimace. Standing at his full height, he towered above Quincy. He took off his cap, wiped the sweat from his brow, and shook his hair, dislodging the loose dirt and hay before putting the hat back on his head.

"I'm sorry, sir, I lost track of time," Quincy sheepishly admitted.

"Well obviously, since ya're twelve minutes late, which is complet'ly unlike ya ma dear. It doesn't look like ya've come ta harm. Though it's hard ta tell with the dark circles under those eyes. Haven't been sleepin' much, have we?" Cigfran wagged a finger at her. "Ah well, ya know your duties luv, so get to 'em."

Quincy hid a smile at his continually changing accent. She walked towards the tack shelf and grabbed a rag. Two days ago he had forgotten the *h* in *hinges* and *haven't*, but today he must have found it again.

"Cigfran, I'm going to exercise the bay," Quincy yelled.

"Mind ya're voice. I'm here," Cigfran groaned, rubbing his ears, and Quincy jumped, surprised by his stealthy approach. He grabbed the horse's tack and handed it to her.

"Listen, luv. We need ta talk."

"Okay," she answered not looking up from her task.

Cigfran placed his hands on her shoulders and gently guided her to face him. "I've handed in ma notice ta the owners a' the stable."

Quincy look at him with confusion. "Notice? You're leaving?" Her heart pounded in her chest, and the blood drained from her head, leaving her feeling a little dizzy.

Cigfran slowly nodded.

"Where are you going? It's not that neighborhood stable in Knox, is it? Haven't they been after you for over a year?" she teased, hoping that she sounded lighter than she felt.

"Quinn, I'll be leavin' New York stables entirely," Cigfran said quietly.

"But...but why?" she asked in a soft, trembling voice. He was her only friend here.

"Ya're no longer a little thing. Ya don't really need ma company anymore," he answered simply.

Quincy wanted to declare that he was wrong, but she couldn't think of the right thing to say. Then she wanted to yell at him, plead that he stay near by. Instead, she could only lower her head in the stall and mumble, "I'm going to miss you."

Cigfran sniffed in reply, "I know, an' I will miss ya too, lassie. Mind yer fingers. That beastie likes to bite."

Quincy pulled her hand back and watched Cigfran walk to the opposite side of the stable. Her nose started to run and she quickly grasped the bridle and rushed out the stable door.

***

Cigfran looked outside and watched Quincy run training exercises with a neighbor's boarded horse. He smiled, pleased with their progress, but then sighed when Quincy's strong facade momentarily weakened as she wiped her eyes. He knew she would miss him. Much to his surprise, he had ended up liking her. More than he chose to admit even to himself. He hated being attached to anyone or anything. It made things...painful. At fifteen years of age, it was time for her to choose for herself the path that her life would take. Difficult, but necessary. He knew that other people would like her if they took the chance to get to know her: however, they had not and *would not* and he knew why. She was different from them and they were jealous of her.

He looked at the darkening skyline and frowned. Being late once in a day was odd for the girl, but twice was inconceivable. He opened the squeaky window and poked his head out.

"Quinn, luv. Ya're done fer today. If ya don't leave now, ya're gonna be late."

The small girl dashed inside and began to take the tack off the horse.

"I'll finish that. Don't be late." Cigfran grimaced, realizing that he had completely forgotten the accent. She looked too hurried to have caught on.

She smiled and gave him a hug. "Thank you, Cigfran!"

He turned around to wipe down the stable bench so that Quincy would not see the upset on his face. He didn't do gratitude, or good-byes, well.

"It's best that ya run, lest ya be late for supper."

"You're right. Thank you again, and I'll see you on Friday," she yelled to him as she sprinted towards the main house.

Cigfran's smile faded as she ran toward the building. Cigfran was leaving her, and by the time she had read the letter that he had placed inside her sweater pocket, the stable keeper would be gone. Cigfran had done his duty and now it was time for a new guardian.

He held back a look of distaste as a man entered the stable to take one of the horses into town. He was glad to be done working at the neighborhood stable. No one rode for pleasure; life was all business to them. They were distastefully similar to the horses in this stable. Boring.

He looked toward the main house where Quincy would soon be eating her supper and hoped she would be ready for the next step.

He wished that he could have better prepared her for the danger and the difficult choices to come.

"Too late now," he mumbled to a disinterested dapple next to him. "It's time to change."

***

Quincy swung open the back door of the main house and ran inside, taking the stairs two at a time to her bedroom. She tore off her stable clothes and quickly reset her hair. As she replaced the bobby pins, she thought of Cigfran closing the stable for the night. Quincy spied Maggie running in the door and quickly dried her eyes on her sleeves. Quincy dashed out the room, sensing that she only had one minute before clock chimed for dinnertime. She slid into the dining room and stopped behind her chair just as the clock began to ring.

When the kids were allowed to eat, she bit into a dry bread roll and grimaced. How she still missed the French bakery across the street from her old home. Her heart ached for the chance to leave this place, to go to school or just run away. Maybe Cigfran would take her as his stable groom when her training was finished? She would have to ask him on Friday.

After dinner, she followed the other girls back to their room to change for bed. As she sat on her bed, she heard a *crunch*. She stood up and looked on her bed. Someone had left a letter addressed to her. Puzzled, she sat back down and opened it.

Dearest Quincy,

By the time you have read this letter I will have packed and said my good-byes. Don't you be sad now love, because I'm certain that we will meet again.

Quincy sucked in a breath, her heart pounding in her chest. What did he mean he will have already packed? But he had just told her that he gave his notice this afternoon? She got up and crept over to the door, paying no mind to the whispers of the other girls. This was more important than their mocking. She poked her head out to find the Crone dealing with an incident between the boys across the hall. *Perfect.*

She hurried back to her bed and slipped on her shoes, holding back a groan when she stepped on something hard and cold. She had forgotten about the key. She ignored the uncomfortable sensation of the metal pushing against her toes and slithered down the stairs and outside and to the stables. She swung open the stable door and paused at the first stall to catch her breath. She looked up and trembled when she saw the empty space. She cautiously walked to the other side of the stable, dreading what she would find. She stopped at the room where Cigfran lived. His bed had been made and the room emptied of his personal items. She numbly sat on the mattress and pulled out the letter again.

I heard about what happened with the music box. I'm sorry that it broke. I know how much it meant to you. I also know that inside the box you kept a key on a silver chain.

Quincy clutched the letter close to her chest and looked outside as the darkness descended upon Miss Heatherwood's. She had told him about the music box years ago, but she had never mentioned the key. How had he known? She smoothed the paper and began reading again.

Don't under any circumstance misplace this key! Keep it with you at all times, and at twelve o'clock tonight, go to the third floor, find the first door to your left, and go inside. From there, locate the window on your left. At twelve-thirty, for one minute only, the moon will show through the window, creating on a silhouette of a door. Go to the door, put the key in the lock, and turn it counterclockwise. But I must warn you, when you put the key in the lock, things will begin to change for you. You must prepare yourself to embrace the unknown. When you open the door, further instructions will follow.

Farewell, Quincy. I wish I could be there to answer all of your questions but I cannot. Only time will tell when we meet again.

~ Cigfran

Flabbergasted, she slipped off her shoe to examine the key, trying to understand its importance. It didn't make sense. The key was a simple trinket her mother used to wear. Wasn't it? Quincy shot another look at Miss Heatherwood's, wondering if Amanda had made this whole thing up as an elaborate trick to get her out of bed and caught by the Crone. That was something she would do without a second thought.

Quincy looked at the handwriting and its elegant swirls and penmanship, and suddenly doubted it. The lettering and the vocabulary were too mature and too smart for Amanda. It was definitely Cigfran's writing. She had only seen his signature a few times, when he would sign off for oats and stable equipment, but she had been impressed with the beauty in his name. Odd for a stable master. She read through the letter again, this time letting his closing words really sink in

This was his good-bye. It was all she had left of him. She put her knees to her chin, clinging to the letter and the key. He hadn't let her say good-bye. Why did everyone close to her eventually leave her behind? Her head grew hot, and her hands trembled. She grabbed Cigran's pillow and screamed into it, the noise dampened by the material.

A horse neighed and it quickly brought her back to the present. She grabbed the key and ran back to the house. She slipped into her bed just as the night bell rang and the Crone poked her head inside for the night's final tally. Gradually the room's occupants drifted off to sleep leaving Quincy to her confusing thoughts.

The way she saw it, she had two choices. Option one meant she stayed in bed and ignored the letter completely. Nothing would change. She would start her professional grooming training—now without Cigfran—and when she turned eighteen, she'd get a job working at one of the stables in the area and leave Miss Heatherwood's. At least she would be working with horses, and being a groom wouldn't be a terrible fate. It just wasn't Oakley.

Her parents had always expected her and her sister to join them in the long line of prestigious graduates. Would her parents understand or be disappointed if she ended the family tradition and spent her life as a stable groom? Quincy curled up in a tight ball and squeezed her eyes shut.

She forced herself to focus on option two: she could sneak upstairs to find a nonexistent door. The worst that could happen would be getting in trouble for being out of bed. Or something could actually change and she'd be transported to a place where her family existed, where she had a Talent, where she was a million miles away from Miss Heatherwood's.

That kind of magic wasn't real, though, so what could Cigfran have meant? How could he have left without telling her how he had known about the key? Why the cryptic letter? She angrily clenched the top of her blanket.

She took a deep breath, trying to calm herself and think clearly. It really came down to choosing the unknown or Miss Heatherwood's.

It didn't feel much like a choice. Stay and be a stable assistant at Miss Heatherwood's, which held nothing for her, or take this adventure Cigfran seemed to be pushing her toward, despite the unknowns and the uncertainties. What would be the harm of at least seeing where Cigfran—if it was truly Cigfran—had been trying to guide her?

Quincy slid out of bed. Tiptoeing across the room, barefoot, she opened the door and began to creep up the stairs, pausing after each step. Her heart pounded in her chest. She felt sure that the Crone could hear it from her room, and if she was caught, she doubted that the Crone would believe Quincy's tall tale. Her stomach began to turn as she drew closer to the room Cigfran had described. When she opened the door, it responded with a groan.

She walked slowly into the dark room, letting her eyes adjust. Quincy's stomach heaved from the rotting smell of moldy furniture and book pages. She hid her nose in the sleeve of her nightgown and scanned the room as it came into focus. It looked like a storage room for long-forgotten odds and ends. In the corner, there was an old wooden chair facing the window. She sat down, a dust cloud enveloping her nightgown. The seconds sluggishly passed as she waited to see the door described in the letter.

The moonlight slowly seeped through the slightly open window, illuminating part of the wall. Quincy gasped and leaped up from the chair. The moonbeams now shone on a massive door, intricately engraved with three birds on the bottom. On the top, the door had been inscribed with words from another language in a spidery handwriting. There were five keyholes, two on each side of the door, and one in the very center of a globe-like object, surrounded by vines. The door dominated the room and covered an entire wall.

This was it. This was her chance.

She swallowed hard as she took the key out her pocket and placed it in the center lock. It fit perfectly. She squeezed her eyes shut and turned the key counter-clockwise, as instructed, releasing the door. Bright light escaped as she opened it slightly, but when she swung the door open wider, the light died. All she saw was a brick wall on the other side.

She closed the door and opened it a second time. Still a brick wall.

She closed the door again and stepped back. Maybe she needed to try a different keyhole. But the door had changed. It was just a plain door. She must be going crazy to have imagined the multiple keyholes, and the birds engravings. But what kind of person imagines that? She mentally smacked herself. What had she really expected? A door that would open to take her away? She wasn't special, she wasn't one of a kind, why would something like that happen to her? She was just another Talentless foster kid.

Quincy resisted the urge to scream in frustration. Instead, she flung the key to the ground. The emotional strain from the past two days had finally took its toll and she crumpled down to the floor and sobbed. She glanced to where she'd thrown the key. It had landed on top of a pile of moth-eaten sheets. She reached over and grasped the key. She wished her mother were here. She'd know just what to say.

Quincy stroked the chain, picturing her mother wearing the necklace. She opened the clasp and put the chain and the key around her neck, letting the weight against her chest keep her close to her mother. She left the storage room and numbly made her way back to her room.

CHAPTER THREE

THE BIZARRE INTRODUCTION

Quincy woke up with the sun and sat up in bed, watching the room's sleeping occupants. Having not been caught from last night, she felt emboldened to sneak out before the wake-up bell. She swiftly moved upstairs to the storage room, again, only to find no door at all. Not even an old door in storage. Quincy looked around the room, confused. Maybe she had the wrong room? But then she saw the corner where the dust had been disturbed, her footprints clear.

Suddenly she didn't want to be anywhere near the key on her neck. Maybe it was a bad luck charm. After all, her mother had worn it during her accident, and it obviously wasn't helping her get out of this awful place. Angrily, she pulled at the chain and searched for the hook to release it from her neck. But it refused to unhook itself. It was as if someone had smelted the metal together. Quincy pulled hard, trying to break it. When the chain still resisted, she searched desperately around the room and found a pair of rusty scissors. She picked them up and carefully slid the blade near her skin and around the chain. She squeezed the handles together. The silver chain still refused to snap. It didn't even scratch the thing. It felt like a noose around her neck, and her heart began to race faster and faster, her breathing shallow. She stepped into the hallway to escape the claustrophobia, and leaned her head against the wall near the staircase. After taking a few deep breaths, Quincy abandoned the room and went back to bed before the Crone woke up.

***

The day passed slowly, and Quincy mechanically went through her chores. Between chores, she had visited the stable and tried the new clippers on her chain. But it still remained intact, and Quincy threw the clippers to the ground with a clatter. She grudgingly sprinted back to the main house to mop the lower classrooms.

When lunch came, Quincy mindlessly turned her lunch broth around with her spoon. Her neck burned from the morning attempts to remove the difficult chain.

"So I hear we're going to get a new stable master." Quincy looked over at the woman who sat across the table from Miss Heatherwood. The lady was new herself, working with the kids under ten, and this was her third attempt to try to illicit conversation from the other teachers and staff.

"Such a pity. I'll miss watching him riding the horses in the morning. I hope the new one is just as good-looking. In a rustic way, of course." She started to giggle but quickly stopped when Miss Heatherwood pinned her with a cold stare.

A new stable master. Quincy's heart sank. Cigfran had only left the night before and they were already talking about his replacement. Quincy put down her spoon, her face set in a scowl.

The front doorbell interrupted the silent meal, and Miss Heatherwood's assistant shuffled out of the dining room to answer. When she returned, all forty students looked up in surprise when she handed Miss Heatherwood a blue telegram. A telegram at Miss Heatherwood's?

Miss Heatherwood pursed her lips as she read the note, and goose bumps popped up on Quincy's arms and legs when Miss Heatherwood's gaze moved from the page to *her*. Quincy swallowed, her heart speeding up. Was it about her mother?

Her fear was quickly answered when Miss Heatherwood shrilly called out, "Miss Harris, be outside my office in ten minutes."

After lunch was finished, Quincy's head swam while she walked in a daze to Miss Heatherwood's office and took a seat next to the door. Twenty minutes later, it creaked open and Miss Heatherwood beckoned her inside. Blinking, Quincy paused letting her eyes adjust to the shaded windows inside the stark office. Miss Heatherwood's chair, twice the height of a normal chair, always made Quincy feel small and inferior. That was probably the intent.

Miss Heatherwood's scratchy voice broke the uncomfortable silence first. "Miss Harris, this telegram is about you." Quincy's body went rigid. Miss Heatherwood slammed the telegram on the desk, making Quincy jump.

"Read this aloud," Miss Heatherwood demanded.

With shaking hands, Quincy grasped the paper and began to read.

"Miss Heatherwood, I am informing you of Miss Harris's acceptance to Oakley Academy. Coming in two days. Will explain everything. Thank you. Mrs. Ellen Adalin, Barrister of the British Isles."

"Oakley Academy! Do you have anything you wish to say about this?" Miss Heatherwood demanded.

Quincy shook her head numbly.

"Why would you be accepted to Oakley?"

"I'm not sure," she admitted. Her mind swam with unanswered questions. Who would pay for it? How had she been accepted if she hadn't even applied?

"I will look into this and see if it is legitimate. We'll have to see how we can get you out of this little…misunderstanding," said Miss Heatherwood.

Quincy's cheeks burned, and she bit the inside of her cheek. She was fifteen and Miss Heatherwood wasn't her mother. She couldn't tell her that she couldn't go.

"A *misunderstanding*? What if it's not?" Quincy said boldly. "If I'm accepted, than I want to go."

"That's not up to you." Miss Heatherwood growled. "Besides, who would donate money for your education but not your foster care?"

Another unanswered question.

Quincy stood up and stared directly at Miss Heatherwood. “I don’t understand why you care. I’m just one foster kid, just another mouth to feed. Why shouldn’t I go?”

Miss Heatherwood jumped up, and Quincy recoiled at the darkness behind the headmistress’s eyes.

“That is certainly none of your business, now is it? You are simply a child, and practically an orphan. That means you have no say in anything. You have rights to nothing. I tell you how to live and think.”

Quincy clenched her fists. “No, you don’t,” she said, and before Miss Heatherwood could reply, Quincy fled the room. She sprinted outside and didn’t stop until she reached the stable.

She paused outside the door, sucking in the fresh air. She caught her breath and slowly opened the door, hoping that no one was around. She released her breath in relief when she saw only the horses were inside. She walked to the end and found a currently empty stall and curled up in the corner.

She breathed in the scents of fresh hay and oats from the stall next to her. She braced her arms around her knees and leaned against the wall. She wished she had a court-ordered family visit today. She needed the familiarity of her mother’s shoulder. Oakley had been their dream and somehow, she *would* go. But she had never imagined leaving her mother behind like this.

“How’s that pity party of yours treating you? Does it make you feel better?” a deep voice humorously asked. “Is that your thing?” The sound resonated off the walls of the stable.

Quincy's shoulders tensed at the unfamiliar voice. She hadn't thought that the new stable master had already arrived. They wouldn't get along well if he used humor at her expense.

She got up on her knees to peek out over the stall door. She looked side to side trying to get a glimpse of the man. But she saw no one.

"But what is your thing? You don't know, do you?"

Frowning, Quincy leaned farther over the railing of the stall. Maybe he was in another one nearby.

"Not over there. Up here."

Quincy jerked her head up to the rafters of the stable, trying to figure out why he would have scaled the woodwork to sit up in the ceiling. But again, no one was there. Only a large bird staring intently at her.

Mud caked the feathers of the stationary creature. Quincy looked on in fascination. What kind of large bird had muddy brown feathers?

As if reading her mind, the bird hopped down to the stall door and cocked its head to the side, still focused on her. "I don't normally look like this."

Quincy's eyes widened, and she looked around the stable again for the speaker.

"Stop searching. I'm right here."

The voice definitely came from above. Quincy stared at the bird, and she backed up when he rolled his eyes at her. A shiver ran up her spine. This wasn't possible.

“B-but birds don’t talk,” she stammered.

“Read my beak because this bird does,” he responded. He made a sound between a snort and a snicker. “Never met a talking bird before?”

Quincy shook her head. She pinched her arm, hoping to wake herself up. She looked up and frowned when she still saw the bird in front of her.

“I take it that you’re not the sharpest tool to be found in the shed?”

“Excuse me? You are really rude, you know.” She paused. “A rudely talking bird. Fantastic,” she berated herself. “I have to be hallucinating. Right on par for this week.”

“Hallucinating an insulting bird. Now *I’m* insulted. I don’t think even your brain could come up with that. Let’s just pretend—just to make things easier on your tiny mind—that I am real and you’re not hallucinating.”

“Okay. I think...,” Quincy answered. More questions began to form in her mind, too many to coherently ask.

“Well, I suppose that’s a start. But you obviously have questions. Typical. Ask now, otherwise you’re not going to hear anything I’m about to tell you.”

“Why are you here?” Quincy asked the first question that tumbled out.

The bird snorted. “Of all the questions in every timeline you could have asked, you asked why and not *how*? Interesting.”

“Why is that interesting? And what do you mean every timeline?”

“Why is it that I always get asked this question?” he rolled his eyes at the ceiling. “Everyone likes to think they’re alone in the universe. Do you really think your little timeline without electricity and your eccentric decision to ride genetically modified eagles instead of zeppelins or airplanes stands alone? It’s the twenty-first century and you’re still using horses for transportation. How quaint.”

“What is electricity? What’s an airplane?” She scrunched up her face, more confused than ever.

“Never mind. Let’s move on. How about I answer your first question and then work our way from there, shall we?”

Quincy frowned and crossed her arms. She didn’t like his sarcastic tone.

The bird continued. “I’m here because I’ve been following you. Before you ask the obvious “why,” let me finish.”

“Actually I wanted to ask how you’ve been following me. I don’t remember seeing you.”

The bird dug his talon into the wood and gave her an annoyed hiss. “Do you have to interrupt me?” He sighed. Or at least gave the closest thing to a sigh that bird could. “It’s not hard to keep tabs on you since you go practically nowhere. And I know how not to be seen.” He gestured towards his dirty chest feathers. “Let’s move on. Now for the why. I've been keeping an eye on you because I have a lot invested in you."

"In me?"

"Yes, you. Let's backtrack and do this properly. First things first, my name is Talin, in case you were wondering. I'm the link to your future and presently—more importantly even—your ticket out of here, at least for the school term."

She narrowed her eyes at Talin. "*You're* from Oakley?"

"Do I look like I'm an admissions counselor from Oakley?"

Quincy pursed her lips. "So if you're not from Oakley, why are you here?"

Another sigh. "I am here for Oakley, just not directly with them."

"That doesn't make sense."

The bird growled. "We don't have time for the question game."

"Suppose I believe you," Quincy started. "and I go with you to Oakley for the term...What happens to me during the summer?"

"You come back here."

Arms still crossed, she took a deep breath. "'Here' as in Miss Heatherwood's? Why would I have to come back?"

"Your situation hasn't changed. You're still a ward of the state and assigned to Miss Heatherwood. You've just been accepted to a nine-month school, so you have to come back to your group house for the summer holiday."

"Unless my mother wakes up."

The bird took in a sharp intake of breath. "Yes, unless she wakes up." The bird cleared its throat.

"Okay, but why Oakley?" She met the bird's gaze head-on. "Not that I don't want to go," she rushed on, "because I do. But I never even applied."

"Someone took care of that for you."

Quincy's eyes widened, "But who—"

"Don't bother trying to finish your question because I'm not going to answer that one. Yes, I can in fact be that rude, and no, I don't *have* to tell you. Anyway, why Oakley? There are some decently mediocre schools around here, but your parents wanted you to attend their alma mater. Since people around here generally choose not to take the route of higher Talent education, your generous donor followed their wishes. School pride is such a *human* trait."

"But—"

"Oh, but you don't know what your Talent is?" he interrupted, finishing her thought.

Quincy bit her lip. She didn't want to admit her fear out loud, but she knew she had to. "Well...what if I don't have one?"

The bird looked at the ceiling and groaned. "Let's set something straight, right now. Every person has a Talent. You have a Talent, your greedy headmistress has one, that guy who sells newspapers on the corner has one. Some are more obvious than others. Like your bully, who can sense people's fear. It's just more noticeable."

"So then, what's mine?"

"I don't know, Quinn. That's your job to figure out."

"Wait, did you just call me Quinn?" That had been a family nickname, and the only other person to use it had been Cigfran.

Talin shifted his weight from one foot to the other, at first saying nothing. "I told you I've been following you. It's been awhile."

Quincy shivered, repulsed by the idea that something had been watching her for years without her knowledge.

"Ew. I'm not watching you all the time!" he shouted as he shook his head. "Gross. I've just been here to make sure nothing bad happens to you."

"Nothing bad like being bullied, locked in closets, or whipped?" she gritted her teeth. Where was he when all those things happened?

"No, nothing bad like you being *kidnapped*, *experimented on*, or *murdered* in another carriage accident."

Quincy's mouth opened, but words refused to come out. The bird grimaced and flew down from the rafters, landing beside her. Quincy bit her lip again, not sure if she wanted to scream, swat the bird, or cry.

Finally, she took a deep breath through her nose and gradually released it from her lips. "What do you mean by 'another carriage accident'?" she whispered.

Talin cleared his throat but didn't say anything.

"What did you mean," Quincy asked again, this time much louder. "Are you telling me that the accident wasn't an accident?"

"Yes, that's what I'm telling you. It wasn't an accident."

"Who would do such a thing?" she whispered, her voice trembling.

Talin looked toward the window behind her. "Someone with no moral code and who has nothing to lose. He will do whatever it takes to find it."

Quincy shivered. "To find what?"

"That." Talin gestured with his wing to her neck.

Quincy looked down, puzzled. Then she recalled her sore neck and the chain that refused to open. She pulled out the chain and the key that hung from it. "This?"

Talin growled. "Yes, that. They wanted it from your mother and she refused to comply. So she and your father fled from England to the States where they had you and your sister, and then finally here to New York."

"I've always wondered why they moved us here." Quincy pondered aloud.

"They thought it was the best place to hide and keep them away from you and your sister. Amongst other reasons."

Nausea washed over Quincy like a wave, and she sat back down in the stall. She curled up and put her head to her knees. Talin flew back to the front of the stall to face her.

"Parents are always a surprise to their offspring," Talin offered, his voice softer and almost compassionate.

She slowly lifted her head to look at him with watery eyes. "Who were they running from? Why do they want my Mom's key?"

Talin looked side to side to each side of the stable before continuing. "That key opens something. Something with the potential for immeasurable good or for great evil."

Quincy gasped. That wasn't what she was expecting. Not that she expected any of this. She shook her head as if that would shake off her disbelief. "What does it unlock?"

Talin shrugged. "No one really knows."

"So, am I in danger, then?" The realization hit suddenly and forced the air from her chest, the fear filling her.

"Probably. Eventually." His eyes narrowed to make his point.

"No," she whimpered. She began shaking and reached for the chain on her neck. She grappled with the clasp, and once again it refused to open. "No, I never agreed to this." She bit her lip, this time in anger. "Why won't it come off?"

The bird watched her intently for a moment, then said, "Now try it again."

Quincy sighed and grasped the clasp. To her surprise, it released the key without complaint, falling onto the hay. "But how?" she whispered.

"I generally have that effect on everything," Talin informed her, rolling his eyes yet again. "The key allows you to decide if you are willing or whatever. In your panicked state, you just needed a little bit of help calming down."

"It's like magic."

"There's no such thing as magic." he retorted.

"Said the talking bird."

"Touché."

Quincy's lips began to curve up into a smile, despite her confusion and anger. She quickly remembered his warning of danger, and her grin dropped. "Honestly, I don't want any part of this."

"That's what your mother said, too...at first."

Quincy reached down to grab the key. "Why does my mom have it?"

"You need to stop thinking of it as your mom's. It's your key now."

Quincy looked up at Talin with big eyes.

"You opened the door," he explained, "which deemed you worthy of blah, blah, blah. But the real question is, do you deserve this key?"

She shook her head. "No, I don't think I do. I opened the door, but there was nothing behind it."

Talin gave a demeaning snort from his beak. "Well of course not. How many keyholes were there?"

"All together? Five," Quincy answered, surprised that she had remembered.

"Right. And that's how many keys it takes to find out what's behind it. The door is not connected to any particular wall. You had the key, and by waiting for it and wanting it, you called it to you."

Quincy looked down at the necklace, again enthralled by the gears in the key's eye. She picked the chain back up and unfastened the clasp.

Talin hissed. "You only get one chance to take off that key, and you just used it. If you close that clasp, that key will never leave your skin until the day your soul leaves this earth or until its duty has been fulfilled. So do you stay here? You can't hide in this stable forever. Or do you go to Oakley and embrace the unknown?" Bile rose in Quincy's throat and she repressed the urge to throw up, but Talin continued. "Here you choose your fate…though, of course, some would argue that the choice has already been made. You don't really want to know it, do you? Where's the fun in that?"

Quincy stayed silent as dizziness swept over her.

Talin sighed. "I can't tell you exactly what you face, but let me be honest with you. There will always be people who will want to use you, but others will strive to protect you." His voice sounded soft and almost familiar to Quincy's ear. "Unfortunately, no matter what, people are going to want you for that key."

Quincy closed her eyes and leaned her head against the side of the stall to stop the vertigo. She needed to think clearly now more than ever before. Why had her mother kept the key a secret? She hadn't even bothered to explain why she wore it and the dangers that came hand in hand with the seemly innocent trinket.

"So why did she agree to wear it?"

"Because I told her what would happen if she didn't."

Quincy gestured to him to go on.

"I'm running out of time. Your *world* is running out of time. You're the only person alive who can open the door and save your universe."

Quincy snorted. "The universe. The whole universe?"

"Did you think I would drag you into danger just for giggles? This is serious."

She sighed, sobering. "So I really don't have much of a choice then, do I?"

"You always have a choice. It's just that this choice has consequences either way."

Quincy's heart began to pound in her chest, and the bile rose in her throat. "But Talin, I can't leave my mother. What if she needs me? What if she wakes up?"

"Oh, Quinn," he said, this time not sounding so condescending. "I know that this is a difficult decision, but even if she were coherent, you would've had to leave her behind for Oakley, anyway. The home will keep you informed: if her condition changes you'll know immediately. There's nothing you can do for her here." He paused a beat. "Quinn, your mother would want you to do this. Believe me, I would know."

She frowned at him. "Oh, and how would you know?"

"Like I said, I've been following you for quite awhile."

Quincy chewed on her lip. "But how are you going to help me get out of here? Miss Heatherwood said she's not going to let me go."

"Leave everything in my careful talons."

Quincy closed her eyes and fingered the key. "And what should I do with this?" She swallowed and looked at Talin again.

"It's actually quite simple." he said, voice now somewhat cheerful. "All you have to do is put the key on...If you're sure that's what you want to do, of course."

"What happens if I say no?"

Talin shook his head. "I'm not forcing you to do anything, Quinn, but I can't just find another Key Bearer. You are my last chance."

"What?"

"That key was meant for you, or someone like you. There are very few of you in the world." The bird rocked forward and backward on his talons. "But I really must get going. I don't have all day."

Quincy walked out the stall and through the stable door and stared at the group house. *Anything is better than this.* And Oakley had always been her and her parent's dream for her. She remembered them placing an Oakley poster over her childhood bed.

She nodded once and looped the chain around her head again and closed the clasp.

Under his breath, Talin mumbled, "Okay, here we go." He ruffled his feathers and for a brief moment looked sad. "That was the easiest part I'm afraid."

Before she could reply, he spread his wings, flying out the door and into the sky.

***

Quincy groaned as she realized what time it was. Her conversation with the bird had made her fifteen minutes late for kitchen duty, her last chore of the day. She never lost track of time. What was it with this week? She sprinted back to the house and paused at the kitchen door.

Just what I need today, another lash.

She took a deep breath, opened the kitchen door, and froze at the doorpost when she overheard a shrill southern drawl yell, "Now ain't you dumber than a stump? I swear I told you to stoke that fire, not murder it!"

Quincy bit her lip wishing that she hadn't caught the cook in a bad moment, and quietly walked towards her. Her light-brown hair was pinned back, and she had a smear of bread dough on her cheek. Her height barely reached the top oven and the shoulder of the poor kitchen apprentice she was chastising. She would have looked comical except that she had a rolling pin in her hand and was brandishing it like a sword.

After a moment of awkwardly standing behind the cook, Quincy tentatively cleared her throat. "I'm sorry that I'm late, ma'am."

She put her rolling pin down and wiped her dusty hands on her white apron. She swung around to face Quincy and stared at her icily. Quincy tensed her shoulders, wondering if the cook was going to pick that rolling pin back up and actually use it on her.

"I'm sorry that I'm really late?" Quincy tried again.

The cook turned around and continued her task of chopping some potatoes. "I heard you stood up to the old coot, " the woman said, her back to Quincy. "As far as I'm concerned, if you start to clean those dishes over there, nothing will be mentioned of your being late."

Quincy's jaw dropped slightly, but she snapped it shut. "Thank you, ma'am," she said as she turned to the pile of dirty dishes. Then she stopped to look back at the cook. "Excuse me, but how did you know?" She felt her cheeks grow hot. It had been three years since she had been permitted to speak candidly to an adult other than Cigfran.

The cook's deep-throated laugh echoed off the walls of the kitchen. "I always know what's happening here, contrary to everyone's belief. Southern hick, indeed. I know especially when that news is related to a top-five Talent school. That greedy headmistress is trying to stop you from getting out of this mud hole."

"I don't understand why she won't let me go." Quincy said softly. "Wouldn't I be one less kid to worry about and annoy?"

"That's true, but she wouldn't be getting anything from the government. She gets a monthly stipend to make sure that you're fed and taught because you're a ward of the state. She uses as little as possible of that money on you."

"Really? What does she do with the money?"

The cook looked around and then put her hands in her apron. "Straight in her pockets."

Quincy wasn't entirely surprised. "How does she get away with that?"

"Well, there's no one to step in and make it right. Not really." She stared outside of the window and wiped her hands on her towel. "Besides, life is rarely fair, my dear. You take what's given to you. It's your choice whether you take it happily or bitterly. I learned that the hard way."

Chapter Four

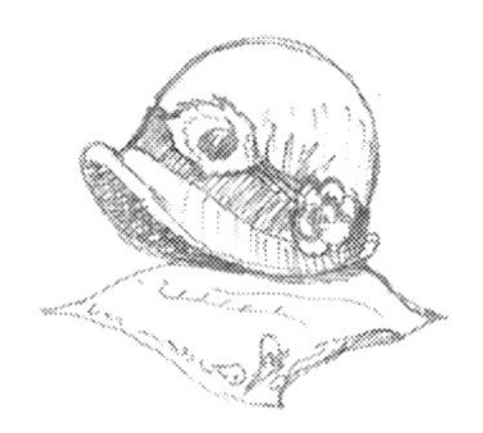

The Difficult Decision

After the telegram had arrived two days earlier, it seemed the entire group house knew what had happened within minutes. She found herself the favored topic of gossip. Yesterday, she had overheard a conversation in the stable between two of her other foster siblings that had also chosen "groom" as their vocation.

"Did you hear that she was accepted to Oakley? You do know what Oakley Academy is, right?" Jason had asked.

"Everyone knows about Oakley. One of the big-five schools." Maris had rolled her eyes. "Isn't it somewhere in Europe, like in England?"

"Wales, actually. Yeah, I once had a foster brother who had a cousin that went there. He told me that there were only three ways that you got to wear the Oakley eagle. You had to be exceptionally Talented—so basically a scholarship student—you bought your slot, or you had to have family or alumni connections."

"So which one is she?" Maris had wondered aloud.

Jason had just shrugged. "No idea." Quincy's cheeks had burned from listening in, and continued to do so everywhere she went. Any time she walked into a room, people seemed to stop talking mid-conversation and gawk at her. Amanda was the only one who wasn't talking about Oakley or Quincy. Instead, she went out of her way to trip her and leave bugs in her bed. Just today she'd even managed to drop a bucket of soapy water on Quincy's head.

She wiped her hair once more before looking at the grimy towel in disgust. She looked up at the mirror, and seeing her reflection, she groaned. Lunch was in ten minutes, which didn't give her enough time to wash out the suds. She would have to serve detention later still smelling like dirty water. The detention was her fault, the consequence of a nightmare the evening before, in which she'd been pushed off a large white eagle. She wondered if there was such a thing as a white eagle.

Quincy grudgingly went down to lunch and to her relief, saw no sign of Miss Heatherwood. Everyone noticed the headmistress's absence and looked at one another in surprise. After the oddly peaceful meal, they all scattered toward their designated chores. Quincy mopped the lower classrooms and removed spider webs from the ceilings without incident.

On her way up the stairs from the classrooms, Anna—who often ran notes around the school—stopped her. "Um, Quincy, excuse me, but Miss Heatherwood wants you." Anna mumbled, intertwining her fingers behind her back. "She sounded kinda mad. You probably should go right now."

Quincy frowned. What had she done now? She turned to thank the little girl, but she had already run away.

Quincy made her way to the office and knocked on the thick door before letting herself in. Miss Heatherwood sat at her desk, and in front of her stood another woman. The stranger turned around and smiled at Quincy, who returned it uncomfortably. "You wanted to see me, Headmistress?"

"Yes, this woman is here to speak to you," she snapped.

The woman smiled a second time, this time showing no teeth. She looked to be in her late thirties, even though her height barely passed Quincy's. Her matching beige sweater and skirt spoke of professional ties, and she held on to an emerald-colored hat with a peacock feather stuck in the side. She wore her hair up and her green eyes sparkled as she introduced herself in a crisp British accent.

"Hello, Miss Quincy. My name is Ellen Adalin."

Quincy stared at the woman's perfectly painted lips until they broke apart to speak again.

"You are to be under my charge until you arrive at school."

Quincy held her breath, now completely focused on the woman. She reluctantly turned away to look at Miss Heatherwood, dreading her reaction. The headmistress stared at her desk, pointedly ignoring Quincy and Mrs. Adalin.

"Miss Heatherwood came into town, just to make sure this wasn't a hoax, isn't that nice? And now I am to take you with me."

"You mean, I'm actually going to Oakley?" She was near to bursting with excitement, but she needed the confirmation.

Mrs. Adalin's smile widened.

Talin did it! She was getting out! She tried to contain herself, keeping her expression the same and her body from shaking.

Miss Heatherwood hissed but said nothing.

Mrs. Adalin turned her attention back to the headmistress and hemmed. "You should be very happy for her. An acceptance to Oakley is quite important, as I'm sure you well know."

Miss Heatherwood threw her a contemptuous look as Mrs. Adalin motioned to Quincy to follow her outside. They left Miss Heatherwoods behind and walked outside into the overcast afternoon.

After a moment of comfortable silence, Mrs. Adalin beamed at Quincy. "Do you know who I am, Quincy?"

"Umm," she started. "You wrote that telegram. You're a..." She couldn't remember the world.

"A barrister," the woman finished. Quincy looked at her quizzically, and Mrs. Adalin gave a small laugh. "It's a term used for lawyers in the British Isles."

Quincy nodded slowly. "Is that where you're from?"

"Yes, I'm from York, England."

"Did Talin send you?" Quincy asked.

Mrs. Adalin looked confused. "Who, dear?"

"Talin?" Quincy cautiously inquired a second time.

"I'm sorry, but I have absolutely no idea who you are talking about."

Quincy frowned. Had she dreamed the whole conversation with the talking brown bird? Who *was* Talin?

Mrs. Adalin changed the subject. "Now, I'm sure that this will be overwhelming, Quincy so I promise to be patient. The first thing that you need to do after we end this little chat of ours is to pack the things you want to take with you. You'll find a decent-sized trunk that is already next to your bed. Only take what you deem is *necessary* for your personal use. Don't bother with clothes." Mrs. Adalin's eyes twinkled. "We will go shopping to get the required things for school."

Quincy twisted a strand of hair between her fingers. So many things were happening at once. She wished her mother were standing next to her right now. She wanted to be going to Oakley the first time with her and her father. Instead, a woman that she had never met would be taking the place of her parents. Quincy blinked rapidly as she tried to stop the flood of emotion.

"I believe that's all for now, and I know that it's a lot to take in. You should go and pack, and please remember to only bring the essentials. I will be back at half past five *sharp* this evening so we may catch the night train."

Quincy eyes widened in surprise. She was leaving tonight? But her weekly visitation with her mother wasn't until tomorrow. Her heart pounded in her chest. She couldn't leave without saying good-bye. "Mrs. Adalin, I'd like to see my mom before we go. Could we please visit her first?"

Mrs. Adalin looked down at her watch. She smiled at Quincy. "Yes, we will have time for that. I will see you soon, and please…be punctual!" She waved farewell and left Quincy alone with her thoughts.

While walking back to her room, she felt mixed feelings of relief and guilt for missing her afternoon detention, especially since she had been its cause. But it passed when she arrived at the bedroom and saw the forest-green trunk with iron hinges and bars waiting next to Quincy's bed with Q.H. embossed in gold on the lid. She brushed her fingers over the letters and watched them shimmer.

She opened her old trunk and pushed the clothes around, trying to find something worth taking to Oakley. She grabbed her sketchbook and the pencils, and then touched the remnants of the music box that she had folded up in a pillow case. She stood there a moment, considering the wooden pieces, but decided not to take them with her. Yet she couldn't let herself throw them away. On second thought, she opened the pillowcase and pulled out the metal music player. Even though its musical mechanism refused to work, she wrapped it in a nightgown and carefully placed it in the otherwise empty trunk going to Oakley. She wanted to take *something* from her actual home with her.

Ten minutes later, the rest of the girls walked into the room to change before dinner. Since Mrs. Adalin would be picking her up before the meal, she didn't have to eat with the rest of them. She looked up, feeling stares from all the foster girls. The news of her departure must have traveled quickly. Amanda's cold stare told Quincy that she would not forget serving detention without its perpetrator.

As the bell signaled five-thirty, she dragged her mostly empty trunk down the stairs. After looking back at the door one final time, Quincy walked away from the house to find a carriage waiting for her.

"You're right on time," said a smiling Mrs. Adalin.

The cabbie jumped down from the carriage and patted his horse on the rump before hurrying to open the back door, and placed her trunk behind the seats. Quincy climbed inside and slid in next to Mrs. Adalin.

"Are you excited to leave?" Mrs. Adalin asked.

"Mostly, but I'm kind of nervous," Quincy admitted.

"Well, that's to be expected. I would be anxious about your state of mind if you weren't."

Mrs. Adalin had Quincy direct the cabbie to Hermistad House, a nearby facility where individuals in varied states like her mother were cared for. When they arrived, Mrs. Adalin stayed with the driver.

"Quincy, dear. I'll wait out here. We have ten minutes before we need to leave to catch the train."

Quincy caught the look of sadness on Mrs. Adalin's usually sunny disposition and nodded, not wanting to say anything. She walked inside the house and was greeted by Michelle, the receptionist and the eyes of the Hermistad House.

She smiled at Quincy. “She’s in her room, sweetheart.”

“Thanks,” Quincy whispered.

She walked down the hallway, peeking at the different occupants of wheelchairs and beds, and the nameplates on the doors. Sometimes they would change if residents woke up from their comas or broke away from the trauma that kept them locked away in their heads. Other times they simply gave up.

Quincy stopped at the door that read CHELSEA HARRIS. Quincy poked her head inside the door and then walked over to the bed. Her mother looked so peaceful that she paused momentarily as if expecting her mother to wake and stretch her arms. When she didn’t, Quincy sat on the bed and held her mother’s hand. Her mother’s eyes flickered open, but they stared emptily at the wall, refusing to recognize her daughter. Even though her mother had not died in the accident, it was almost as if she had. Quincy hated to admit that even though her mother could occasionally move her eyes, she couldn’t do anything else.

“Hi, Mom.” she said softly, her eyes burning as tears welled. “I was accepted to Oakley. Someone paid for my tuition. Though I’m not really sure why...”

She curled up next to her mother, stroking her hair until she heard a soft knock sounded at the door telling her that it was time to leave.

A hot tear rolled down Quincy's cheek as she kissed her mother's forehead. "I love you," she whispered.

She stood up and walked two steps away from the bed before pausing and looking back at her mother. Mrs. Adalin knocked a second time, and Quincy sighed before slowly leaving the room.

"I'm sorry to make you hurry, love. But it's been nearly fifteen minutes and we must catch the train."

Quincy nodded and tried to hide her wet eyes on her sleeve.

Mrs. Adalin handed her a silk handkerchief engraved with a lily.

"Thank you," she said. She dabbed her eyes and then offered the handkerchief back.

Mrs. Adalin smiled sadly. "Please keep it."

Quincy placed the kerchief in her pocket and followed Mrs. Adalin back to the carriage. She sat silently, looking out the window at the receding Hermistad House and familiar neighborhood.

Mrs. Adalin's own silence allowed Quincy to continue looking at the passing storefronts. Buildings became taller as they moved toward the city, matching her growing anticipation, and more and more people began to clutter the sidewalk. She grimaced at the smog in the air and trash on the ground. The approaching evening closed down most of the businesses and darkened the windows of the surrounding buildings.

Quincy had never liked the city center of Albany, preferring her cleaner childhood city of Portland. She grimaced, remembering the tantrum she had thrown at twelve years old when they moved to Albany. She had taken a vow of silence that had lasted for two entire days.

The cab stopped in front of the Albany train station to drop them off. The cabbie pulled down Quincy's trunk and a small canvas bag of Mrs. Adalin's possessions.

Mrs. Adalin looked up at the clock in the train station. "Wonderful. Excellent timing! The train should arrive soon."

Quincy nodded and sat down on the bench next to Mrs. Adalin.

"Oh, before I forget." Mrs. Adalin rummaged through her bag and handed Quincy a piece of paper with a list of clothes, books, and other objects. Above the list was FIRST YEAR SUPPLIES FOR OAKLEY. Quincy glanced over the page.

"What's Oakley like?" she asked.

Over the years, Quincy had heard rumors of golden doorknobs and lavish dinners teasing her and other foster kids who dreamed of attending. She wondered what was real and what had been exaggerated.

Mrs. Adalin paused. Then she patted Quincy on the shoulder. "It's a wonderful place to learn. It's one of the top five schools in the world, after all."

"So you like it, then?"

"I myself never attended Oakley. My brother did, though. He loved it."

Quincy perked up. "Could your brother have known my parents?"

"I doubt it, dear. Different ages, I believe. And it's a fairly large school."

"Oh, right."

Mrs. Adalin squeezed Quincy's shoulder while glancing her watch. "It's almost time. But to warn you, Quincy, this is a slow train with five stops. As long as it is not delayed, we will arrive in New York very early tomorrow morning. Then we'll fly to London the day after."

Quincy looked up in surprise. London was her father's birthplace! The city's large streets and buildings had been the backdrop of her favorite stories.

"Why aren't we flying into Cardiff?" Quincy wondered aloud. That's where her mother had always mentioned going.

"There are more stores in London, and it's the main hub for students to take the eagle to their individual schools. It's an excellent chance for you to meet your classmates."

Quincy leaned back on the bench and closed her eyes. She couldn't believe that she was finally leaving North America. She sighed, wishing that they were taking an eagle to New York City instead of the slow train.

Mrs. Adalin gently tapped her shoulder, startling her from her daydream. The train pulled up to the platform at midnight, and Mrs. Adalin ushered Quincy onto the train. And just as the whistle sounded, Quincy fell fitfully asleep in her seat, lulled by the groan of the train.

Chapter Five

Lord Wilbright E. Fairnight

Lord Wilbright E. Fairnight, master planner and lord of the grand Fairnight estate in the wild Scottish highlands, sat in the dark room staring at the presently illegible writing on the walls. He didn't need the light to know what he had written on them. He had the information safely tucked away in his head. He only wrote it down for the visual point of view and the pleasure of adding and erasing his words. His brow furrowed, trying to decide which next step was the most logical of his choices.

Two years had already been wasted on this blasted project with him hitting proverbial wall after proverbial wall. Finally, last week, he had realized his blunder. He stared angrily at the corner of the room where the names of all the O'Sullivans were listed. What kind of father handed down something so precious to the youngest of his three children, and more shockingly, to a woman. Family heirlooms were always given to the first son. At least that's how they did it in Scotland.

Wilbright shut his eyes and pulled a silver locket from his breast pocket. He slid his fingers against the metal. The familiar feeling simultaneously gave him comfort and great anguish.

I will get you back, he promised. We will be together again.

"Shh," someone whispered outside his closed door, rudely interrupting his reminiscence. His eyes flicked open, and he looked toward the door.

"What if he's in there?"

"He's not," another brazen voice answered. "He leaves the room lit if he's working in there. But, Leslie, it's dark, see?"

"Oh."

"So have you been inside?"

"Of course not, Miranda! I thought that only his personal valet and the housekeeper were allowed in there."

"Oh, everyone does it. As long as you're not caught," Miranda replied.

Wilbright stared in the direction of the voices. He shut his eyes, going through his mental list of all of his employees. Ah yes, his two under maids.

"What's in there? He doesn't have...dead bodies or somethin' right?"

Wilbright's lips twitched into a tight smile. From time to time he wondered what his staff thought of him.

"No, it's even more peculiar. Three walls in there are white, as snow. It's not normal paint, neither. It feels cold and your fingers slide right off it. And on those walls are different colored lines with nonsense writing and dates on them. It's erasable, too, because sometimes the writing changes. One day it's there and the next day it's not."

Wilbright frowned. Maybe it was time to invest in a lock for his office. He didn't want under maids poking through his notes. Even if they couldn't understand it.

"So curious! What do the lines mean? What does he do in–" But before Leslie could continue, there was a brusque "ahem," from a third person outside.

Wilbright was almost disappointed. He had to admit he was just a little bit curious what his under maids thought his "lines" meant.

"Don't you both have work to do that does not include loitering next to the master's office?"

Wilbright recognized the voice of his valet, Hatchet, before he heard a *tap* on his office door.

"Enter," Wilbright replied.

The valet opened the door, and Wilbright caught a cursory glance at the two quivering maids. They fled before he could reprimand them.

The valet walked into the dark room and cleared his throat, "May I light the room, milord?"

Wilbright paused, deciding he wanted the light. The dark room usually helped him to think, but it wasn't providing him much insight today. "By all means," he finally replied.

The valet set the tray he was carrying next to his master and handed him the tea cup, and a letter before opening the previously shaded windows and lighting the candles. Suddenly the room became bright, the light bouncing off the oddly white walls.

Wilbright frowned at the letter. It seemed that everyone was going to interrupt his thinking this afternoon.

"Will there be anything else, milord?"

"No, Mr. Hatchet. That will be all," Wilbright said, dismissing the man.

The valet bowed and walked toward the door.

"Actually, there is one thing."

"Sir?'

"Give those two maids a final warning. I don't want them near my office again. And they will not get any letters of reference if they're terminated."

"As you wish."

Hatchet left without another word and closed the door behind him with a *click.*

Wilbright took in a sharp breath of air and slowly released it from his nostrils. He paid servants to serve, not to stick their noses into his personal business. He took the letter opener and sliced the envelope. He swore as he began to read, and then ripped the letter to pieces.

"Curse you, Prendergast," he grumbled darkly.

He stomped toward the corner of the wall and erased generations of the O'Sullivans. He grabbed a pen and in the now-empty space wrote the name Katelyn Prendergast.

Wilbright pointed his finger and narrowed his eyes at the name. If he was correct, Prendergast had the O'Sullivan key. With help from the Dublin library, he had followed the family line from daughter to daughter. Not easily done with their married name changes.

"I will find your key," he swore.

He ran a hand through his almost-completely white head of hair and rubbed between his eyes. After sighing at the board, he walked back to his chair, took off his tweed jacket, and sat down.

He clasped his hands, frowning at his reflection in the window. His white hair always surprised him. Sometimes he found it difficult to believe that he was not even forty-five.

He pulled out an expensive fountain pen and a notebook from his jacket pocket and held the pen poised over the paper. He stared at the pieces of the torn letter. What to do? Katelyn Prendergast was *dead*. She had lost her life to severe pneumonia almost fifteen years prior. With her death, the key had disappeared. She should have placed it in the family vault, as all the women of her family line had done before her, but according to the letter, his man in Dublin had said the key was not there. Where had the minx put it?

And the plot thickened, too. She hadn't left behind a daughter, only a son. A son who was perpetually ill and always trailed by two security guards. Would she have broken the tradition to entrust it to him?

Walking up to another of the lined and scribbled-upon walls, he angrily erased one of the lines. Then he slowly returned to the opposite side of the room and stared at yet another list of names. He focused on the final name: Quincy Harris. The girl incited in him both relief and frustration. Relief in that she had lived. He had instructed the man in New York to *find* Chelsea Harris, not to accidentally ram into their carriage, eliminating two of the three Master-Key Bearers. They were exceedingly lucky that Chelsea's eldest daughter had been home sick with a cold.

His relief turned to frustration at the memory of his servant. Instead of quietly following the girl to see where she had been placed in the foster system, he'd fled in fear, thus ending any hope of redemption. The girl had slipped right through his fingertips! It seemed that whenever Quincy Harris coincided with his timelines, she foiled his carefully laid plans. The servant's selfish behavior had lost him the only living Master-Key Bearer.

Good servants were difficult to come by these days.

Wilbright angrily slammed his palm against his whiteboard. As a result, his perfectly created calculations and been ruined! Again! It almost annoyed him more than the failure of the mission. His business partner had become very angry when the news had been brought to him, as well. Or at least he thought Prieler had been angry, but it was becoming more and more difficult to read his true emotions.

That's what happens when you experiment on yourself, Wilbright thought, crossing his arms and restraining himself from rolling his eyes.

He had eyes in every major NEFS station on the East Coast and all over Europe in case she would appear. According to his favorite line on the wall that she would eventually make her way through New York. Now it had become a game of waiting.

He reached into his pocket and grimaced as he touched the cool metal, a sense of dread hanging over him. He pulled out the key and stared intensely at the keyhole lined with antlers like the red deer of his family crest. His options were running out. It would be only a matter of time before he would have to use the key and search for the others from the set in the past. Time traveling came with severe consequences, but they couldn't outweigh results.

He pulled out the locket and stared at the two objects in each hand, dreaming of what he could do once he had all the keys. He smiled slowly and placed them back in their individual pockets.

She was worth the risk.

He had a sip of tea and closed his eyes, waiting for further news before he rewrote any more of his precious timelines.

CHAPTER SIX

THE TRANSLATION FOR GIBBERISH

Quincy woke up from her light doze when the train squealed to a stop. The train had stopped at Poughkeepsie for over an hour from rail failure. She hadn't slept well and she longed for a bed that didn't move. Rubbing her eyes, Quincy stretched and looked outside the window. She spied a second train leaving the platform of a station. "Are we there now?"

"Yes, we have arrived. Grab your things. We'll go pick up our trunks in the back." She smiled at Quincy before collecting her own belongings. "I wonder what time it is."

"It's 5:17," Quincy absent-mindedly mumbled.

"Oh really? And how do you know that?" Mrs. Adalin asked, amused.

A conductor stole Mrs. Adalin's attention by offering to help with their belongings. She paused outside the train when she saw the large station clock. "Oh, you must have seen the time from the train?"

"Must've been it." Quincy conceded with a yawn.

Mrs. Adalin directed her toward the outside of the station and into the morning air. Quincy's stomach grumbled and Mrs. Adalin bought two apples from a fruit vendor. Quincy bit into the sweet apple, savoring every mouthful. She looked sadly at the apple core when she finished, wishing that it had been larger. Once Mrs. Adalin had finished hers, too, she hailed a carriage. They were settled inside, and Mrs. Adalin outlined the next part of their journey while Quincy rubbed the grogginess from her eyes, fighting to stay awake.

"We need to go to the identity office today to set up your school papers and renew your passport." After *passport*, Quincy stopped listening. Her eyes widened and she was certainly not in danger of falling asleep now that the excitement was creeping back in. She stared at the large buildings, the sleek carriages, the water fountains, and the stylish window models. She'd never seen anything like it. The carriage dropped them off at large building with a sign that read, THE NEW YORK CITY HOTEL.

As she stepped inside, her jaw dropped. Marble tiles gleamed underfoot, and serene paintings hung on the clean white walls. Small rainbows danced on the floor and up her arms. She looked up to find a crystal chandelier.

"Wow," she breathed.

"Wait here, please, dear," Mrs. Adalin said before she headed to the front desk, leaving Quincy in the foyer. She stared at a large statue of a lion in the center of the room. A few minutes later, Mrs. Adalin lightly grasped her arm and led her to the room. When they reached the door. Mrs. Adalin handed her a wrapped package. "There are two nightgowns in here that should be about your size."

Quincy nibbled her bottom lip. "Thank you, Mrs. Adalin. But I actually brought a nightgown with me."

"That was thoughtful of you. But I have already bought this with you in mind. I don't believe this would fit me." She smiled. "Please accept the gift. I encourage you to get some sleep now. I'll wake you up in a couple of hours for a late breakfast. Rest well."

Quincy doubted that she could fall asleep with all the excitement, but she changed out of her grimy clothes into a rose smelling nightgown and sat on the bed. She couldn't remember a mattress so soft and despite her excitement, curled up and fell asleep on the large bed.

***

Quincy recoiled from the biting wind that drowned all other sounds. She couldn't see anything for miles upon miles except the heather that covered the ground like a plague. It was as if she were the only one alive in the vast wasteland. She pulled her flowing dark-green coat tighter to fit her wiry figure. Wings rustled as a bird landed on her shoulder, pinching through her coat with his talons, holding on. The large black bird—a raven or possibly a crow— pointedly ignored her. Her hazel eyes searched the purple horizon. She pulled out the silver braided chain from under her shirt, and making sure it was still there, grasped the key. The black bird shifted its weight back and forth on her shoulder, and she shivered.

She had been here before, she realized.

A flash of light burst into the starless sky, then, and suddenly the landscape around her began to change. She was hurled through a vortex of vibrant colors and she watched the blurred images fly past her until she couldn't distinguish her current location anymore. She saw herself reading the paper on her father's lap and playing with paper dolls with her sister in the kitchen.

For a moment she was blissfully happy, and then her sister began to dissipate. Screaming her sister's name, she reached for the smaller girl but the tiled ground enveloped them both. Quincy fell through the floor and landed with a thud on wet grass. She was sitting across from two tombstones in an otherwise empty field. Raindrops hit her cheeks, slid along her face, and dripped from her chin.

They had all left her behind.

The scene around her changed again, and this time the black bird was back on her shoulder. Another—and a much stronger—gust of wind grabbed the two of them and blew them away into the sky. People she had never seen before spun around her. They kept screaming her name, begging for her to save them. But she didn't know how to help them. Her face felt muzzled as if some invisible creature had flown up behind her and put its shadowy hands over her mouth.

Just above her, a hawk swooped and laughed at her agony. The black bird snarled and launched from her shoulder, leaving her alone once again. This ghostly embrace would be her end.

A chilling voice swallowed the other sounds as Quincy tried to scream. She knew that voice. It belonged to the man in the burgundy suit. The accented, monotone voice spoke directly in her ear, "You and only you can make the choice and follow it. But the question is... what will you choose?"

A loud knock jerked Quincy awake. Her eyes flickered, disoriented, around the strange room. Her hand was clenched around the key, and she forced herself to release it.

"Who is it?" Quincy cautiously asked.

"Don't be silly, dear. It's only me." Mrs. Adalin opened the door and walked inside with more brown packages in her arms.

"Open these and decide what you wish to wear today. Meet me downstairs to eat in fifteen minutes, all right?"

Quincy nodded tensely, and Mrs. Adalin left to give her some privacy.

Inside the packages were a skirt, khaki pants, a sweater, and some shirts, and a pair of brown oxfords. These were her first new clothes since before the accident, and she touched each item gently. After sorting through them, Quincy decided on the skirt and a sweater and walked downstairs to meet Mrs. Adalin. She winced on the stairs, stopping to adjust her new shoes. It would take some time to break them in.

Mrs. Adalin greeted her with a smile as Quincy sat down at the table she'd reserved. After a nice meal, she followed Mrs. Adalin back into a cab and watched the street signs that pointed them toward the central part of the city.

"Where are we going first?" she asked.

"To get your passport sorted." Mrs. Adalin explained. "It will take awhile."

Quincy sat straight up, suddenly glad she had new clothes to wear if she was going to have her photo taken, and gazed out the window of the carriage. The city seemed to go on forever, and she gawked at the buildings that touched the sky. She had no idea cities could be so vast. She finally lost count of the large streets they passed when the carriage suddenly stopped in front of an oddly shaped building that was a half-square, half-circular. A large sign in front of the building read, TRAVEL AND REGISTRATION OFFICES.

Quincy quickly followed Mrs. Adalin into the government building. They waited in line for her photo, and then headed upstairs to the Records department. They took their place in line again, and Quincy stared down at her picture. An emotionless face looked back at her.

Quincy sighed and looked up at the family in front of her. The father was balancing a pen between the top of his lips and his nose. The kids burst into fits of giggles, and their mother pretended to be exasperated with her husband. Quincy smiled, amused by them. Her enjoyment soured again, though, when she looked down at her lonely photograph. The time she had sat for a photograph, it had been with her younger sister.

She wanted to ask if Mrs. Adalin was close to her own parents or if she had any children, but prying into the barrister's life when she hadn't offered any details about herself probably wasn't a polite thing to do. Instead, she focused on a more realistic question.

She looked over at Mrs. Adalin. "Where is all the money for school and my expenses coming from?"

The barrister cleared her throat and kept her gaze straight ahead. "Your tuition and travel expenses have been paid for by a wealthy benefactress who wishes to remain unknown. She wanted to follow your parents wishes."

"She's a *she*?"

Mrs. Adalin pursed her lips. "Because I am under her pay, I am required to keep her wishes. I am, however, also helping you keep charge of your estate until you turn eighteen. You're not exceedingly wealthy, but you have enough money to spend every year with some leftover on your eighteenth birthday."

"But I was told I wasn't allowed to touch that money."

"They do that because they feel that they cannot trust fifteen-year-olds to spend their money wisely. With the help of a barrister like me, you are allowed an annual stipend for books and clothes."

Quincy nodded, relieved that she was spending some of her own money. Guilt filled her at the idea of this mysterious benefactress paying for her education. If the woman cared enough about Quincy and her family, why wait so long to help and then not take any credit for it?

When they were finished with the second line, Mrs. Adalin guided Quincy to the third floor to wait in their final line. Thank goodness, too, because Quincy's feet were really starting to scream in the brand-new oxfords. She paused and looked around. Two built men wearing black suits and sunglasses watched the room and the people waiting.

"Why is this line longer than the others?"

"This is the customs line, the final thing you must do to acquire your travel papers. In order for students from other countries to travel in the States, they need to get permission to come and go. Since you are going to London, you also need permission."

Mrs. Adalin scanned the line, looked at her watch and pursed her lips. "This is taking us longer than I had expected, though. I need to send a telegram ahead before the post office closes. I saw one across the street so I will be back momentarily. Stay in line and hand them your papers when it's your turn. I'll meet you in the waiting room when you're done."

Quincy nodded, and Mrs. Adalin waved as she left. Quincy leaned out of the line for a moment and counted the people in front of her. Fifteen. And there was another family already behind her. This would take awhile with only one person working the counter as there was. The woman behind the desk seemed like she might be new, too, because she kept dropping things and stuttering apologies. Quincy stifled a yawn and rubbed her neck. Slowly the line began to move and the room started to empty as it got later and later in the afternoon. Finally, only two families stood in front of her.

After sixteen minutes of waiting for the first family to finish, Quincy became restless. So did the man in front of her. She hadn't noticed him before because he blended in with the large family in front. He dropped his book to the floor, and for a full minute, paused before picking it up. Quincy almost reached down to get it for him, but before she could do so, the woman standing next to him tapped him on the shoulder. He slowly nodded, and bent over to retrieve his book with shaking hands. He wore a long, dark-blue jacket that went past his knees, and his white-haired head only reached the woman's shoulders at his full height. He was even shorter than Quincy. Maybe he was the children's grandfather? She peeked at the side of his face and her eyes widened in surprise to see that he was a boy not much older than she was. She narrowed her eyes and gave him a closer inspection. The hair she'd thought was white was actually light blond.

The voices ahead of them rose as multiple people spoke at once until someone cleared his throat loudly. The few people left in the room turned to stare at the boy in front of Quincy.

In a silky accent, he began to speak. "Which location are you trying to attain travel papers for?" he asked the other family. "The lady behind the counter has been unsuccessfully trying to tell you that code you are using is for Agagos, the school in South Africa. Is that where you are planning to attend?"

Before anyone could answer, he continued.

"No, I thought not. The papers that I believe you are attempting to obtain are for Australia which has a similar code but deviates by two digits. Secondly, you may not use a picture taken two months ago from another location because everyone from this area of the world must have the identical backdrop. And finally, the paper that you are so desperately searching for," he added, turning toward the lady behind the counter who was now flabbergasted, "is located in the second filing cabinet, not the fourth one."

Everyone was silent for a moment. "I believe all your questions have been answered?" he added stiffly while rubbing his forehead.

The adults in front nodded dumbly, and after another awkward pause, they continued with their business, but this time much faster.

The boy's mother leaned over to him, and Quincy tried, and failed, not to overhear the whispering woman coldly berating him.

"I thought that I told you not to do that in public," she hissed in the same accent as his.

The boy shrugged. "I do not wish to spend any more time in this queue than I must," he said simply.

Quincy's eyes widened. She wondered what kind of person would be reprimanded for helping people but not for speaking disrespectfully to an adult. She would have been grounded by her parents or whipped by Miss Heatherwood if she had spoken like that to anyone in charge. But now it was their turn. The family's business was finished quickly and as they were leaving the room, the boy turned his head in Quincy's direction, and for a brief moment, their eyes met. The moment passed too quickly for Quincy to distinguish any details, but the encounter left her with goose bumps on her arms and legs. As the boy walked away, the two men in black suits followed.

It was finally Quincy's turn. She showed the records lady her papers. The frazzled woman reached down and picked up Quincy's picture.

"You chose to use an American passport instead of a British one. Is that correct?"

Quincy nodded. They'd given her the option to get a British one because of her parents, but it wasn't her home.

The woman pulled out a blue book with a green eagle on the corner and pasted Quincy's picture on the first page with her personal information. She stamped the first page.

Don't forget to have your book stamped every time you enter or leave a country, okay?"

"Okay. Thank you."

The woman smiled tightly and rubbed her forehead, and Quincy took that as her cue to scurry off. She headed toward the waiting room but found Mrs. Adalin sitting just outside the doorway.

"All finished," Quincy told her.

"Excellent. I would prefer not to have to do this again anytime soon," Mrs. Adalin daintily yawned into a handkerchief and stood up.

"I second that," Quincy muttered, her legs sore from standing in lines all day. She grasped her passport tighter as they left the building. Pausing outside, she took a deep breath of the crisp evening air, relieved to be done. While waiting on the curb for a carriage, something flew past Quincy's face, and her gaze followed the bird as it landed. Was it Talin? She looked closer, and her shoulders slumped. It had only been a pigeon.

Finally, the cab arrived and they went back to the hotel and ate hearty pot-pies for a late lunch. Quincy took a bite of the steamy pie and slowly chewed. Despite the crispy piecrust, she found it difficult to enjoy it. The crust was missing an ingredient, but she couldn't figure out which one. Her mother would know. Quincy sniffed and wiped her nose on her napkin. Longing for her mother would come in waves, and she tried to hold this one back.

Mrs. Adalin gently placed her hand on top of Quincy's. "Do you enjoy reading?"

Quincy slowly nodded, not saying anything.

"Well then I have excellent news for you. Tomorrow, before our flight, we'll buy some books for the journey."

Quincy tightly smiled. "That sounds great." But her heart still ached. Tomorrow she was truly leaving her mother behind. She finished her meal in silence and then excused herself to try to sleep.

Chapter Seven

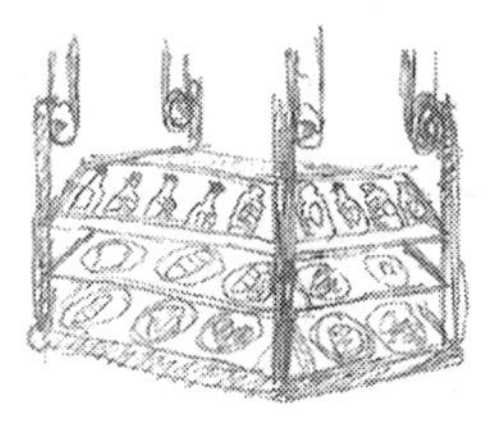

The NEFS

Mrs. Adalin woke Quincy up in the early morning, long before the sunrise. Quincy chose a comfortable sweater and khakis to wear before meeting Mrs. Adalin downstairs for breakfast. She found it difficult to sit still and forced herself to eat her cinnamon oatmeal. It had been over five years since she had ridden an eagle from Portland, and she felt restless with travel anxiety. Once she had managed to finish her meal, they caught another carriage to take them out of the city. Quincy watched the shadows of the large buildings slowly disappear until she began to see fewer lights and more trees. Quincy yawned into her sleeve. She wished that the darkness didn't make it so difficult to see the countryside.

After a twenty-minute ride, the carriage stopped right in front of a sign on the roadside that read, WELCOME TO YOUR LOCAL NATIONAL EAGLE FLIGHT SERVICES SERVICING NEW YORK CITY.

Mrs. Adalin paid the cabbie while he pulled their luggage next to the sign. He took his money and urged his horse to carry on. The two waited in silence as other carriages continued to drop off passengers until six people waited by the road. After eight minutes, a different, larger carriage came from the opposite direction and picked them all up. The driver took them past the sign toward what looked like a forest. After they passed the barrier of trees, they entered into a clearing with a large glass building.

Quincy's heart began to thump as she got out of the carriage.

"Come along dear," Mrs. Adalin said as she grasped Quincy by the shoulder and led her into the glass building.

Quincy looked around in surprise at how many people were bustling around the station, grabbing coffee, checking the station clock, and buying tickets. Mrs. Adalin stopped by a small shop near the main doors and gestured Quincy inside. She suggested that Quincy pick out a couple of books that looked interesting to her. One of the books she chose had gold engravings of fairies on the binding, and the second was about the flora and fauna of forest life.

Afterward, they set their bags down in another glass room that said WAITING AREA over the door. Mrs. Adalin gave Quincy some money and sent her off to pick out a beverage and one snack from a small café in the corner of the room while she checked to make sure their flight hadn't been delayed.

"Whatcha having today, sweetheart?" the lady behind the counter asked. She popped her gum, and her large hoop earrings moved with the slightest tilt of her head. One even caught in her curly hair.

Quincy looked up at the menu behind the woman and saw many unfamiliar types of beverages and snacks. “Hot chocolate, please.” She at least recognized that. “Oh, and also a blueberry muffin,” Quincy grinned at the large muffin in the case.

“Would you like some peppermint or raspberry syrup with your hot chocolate, sweetie?” asked the woman while wiping her hands on her apron.

Quincy’s eyes widened at the thought of something added to her hot chocolate. “I’ve never tried that before,” she admitted. She tapped her fingers on the counter. “Okay, raspberry, please.”

After her first sip, she smiled. She drank it slowly, trying not to guzzle it down. She found Mrs. Adalin back at their seats and sat down next to her. Mrs. Adalin handed her a ticket, and they looked through Quincy’s books while they waited to board.

Fifteen minutes later, her reading was interrupted by a piercing bird’s call. Quincy looked up just in time to see the station’s ceiling begin to open. An extraordinarily large gray bird swooped in and landed on a large patch on the bottom of the room. The conductor began to yell, “Passengers disembark!” while waving his hands.

The eagle bent down in a nesting position, giving Quincy a glimpse of the three boxes stacked on its back and the thick leather straps around its wings. The bottom two boxes were larger than the smaller one on top. That one had a long tube connecting it to the side of the eagle’s head. The two larger boxes opened and twelve people, six from each compartment, disembarked from a ladder that led to the floor of the station. Two more people, both in NEFS uniforms, dismounted from the top box next, and then the same conductor yelled, “All aboard! This flight travels through Amsterdam and then on to Paris!”

Twelve new people mounted the bottom two compartments as a large water pan was wheeled over to the eagle so it could be hydrated. Ten minutes later, after everyone had settled in, another set of people wearing NEFS gear entered the top compartment. After a final minute, the eagle stretched out its wings and tail feathers before taking off into the sky bound for Amsterdam.

Quincy rubbed her fingers and looked at the board of arrivals and departures, wishing that the wait time would speed up. But it was thirty more minutes before another eagle descended and London was finally called. The conductor looked at their tickets and travel books before ushering them onto the ladder for the bottom compartment. Quincy took her place next to Mrs. Adalin in the center of one of the two benches and patted the soft plaid fabric. It hadn’t changed since her early childhood. It reminded her of the room inside overnight trains. The compartment itself was made of varnished wood with four slots for candles at night.

Quincy’s stomach heaved as the eagle tensed and then took off through the open ceiling. She closed her eyes tightly and wondered if it was possible for her heart to leap through her mouth. When the eagle stopped ascending, she slowly opened her eyes, relieved that she had not lost her heart or her muffin. She looked out the small window on the side of the compartment and watched New York

City grow smaller in the dim early-morning light. After the eagle had flown into the clouds, she began to look around at her fellow travelers.

On the other side of Mrs. Adalin, sat an older lady who began to knit, and on the other bench opposite them a couple whispered and giggled profusely. The man sitting directly across from Quincy wore black—*all* black. He rested his hand on a dark-wooden walking stick and leaned back in his seat. His bowler hat had a feather in it. A black feather. An odd embellishment, Quincy thought. He placed his hat over his eyes as if knowing he was being observed. Embarrassed, she pressed her face to the glass to see the sky brighten.

After watching the fluffy clouds for half an hour, she made designs on the condensation of the window, bored. "Mrs. Adalin?" she whispered.

"Yes," she replied without looking up from her newspaper.

"How long is this trip going to take?"

"About seven hours give or take the air current."

Quincy held back a sigh. "That long?"

Mrs. Adalin patted her hand. "How about you read this while you wait?" She handed Quincy her newspaper. She stared at the paper titled, *The Chronicle*, and felt her heart beat faster. She recognized it. She used to pick up this paper every morning just before breakfast on the corner market in Portland. She and her sister used to put their foreheads on the glass of the doughnut box that had been strategically placed next to the papers. Occasionally they were rewarded with something sweet. She hadn't seen this newspaper since her father had died.

The news headline read, *Missing key found?*

Quincy's throat went dry as panic swept through her. Did people know about the key?

She read on:

In an attic in Manchester, England, a Mr. Geneva claims to have come across what could be a minor key during a late-spring clean. But before he can claim the coveted title of Minor Key Bearer, the key will have to be tested and then certified by the Board of Patents in Oxford.

Melody Mauvaise, an expert of the lore of the keys, believes that this could actually be one of the four minor keys since, rumor has it, a key must be floating around Great Britain. Gerald Kimsey a well-known scholar and graduate from Oakley Academy, disagrees, arguing the validity of such a rumor. After all these years, he believes the keys have now been permanently lost, if they in fact existed at all.

Here's a short refresher for those of you who have forgotten the childhood tale of the Man Who Created the Keys. The first key he created for himself, which only he could use. The other four could be used by any, their power believed to open any locked door. According to legend, the purpose of these five keys was to hide a device so powerful that it would have been detrimental to the entire world and all of time if in the hands of the wrong person. Its creator believed that it would either start a devastating war or create peace, so he built a door that would only open with five keys at the hand of a deserving Master-Key Bearer.

The tale is believed to be about GMC Engineer Wallace Masterson. All other details have long been forgotten, lost in the passage of time. This story has been passed down for so many generations that no one truly knows the fact from fiction.

Could this key be one of the four minor keys? At this point it's anyone's guess.

Quincy grasped her key, remembering how Talin told her she was the only one able to bear the key. She swallowed. Why had she never heard the tale of the five keys? And where were the other four?

She looked back down at the paper and turned the page to the gossip column. A woman wearing a robe and a curly wig seemed to be addressing an unseen audience. Underneath the picture, the writer questioned why a Third had been seen in Wales instead of in Oxford where she should have been busy with Parliament. Quincy had never met a Third. She knew that Thirds were an elected body of government that created the Talent laws, but they'd never had anything to do with her and had little power in the more remote cities. Maybe she would meet one at Oakley, though, and maybe that Third would know why her Talent hadn't presented itself yet.

***

After a couple of hours of reading, Quincy heard something above and below rumbling simultaneously. Then a trap door in the center of the floor and the ceiling opened up, and a device, like the broken dumbwaiter at Miss Heatherwood's, came through. A tray with different foods and drinks on it had been carefully arranged on the device.

Quincy looked over but touched nothing. She wanted to save her money in case she really needed it later. When asked if she wanted something, Quincy shook her head. "No, thank you."

"A sandwich and drink are complimentary on the flight," Mrs. Adalin nudged.

"Oh," Quincy grinned. "Thanks."

She reached for a sandwich and a fizzy, electric-green drink in a glass bottle that she was unable to identify. She opened the cap and looked inside at the slimy-looking green concoction. She brought it to her lips for a small sip, and then immediately gulped down the rest. The taste was unlike anything she'd experienced before. It attacked all her senses at once, and she couldn't decide if it was salty, bitter, or sweet. The drink fizzled on her tongue, making her want to laugh aloud. She held off for almost a full minute, not wanting to bother the other passengers, but finally she gave up and burst into giggles.

The young woman in the far corner smiled. "It usually only takes me twenty-five seconds before I start to laugh. I'm impressed you lasted so long."

Her husband patted her knee. "She's exaggerating. She's lucky if she makes it that long." She pretended to slap his shoulder and they went back to their romantic whispering. Quincy giggled again and looked at her smiling reflection in the window.

Chapter Eight

Plan D

The master in the three-piece tweed suit took one final turn around the garden in the crisp morning air before walking into his grand home. Opening the door, he found his manservant waiting for him at the bottom of the stairs. The servant shifted his weight uneasily from one leg to the other until he saw his master, and then stood up straight in attention.

"There's been a telegram for you, Lord Wilbright." he said, handing his master an envelope.

Wilbright waved his wrist to dismiss the man and opened the letter as he slowly made his way toward another part of the estate. He looked down, recognizing the sender. It was from his eyes in the London NEFS station.

He looked down at the telegram, and for a quick moment his face lit up. His uncle had often told him that he could be a handsome man if he frowned and schemed less, but with master planning as his Talent, scheming and frowning were simply symptoms of his genius. Not just anyone could see the whole picture. He lived in the hypothetical. All the hypotheticals.

He tightly smiled to himself. Quincy Harris had taken off in New York for London. He would have his eagle prepared and leave within the hour. He needed to talk to her, to find out how much she knew. What if she knew what was behind the door?

He tightly grasped the locket in his breast pocket. He needed to open the door if he was to save his love from her past mistake. He must speak with the Harris girl. If he left soon and planned correctly, he could overtake her before she arrived at school. Meeting her at Oakley would certainly be a bother. They kept the academy too secure, its borders well protected.

Or did they?

Wilbright smirked. Even Oakley's guardian wasn't without his own mistakes. There were still a few cards in play. And at least at this moment, time was on his side.

He made a mental note of items to pick up before takeoff, but first, he needed to inform his partner of the change of plans. Wilbright walked to the far side of the mansion and locked himself in one of the old guest rooms. He pulled a brick from the fireplace that triggered the heater to open into a hidden room. Sucking in his courage, he took a deep breath before walking into Prieler's office.

It was time to begin Plan D…

Chapter Nine

The World Beyond

A loud sneeze echoing in the cabin jolted Quincy awake just over four hours later. Her reaction then woke Mrs. Adalin, who blinked and checked her reflection in a small pocket mirror.

"You wouldn't happen to know what time it is, would you?" Mrs. Adalin teased Quincy. "Since you always seem to."

Quincy paused and frowned. "It is 1:12 pm. No, wait... it's 6:12 pm. Have we changed time zones?"

Mrs. Adalin looked at her in surprise. "I believe you are correct. It's probably one in the afternoon in New York and six where we're at now. How did you know?"

Quincy shrugged. "I just usually know what time it is."

Mrs. Adalin's eyes widened. "Really?"

Quincy looked over at Mrs. Adalin. "Is that a Talent? Knowing what time it is?" It seemed like a silly Talent to have, but she would rather walk into Oakley with any Talent than none at all.

"Not that I know of."

"Oh," Quincy answered, slumping her shoulders.

Mrs. Adalin patted her hand and then closed her eyes to fall back to sleep. Quincy sat up, now wide-awake. She looked over at the bench in front of her and saw the man wearing all black staring intently in her direction. She had an odd sense of déjà vu, as if they had met before. Embarrassment burned on her skin with his gaze on her like that, and she peered outside. By the time she looked over again, he had closed his eyes.

After another hour, the eagle descended into the twilight of the London evening. Quincy looked outside the window, trying to get a glimpse of her father's city. She crossed her arms in disappointment at the fog outside.

The street below opened for them and they flew into a dark tunnel.

"Where are we?" Quincy asked, her eyes wide in amazement.

"Underneath London. At the NEFS London Central Station."

Candles and mirrors filled the underground, reflecting light into the whole station. Quincy walked down the ladder and stood near the head of the eagle. She peered at the metal bar that connected it to the top compartment. She had never realized that the bar was hollow before. Above the din of the station, she just barely overheard the conductor thanking the eagle through the rod. She too decided to thank the eagle and looked up at its large intelligent eye. She might have imagined it, but she thought it winked at her.

"This way, dear. We need to go upstairs to have your book stamped," Mrs. Adalin said as she whisked her away through the crowd. Two burly young men burst out, bumping into Quincy and tripping her. She fell against the wall of the station.

"Sorry!" one yelled back as he followed his friend.

She stood up and leaned against the wall to get away from the rush hour jostle. She rubbed her skinned elbow while standing on her tiptoes trying to catch a glimpse of Mrs. Adalin's peacock-feathered hat. She whirled around, but she was nowhere to be found.

Quincy retraced her steps to the platform, but the eagle had already left. Quincy's heart began to pound and she felt lightheaded. She staggered toward a bench and gratefully sat down, hoping that an, NEFS member would walk by and she could ask if they'd seen Mrs. Adalin. But everyone seemed too busy for her to flag anyone down. Quincy curled up on a bench after deciding that waiting here for Mrs. Adalin would be better than getting completely lost. The ceiling creaked open and another eagle landed, but she ignored her surroundings and, instead, pulled out her key and began to rub it between her thumb and pointer finger. For some reason it made her feel connected to her mother and helped keep her calm.

Are you lost again, little one?

Quincy's eyes shot open at the voice, expecting to see a station worker waiting for her response. She frowned. No one was looking at her, let along talking to her. No one, except the largest eagle that Quincy had ever seen. The eagle was at least double the size of the other eagles she'd seen that day. Instead of three compartments on its back, it had six. Eyes of pure blue with small specks of gray gazed at Quincy, and she stared up at it, in awe of its size and great beauty. She felt so insignificant next to the bird.

They locked eyes and the eagle quickly blinked one of it's eyes. Did it just wink at her?

Then she gasped. *The eagle*, had it spoken to her! She had never heard of an eagle talking to its passengers, but after Talin, how could she be surprised?

Are you lost again, little one? it repeated, as if to confirm for her.

"Again?" she whispered. She knew that she had never seen this eagle before in her whole life. She would not have forgotten such a meeting.

That is true. You have not met me yet. I do apologize.

She looked around to see if anyone else had heard the voice, but no passersby had stopped to stare in shock. Quincy looked back at the eagle, pausing on its massive talons with a shudder.

You have no reason to fear me, it said. I just wanted to let you know the man at the door is here for you.

Quincy blinked, puzzled, and looked over toward the door. A man in an NEFS uniform was scanning the room and then met her eyes, relief sweeping across his face.

"Miss Harris?" he asked with a London accent.

"Yes," she answered and jumping up from the bench. She slowly backed away from the eagle toward the man. "Thank you," Quincy whispered to it.

NEFS LONDON
GATE-02

The eagle winked again and then closed its eyes. She turned away and followed the man up the stairs and into the custody of Mrs. Adalin.

"Oh good," she sighed. "I didn't know where you got off to!"

Quincy gave her a little smile as they waited in the international line. Once the customs officer stamped her book, allowing her into the country, they followed the throng of travelers and made their way out of the station and into the London night. She went from hot to freezing cold in a matter of seconds, and she rubbed her arms for warmth. But when she saw the London skyline, she instantly forgot about the cold, its lights mesmerizing.

The city streets were filled with people and noises. It wasn't fully dark, yet, but the lights on poles faced one another across the street so that anyone could go about their business when the sun fell the rest of the way behind the horizon. When she looked up, she could barely see the tops of the gigantic buildings. Mrs. Adalin took her hand and gave her a quick, gentle tug, and the two of them began to cross the street, trying to dodge people while guiding their luggage.

"Oh, I'm sorry," Quincy apologized.

"Mind where you're walking."

"Watch yourself!"

The shouts kept coming, but Quincy had difficulty understanding all the different foreign accents and finally gave up on trying to decipher them, instead focusing on the buildings. She saw fountains, small sidewalk cafés—most of which were now closed—pubs filled with laughter, and countless scores of people and animals out and about. Many carriages filled the roads and they stopped for pedestrians who got in their way. Yelling often followed from both sides, with the occasional addition of rude gestures.

"Are we going to get a cab?" Quincy yelled into Mrs. Adalin's ear.

"Not this time. We're almost there."

They crossed the street, barely being missed by a speeding carriage, and entered into a quiet neighborhood. They stopped outside a charming yellow home with a sign that read, BAILEY'S B&B.

The cozy building reminded Quincy of her childhood house with its warm golds and cheery rugs. She closed her eyes and breathed in the scent of freshly baked cookies.

A jolly woman with bright red cheeks walked in from the kitchen with a tray of those very cookies in her hand. "Welcome to my B&B! I'm Bailey, of course. Cookie?" She offered them the tray.

Quincy grinned and took one. "Thank you," she said before biting into the gooey cookie.

Bailey smiled. "You both look exhausted. Leave your things by the staircase and my son Mason will bring your luggage upstairs. Would you prefer to have food brought up to you, as well?"

Mrs. Adalin looked uncomfortable, and Bailey laughed. "We don't stand on ceremony here. We won't be offended if you choose not to eat in the dining room."

Mrs. Adalin smiled, and Bailey grabbed some keys from behind the counter. "Follow me."

Quincy followed the owner and Mrs. Adalin up the stairs. An assortment of landscape paintings lined the hallway at the top of the staircase. Quincy couldn't keep from studying the colorful pictures and nearly ran into Mrs. Adalin when she stopped in front of a room marked THE HOLLY ROOM.

"This is you, dearie." Bailey gestured to the door. "And for you, the Juniper Room." She pointed at Mrs. Adalin and then smiled at them both. "We'll bring you your supper momentarily. Please let us know if you're in need of anything." Bailey waved and walked back down the stairs.

When she was gone, Mrs. Adalin turned to Quincy. "I need a little bit of quiet time tonight, if you don't mind. Knock if you need me."

Quincy nodded and watched Mrs. Adalin walk into her room. She opened her own door and smiled at the lace curtains and matching bed covers. Before she could close the door, though, she heard a thump outside, and she whirled around to see a young man with a crooked grin balancing her trunk and a tray of tea and soup.

"Here's your things 'an supper." He smiled at her, and she felt her cheeks redden.

"Thanks," Quincy said as she grasped the tray.

"Well, good night." He smiled again, this time blushing. Quincy waited for him to leave before sitting on the bed and taking a sip of the calming tea. She sighed contentedly when she saw a second chocolate chip cookie on the tray. She yawned and curled up on the fluffy pillow with her new books and decadent treats.

***

Quincy sat curled against the chilly window watching the sunrise over the street. The foreign room had left her out of sorts. She missed her mother, and even the familiarity of Miss Heatherwood's.

Quincy grudgingly stood up to begin her morning routine. As she debated leaving her hair down or tying it up, someone knocked on her door and in a cheery voice called out, "Good morning!"

Quincy opened the door and Mrs. Adalin poked her head inside.

"Good morning!" she said again. Then her smile fell. "You look tired, dear."

Quincy nodded. "I feel it this morning."

Mrs. Adalin walked in and squeezed her shoulder. "Well then naps for us both this afternoon! Let's find you something hot to drink to wake you up."

Quincy grabbed a sweater and walked down the stairs into a dining room filled with mismatched tables and chairs where they ate an authentic English breakfast. When Quincy finished her cup of hot chocolate, Mrs. Adalin ushered her out of the building as she explained the schedule for the day.

"First of all we need to buy your books. Then we really ought to get your uniform, then we probably should have lunch, and then that will give you a chance to look through your new things, have supper, and then you really should get to bed at a decent hour since tomorrow you leave for school." Mrs. Adalin took a deep breath, finally done with her long rambling list.

Quincy's stomach began to twist. "I'm really going to school *tomorrow*?"

"Yes, of course. Come along now, Miss Quincy. We really haven't all day to dillydally."

She ran to catch up to Mrs. Adalin and kept close to her until a flower market stall caught her attention and she paused.

"Stay close," Mrs. Adalin yelled over her shoulder. Quincy hurried after the barrister again. She watched the streets pass, wishing that she remembered which one her father had lived on so that she could visit.

Mrs. Adalin stopped at a storefront. "Excellent. We've made wonderful time," she said, delighted as she closed a small pocket watch and placed it back in her pocket.

Quincy was going to ask where they were until she looked up and saw a sign that read, MR. BAUER'S BOOKSHOP…FOR BOOKS COMMON AND NOT SO COMMON

"We're seriously going to find my schoolbooks in here?" Quincy asked after sizing up the tiny storefront. "It looks so small."

"Looks can be deceiving," Mrs. Adalin winked. "Yes, we're going to find your books here."

When Mrs. Adalin opened the door, Quincy heard the tinkle of a small bell. A large desk met them at the front of the shop with a sign that warned the customer that the owner would be back in a matter of minutes.

"Why is he never where he should be?" Mrs. Adalin said under her breath, clearly annoyed. "Quincy, why don't you look around? I'll call you when Mr. Bauer arrives from…his break. But don't go far and don't leave. People tend to get lost in here."

Who could get lost in such a small shop? Quincy vaguely wondered if Mrs. Adalin was teasing her again.

She slowly wandered away from the front room, enthralled by the spines of the countless books. Occasionally she would stop and pull a book from the shelf to take in the different languages and printing styles. She breathed the wonderful scent of the musty pages as she went.

She walked into a number of different rooms, and it seemed as if the bookstore never ended. She paused at a large mirror, thinking it oddly placed, and looked at her reflection. But instead of seeing herself, she saw a young woman. Quincy guessed she must be in her early twenties. The woman winked at her and walked away, leaving a picture of an empty view of the shop for a moment.

Quincy frowned and stared at the empty mirror. Her own image suddenly popped into the mirror and she jumped and hurried out of the room and into another, trying to find her way back to

Mrs. Adalin. She must have taken a wrong turn so she began to desperately look for an exit sign. Finally she saw a glass door and grabbed the handle to walk outside. But it opened before she even turned the handle. She gasped, and a man with salt-and-pepper hair walked through the door with a steaming cup of something.

He groaned and placed himself between Quincy and the door. He firmly moved her away and shut the door behind him. "Wrong exit. Believe me. You don't want to go through that door," He laughed. Spectacles partially hid the laughter wrinkles near his eyes, but not completely.

"Quincy," Mrs. Adalin yelled, her voice echoing through the store.

"We're coming," the man next to her hollered back.

She followed the middle-aged man as they walked through room after room of books.

"I'm impressed," he said to her. "Not many people make it to the far side of the book shop."

"Where did that door lead?" Quincy asked.

"To another section of London. I'd hate for you to get lost, especially with you being an American and all that." He winked at her.

"Why is it different than the other door?" Quincy asked. The man hummed as if deciding what to say. They walked past the mirror, and Quincy stopped to look inside again. The man paused and stood next to her.

Quincy frowned. "There was a woman in the mirror before. Who was she?"

The man grinned. "It's like the glass door, the one I said not to go through. It's a bit of an amusing story, actually. I inherited this shop with a novel's worth of warnings. You see, this store was built on a time vortex."

"Meaning?" she prodded.

"Meaning that woman could have been a customer from the past, or the future or a person from a different dimension."

Quincy's head throbbed at all the possibilities. And she'd heard that word before...*timeline.* From Talin. "So like another world?"

"Exactly."

"How many time vortices are there?"

The man groaned. "You like asking questions, don't you? Honestly, I don't know how many there are."

Quincy thought about other worlds and these "timelines" as they continued on to the front of the room.

Mrs. Adalin sniffed when she saw the man appear next to Quincy. "How many cups?"

"This? This is only my second cup of coffee."

Mrs. Adalin folded her arms and frowned.

The man's shoulders slumped. "Fine. It's my fourth."

"It's only ten-thirty in the morning. You have an addiction," she snapped.

"I never said that I didn't have an addiction," he grinned mischievously.

"You're impossible."

"Oh, I'm impossible?"

Both stopped talking when Quincy respectfully cleared her throat. Mrs. Adalin unnecessarily smoothed her dress.

"Welcome to Mr. Bauer's Bookshop...for books common, and not so common. How might I be of service today?" he droned on, clearly having the speech memorized.

Mrs. Adalin answered for Quincy. "Schoolbooks."

"Indeed." Mr. Bauer's eyes left Mrs. Adalin, and he studied Quincy carefully.

Mrs. Adalin uncomfortably laughed. "Oh, I'm sorry. This is Quincy Harris, a new student at Oakley."

Mr. Bauer peered over his spectacles and seemed to gaze right into Quincy's most personal thoughts. She felt her cheeks flush.

"She found the other exit." he told Mrs. Adalin.

This time Mrs. Adalin coughed, and he ended the uncomfortable silence by addressing Quincy directly.

"Hello, Quincy," Mr. Bauer narrowed his eyes. "Or is it Quinn?"

Quincy gawked at the man. First Talin, now this man? How did everyone know the name her parents had called her?

His lips curled. "Talent for knowing preferred names. Not the most exciting Talent to be had, but it's mine. Please follow me."

Quincy no longer doubted that she could get lost in this shop and gladly followed them down the hallway. After a left turn followed by an immediate right, she lost track of the path they took. When they finally stopped, Mr. Bauer bowed his head slightly and left them alone. He closed the door behind him, and Quincy's mouth dropped in surprise when she surveyed the room.

The shadows of candle flames danced across the room. Two overstuffed chairs sat in front of the unlit fireplace. Quincy looked up and saw that the bookshelves reached to the high ceiling. How could such a large room fit in such a small shop?

"How…Is this from the time vortex, thing?" Quincy asked.

Mrs. Adalin looked over and laughed. "I'm not entirely sure to be quite honest. I've never bothered to find out," she sheepishly admitted. "Some kind of illusion, I suppose. It doesn't make too much sense to me, I'm afraid. What I do know though is that it allows him to use his Talent to do…" Mrs. Adalin's hand motioned to the size in the room. "All of this. But what do I know, I'm obviously not a Creative Engineer."

Just as Quincy had never met a Third, she had never encountered a Creative Engineer. When her father had been a young man, he had once dreamed of attaining Creative Engineer status.

"I wonder if this store was a Creative Engineer's final achievement?" Quincy asked.

Quincy's father had told her and her sister that in order to receive the title a person had to pass the series of tests. Almost anyone could work toward becoming a Creative Engineer, but it was not easy to earn the name. Quincy had heard of musicians, mathematicians, and actual engineers joining the CE branch of the government. The recognition of the title allowed people to vote on Creative Engineering issues, patents, and laws regarding the government. It was a title that usually took years to earn.

"Who knows?" Mrs. Adalin said, clearly uninterested.

"Okay, so which books do I need?" Quincy changed the subject. Daunted by the task, she took another look at the large bookshelves.

"We have a list here and there are more of those small tags around the room to help us find what we are looking for. Let me see, Arithmetic for Year Ones are over there, and Latin books, and wait, go over here for this book…"

Mrs. Adalin continued until they had a large pile. They hauled the books out of the room and went to buy them from Mr. Bauer.

When they were back in front of the shop, Mrs. Adalin paused in front of the bookstore owner.

"Farewell, Ellen." Mr. Bauer grinned at Mrs. Adalin, who at first tried not to respond, but in the end gave up and smiled back at the bookseller.

"Tell Mum hello please," Mrs. Adalin added.

Quincy scrunched up her face, confused. But before she could ask about it, he nodded and turned towards Quincy. "Pleasure to meet you, Miss Quinn."

"Thank you." Quincy gave him a tight smile.

After they were out of hearing distance of the shop, Quincy turned to Mrs. Adalin. "Is Mr. Bauer related to you?"

"Actually, yes he is. He's my older brother."

"Oh," Quincy said simply. She shoved her hands in her pockets, envious of the woman's family and their teasing banter. Mrs. Adalin seemed to understand Quincy's suddenly sober countenance and left her in silence.

***

After dropping off their purchases at the B&B, the barrister swept Quincy off to another part of London. They arrived at a much larger storefront with windows framing pinstripe suits and multi-layered skirts. The sign read, *Le Magasin Trés Chic de Madame Joyeux*. They walked through the door and into the clamor of people. Individuals of all ages and backgrounds were looking at different styles of clothing, many of them laughing together.

"Why are there so many people here?" Quincy asked. She grimaced as she got bumped into for the third time.

"They're all getting clothes for school, of course." Mrs. Adalin answered as if this was completely obvious.

"But then why wasn't the bookshop busy this morning? Don't they all need schoolbooks, too?"

"It was. It just hides people well so that they can have peace and quiet while they're looking for books. You only see the people you came in with, and Mr. Bauer, of course. It was built that way over fifty years ago. It's something to do with mirrors, I think."

Before Quincy could ask anything else, Mrs. Adalin pointed toward the main desk. The tall woman behind it tapped her pen while talking to a customer. Eventually she lifted the pen and twisted it up in her brown hair. When she saw Mrs. Adalin, the woman smiled delightedly and pulled out her writing utensil from her head.

"Ellen my dear, you are looking lovely." The lady wagged her pen. "But far too professional for my taste. Now what school are you 'ere for today?"

"Quincy, this is Madame Colette-Pierrette Joyeux. Would you like to tell her which school?" This time Mrs. Adalin looked at Quincy expectantly.

"Oakley, please." she answered tentatively.

"Ahh, *les aigles*. Follow me, *chérie*."

Quincy struggled to follow the French seamstress down the busy halls and past the packed rooms and was grateful when they arrived at the woman's planned destination. "'Ere I leave you both. Enjoy!" Madame Joyeux waved and headed off to help another customer.

Quincy turned around to look at the room. At its center, stood a statue of a large eagle, as if it were about to take flight. The circular room was covered with shelves filled with different types of school uniforms.

"This is the Oakley Academy patch," Mrs. Adalin told her, pointing to a patch sewed onto a nearby jacket. The patch showcased a *white* eagle midflight, its wings spread out and dangerous talons at the ready. It had big, all-knowing eyes that stared directly at the onlooker. It was as if it could fly out of the patch and cry out at any moment.

It was just like the eagle that had helped her yesterday, she realized.

A student near Quincy groaned and frowned at his father as they stood in front of a new piece of his uniform. “An apron? But, Dad, I’m never going to have to cook anyway. That’s a woman’s job.”

His father laughed. “Hardly. Besides, you might find that you actually enjoy it.”

Quincy looked around the room and bit her lip. She stared longingly at the art aprons. She’d always enjoyed painting, but Miss Heatherwood had never allowed it. She said it was “too messy.” So Quincy just drew in her sketchbook when she could sneak the time, which wasn’t often. She was suddenly very glad she’d packed her pencils and sketchbook. She had so much she wanted to draw, now—memories of her family she didn’t want to forget while she was away.

Contagious giggles grabbed her attention. Three girls compared skirts and one was trying on a science lab coat. Quincy wanted to try on clothes and laugh with them.

Mrs. Adalin tapped her shoulder. “Don’t worry. Next year, you’ll know just about everyone in here.”

Quincy forced a smile, nerves suddenly swallowing her whole, and turned to face Mrs. Adalin. A store attendant walked up to them, and helped Quincy choose clothes appropriate to her size and her year.

After they had paid for her new clothes, Quincy and Mrs. Adalin went back to the B&B and sat outside for a late lunch. Quincy watched two boys and a girl throwing a ball back and forth, their laughter echoing off the houses.

"What is there to do at school? You know, in case I don't make friends. Do they have a stable there?"

"There are plenty of things to do at school. There are libraries, as well as after-school sports and activities. And yes, they do have a stable," Mrs. Adalin nodded. "Though, to be honest with you, my dear, I have no doubt that you will be able to make friends at school. Things will be significantly better there than at Miss Heatherwood's."

Quincy hoped she was right. "So how long will it take to get there?" she asked between spoonfuls of vegetable soup.

Mrs. Adalin tried to stifle a yawn, but Quincy caught it. "From here to Oakley? It's a couple of hours on an eagle from London to the countryside in Wales."

Quincy nodded and looked outside, wondering what it would be like at the Welsh school as excitement and anxiety swirled in her stomach. As she watched through the window, a bird glided across the street and dropped a nut for the incoming traffic to break open. It wasn't a brown bird, like Talin, but it seemed as bold as the dusty bird she'd met in the stable at Miss Heatherwoods. She wondered offhandedly if she would see Talin again. Did she even want to? She still didn't appreciate his sarcasm, even though he had come to help her.

Mrs. Adalin rubbed her forehead.

"Are you feeling okay, Mrs. Adalin?"

"Yes, thank you, Quincy. But I am suddenly feeling tired from our morning."

"Maybe you'll feel better if you take a nap?" Quincy offered.

Answering her question, Mrs. Adalin yawned again. "I think that is a good idea. Here are two pounds if you'd like to buy something. You are welcome to look around, but don't go far, okay?"

"Okay. Sleep well," Quincy said.

Mrs. Adalin waved weakly and staggered upstairs.

Quincy finished her soup and walked outside intending to explore the nearby park. She paused on the corner of the street, breathing in the scent of freedom. She wrinkled her nose. Freedom smelled like a mixture of sweating horse and fresh bread from the local bakery. She giggled despite the strange smell, reveling in her free time.

She found the park quickly and sat on the bench to watch some kids play a game that she was unfamiliar with. Then she picked a wild flower and walked to the other side of the park. Soon bored, she left the park grounds and found a small shopping district. She loved the glimpses she'd gotten of London life so far and wondered what it would be like if *she* lived in the city.

She looked in windows and people watched. Couples held hands and fathers hoisted their daughters up onto their shoulders. Quincy's heart ached, but she pushed it away. She needed to enjoy this time. She felt around her pockets and touched the two coins that Mrs. Adalin had given her. She hoped to find an art shop to buy new pencils.

A burst of wind caught her off-guard, and she shivered, wishing that she'd brought her sweater. A raindrop landed on her nose, and she looked back toward the B&B. Not feeling like running back, she ducked into a storefront to wait for the rain to end. Hopefully it would just be a short shower. But the rain began to fall more rapidly, and soon the street echoed with the sound of raindrops. Without thinking, Quincy pulled the key from under her shirt and ran her fingers over its eye.

"That's a fascinating key around your neck."

Quincy jumped when she felt the breath of the voice next to her ear. Her legs stiffened and refused to move, as if rooted to the spot. His accent was like her own, an American West-Coast accent. What was he doing here in London? What did he know about her key? Was this one of the men who had been a part of the plot to go after her family? Was he after her now?

She tried to hide her paranoia from him, but she trembled anyway. "Th-thank you?" her voice quavered. She slowly turned to confront the speaker, but there wasn't anyone there. Again.

"Please tell me where a young girl like you came into possession of such a trinket?"

Quincy whirled around and nearly bumped into the man. He grasped her shoulders, steadying her. As soon as she had regained her footing, he pulled his dark cap over his eyes his dark wool coat closer to him. His black hair stayed stationary under his cap, unlike her own, which was wet and windblown. She wished she could see his features clearly, but the rim of the hat hid his face as his gaze darted right and left as if searching for someone. She looked down and saw a walking cane hooked to his elbow.

Finally, she softly replied, "It's my mom's. I don't know where she got it."

"If I had such a key in my possession, I would want to keep it out of sight and away from prying eyes. It's a good thing I have no interest in owning one myself."

Quincy bit her lip and slowly took steps away from the man toward the rainy street.

"I am here to warn you, not to harm you," he said quickly.

She stopped walking away but kept her distance as he continued.

"You are right to be afraid. There are people who would see that key and try to steal it, or even kidnap you. Fortunately, they need you alive. But that doesn't keep you free and safe. Do you really need another warning?"

The rain stopped then, but the wind began to howl and Quincy's eyes watered. She wasn't sure it was from the biting wind or from fear.

"Listen carefully. Go back into the protection of your guardian. Don't trust anyone who is not within the walls of your heart and your school. Keep an eye on your judgment, as well. Remember, they are watching you."

Before Quincy could ask who exactly was watching her, the man disappeared into the London streets. She looked around for him once more, and when he was nowhere to be found, she took off back to the B&B.

***

Fiddlesticks!

Wilbright watched as his beautiful blue line, the one known as Plan D, disintegrate before his very eyes. He watched the girl run down the street and away from where he stood. Who was it that was keeping a wary eye on her? Was that *him*? That had been the best opportunity to talk to her alone. From now on, it would only become more difficult. They would train her and brainwash her. All he wanted to do was show her a second path and give her his side of the truth.

Her guardian had not been with her, thanks to a paid employee and the sleeping pill that had dissolved in the woman's lunchtime drink. The girl had now undoubtedly been warned, and this would make his job much more difficult. He would have to come up with a Plan E... and quickly.

He pulled his tweed jacket collar up to his chin and walked away through the darkened alley, grumbling about Plan D as he headed toward the private eagle station for society's elite. He couldn't hold it off any longer. It was time to travel backward.

***

Talin landed on the rooftop and paused to catch his breath before growling. What was Wilbright doing here?

He knew Lord Wilbright very well. As a child, Wilbright had been serious but inquisitive, delighting in learning and knowledge. Talin had met few men as intelligent and driven as him. Except for maybe the other Fairnight. Jealousy—perhaps that was where the problem stemmed from? Despite the fact that this particular "spy" was in the top tier of intelligence, Wilbright's immaturity and bitterness kept him from achieving the greatness that he desperately desired. He should be circulating parliament, rising to power instead of sitting alone in his manor, pouting about his lost love like a child.

Quincy couldn't get to Oakley fast enough. Especially now that Wilbright was poking his pointy nose where it didn't belong.

What was he trying to accomplish?

Talin slammed his talon against the cement wall. His failing foresight was becoming a problem, as was his history with Lord Fairnight. Oh why had he been put in charge of this key business? He knew with complete certainty that he had his work cut out for him, but he always did, and he usually did a good job finishing what needed to be done. *Usually*.

Talin grimaced to himself.

That last time was not completely his fault. He'd had a moment's glimpse of a young woman, not much older than Quinn, looking up at him and smiling.

He quickly shook the memory away. He needed to be here right now. His thoughts returned to Quinn and he reminded himself that as soon as she arrived at Oakley, she would be safe. Well, safer anyway. Hopefully.

Oh why did he end up with the toughest job?

But he already knew the answer.

He was the only one left.

***

Quincy only stopped running when she reached the doorstep of the B&B. She smiled at the Bailey, but her fake happiness didn't reach her eyes. She quickly walked upstairs and into her room. She caught her breath as she remembered the man's haunting words. *You are right to be afraid.*

She shivered and curled up on her bed, then pulled out her mother's key for the hundredth time. If what was behind the door threatened the universe, why would someone fight against her and go through such lengths to follow her to London?

She looked outside, imagining that everyone walking by could be potentially watching her. Would she be safe at Oakley? She should have demanded answers from the man. He surely knew things she didn't. She shivered again and wrapped a blanket around herself.

A knock outside her door made her jump.

"Yes?" she called, looking for something to protect herself with.

"May I come in?"

Mrs. Adalin. Her body slumped in relief. "Yes, come in."

The barrister came into the room and sat on the bed beside Quincy. “Bailey informed me that you looked tense when you arrived back tonight. Are you all right?” She put the back of her hand against Quincy’s forehead to check for a fever.

Quincy nodded. “I’m fine. I just got caught in the rain.”

“Oh, okay. Do you want to go downstairs for some food?”

“I think I would rather stay up here. Is it okay if I eat in my room?”

“Certainly.”

Quincy smiled, relieved. She didn’t want to talk about any of it.

“Sleep well,” Mrs. Adalin said. “for tomorrow we will be getting up early for school. Good night.”

“Good night,” Quincy called, clutching the key to her chest once more.

Chapter Ten

The Inconvenience of Family

Wilbright took a seat in the plush chair of the private section of NEFS London. He pulled out the circular silver locket and rubbed the engraved cherry-blossomed branch. Wilbright stared as the gentleman in front of him ascended the eagle. He focused on the clock, thankful that he would depart soon. He politely covered a yawn and placed the locket back in his pocket. He furrowed his eyebrows as he mentally erased his line and plotted his next action. The Harris key wasn't going anywhere. He would only have to be more persuasive when their paths eventually intersected.

"Hello, Wil."

Wilbright whirled around in his chair at the sound of the Scottish brogue identical to his own. He found himself staring at the back of a man in a black bowler hat, sitting behind him. The man refused to turn to face him.

Wilbright sat face-forward in his seat again. "Hello, uncle. I wondered if that was you this afternoon," Wilbright bitterly answered.

"Yes, you thought correctly."

"What are you doing here?" he asked, already knowing the answer.

"I'm trying to protect a teenager," his uncle spat. "The same could be asked of you. Why the hell are you here?"

"Research."

"Research?" the man snorted. "What do you want with the girl?" He sighed. "I mean, of course, what do you want with her *key*?"

Wilbright gaped, and his uncle behind him laughed humorlessly. "I'm not so entirely oblivious that I don't know what you're doing. I know you've been having information channeled to you from Ireland. Why are you key-hunting?"

Wilbright remained silent and stood up to leave.

His uncle sighed. "What are you hoping to accomplish with all of this?"

Wilbright turned around and stared at his uncle's back again. "I'm going to rewrite time."

"What did you say?" His uncle's voice was cold and steady.

"I know you heard me," Wilbright said dryly.

"Why would you wish to do such a thing?"

"You know why."

His uncle shook his head. "Please don't tell me this is why you're doing this? After all this time?"

"What do you mean 'after all this time'? He took everything from me," Wilbright howled while standing up. His uncle slowly stood up and turned to look at Wilbright. His dark eyes stared into his nephew's and Wilbright took a step back, having forgotten how tall and scary his uncle could look when angered.

"Everything? Look around you Wil!" He gestured around. "You inherited the lands, the title, you're incredibly intelligent, and you could have had any *other* woman you wanted. Yet you deeply desired what your brother had. *Had,* Wilbright. He has nothing and you have everything. What else do you want?"

Wilbright brushed his hand against the locket in his pocket. "I want the other title, I want her."

His uncle's shoulders slumped in defeat. "Is that what you think is hidden behind the door?"

"So I've been told."

"And you believe everything you hear?" his uncle sneered.

"I believe it this time." He locked eyes with his uncle again, and for the first time, he noticed exhaustion within the dark intelligent eyes.

"I'm sure that you're well aware that the key wasn't buried with her and she didn't leave it in her family vault. And she made sure that you couldn't get your hands on her son, either. So what to do?"

"You forget what I have."

"No, believe me, I haven't forgotten." He narrowed his eyes at his nephew. "When you and your brother were fifteen I told you the story of Chenoweth specifically so you wouldn't dream of doing this exact same thing. Do you not remember what I said?"

"You told us that the consequences of playing with time stopped his mental clock from working to the point where he no longer knew where or when he was."

"Yes, and every person is different. For some it could take five trips; for others, only one could do irrevocable damage. And the further back you travel, the worse the aftereffects are. Are you sure you really wish to gamble with your sanity?"

Wilbright's fingers brushed the metal of the locket and he stared defiantly into his uncle's eyes. "I choose my own fate."

"Perhaps, but is this the fate you truly wish?"

"It's better than a fate where I play lackey to a bird?" Wilbright taunted.

His uncle's voice grew softer. "Is that all you believe I am?"

A shrill whistle warned Wilbright that his eagle was ready to depart, and he looked over. He turned around one more time to bid farewell to his uncle, but he had already vanished.

CHAPTER ELEVEN

AVIATOPHOBIA

She walked back to the park and sat beneath a magnificent weeping willow. She reached over to a grab a handful of daisies when something caught her attention in the distance. Holes began to appear, pulling the landscape and trees down into the Earth. She stood up to stare at the disappearing horizon. Cracks from the holes began to grow, reaching out to her like a skeleton's fingers. She began to run away, but the fissures followed alongside of her. Hands made of shadows slinked from the caverns and reached for her neck. She placed her hand around the key, trying to protect it. Then she ran full speed into an object, and she fell on her backside. She looked up to face the black silhouette of a man with messy hair. He extended his arms and grabbed her by the neck, choking her. He didn't want just the key, after all.

Quincy woke up screaming into her pillow. After a moment of waiting for Amanda's rough handling, she realized with relief that she was half a world away. She rolled out of her messy bed and sweaty sheets and stood on the cold floor. Shivering uncontrollably, she decided to warm up by taking a bath.

Surrounded by bubbles, she logically knew the absurdity of her dream. Shadows could not materialize to grab her. But this nightmare reminded her of the very lifelike night back in Albany where she had found herself face-to-face with the shadowy man. She trembled despite the hot water in the tub.

She fingered the key. She couldn't do this. She wasn't built for it. Despite Talin's warning and her previous failures, she once again attempted to take it off the chain. She wasn't surprised when the clasp refused to open.

She finished her bath and sat on her bed waiting for Mrs. Adalin. She looked down at her new school uniform, stroking the soft sweater and savoring the smell of never-worn clothes. At eight o' clock sharp, Mrs. Adalin knocked and called out, "Quincy, are you ready to leave?"

"Coming!" Quincy said, jumping up to drag her now-heavy trunk out of her room. With Mason's help, she managed to get her belongings outside. A sleek cherrywood carriage waited for them in front of the B&B.

Mrs. Adalin walked to the front of the carriage and motioned for Quincy to sit in the backseat. After all the doors were closed and Quincy's luggage had been securely placed in the trunk—or "the boot" as Mrs. Adalin called it—the cabbie clicked his tongue and they joined in the bustle of London's busy streets. Quincy watched the passing cityscape, noticing how different the architecture was from New York.

They drove past the NEFS station, and she poked her head to the front of the carriage. "Didn't we just pass the station?"

"That one is for the city eagles." Mrs. Adalin explained. "Today you're going to a special field reserved for school travel."

Quincy sat back and pressed her face to the window. Soon she began to see fewer buildings and more trees as they entered the countryside. After leaving the main road, they swerved into the forest and onto a small dirt path. They traveled on the path for fifteen minutes before stopping at the edge of a clearing.

"Four times a year, a number of eagles are contracted out for an entire day just for students and teachers to be taken to their designated schools," Mrs. Adalin informed Quincy.

She heard the echoes of laughter, and conversations, so she opened the window to peer out. To her surprise, the clearing teemed with people of many different accents, most of who were around her age.

Toward the far end of the clearing, students congregated near ten empty doorposts. They looked like doorways without the doors.

"Are all of these people going to Oakley?" Quincy asked in awe.

"Heavens, no. Of those ten posts at the end of the field, only one belongs to Oakley. The other nine will go to other schools nearby or to a specific continent. The fourth one from the right would take you back to New York for the three schools in your home country, for example. You could have taken the eagle from New York today, but I wanted you to have a few days to do the necessary shopping and for you to acclimate to the time change. Not that you seem to need it." Mrs. Adalin noted with a smile. "The other doorways are going to Asia, Africa, and different places in Europe—all over the world. Your trunk will be placed with the rest of Oakley-bound luggage and will be left in your room before you even know which floor you will be living on. Look for the post with an eagle engraved on it." Mrs. Adalin dug around in her purse. "Here is a sandwich for the ride," she said, handing a brown bag to Quincy.

"Thank you, Mrs. Adalin," Quincy said relieved that the barrister had thought ahead for her. "Will I see you again soon?" she asked hopefully.

Mrs. Adalin gave her a small hug, surprising Quincy.

"Not for a while I'm afraid. I will ask about you to see how things are going and will be cheering for you this year, though. Check the post office for letters from me, and I hope you'll write back. I'll meet you right here at the end of the school year. Have fun, Quincy!"

She waved as Mrs. Adalin got back into the carriage. The barrister poked her head from the window. "Please be safe, too, all right?"

Quincy nodded and watched as the carriage left her behind. Her heart began to pound as she realized that she was now on her own. She inhaled the morning air and then turned around to assess the situation. She looked at all the students' cloaks, trying to see their colors. Students mingled and met other students from various schools. She saw patches with rabbits, tigers, bears, dragons, scorpions, bulldogs, marlins, and finally a couple of eagles. Each animal seemed alive and ready to jump off its patch.

Countless types of people speaking in their native languages and dialects walked past her. Like she was, some seemed nervous and uncertain, while others found friends and laughed as if they had known one another for years. She slowly began to walk around watching the activity. Quincy saw parents meeting other parents while staff answered last-minute questions. In one corner of the field a snack bar sold small school items to forgetful students, such as notebooks and pencils. Students bought water bottles stamped with assorted school logos.

After walking the field for a bit, Quincy found herself in a somewhat secluded area. She looked around anxiously, searching for an eagle or an adult to give her directions. She felt a tap on her shoulder and jumped in surprise. Whirling around, she found herself face-to-face with a taller girl with frizzy, short blond hair. Her dancing eyes caught Quincy's attention: one eye was a dark blue, the other a deep hazel. The girl broke into a mischievous smile and then laughed out loud at having surprised Quincy.

"Hiya! Sorry if I startled you! I'm Mikaela Trindle. It looks like we both attend Oakley." She pointed to Quincy's patch. "But you look lost. What's your name?" Mikaela had spoken quickly, all in one breath, with no pauses between sentences.

"I'm Quincy Harris, and yeah, I'm kind of lost." She anxiously chewed on her lip.

"Quincy it is! Isn't that a boy's name, though?" Mikaela prodded.

"I think it works either way," Quincy admitted.

"Oh, how cute! By the way, don't be bothered. Just about everyone gets lost on their first day."

Quincy smiled at the older girl in relief. "So what do we do now?"

"We wait," Mikaela replied.

Quincy nodded and stared at the door-less doorways. "When are they coming?"

Mikaela didn't immediately respond to Quincy and instead stood straight up and looked to the horizon. After a pause, she turned and grinned at Quincy. "Now."

Mikaela's grin grew even wider as her excitement grew. It was contagious, and quickly the entire field of people grew silent with anticipation. The clearing reverberated with a bird's call. Immediately afterward, many eagles called back in answer as they began to fly in from different directions. They bobbed and weaved, sometimes just missing another eagle's wing. Quincy had never seen anything so magnificent.

The eagles gently glided on top of the wind and landed elegantly near the doorways at the end of the field by the empty doorposts. As Quincy followed Mikaela closer to the eagles, she glimpsed small ladders near the posts, presumably to mount the huge birds. The first ten landed, and the others continued to tread the air above. On the ten skeleton doorways, in front of the eagles, different mascots or continents had been stenciled on top of the doorways, just as Mrs. Adalin had said. As soon as the first ten eagles had landed, a staff member flagged everyone forward. Quincy turned to talk to Mikaela, but her schoolmate had already disappeared into the crowd. Quincy frowned and joined the line with the other students with eagles on their patches.

After the first three eagles had left, she found a chance to get a closer look at the massive birds again. Quincy decided why her school had chosen the eagle as its mascot. Only a fool would want to pick a fight with one. One large compartment was strapped securely to the back of each bird. They were different than the one Quincy had ridden in from New York. The compartment, stamped with a golden number, sat six people comfortably, but Quincy saw as many as eight giggling friends squeeze into one. After the six or so people sat down, the eagles left for their designated destinations. After standing on her tiptoes to look ahead of her, Quincy saw Mikaela's blond hair as she left on an eagle in front of her.

"Well, at least I know I'm in the right line," she mumbled to herself. After two more eagles left, it was Quincy's turn to jump into the compartment randomly labeled with the numerals 003. She showed her travel book to the attendant by the doorway, who waved her in. She chose a seat at the far end of the compartment and watched as the other five people boarded.

The first passenger—a small girl probably around Quincy's age—hopped in and sat in the bench across from Quincy in the spot nearest the door. She immediately hid something next to her seat. She held on to the handle of the object so tightly that her knuckles turned white. It was rude, openly staring at the girl, but Quincy couldn't help herself. She couldn't decide what she found more surprising, the purple streaks in her dark-blond hair or the matching purple shoelaces and purple fingernails. Then Quincy figured out what the girl was clinging to. Why had she brought an umbrella with her on a sunny day when she could have left it behind with her luggage?

Quincy shrugged to herself and looked back at the door as the final passenger was getting on. The tall boy sat down next to the girl with the purple streaks in her hair. He didn't seem too happy about this with his crossed arms and frowning face. It was the only spot left and in the middle of the bench. Next to him, a boy hid himself completely by a newspaper. The only thing Quincy could see were two pale hands clutching the paper. From time to time she would hear the sound of pages turning.

A girl and a boy—twins, Quincy thought— had sat down next to her and smiled. They all grabbed on to the hand holders on each bench, and the eagle took off in the sky toward Oakley. Once they were safely in the air, the students began to talk and introduce themselves. The twins introduced themselves simultaneously, in with what Quincy found out were Danish accents, and offered the names Anders and Astrid. The girl with the purple hair, had an English accent and introduced herself as Eloise. The older-looking boy in the center with a gruff Irish accent gave the name Sean.

Quincy finally introduced herself and gave a quick explanation about her unfamiliar accent. None of them had met an American before. The boy hiding behind the newspaper said nothing, of course. He didn't even make a sound. *As if he were frozen,* Quincy thought. Sean rolled his eyes at the newspaper, but didn't say anything.

Eloise opened her bag, pulled out a small box, and giggled with delight. She ate a slice of chocolate cake before turning to a salad. The twins likewise pulled out food and began to chat in their native tongue. Sean reached into his bag, and Quincy grabbed her sandwich, too. She smiled when she smelled tuna fish. Her favorite.

She looked over at the boy with the newspaper. He was still reading and hadn't even looked for his lunch.

"Excuse me," Quincy said timidly, "Have you forgotten your lunch?" She gently tapped on the paper. He didn't reply. She shrugged and sat back down. She looked in the corner and saw that Sean's frown had deepened. He must have forgotten his lunch, as well.

"Sean," Quincy asked, "Would you like half of my sandwich?"

He looked up at her and growled, "I don't need his castoffs." He motioned to the unmoving newspaper. "And I certainly don't need charity from *you*." He knocked the whole sandwich from Quincy's hands, and it fell to the ground.

Eloise choked on her salad, and Anders and Astrid watched with open mouths. But no one said anything. Quincy stared at the sandwich, not knowing how to react. Before Sean could move any closer to her, an obviously fake cough came from the previously silent boy across the way.

Without moving the paper he began to speak with a silky accent that Quincy immediately recognized. What were the odds that she and the boy from the records office were going to the same school? She squirmed uncomfortably as she remembered his cold behavior.

"Perhaps we should analyze why you so enjoy causing dramatic scenes. Or even better, why you feel the need to release the embarrassment you feel from having left your meal behind, especially while sitting near me," he nonchalantly commented. He folded the paper neatly and stood up to face the larger boy. He crossed his arms and raised his nose disdainfully.

Sean bent down to look the smaller boy in the eye and sneered. "Oh, now the little lord speaks. Coming to the aid of a damsel in distress?"

The smaller boy sighed. "Must we do this again? I am not a lord. My name is just older and more influential than yours."

"Yeah, but only in Wicklow. Besides, Monty, aren't there more important things than money? It wasn't my da who left me behind to gallivant across the world." Sean gestured to Monty but looked around at everyone else in the box. "Take a look while you can, mates. Here is the future lord of Wicklow. Too bad he won't live long enough to even inherit the title."

In answer to Sean's insult, Monty turned his head to the side as if he had been physically stuck. "I am still alive, am I not?" He glared up at the taller boy, lips pursed as if bracing for a fight.

Sean laughed. A mean laugh without any warmth. "True, but for how long without your bodyguards? At Oakley, you're just like everybody else."

Quincy tensed her shoulders, anxious for Monty's safety. After a moment of uncomfortable silence, he sat down and, despite his straight posture, looked exhausted, as if he had just ran a marathon instead of having an argument. He rubbed his brow and then wiped his forehead with a handkerchief before slipping it back into his coat pocket and turning away from Sean. The larger boy looked bored now, and sat down and feigned sleep while the other three in the compartment pretended to ignore the entire argument. No one seemed comfortable enough to talk anymore.

After five minutes of silence, Quincy relaxed her shoulders, relieved. At least Sean had left her alone, even if it had been at Monty's expense. She appreciated his help and made a mental note to tell him so later. She looked down at the ruined sandwich and sniffed quietly. She couldn't remember the last time she had eaten a tuna fish sandwich with tomatoes.

Monty politely coughed, and Quincy looked up into his frosty gaze. Even though he had stood up for her, she still felt uneasy around his calculated stare. After a minute of him seemingly sizing her up, he offered his hand to her. "Greetings. My name is Monty McCalister."

Monty was constantly pushing his wispy blond hair from his face. And every time that he did, Quincy caught a glimpse of his small, thick, black-rimmed glasses and deep-blue eyes. Monty's paler-than-normal complexion gave her the impression that he spent more time behind a book than outside. Maybe that's how he had known all the answers in New York. She wondered if he remembered seeing her last week, too.

"Hi, I'm—"

"Quincy, yes. You mentioned. It is a pleasure to meet you." Monty said. He then immediately apologized for interrupting her.

She looked at the rest of the occupants in the compartment and apologized. "I'm sorry if I created a problem."

"It is not so much that you created one as it is that you touched upon one. Some have the misconception of their place in society and what social graces come with them." Monty replied, taking off his glasses to wipe them on his handkerchief.

Quincy didn't know exactly what he meant, but it sounded cryptic. Obviously, it had been directed Sean, who continued to feign a nap.

Tentatively, she asked Monty another question. "I don't know if you remember, but I saw you the other day when I was getting my travel papers. What were you and your mother doing in New York if you're from Ireland?"

Monty's expression grew colder, and he sat up straight in his seat. "That was not my mother. That was my aunt. I live with her and my uncle."

He clearly did not want to talk about his home life so Quincy just nodded.

Then his shoulders slumped, and he sighed. "I was in New York to learn about your history firsthand while my aunt had a business convention," he mumbled. "I wondered why you looked familiar." He looked up at her and frowned. "Your accent does not sound like a New York accent."

"It's not. I'm from the West Coast. Portland, in Oregon."

"Fascinating." Monty answered. He didn't ask any more questions, and Quincy didn't press. Her stomach grumbled, and her cheeks grew hotter.

Monty reached into a leather bag and pulled out a sandwich. "I apologize again for Sean. Please take my sandwich in its place of your own."

He handed Quincy the whole sandwich, and she thanked him before opening it.

"Do you want to share it?"

Monty shook his head. "I had a large breakfast already and was not planning on eating it."

Quincy wasn't sure she was supposed to feel thankful or insulted by that. Monty went back to his paper, and Quincy took a bite out of the sharp-cheddar sandwich.

***

The second half of the trip was much more enjoyable as people began to share where they were from. Even Monty put his paper away to take part of the conversation.

"I live in Oxford. I walk past the parliament buildings everyday," Eloise wistfully said. "One day I'll have a seat there." She turned red and mumbled, "I hope." She turned and smiled at Quincy. "I've never been to America, where is Orygon?" she questioned, mispronouncing *Oregon*.

Quincy giggled. "It's in the northwest."

"Is it near Florida?" Eloise innocently asked.

"Other side." Quincy said, fighting to keep her face straight.

Eloise nodded, pretending to understand. "Monty, may I see your newspaper?"

He nodded and silently handed her the paper, and Eloise pulled out neon purple reading glasses. After a moment, she sighed.

"What's wrong?" Anders asked.

"The key turned out to be a fake," said Eloise, disappointed.

"A fake implies that there is something that is real. Perhaps the keys, are in fact, simple fairy tales for children." Monty responded curtly.

Quincy resisted the desire to reach for her own key, and instead played with one of the buttons on her cloak. The conversation turned to other topics and soon Quincy started to feel the slight descent of the eagle.

"We must be arriving at Oakley." Astrid said as she stared out the window.

"Almost. We have to land on a field near the town of Oakdale because the eagles are too big to land comfortably on the school grounds." Eloise answered. She seemed to be well-informed. Quincy figured that it couldn't hurt to ask her questions.

"So, Eloise. What do we do when we're not in class?"

"You mean, what do we do for fun?" Eloise said while playing with a purple strand of hair.

Quincy nodded.

"Well, it really depends on the person. Everyone can join a club, but if there's something you want to do but don't see it offered, you have to wait until your third year. Then you are allowed to create a club or extra-curricular activity, which many do because they can. Oakley has a yearly book that lists all activities around the school. *Oakley A to Z*."

"Is there an equestrian club?" Quincy asked.

Eloise didn't answer and instead looked out the window, her face turning white.

"What is it, Eloise?" Quincy prodded.

"It's probably nothing, but last night my older brother, who graduated last year, told me that every year, a Year One forgets to hold on to the handrails—" Eloise clutched her umbrella. "—and flies out the window."

Monty coughed politely into a second handkerchief. "I believe you have been had."

"Maybe…?" Eloise grabbed the handrails and tightly shut her eyes.

Quincy and the others also held on as the eagle descended. Quincy looked outside and then immediately back to the floor beneath her feet. The quickly approaching ground and the speed made her nauseated. She looked over at a pale Eloise, whose hand had turned white from holding on so tightly. Quincy closed her eyes until she felt a final hard jerk and a bump as the eagle came to a stop.

CHAPTER TWELVE

OAKLEY

Quincy slowly opened her eyes and looked around. Her fellow students had already begun to climb down from the compartment. Once Eloise exited, Quincy was the only one left inside.

"What are you waiting for?" Monty asked, waiting by the door. His piercing gaze made her blush.

Quincy slid over on the bench and stood up, her whole body trembling with nerves. Her new shoe caught on the edge of the compartment and she tripped, landing on her backside, shocked but not hurt. Her cheeks burned. She just *had* to trip in front of the Irish boy.

Monty offered her his hand politely and said nothing until she was back on her feet. "We should hurry."

Quincy looked past Monty and saw a line of carriages picking up students. Eloise was waving them over toward her carriage with her umbrella.

As they walked up to the carriages, Quincy smiled delightedly, the embarrassment forgotten. The one in front of her had been uniquely handcrafted and painted in different colors. Mosaics made from cut glass were added to the outside, too, showing different scenes of the night sky. The second carriage had been similarly crafted with its own unique glass placement of a flowing river. The horses' coats gleamed and ribbons had been tied in their manes. They nickered to one another, as if having a discussion before departing.

Quincy could hardly wait to see the stable if this is what the carriage horses were like. Cigfran would have loved these horses. Her throat tightened at the thought of the stable master. She didn't even know where Cigfran lived now.

"Us Year Ones should stick together," Eloise said while patting the carriage.

Quincy, Monty, and Eloise jumped in and sat down nearly bumping into Mikaela.

"Hey, imp, these seats are saved. Find your own carriage," Mikaela snapped at Eloise. Quincy's jaw began to drop at the older girl's rudeness but then Mikaela's annoyance immediately changed when she saw Quincy. "You made it! You and your friend can sit here."

Mikaela frowned again at Eloise, who quickly replied, "I'm with them," while gesturing toward Quincy and Monty.

"Fine. But don't you forget..."

Eloise rolled her eyes. "I haven't forgotten. We've never met, we don't live in the same house, I have no idea where you sleep, and I am to never refer to you as 'sister.'" Eloise and Mikaela stuck out their tongues at each other and then both giggled. Quincy couldn't help but smile. It all made sense now.

Mikaela looked over at Quincy. "I thought I'd lost you back there! How was the trip?"

"Um, it was fine, I guess. By the way, this is Monty, and it seems like you already know Eloise."

Mikaela glared at her little sister. Monty cleared his throat and offered her his hand. She took it and gave him a firm shake. "Monty is short for Montgomery, am I right?"

Monty grimaced visibly. "Monty will do quite all right, thank you."

Four girls poked their heads in, then, and frowned unhappily when they saw that the carriage was nearly full.

"Aw, Mikaela. You were supposed to save us seats," one of the girls pouted.

"Sorry, ladies. I'm taking pity on some tiny Year Ones."

The girls looked disappointed and left to find another carriage. In their place, two more boys jumped in to take the last two remaining spots. Once everyone was seated, the carriage took off for Oakley.

Mikaela smiled and then looked out of the window. "It's wonderful to be back. This place is gorgeous first thing in the morning with the dew covering everything. It's even pretty under snow." She turned back to face them. "Are either of you going out for sports? What after-school classes or activities are you both taking?" She spoke so quickly and changed subjects with barely a pause, that it took both Quincy and Monty a moment to answer.

"At this point, I do not know what I am going to do or take. I have decided to wait for orientation to look through the school book first." Monty answered.

"Same here," Quincy added, deciding that it sounded like the right thing to say. She stared outside at the passing forest. What if she couldn't find anything that she liked at Oakley?

"That's a good idea. There are so many things to choose from," Mikaela answered.

"Well I'm—" Eloise started before Mikaela interrupted.

"Imp, I can already guess what you're doing. I'm not interested in you."

Eloise stuck out her tongue again.

"So may I inquire what you do with your free time?" Monty asked, as if attempting to change the subject.

Mikaela was more than happy to oblige. "I'm on the debate team."

"Really? So what do you debate?" Quincy inquired.

Mikaela gave her a mischievous grin. "Anything. Everything."

"Are you a gifted debater?" Monty asked her politely.

Mikaela laughed. "You could say that," she replied and then laughed some more. Eloise rolled her eyes. The smaller girl sat up and looked over Quincy's shoulders. Her squeal echoed in the carriage, and she began to bounce up and down. Mikaela rubbed her ear and scowled at Eloise's ear-splitting excitement, but Eloise just pointed out the window. Quincy turned to look. A magnificent stone drawbridge lay over a river that flowed into a large waterfall. Quincy gazed at the large arch as they drove through toward the bridge.

"We're here!" Eloise clapped her hands, completely unabashed by her sister's annoyance.

Quincy looked past the arch and got her first glimpse of Oakley. Her mouth got wider and wider as they came closer to the school. She grew teary-eyed as she surveyed the grounds. Her parents, just like her, had once been students here. They'd walked on that grass and studied in those buildings. She wished they could see her now.

"Welcome to Oakley," Mikaela proclaimed.

Before the carriage passed through the entrance, Quincy caught a glimpse of an intricately engraved eagle in the arch, talons drawn, as if guarding the school. They went through the open gates under the arch and into a different world. A dark-brick castle surrounded mismatched buildings, its architecture from different centuries. Above the doors of the first building, there were glass windows in the shape of a clock face with an eagle in the middle. At the bottom of the windows, there was engraved text. It was written in a language that looked like gibberish to Quincy.

"What does that mean?" She motioned to the words as she whispered to Mikaela.

“*Ddefnyddio’r amser yn ddoeth.* It’s Welsh. It means, ‘Use the time wisely.’” Mikaela rolled her eyes and looked up at the ceiling. “School motto. Better get used to it. You’re going to hear it *a lot*.”

The arriving students left the carriages and walked in the first building. They stopped when a squeaky voice called out, “First Years, follow me to the orientation room, please!”

“Have fun, kiddos!” Mikaela waved farewell and ran off with her older friends.

“Please don’t dawdle!” the voice squeaked again.

Quincy desperately tried to find a face to match the voice but could not. She gave up and followed Monty and the group down one of three corridors. They all stopped suddenly and gathered in a large, high-ceiling room. Rows of chairs faced a podium and a chalkboard.

“Greetings, Year Ones! We will meet here weekly to discuss school business. This room is considered your homeroom also known as Advisory.”

Quincy still could not find the disembodied voice and got on her tiptoes to look again.

“Students, please take an open seat.”

Quincy found a place in the middle of the room and finally noticed a small man barely standing over the top of the podium. Once he saw that he had the audience’s attention, he jumped down as he began to speak. He tried to pace the length of the platform, but from time to time, his light-grey robe would catch on his feet and he would gently trip without falling. The small man’s long white hair was tied behind his back, and when he smiled at them, the wrinkles of his face reminded Quincy of small rivers. His green eyes twinkled as he surveyed the new students.

"Please allow me to introduce myself. I am Professor Agglebee, and today I have the pleasure of introducing you to all the important things you need to know about Oakley, not all of which are fascinating to young people like yourselves."

The professor wagged his finger at the students. "But they are important things nevertheless. Like school rooms, a tour of the school, and floor assignments. Afterward we will all go to supper together. Do we have any questions that need immediate answering?"

One of the male students shot up his hand and was immediately called upon. "When do tryouts start for polo?"

Someone in the back of the room whispered, "Not until spring, moron."

The professor chided the student. "He is right, though his delivery should be improved upon." He frowned. "A better answer, though, is that you all will be given an introduction in Physical Education. Unfortunately, Year Ones and Twos are not allowed to participate in polo on a competitive level."

Some of the students groaned.

"I know, it is terribly disappointing, but this is to ensure your priority for high marks and excellent study habits! Are there any other very important questions that cannot wait for me to answer them later?"

The professor paused but the look on his face discouraged further questions. Quincy definitely wasn't going to ask one. She just folded her hands in her lap and listened quietly.

"No? Splendid! Now where was I? Oh yes! School introductions. Tomorrow you will receive your class schedules. The schedules will also include your student handbook with a list of rules in the Oakley Code of Conduct. Please do read it. Follow these rules and your years here will be pleasant and stimulating." He glanced around the room. "Now, please follow me."

***

At five p.m., the hour-long introduction to the Main Hall and its immediate surroundings had finished, and the First Years were left standing next to the school bulletin board. On the board were times for guest lectures, tournaments, and other happenings that were taking place on the grounds. One paper offered tutoring in the Main Library in the afternoons, and in the middle of the board was a list of names and next to each one was a number.

"Oh! They've posted our floor assignments," someone yelled from behind Quincy.

Immediately all the Year Ones swarmed the piece of paper in excitement. Quincy grimly remembered swarming another list at Miss Heatherwood's, but that one was not nearly as interesting as this. A girl near her reminded her of Anna, and Quincy's heart tightened, wishing that the foster kid could have the same chance of leaving Miss Heatherwood's for the school and life of her choice.

Quincy forced herself back to her new reality and managed a glimpse of her name and the number three next to it. She continued to glance down the list of her floormates and grinned when she saw Mikaela's name as well as Eloise's, a couple of names after her own. Mikaela and Eloise Trindle.

"Ugh," Eloise dramatically moaned. "How did I get put with my sister? I'm dead for sure."

"At least you're with me?" Quincy pointed at the list.

Eloise instantaneously recovered from her fake fainting spell and looked up with glee. "We're going to have such fun!" she squealed.

Quincy laughed and glanced at the boy's list. She paused at Monty's name, and her cheeks burned. It looked like she would be seeing a lot of the Irish boy whether she wanted to or not. At least Sean wasn't on her floor.

The bells rang, and the Year Ones looked around confused. Older students bounded from all corners of the school, all moving in the same direction.

"Food!" a nearby student hollered.

With all confusion gone, the rest of the Year Ones excitedly followed the throngs of students. Quincy and Monty did the same. Then she stopped, suddenly, pausing in the middle of the hallway. The door in front of her was unique, but to her it was also familiar. *But how...?*

"Are you coming, Quincy?" Monty asked.

She didn't turn to look at him. "Uh, yeah... I'll be there in a minute."

Monty shrugged and walked away. Her heart pounded as she took in the sculpted details of the door—the writing and the five keyholes. She stared numbly at it as the rest of the student body filed by, forced to go around her.

She jumped out of her stupor when something jabbed her in the calf. She whirled around to see Eloise and her umbrella, smiling.

"What are you staring at?" she asked.

Quincy tilted her head at the door. "What is this?"

"What do you mean? It's just a door."

"It's not a…magic door?"

Eloise looked at Quincy like she was crazy. The smaller girl grabbed her by the elbow and began to pull her into the dining room. "It's been a long time since you had anything to drink, right? Maybe you just need some water."

Quincy nodded. She wouldn't mention the door again.

She walked toward the dining room, nearly bumping into Eloise, who had now paused in the center aisle to look at the creative architecture inside. Quincy shook her head. It seemed she wasn't the only one enamored by the building.

The ceiling rested on long beams from the four corners of the room and connected at a pinnacle high above. On the four walls, an enormous mural of glimmering trees reached the beams of the ceiling. The trees seemed to sway as if they were caught in a breeze. The painted clouds also changed positions, as well as shapes, around the blue parts in the ceiling and upper walls. The lower walls had been painted with different shades of green, and Quincy saw each brush stroke as if each one was a different blade of grass.

Quincy gasped as a fox bounded into its den in the painted grass underneath a large oak tree. She looked at the sky again and saw birds flying through the blue.

"Hey!" called a voice that sounded like Mikaela's. Quincy turned to find the older girl directing them to a table. "You two look the way I felt on my first day. Just wait—it changes with the weather, too." Mikaela burst out laughing. "Though sometimes it likes to randomly snow."

"How can someone do this?" Quincy asked aloud.

"It's an illusion. It's almost difficult to imagine having this Talent, though and mixing it with a passion for art. I'm guessing a former student probably did it. Apparently it's been here for quite some time. It never has to be retouched or anything. Almost as if it's alive," said Mikaela reverently. "Anyways, enjoy the meal." She grinned and waved, leaving them behind to find a seat with other friends.

Quincy shrugged and sat down next to Eloise. She was about to look around for Monty when he sat down next to her. Her body tensed, even more so when his leg brushed hers. She sat straighter and focused on the table in front of her. It was set up with an array of delicious-looking soups, meats, and breads. Her mouth watered when she glimpsed the cheese-and-broccoli soup. She hadn't had that since before...well since *before.*

She looked back at the walls and then over her shoulder toward the door. A middle-aged man with salt-and-pepper hair and a short, well-kept beard stood in the doorway and then slowly made his way through the room toward the staff tables at the opposite end of the large room. He kept one hand in his green velvet coat and would fish it out to wave or shake a student's offered hand. Despite his quick smile, the lines around his eyes made him seem sad.

"Who's that?" Quincy asked, leaning forward toward Eloise.

She looked up and smiled. "That's our headmaster."

Quincy continued to watch him until he sat down at his seat. He took a sip of water before standing up again. The headmaster cleared his voice, and all the conversations in the room stopped midsentence.

"I would like to welcome all of you to Oakley, whether you are a professor here or if this is your first time riding through the stone arch. For those of you whom I have not yet had the pleasure of meeting, my name is Luther Marquam and I am the headmaster here at Oakley. I trust that you all have chosen seats appropriate to your floor?"

The headmaster's soft but commanding voice sounded like the gentle cadence of music. He waited for scattered nods before continuing. Quincy hoped they were in the right spot. Surely Mikaela wouldn't have sent them to the wrong place. Right?

"Now, for you Year Ones, this always feels…just a tad *odd.* If at any time you feel ill, please look down at your table and focus on your empty plate."

Quincy's eyebrows quizzically rose as she looked over at Monty, who shrugged and then to Eloise, who giggled. After they had been warned, Quincy finally felt the odd sensation he'd been talking about. It was as if the whole room was moving around her. Once the feeling stopped, Quincy's eyes widened when she couldn't see any other tables next to her own. She looked up and saw the fourth floor slightly behind and above her. The table looked like it had been suspended in air, and Quincy laughed as she saw student's feet dangling on top of her head. At closer inspection, Quincy saw a pink substance stuck to one of the shoes. She looked across the table and saw the top of heads from the second-floor students. Her eyes met another Year One's from the second floor, who had the same shocked expression on her face as Quincy did. She looked down at her shoes, confused. Her feet were still touching solid ground. She looked to her right and saw the same three round staff tables, also on the ground..

"Why isn't our table floating like everyone else's?" she asked.

Monty promptly replied that, "Each table is on a separate plane, but each *floor* feels that they are on the ground with the staff in front of them. The staff actually sees all of us on the same plane, so it is only the students who imagine we are separated from the other floors."

"The illusion ends as soon as we leave from the main door," Eloise added. "and the room resets itself when the headmaster has finished eating. We're encouraged not to be late to the evening meal because it's awkward to walk in and see all the different levels. It's the same for leaving early."

"But why are we separated?"

Eloise grinned. "Food fights were too common between the separate floors thirty years ago. Eventually, it just became a tradition. Don't worry too much though; this only happens at supper. The room doesn't shift for breakfast and the midday meal."

Quincy could not imagine a food fight taking place here.

The headmaster continued his speech then. "Please take a moment of silence and enjoy your meal."

After the moment of silence, the students dug in.

"Please pass me the oxtail soup," Eloise asked a redhead that had sat next to her.

"The what?"

"The kettle in front of you," a third voice chimed in.

The redhead looked at the soup suspiciously but picked it up and handed it to Eloise. When he saw her, his eyes widened. He pointed at Eloise's head. "You have purple in your hair!"

Eloise looked shocked. "Gasp!" she said as she grabbed a strand of her hair and looked at it. "So I do! How did that happen?" She burst into a fit of giggles.

The boy joined her laughter and offered his hand. “My name’s Russell, Russell Baker. But you can call me Rusty. ‘Cause everybody else does.” He pointed to his red hair.

Eloise and Quincy shook hands with him and smiled.

“So do y’all eat oxtail round these parts?” Rusty asked, grinning.

“Just try it,” said the handsome boy sitting beside Rusty. He rolled his green eyes and offered him a spoon.

Rusty narrowed his eyes at his friend, but accepted the spoon. He took a sip and laughed loudly, his eyes seemingly dancing. “That ain’t half bad.”

Quincy watched Mikaela, whose eyes were fixed to their table, navigate her way over to sit next to Quincy. She tripped and landed on the bench with a *thump*.

She looked down, angrily. “What is that box?” she asked the table accusingly.

Rusty’s face turned a bright red that complemented his hair. He reached down and placed a box on his lap. Quincy hadn’t noticed it before. “I apologize for Savannah. She ain’t mean ya no harm.”

“Savannah?” Eloise asked, playing with one of her streaks of purple in her hair while staring at the box. He grinned and pulled it protectively to his chest. “My dear Eloise, meet Savannah, my trusty trumpet.”

“Did you have to bring her to dinner?” his friend asked with a grin.

"Of course. I might have a chance to practice. I haven't played in two whole days!" Rusty said with over exaggerated emotion.

They all met his declaration with awkward silence until Rusty started to laugh, permitting the rest of the group to laugh, as well.

His friend shook his head at Rusty. "My name is Colin Knight, by the way," he informed the group between breaths from laughing as Rusty cuddled his trumpet case. He spoke with an upper-class British accent and sat up with perfect posture. Despite the obvious class difference, his genuine smile encouraged friendly conversation. Quincy's heart quickened when he smiled at her.

Quincy peeked over at Monty who stared at the British boy suspiciously. Colin returned the cold stare but instantaneously switched to a wide smile for everyone else. The change had been so fast that Quincy began to doubt that he had ever been cold at all.

"So are you all Year Ones?" Colin asked.

"Nope, not me. That was so last year." Mikaela rolled her eyes.

When the other boys found out that Mikaela was a Year Two, they immediately began to ask her questions about Oakley and her experiences.

"Are you taking any music classes, Mikaela?" Rusty asked hopefully.

"Me? Music is definitely not my thing."

"Do you like any type of art?" Colin asked.

"Mikaela doesn't have time for art." Eloise pitched her voice to sound like Mikaela. "I live, breathe, and eat debate."

"Oi, imp, don't talk. I still haven't forgiven you for ending up on my floor. Besides, debate *is* art, you plonker."

"Wait, are you actually saying that debating should be considered on the same level as music or art?" Eloise questioned.

"How is debate like music?" Rusty asked obviously curious.

"It's probably better not to get involved," Colin said under his breath.

"As opposed to what you do in your head all day, Eloise?" Mikaela fired back.

Eloise frowned. "I never said that what I do is art." Then she muttered, "Even though it is."

Quincy wished she could disappear through her seat.

"I apologize for interrupting, but perhaps you could place music, art, debate, and whatever you enjoy, Eloise, and file it under the term 'hobby,'" Monty smoothly interjected.

"So what *hobbies* do you have, Monty?" Mikaela asked.

He paused and thought about it as he chewed on his bread roll. "I do not have any," he finally admitted.

"Everyone has things that they like to do. How about you, Quincy?" Colin questioned her.

"Horseback riding and drawing." Quincy answered without having to think.

Colin grinned at her. "I draw too. I prefer to paint with acrylics, though." He paused for a moment. "By the way, did you know that the art rooms are open for everybody in the afternoons? Even Year

Ones and Twos are allowed in. We should go this week. If you want to."

Quincy grinned, her heart racing again. "Sounds great."

"So how about you?" Eloise asked Rusty.

In a voice similar to an operatic baritone, he answered by singing, "I love music."

Everyone nearby groaned except for Eloise, who again, burst into giggles.

"Your turn, again, Monty." Colin nudged.

Monty pursed his lips but his face remained passive. "I enjoy learning."

"So you *actually* don't have any hobbies," Colin teased, but the humor didn't reach his eyes.

"I believe I just said that," Monty wiped his glasses yet again and refused to look at anyone.

"If he likes it then it's a hobby, right? Isn't that what a hobby is?" Quincy said, surprising herself by speaking up. She looked over at Monty and noted his widening eyes.

"Perhaps we'll have to debate it." Mikaela said, and Eloise pretended to faint in her soup.

The noise level in the dining room gradually grew louder over the course of the meal. Quincy kept looking over at the staff table, wondering when someone would tell them to be quiet. It never happened. Quincy gasped when she realized that some of the loud noises came from the adults. They laughed just as loudly at one another's anecdotes, and one professor slammed his palm down on the table with glee. Quincy smiled when she saw one of the professors throw a dinner roll to a coaxing professor from one of the other tables. This was nothing like Miss Heatherwood's.

When the meal began to wind down, the headmaster clapped his hands twice and all the tables landed back on the main floor. Some student's jaws hung open as they stared at the other students now on the ground next to them. The staff and the professors began to leave the room, and the students headed for their assigned floors. Quincy, Eloise, and Monty followed the horde of students who looked like they knew where they were going.

They walked toward a magnificent mahogany and rod-iron staircase. Candles were securely housed in various small hollow places, lighting the way for the students. Each one burned a different color than the one before it and flickered uniquely. On the left side of the staircase, each floor had its number intricately engraved above its entryway. At each level, someone would call the floor number and a portion of the student body would separate and walk through.

When they had reached the third floor, a voice at the front of the mass of students shouted, "This is the third floor. Please follow me!"

A group of thirty or so students left the main thoroughfare and walked underneath the number three on the entryway.

"Year Ones, meet me in the family room at the end of the hallway," the same voice called. Quincy and the rest of the Year

Ones stopped at the end of the hallway while the rest of her floor mates presumably went to their rooms.

"Well, come inside," the voice invited, and they all congregated in the well-lit room in front of the fireplace. There were six Year One students on the floor: three girls, herself, another girl who introduced herself as Genevieve, and Eloise; and three boys, Rusty, Colin, and Monty. From the corner of the room, a fourth boy cleared his throat. Quincy yawned and hoped that the speech would be brief. Her eyes grew watery and fought to keep them open.

"Welcome to the family room. My name is Bry and I'm the floor leader here on three. If you need anything, ask me. Now, for those of you who fancy yourselves as night owls, I warn you that Oakley is really difficult to navigate at night. And for you crazy A-types, please remember that the library closes with the lights-out bell." His eyes skimmed the small group. "Now, when you walk out of here, the boy's rooms are to the right and the girl's are to the left. If you get confused, look to on the walls—flower gardens for girls and a forest for boys."

Eloise huffed, and Bry shot her a look before continuing. "The family room is always open for quiet conversation and studying. But I suggest that tonight you unpack and become acquainted with your beds. I'll see you tomorrow at the eighth bell, which is, of course, at eight o'clock. Good night, I look forward to getting to know all of you tomorrow."

Everyone said good night and headed down the relevant corridor. Quincy yawned and rubbed her eyes as she went. She began to imagine a pillow, any pillow.

With a burst of energy, Eloise twirled her umbrella, grabbed Quincy's arm, and began skipping towards the girl's dormitory. Quincy was surprised to say the least, and she looked around, embarrassed to be a skipping-fifteen-year old, but Eloise's excitement was contagious and Quincy smiled, happy to have made a friend already.

Genevieve ran after them, trying to keep up. The three paused when they came to a door, breathing heavily. Quincy looked around at the painted walls while she caught her breath. They showcased different flowers and vines that looked so real that she was sure she could smell them. She looked to the closed door in front of them.

"Is this it?" Quincy wondered aloud.

The engraved doorframe was made of intertwined wooden vines and roses in full bloom. Someone had painted one rose a dark red. Behind the door, they could hear giggling and gossiping about the summer's events. This was definitely it.

With a deep breath, Eloise flung open the door, and everyone in the room silently stared at them.

"New floor three girls," someone in the room squealed.

In response, the other twelve girls squealed, too, and encircled Quincy, Eloise, and Genevieve. At first, Quincy felt uneasy with the attention and then she actually started to enjoy the feeling of being welcomed. She recognized the four girls who had tried to get on the carriage with Mikaela earlier. One of them was an Asian girl who waved.

"My name is Chae Mon-Aye. It is okay for you to call me Mon-Aye."

"Why not Chae," Quincy asked.

She smiled. "Chae is my family name. It is the other way around where I am from."

Another girl came up from behind them and grasped her and Eloise' arms. She ushered them to the remaining open beds. "*Mis corazónes*, I'm Alba. I'm a Year Three, so you ask me for help when you need it, yes? Here are three beds to choose between yourselves. You are all taking the places of three most loved girls, and for your sakes, you had better be worth the loss." She winked at them.

Mikaela giggled in Quincy's ears, "I love Alba, she tells you like it is. That's her best friend, Lindy." Mikaela pointed over to a tall blond who was sprawled on Alba's bed. "She's from Italy and loves to talk with her hands. So between the fluctuation of Alba's voice and Lindy's extravagant use of her hands, I can never tell if they're fighting or having a normal conversation."

Another student cleared her throat, stood before the three Year Ones, and crossed her arms as if sizing them up. She had long dark hair, plaited in braids, and her hair matched her brown skin. The girls went silent and stared at the girl as if waiting for her final decision. Finally, she smiled, and everyone began to talk again.

“My name is Rachel,” the girl said. “and I’m in charge of the girls here on three. I look forward to living with you.”

After the “new-student shine” had worn off and they all went off to their own beds, Quincy found some quiet time on her bed and started to unpack. She had chosen the last open bed and to her relief, she found herself next to Mikaela. She didn’t know the girl on her other side yet, but she was excited to get to know another new person. Eloise had been chosen the bed across from her and waved when she saw Quincy scouting out the room.

Quincy looked at the cream-colored walls and the fifteen beds that made a semicircle around the room. She loved how comfortable she already felt here. There were hooks on the ceiling that held a square of metal poles that allowed two rusty-red fabric drapes to surround each bed. The same fabric was used for draperies for the windows. She looked to the beds next and noted a small side table with lit candle and a cup of water on each one. Underneath the side tables, a place for books and other belongings had been built and next to the side table, a small wardrobe housed clothes and each of the girl’s trunks. Finally, on the other side of the beds, each girl had a small bureau that opened up to a desk.

While each miniature “room” was the same, each girl’s furniture was made of different wood to match their specific set. Quincy ran her hands over her furniture. Fleur de lys and birds graced the dark-red furniture set. As she emptied the contents of her trunk, she quietly laughed. It was all her own, and she could put whatever she wanted inside the drawers. She opened her trunk and placed the broken music box on the top of her desk. She smiled sadly down at it. *Such a small piece of home*.

Once Quincy put her things away, she took off her shoes, expecting her sore feet to touch a cold floor. She yelped in surprise when she set them down, though.

Mikaela laughed at Quincy's shocked expression. "Brilliant, yeah? They take the heat from the ovens in the kitchens and fireplaces all around the school and let the excess heat escape to a vent that goes under each of the dormitories on all the floors. Most of the classrooms, as well. So the floor is always warm during the colder seasons."

The other fourteen girls laughed as they showed off their new clothes and books. Even though she still shared one large room with multiple girls, it couldn't have been more different than Miss Heatherwood's. She smiled with contentment before drawing her curtains and collapsing in bed.

Chapter Thirteen

One

Lord Wilbright spat out the overly sweet tea back into the teacup and pulled out a handkerchief with the initials WEF embroidered on it. He wiped the corners of his lips. *There must be a new kitchen assistant*, he thought. *No normal person would drink tea this sugary.*

He would not, anyway.

He set down the cup, clasped his hands, and looked out into the darkness. The cold from the outside and the heat from the fireplace left droplets on the window. He slowly stood up and began to draw one long vertical line on the condensation. He stopped to study his handiwork.

One.

He breathed in and out deeply while trying to do battle with the dull ache in his head. He no longer had any choice. It was time to travel. His uncle's warning of the negative side effects ran through his head.

He knew the human makeup, though. As a master planner, he understood human reasoning and intellect better than almost anyone of his generation. He knew what he could potentially be doing to himself and how unnatural it was. He also knew the penalty for his actions. The human brain was not built for time travel. His brain was simply not wired for the abuse. Time travel had driven Master Creative Engineer Marcus Chenoweth completely mad. His sanity and his reasoning completely destroyed. And then one day he had simply disappeared.

How long would it take for Wilbright to lose his Talent; his most precious thing?

A sharp rap on the door interrupted Wilbright's thoughts. He growled in annoyance, but was secretly relieved to redirect his train of thought.

"Enter."

"You called for me sir?" his valet asked, poking his head through the door.

"Did I?" Wilbright frowned. "Ah yes. Prepare my eagle. I wish to leave at dawn."

"Where should I say that you are going, milord?"

"Oakdale."

It was time to travel back to Dublin and to meet Katelyn Prendergast face-to-face.

Chapter Fourteen

Observant Behavior

Quincy woke up to the smell of freshly baked bread. She breathed it in deeply and then opened her bed-curtains to watch the sun stream through the windows. She touched the thick, dark-red material. She had dreamed about the man in burgundy again. *They can't protect you,* he had laughed at her. She had woken up screaming, but no one in the room had even stirred at the sound of her cries. With all the magic this place seemed to possess, maybe the drapes were soundproof. The thought of not having to worry about waking the other girls made her smile.

She closed her eyes to enjoy her moment of peace when she heard a muffled scream. Quincy quickly sat up, her heart pounding from the adrenaline. Before she could jump out of her bed to help whoever had screamed, a huge pillow hit her directly in the face. She pulled it off her and looked around for the culprit. She couldn't distinguish who had thrown the fluffy projectile, because everyone had decided that it was her duty to wake up her neighbor with a hard smack of a pillow. Feathers began to fly across the room with a chorus of “Ow,” “oof,” “hey!”, “en guarde,” and “take that!” Quincy watched, eyes wide, and laughed.

This continued until a loud knock on the door interrupted them. Feathers and pillows instantly dropped to the floor. Except for Eloise’s, who managed one last smack as she whacked Mikaela’s back with her pillow. Quincy recoiled at the foot of her bed. What punishment would she receive from Oakley on her first day?

Rachel answered in a singsong voice. “Ye-es.”

“Good morning, children.” a male voice shouted through the door.

Bry, Mikaela mouthed to Quincy, rolling her eyes.

“As your floor leader,” he went on, “I’m here to remind you five-year-olds in there that breakfast will be in an hour, and first day means we all have to go down together.”

Kalleigh, Quincy’s neighbor, grabbed a pillow and swung open the door. She discharged her weapon at the unsuspecting Bry, and a gasp of surprise came from the hallway before she slammed the door shut on him.

“Oh very mature, Kalleigh. No, really, I’m impressed. Now come on ladies. Please get ready. I know that *we* would prefer to be on time.”

Scattered giggles and rolling eyes met his statement.

“By the way, we need to meet in the family room before we go down. Thank you.” He paused for a moment. “Why don’t I hear the patter of little feet. Get moving!”

Once he left and his lone footsteps faded, the older years broke into laughter and slowly began to clean up the room and replace their pillows.

"That's my pillow."

"No it's not."

"Please, they're all the same."

"This one is wet! It's Lindy's. She sleeps with her mouth open." Mon-Aye opened her mouth wide. "Do you know how I know that, Lindy?"

"No Mon-Aye, please tell me."

"Because I can hear your loud snoring even through the curtains!"

Quincy felt the dense drapes again. They must really be soundproof, then.

The other girls giggled, and Lindy rolled her eyes.

"Did you guys hear Bry? 'Why don't I hear the patter of feet?'" Rachel mimicked.

"Please. He's just rubbing it in because Year Threes never get to be a floor leader," Lindy nudged Alba.

"Yeah, why *is* he floor leader? I thought you were going to be chosen, Rachel?" Kalleigh asked.

"Me? Seriously? I don't have enough time to be floor leader."

Mikaela was tiptoeing away when someone caught her.

"Oi! Sneaking off, are you?"

Suddenly, like a herd of wild animals, the room erupted in commotion as the girls raced to the bathroom. Quincy caught up with Eloise in the line. Eloise looked up at the ceiling and moaned. "Only three toilets, two showers, and one large mirror for fifteen girls. Boys must have engineered this bathroom."

From inside the bathroom Quincy heard someone shout, "They ought to be sacked!"

After about forty-five minutes, the girls made a procession to the floor three family room. Daylight had flooded the previously dark hallway so that Quincy could see the flowers in better detail. Like in the dining room, the details on the petals were immaculate, all the way down to the droplets of dew on the leaves.

Mikaela rushed past her in the hallway, and she paused just in front of Quincy. "Come on, molasses."

Quincy grinned and followed her down the hall. They walked inside the family room, and she grabbed a seat with Mikaela in the well-worn couches while Eloise curled up on the floor by the fire. Quincy looked over at the fireplace and saw that someone had taken three polo mallets and formed them into a star.

Bry clapped his hands three times and cleared his throat. "Welcome back! I trust we all had a pleasant and productive holiday."

A couple of girls giggled. Someone behind her shushed a neighbor because, "the almighty Bry is speaking."

"I hope we have all introduced ourselves to our new students. Welcome again to floor three!"

His statement was met with cheering, groaning, and someone who randomly began to fake snore. Quincy took a good look at the floor leader and immediately understood why all the girls had rolled their eyes and giggled behind his back. He had light-brown hair that seemed to be glued in place. Some of it stuck straight up, while random sections were flat. He was shorter and stouter than everyone she'd seen so far, but he had a determined look in his eyes emphasized by the crease in his forehead.

As he began to speak again, he paced the room, looking each student in the eye. Despite the fact that his floor mates—especially the females—teased him, his charismatic voice commanded respect, and like Lindy, he spoke with his hands. As he continued to lecture, even the loud Mikaela honed in to his voice and silently listened.

His brown eyes glanced over at the mantelpiece as he began to speak about floor pride. "Randomly, once a month, all dorms are inspected. If our floor is considered "lacking" the whole floor has to clean dishes and other fun things for a month."

Quincy caught a glimpse of Monty looking disgusted at the thought of cleaning duties. She wondered if he had ever done any chores in his life.

"So, it's our job to keep our floor tidy," Bry wagged his finger at the students. "After breakfast we will congregate outside the Learner's Citadel for the annual Student Welcome Ceremony. Then everyone will get their class schedules and clubs list. If you can't find your classroom, feel free to ask a porter or a student wearing an orange shirt. They're part of the student government and are there to help you. I have also been told to remind you that the scouts are not our maids and if we leave things too messy for them around here, they will refuse to light the fire in our family room."

Rusty awkwardly raised his hand. "What are porters and scouts?"

In the back of the room, someone loudly whispered, "Scholarship student," and Rusty's face turned bright red.

"Enough! I happen to know what your Talent is, Max, and I wouldn't be speaking up if I were you. Russell, they're the adults that keep this place running. Any other questions?"

When no one else made a move to ask, anything. Bry nodded approvingly. "Now, let's go down to the morning meal."

Quincy followed Colin, walking near Rusty, with the rest of the floor out the staircase. Outside the 3, they met a couple of the other floors walking briskly down the stairs. An air of excitement permeated the entire school catching Quincy up in the camaraderie. At breakfast, she sat down in the same place again, but this time she was between Mikaela and Monty.

Monty took off his glasses and wiped them on his sweater. He had dark circles under his eyes, and his stormy blue eyes stared at the lens.

"Did you sleep okay, Monty?" Quincy asked.

He shrugged in reply, not looking up from his cleaning.

Quincy jammed her knife into the butter with frustration. As the meal continued, he said little other than asking for orange juice.

He was being awfully rude again, like he had before they'd officially met. And she'd thought they were becoming friends.

"Please pass me the ketchup," Rusty said politely. *Now there was a boy with manners.* Quincy thought as she handed him the bottle.

Rusty loaded the red sauce onto his eggs, and the rest of them stared at him in shock. Colin looked disgusted but quickly hid it with a bite of toast. Rusty grinned and took a large bite, exaggeratedly smacking his lips.

Eloise reached for the jar of honey and began to liberally spread it on her toast.

"Ugh, Eloise. That's obscene. Do you want some toast with your honey?" Mikaela rolled her eyes.

Eloise giggled and reached for her sister across the table with her sticky fingers. "Come here, sister dearest. I feel like I need some sisterly love."

Mikaela squealed and Quincy laughed. Then she dodged Eloise, who was now reaching in her direction. She could not remember such a wonderful breakfast.

But as she watched Mikaela and Eloise together, a heaviness settled over her heart. This should have been her and her sister. Quincy would have been a Year Three when Emily would have been a Year One. She quickly gulped her orange juice and grabbed an apple.

She looked over at the table next to her, relieved to see it firmly on the ground. She was glad that that the tables were only suspended in air during dinner. Why anyone thought it was a good idea, was beyond her comprehension.

When the meal ended, the student body intermingled as they made their way outside toward the Learner's Citadel, which housed most of the classes held at Oakley. The citadel was made of white stone, but it seemed that a pale-blue hue radiated from the stonework. Six steps led up to two large doors, and on each side of the stone staircase an eagle sat, one facing the other. The mob of students stopped in front of the first step. The school bell rang in the far distance, and an older student struggled against the crowd to stand on the second step.

"That's Ian." Mikaela whispered to Quincy. "On the last day of the school term, a lucky Year Four is chosen to recite the starting mantra for the next year."

Ian saluted and grinned at everyone behind him before taking a deep breath, turning and staring at the closed door. "Givers of wisdom, the bell of knowledge has been rung to indicate that the new year has begun. Open the doors of Rowan grown to let the learners in."

In reply, The headmaster's cheery voice answered. "If all of you are all ready to learn and listen, follow the rules, to honor those above you, and make your own place here within the school walls, please open these doors and prepare yourselves for the new year."

Ian yanked the doors open as the bell began to ring continuously for a full minute. When he took the first step inside, the rest of the students began to follow him into the building. The professors sat at the end of a large room behind tables to sign in students and pass out class schedules and green-bound books.

As the ten-o'clock bell rang, conversation ended and someone on the opposite side of the room clapped four times. Quincy watched the woman who was now giving directions. Her white hair had been braided into a crown around her head. She had long, wispy white eyelashes and eyebrows despite her young age. She held a large book in her slender hands. Quincy noticed her shimmering dark blue robe that started at her neck and fell down into long bell-sleeves that ended near the floor. She was the most beautiful woman that Quincy had ever seen.

"Attention, students." the woman called out. "If you cannot find your way around please ask instead of getting lost. Tardiness will be excused today and tomorrow, but after that you *will* be penalized. You all have ten minutes to find your first period classes."

"That is Professor Archer. She is the headmaster's second and teaches Language Arts." Quincy had been so focused that she had missed Monty walking up to her. "She wrote a book on the evolution of language that I found most informative. So what is your first class of the day?"

Now why had he decided to talk to her? Quincy resisted frowning at him, instead looking down at her schedule to see the list of classes, times, and room numbers. Her eight classes weren't much of a surprise. She had Mathematics, Language Arts, Latin,

Physical Education, Social Studies, Science, Study Hall, and Independent Study.

"I have Latin first," she answered. "You?"

"Same," he said as he sorted through his own book.

She continued to read through her class list but paused when she saw her period eight class: Independent *Talent* Study. She frowned at the paper. "So who teaches that?" she asked Monty.

"It depends. There is a survey on the back of your schedule to fill out before supper so that they can pair you with the appropriate professor."

Quincy wondered who taught students without Talents. She sighed, and looked at Monty. "So, what don't you know?"

Monty looked at Quincy and rewarded her with a grin. His face lit up and his blue eyes danced. Quincy blushed with embarrassment, hoping that she would get a chance to see it again.

But then Monty's face hardened. "Enough things that I still have to attend school. Unfortunately."

She pondered his quick change in temperament as something hard slammed into Quincy, forcing her to bump into Monty. He hit the wall beside him and frowned at the small culprit.

"Sorry," Eloise said sheepishly as she bent down to tie her shoes. "Have you guys looked at the green book yet?"

Monty stretched his shoulder where it had hit the wall while Quincy rubbed the part of her rib cage where Eloise had rammed into her. Both shook their heads no.

"Inside is the list of all the current clubs."

Quincy opened the book and started to flip through the pages. The list of clubs seemed endless, and each name was followed by a brief description.

Monty scratched his head. "Why are there so many?"

"Year Threes are allowed to start clubs, remember." reminded Eloise. "And if you don't see it here, you can start it in your third year. Anyways, I have Language Arts first, so unless you guys have that first too, I'll see you both later!"

Quincy waved farewell as Eloise skipped off toward the staircase, her umbrella bumping into everyone she passed. The school bell rang again, and Quincy looked at her schedule.

"Latin is in room forty-one. I'm hoping its location isn't one of the things you *don't* know," she teased with a grin.

He rolled his eyes, but the corner of his lips rose in a tight smile. "It is this way," he gestured to the stairs. "I believe."

***

After getting lost twice because they both had refused to ask for help, Monty and Quincy made it to the Latin classroom. They stopped by the door and watched the professor talking animatedly with his hands accentuating every point. Though he sounded excited, his face remained completely void of any and all emotion. Quincy wondered if they were in the right classroom.

"Are you sure we're in the Latin room?" Quincy whispered to Monty. He shrugged in response and tilted his head toward the Latin posters on the walls.

Both paused, unsure what to do, until the Professor looked up at the two of them.

"Oh, lovely. Two more of you. So glad you could finally make it. Please find an open seat."

She couldn't tell if he was being sarcastic or genuine, so she tensed her shoulders and finally nodded. She and Monty sat down toward the back of the classroom and placed their bags underneath their desks.

"Moving on, we will start with basic adjectives and then go in depth into grammar. By the end of your third year everyone in the classroom should have a firm grasp on the Latin language. If not, it will not be my fault."

As the professor continued to lecture on language study habits, Quincy's mind—and eyes—began to wander around the classroom. The Latin alphabet had been painted on the borders of the walls. The characters flowed in a beautiful, spidery form. As she focused more closely on the intermingling alphabet, the letters started to pop out from the walls. Her eyes widened and she jumped back quickly, forgetting that her seat was connected to the desk. She rammed her back roughly against the top of the chair. She bit her lip to keep from crying aloud, and tasted her own blood when she finally felt safe enough to let go. Her cheeks reddened when she heard snickers from around the room.

"Oh splendid," the professor said. "Someone noticed the alphabet on the walls. Quite fascinating, is it not? I was bored last year and created it myself. It's just a simple illusion, nothing fancy, but it is difficult to see unless you are very aware of minute details and see things with the right frame of mind. I congratulate you. Now, back to the very exciting world of Latin."

CHAPTER FIFTEEN

AN OAKLEY EDUCATION

After her second class of the day, she quickly walked out of the Learner's Citadel and headed for lunch. She saw Monty looking for her, and he waved her to an open seat next to him. Monty had already eaten half of his sandwich and was looking at his still-blank Talent form for Independent Study.

She sat down next to him at the table. "Hey, Monty."

"Hello. I have to say that you were very suave this morning in Latin."

At first Quincy thought he was making fun of her, but when the corner of his lips curled up slightly, her embarrassment faded and she grinned.

"Why, Monty, thank you very much. I hope that observing small details is a compliment."

"Oh I have no doubt."

Quincy reached for two pieces of bread from the fixings on the table to make a sandwich.

“Please tell me that you did not do something like that in Mathematics,” Monty said, wiping his mouth with his napkin.

“Not to worry. One scene is enough for today. I am quite happy not to be the center of attention. It might be too late though, I’m going to be eternally remembered as the ‘one who sees odd things.’”

“Who knows, it might become useful?” Monty said as he unsuccessfully tried to hide a smile by pushing up his glasses. “Besides, I doubt that it will be quite that long. School is only four years.”

‘Ha ha.” Quincy scrunched her nose at him, trying to figure out why he was being friendly now when he was so distant at breakfast.

“Well anyway, it is my turn for Mathematics, and I hope it is not as boring as everyone makes it out to be,” Monty said as he stood up.

“Can’t help you there. Mathematics really is that boring. See you later.”

“Oh, I doubt that it is completely uninteresting. Until Physical Education.” Monty made his exit with a slight mock bow and left the room going in the wrong direction.

Quincy sighed and began to build a turkey sandwich. She took a bite and laughed. “Well, at least he remembered to take his Talent form,” Quincy smiled to herself.

“What’s so funny? Did I miss something?”

Quincy felt someone slide onto the bench, next to her. She looked over at her friend.

"Hi, Eloise. You didn't miss anything. Monty walked off in the wrong direction."

Eloise giggled. "Anyway, I'm off to Social Studies, how about you?"

"Oh, me too. Eloise. Did you eat yet, though?" Quincy hadn't seen the smaller girl eat a single bite.

"Sort of. Mind if I tag along?" Eloise asked hopefully.

"Not at all. Let's go." A warm feeling of finally having a friend spread over Quincy's body, and she motioned toward the door as Eloise jumped up. Quincy did the same, turning quickly, and bumping into someone. That someone fell, and his books and papers, which were not in a bag, flew across the room.

Quincy tried to apologize, but stopped midsentence when she saw that she had bumped into Sean, the boy from the eagle ride.

He sneered at her and pointedly looked down. "So I see you aren't always under the protection of your little guardian. Where is that chancer, anyway." Sean fake spat at her. "Have you even asked yourself why he bothers with you? 'Specially since he doesn't do *friends*."

Before Quincy could respond, Sean strutted away toward his friends, who were all staring at Quincy. Her heart pounded, and she desperately wished to run from the room. But her legs shook and refused to move, as if they had become frozen to the ground.

Eloise broke the moment by grabbing Quincy's arm and dragging her away.

When they were out of earshot from the students, Eloise let go of Quincy's arm and sighed in relief. "Chancer himself. Yuck. Let's go."

Quincy nodded, and Eloise released the tight grip on her umbrella and began to twirl it.

"Ouch! Mind where you spinning that!"

"Sorry!" Eloise called back as they walked toward the Learner's Citadel.

Sean did bring up an important fact, Quincy thought as they went. Why had the calculating Monty seemingly singled her out if it was out of character for him to make friends?

"Eloise, what's a chancer?"

"My cousin's from Ireland and he uses that word all the time. It means a dodgy character. Like a con man, someone you don't trust."

"Oh," was all Quincy could say to that. She wondered which of the two boys was the real *chancer*.

Once inside the citadel, they passed a small group of students on their way to class. Quincy and Eloise stopped and gaped at the strange scene taking place in front of them. Five upper-class boys trailed after Kalleigh. One blond-haired boy carried a pile of books that was large enough for two people. He also sported a girly messenger bag with flowers made from buttons.

"Oh, come on, Luke! When is my turn to carry Kalleigh's books?"

Luke smiled smugly and continued on as if he hadn't heard anything.

"What's going on with Kalleigh?" Quincy asked Eloise.

"What does she know that we don't? *Five* blokes?" Eloise giggled.

Quincy shrugged.

"Hello, kiddies!"

Both Eloise and Quincy jumped, and Eloise brandished her umbrella like a sword and tried to stab Mikaela. She easily dodged it, and Quincy had a suspicion that this happened regularly.

"Hi, Mikaela," she said with a smile.

"How are classes?" Mikaela asked as she put her arms over the girl's shoulders.

"Good so far, thanks. What's happening there?" Quincy pointed at Kalleigh's retreating figure and boys surrounding her.

Mikaela peered at the group that was now walking up the stairs. She laughed. "Oh that? That's her fan club."

"Fan club?" Both Quincy and Eloise asked in disbelief. There were all kinds of clubs at Oakley, she knew, but she couldn't have imagined this one.

"Yup, you can find it in the Oakley A to Z and everything."

Quincy looked surprised and tried to stifle a laugh but ultimately failed. Eloise and Mikaela joined in the amusement.

Some of the other students stared back at them, but Quincy felt safe walking with the two Trindle girls.

"This is my stop. See you both later!" Before they could say good-bye, Mikaela had disappeared down a hallway.

"Oops, I read this wrong." Eloise admitted with a grimace. "The room isn't on level two. It's *negative* level two, room one."

"How can a level be negative?" Quincy wondered.

"Underground maybe?" Eloise asked hopefully.

"There's only one way to find out."

Quincy and Eloise began searching the ground floor for a staircase. The only thing they saw was a small flight of steps with lanterns in the far side of the first floor. They walked down the precarious-looking stairs and saw more classrooms. Each had a negative one preceding the room number.

"Where is the minus two?"

Quincy's question was answered when she saw fifteen students congregated at the end of the hallway.

"Apparently we're not the only ones who have no idea," Eloise whispered.

Quincy noticed the sign with a negative two on it as they approached, but she couldn't see a staircase or a door. All fifteen students were tapping on walls and looking at the floor with confusion pasted on each of their faces. The students became still when they heard a *tap tap tap* coming from beneath them. Much to their surprise and amazement, a big square piece of the flooring creaked and shook. Everyone jumped back when the square swung up, revealing a dark passageway inside.

A light-red-haired head poked up and smiled at the encircled students. "Ah, Year Ones. I forgot to open the passage. If you please, follow me."

The students followed the professor down the dark passageway and deeper into the ground. Every ten feet, a lantern had been posted on the wall. Much like the candles near the dormitories, the lantern's colors and flickers were all unique, and it gave the passageway an eerie glow. The walls had roots growing in and out of them, forcing some of the taller students to duck underneath.

After walking down for a couple of minutes, Quincy felt the passageway move up again. At the end of the tunnel, the students were momentarily blinded by the natural light. When Quincy's eyes adjusted, she found herself in a large room. She looked up and saw that instead of a ceiling, they were under the roots of a tree. The roots extended around the room and left large open gaps. In the middle of the ceiling, a large candelabra with lit candles had been installed. There were glass baubles over the flames to protect the tree.

Quincy looked down at the floor of dirt, grass, and wood chips. Five rows of six desks sat in neat lines on the floor while a large glass bookcase stood in the front of the room next to a desk and a large blackboard. Some of the students looked at the spaces between the roots nervously while rubbing their bare arms against the chill.

"Not to worry. When winter hits, glass will cover the gaps to keep us protected from the cold. Even then, I encourage you all to bring extra layers to keep yourselves warm. You may take the outer entrance if you feel that it is faster for you than the underground one. Anyway, welcome. My name is Professor…eh…Professor…"

He rubbed his head absentmindedly. After a couple of seconds, he deemed it unimportant and walked to the front of the room next to the chalkboard which read, WELCOME TO THE CLASSROOM OF EXTRAVAGANT LEARNING AND MELODIOUS INTELLECTUAL ATTAINMENT.

Some students looked at the board, confused, while others stifled laughter unsure if this was a joke or a serious statement. A student behind Quincy whispered, "I thought this was Social Studies. Is this Language Arts?"

The professor interrupted the student by requesting silence with one finger over his mouth. "Please allow me to read the seating chart. Which, um, was right here."

He rummaged through his pockets and turned them inside and out. After giving the students a sheepish look, he flipped the chalkboard over to the other side, and smiled at the class. The board read, PROFESSOR HUTCHMAN'S 5TH PERIOD CLASS, and it listed the fifteen students in order of where they were supposed to sit.

Two girls in front of her giggled, grabbing dandelions from the earth and peeling off petals. "Ah. Learn your seats, but don't bother sitting down. We're not staying here. Leave your things at your desk and follow me."

Everyone followed the professor with bewildered expressions on their faces.

"Can anyone tell me how old Oakley Academy is?" Professor Hutchman yelled to his class.

Quincy's classmates shrugged at one another. Finally, one ventured a guess. "Uh, seventeen hundred and something?"

"Not even close, but good try. Anyone else?"

When nobody else spoke up, the professor laughed. "Oakley's first classes were taught in 1240. Though none of the buildings you see here are that old, save a piece of the original foundation built in somewhere near the Main Hall, though it has long been forgotten. Each hundred years or so, another building is added or renovated here at Oakley. Interestingly enough, the Learner's Citadel is the newest addition. Though the stable has had a recent artistic renovation forty years ago."

Quincy's ears perked up. *The stable.*

"Ladies," Professor Hutchman said without turning around, "you will be tested on this information." They dropped the flowers and focused on walking behind the professor.

"Good. Now, this year our focus will be on Oakley and its history," he continued. "It's important to know where you come from in order to understand where you are going. We will also discuss the history of the creation of the school and your choice of going to a school where your focus is your Talent."

Quincy grasped her school bag tightly, her joy at hearing of the stable fading fast.

The professor ushered them to a courtyard behind the school and near the forest. He motioned to the center, but no one needed to be told what to look at. A magnificent clock made of dark stone stood alone in the middle of the courtyard. Quincy's eyes widened at the clamor from the loud ticking. A large pendulum swung side to side, barely missing the ground. She looked higher up and saw multiple clock faces stacked on top of one another.

All the students stared in awe at the large clock.

"Meet Chenoweth, informally known as the Timepiece."

Quincy frowned as she looked at the clock, trying to read the different faces. It didn't make any sense. She tried to find the hands to see the time, but there were none. She watched the dials turn counterclockwise. The tiny moving roman numerals made it even more difficult to read.

"Excuse me, professor? But how do you read the time? Where are the hands?" someone asked. Apparently she wasn't the only one struggling with the clock.

The professor laughed. "It's a difficult clock with four faces and, yes, without any hands. Start from inside and work your way out. The first face in the center has the numbers zero to eleven, and it changes every hour. The second face has the numbers zero to fifty and changes every ten minutes. The third face has the numbers zero through nine and changes every minute. And the fourth face, and the largest, outer face, is for seconds in increments of three. Sixty seconds to be exact, despite the fact that the face begins at zero and ends at the number fifty-nine. See how it turns counter clockwise every second? That's the dial that is ticking. If you concentrate, you can hear the ticking of the Timepiece anywhere on Oakley grounds. Occasionally a student will tell me that even after they've graduated, they still hear the clock's ringing and ticking."

Quincy stared in awe at the clock and closed her eyes to listen to its ticking.

A student next to Quincy laughed and said, "Wait, so since there isn't twelve on the clock it's never noon and never midnight?"

The professor nodded his head. "The clock instead reads it as zero hours. Because there isn't a zero in roman numerals, the engineer left the spot blank. Now, if you look even more closely at the pendulum moving at the bottom of the clock there are three more clock face plates. The largest one is for months, once again zero to eleven."

Quincy scrunched her nose. All the months had been numbered differently, then.

"Yes, it's very confusing for everyone, but you can't argue with a Master Creative Engineer. Especially one who was so…creative."

no numeral
no clock hands!!!
The Timepiece

Quincy grinned and wondered what the engineer had been like. He must have been very accomplished to have surpassed Creative Engineer and become a Master. If her father had lived to be promoted to Creative Engineer, she wondered if he would have graduated to a Master. He was smart enough.

"Continuing on, the second set underneath have three more plates. The center face is for days, and the foremost face is for the year. The month dial has thirty-one days and automatically knows, depending on which month, how many days until the new month begins."

"Why the name Chenoweth?" another student asked.

"Because that's the name of the inventor," Eloise answered with satisfaction.

"Yes, well done," the professor said, pleased. "Very few use its name now, though. It's simply referred to as the Timepiece. We'll discuss more about Chenoweth and Master Creative Engineers in the next few years here."

The professor looked up fondly at the clock before turning around to face the class. "Any more questions?"

Eloise shot up her hand.

"Yes?"

"Do you believe that Chenoweth had one of the minor keys?"

Quincy looked over at Eloise and then at the professor. Students around her began to chatter, some rolling their eyes, some looking up at the professor to hear his thoughts. The professor pursed his lips, pausing as if deciding what to say. Finally, he cautiously said, "It's true that there are some who believe that he owned a minor key, though there aren't any facts to back up this theory. When he disappeared, no key was found in his belongings, so no one really knows the truth."

Eloise and the other students looked disappointed. Quincy looked up at the clock with new interest. If the clock's inventor really had one of the keys, what had happened to it? She yearned to reach for the chain at her neck, to grasp the key her mother kept safe for so long, but she fought the desire. The last thing she needed today was for someone to see her key and ask her questions.

"Back inside now, children," the professor directed. He turned to lead the way, and everyone followed.

Once back in the classroom, they all found their designated seats.

"Please pull out your books and read the introduction," the professor said, pulling out his own tattered copy.

After ten minutes, the Timepiece rang in the distance, realeasing them from class.

"Well, that's all for today. For homework, read Chapter One and be prepared to discuss it in our next class."

Quincy and Eloise stepped out of one the larger gaps in the tree and walked toward the main field for Physical Education. On their way, they met up with Monty, Colin, and Rusty.

"So what did you think of the Timepiece?" Colin asked Quincy.

"It's fantastic." she said, not able to help the smile on her face. "I'm guessing you've already had Social Studies then?"

Colin nodded. "It's one of my favorite subjects."

"I understand why."

Rusty caught up to them and groaned. "Hey, Colin? Eloise is calling me ginger and is refusin' to tell me why."

Eloise burst into laughter, and even though Quincy wasn't sure why either, she couldn't help but laugh along.

Colin rolled his eyes. "Ginger is slang for the color of your red hair. I reckon you don't use that back home?"

Rusty shook his head. "Why would anyone call me a cookin' spice?"

Monty lagged behind them, and Quincy slowed down to let him catch up. But he didn't even look at her. Again. Then Quincy remembered Sean's lunchtime accusation and wondered if she should say something. Maybe he was upset about something? But if she were upset, and didn't want to talk about it, she wouldn't want people asking her. She'd want a distraction.

She matched his slow footsteps. "Hey," she greeted him.

"Unfortunately, Quincy, I cannot this afternoon," he said without looking up from the pathway.

Her brow furrowed. "Excuse me?"

"Oh, right. I apologize. What was your question?"

"Uh, I was going to ask if you wanted to go explore the school grounds after class." She looked at him, perplexed. She hadn't even asked him, but he'd already answered.

Monty wrinkled his forehead, and for a moment, he squeezed his eyes shut before staring directly at Quincy.

"Not today, I have already designated my time in the library. Perhaps we might visit the school café this evening?"

"Okay, but how did—"

"I do not wish to talk about this. Please? It is a..." Monty paused awkwardly and pointed to his head. "It is my Talent, knowing things that I should not."

Quincy opened her mouth, not sure how to respond, but she was saved thankfully by Rusty. He interrupted any further conversation by stopping near a small building and hollering, "Ladies, this looks like you, so I bid thee farewell." He saluted and continued walking toward the opposite end of the building where the boy's locker room presumably was.

Quincy followed Eloise toward the door of the girl's locker room while trying to sort out her feelings. What was a Talent for knowing things? She hadn't heard of that one before. She watched Monty walk away, disappointed that he didn't want to explore this afternoon with her, but strangely excited to visit the café with him.

How could one person make her so confused?

Quincy watched Colin run after Rusty, and Monty silently followed them, rubbing his forehead before she walked inside.

"See you all in a bit," Eloise called after the boys.

Quincy clung to her bag as she walked into the locker room. She saw the entire First year class of girls changing and giggling as they were getting ready for class. A note had been posted near the door listing the girls and their designated locker numbers.

Once their things were put away in their personal lockers, Quincy and Eloise slowly made their way to the opposite door, just as the girls before them had. They opened the door and entered into a larger room in the center of the building. Many of the boys had already changed and were clamoring around some glass cases. Quincy joined the group to see what was so captivating.

Trophies filled the cases, and Quincy gazed wide-eyed at the ones with tiny horses on top. There were also a bunch of ribbons stung in a row. She daydreamed that her name would one day be printed on the list of award-winning jumpers. She looked around the room. There were shelves everywhere, filled with awards that were stamped with current dates and others that went back nearly two centuries. Some said things like "honorable mention", "1st", "2nd", "3rd" and other things to that effect. Some shone brightly while others lacked that new luster. There were trophies for polo and rugby, and even more cases designated just for horsemanship. She glanced at another shelf lined with soccer trophies. Or *football* as people here called it.

Colin sighed. "I wish we could compete in polo this year."

"I've never played," Quincy admitted.

"That's okay," he grinned. "Since you know how to ride horses, it should be easier for you to learn. Did you know that Oakley participates with other schools that do polo Talents-style?"

"What's that mean?" Rusty asked.

"Basically, it's not against the rules if you use your Talent to aide you in the game. As long as you don't break the cardinal rules or foul anyone."

Quincy's eyes widened at this new piece of knowledge. Talents could be used in polo?

"Attention, please!"

The students whirled around to find the speaker, and many had to work at keeping their faces passive and their mouths shut. She had a stern look on her face and kept her hands behind her back like a drill sergeant. Quincy found herself drawn to the woman's eyes. They were dark green and matched her neatly pressed brown slacks, and olive-green shirt. Her eyes darted around the room, sizing up her new students. Her pursed lips slowly changed to a sneer.

After looking at her strict posture, Quincy—as well as many others—bit their lips to keep from laughing when they saw her hair. The woman's fiery red hair curled out of control, in complete opposition to her otherwise precise and neat behavior.

It must drive her crazy.

The professor had also placed riding goggles over the top of her curly head, and the countless freckles covering her face, making her look very young. Some of the students ignored her and started to talk amongst themselves. Had they really not figured out that this woman was their professor?

"I said...attention!" roared the woman. She pulled something out from behind her back, and Quincy cowered instinctively. With a large *crack*, the horsewhip hit the wall with great force.

The Deathstrike had followed her to Oakley.

The whip did its job because suddenly the room became deathly silent. After waiting for a few moments to make sure she had the entire room's complete attention, she cleared her throat and continued.

"I suppose I should welcome you to Physical Education, but by the end of the week, none of you will feel so welcome. Year Ones will have an introduction to all the major sports offered here at Oakley. And to answer a question that I get asked every year, *No*, Marching and pep band are not sports. They're school activities, so those are not my areas of expertise. So don't ask me what time your 'practice' is and where it's located."

Quincy felt Rusty, who was right next to her, tense his shoulders.

"And finally, Year Ones and Twos may *not* play polo outside of class! So *no*, none of you are allowed to tryout for the Oakley team. I don't care that you've been riding since before you could speak. I'm not interested!"

After looking at all the students' faces, the professor's own face changed into a smug expression. She waved her hand around the room toward the various trophies. "As you can see, Oakley is known for its ability in many areas, from chess, yet another *activity*, to the horse sports of dressage and polo. We expect you to find your place here and excel. This is Oakley, after all. Now, each of you will pick up your equipment and leave it in the lockers that have been assigned to you. Form a single file and follow me to the Equipment Room."

She began to walk away and then paused. She whirled around and clicked her heels as she faced them a second time. "Oh, by the way, call me Professor with my surname Pertinax. None of that 'Professor P' rubbish."

Quincy looked over at Rusty and saw him trying to mimic Professor Pertinax by straightening his usually slumped-over posture and foolishly parting his lips to form fake words. Colin slowly slid away from his friend, not wanting to get in trouble on the first day. Quincy decided to follow suit and nonchalantly slid over toward Monty, who had seen the whole event and again failed to hide his smirk by cleaning his glasses.

Quincy followed the rest of the class and joined the single-file line.

"There is a list on the board over there that indicates what team you will be on for football, which will be our first focus of the year. Team one will take blue jerseys, team two takes yellow, team three will take red, and team four takes orange." Someone groaned and declared that yellow clashed with her hair but stopped when Professor Pertinax gave her a cold look.

“We start with football for the fall, and then we’ll work with horses in the early spring. Even though you cannot play for the school team, we will still learn polo basics this year. Today will be the only short day you get all year, as we will also be assigning your horses and tack. We won’t be working with horses until after the winter holiday, but it will be your duty for this class to get to know your charges *before* we work with them. This will be done on your own time. Think of this as homework, for you will fail this class if you cannot ride your horse appropriately for polo.”

Quincy smiled in relief. She looked over at Colin and shared a grin. This would be one class where the homework would be fun.

Professor Pertinax clapped her hand twice. “Follow me.”

Everyone walked outside and crossed the empty field and spectator stands toward a large building near the edge of the forest. When the stable came into full view, Quincy stopped and stared. She instantly knew this would be her favorite building. She didn’t even need to see the rest of the campus.

It was nothing like the stable at Miss Heatherwood’s. Even though this stable looked old, the recently stained doors told Quincy that it had been cherished. She walked up to it, and like on the school carriages, pieces of beads, pottery, and broken china adorned the walls. She stopped when she saw a silver spoon on the wall.

Shivers crawled down her spine and into her legs. Cigfran had told her a story about living near a stable just like this. Had the old stable master once worked at Oakley? If he had, why hadn’t he ever said anything to her? She rubbed her arms to rid herself of the goose bumps and walked up to the open silver doors that stood between two round windows.

"Students, pick your horses. But I warn you, pick them well. They will become yours while you are students here at Oakley. If you need help with your mount, there are stable keepers and grooms that will be able to help you. There are five rows of stalls, and Year Ones, I hope that I don't have to tell you from which numbered row to choose your horses. Here are stickers with your names on them. Put yours on the door of the horse that you choose, and then you are all released for the day."

As soon as she finished talking, there were cheers and then a mad dash to grab the stickers and find the perfect horse.

"Oi! Careful not to frighten the horses!" someone called, from the side, but no one slowed down.

After a few moments of looking at the horses, Quincy found her. She'd remembered the lessons from her father and Cigfran, and she'd checked the teeth, the hooves, the eyes, and finally, the coat. She was a beautiful dapple with friendly eyes. This was the one. She started to put the sticker with her name next to the nameplate that read, APPLE. But before she could stick it on, her hand was pushed out of the way and someone else's sticker took its place. It read, GENEVIEVE.

Quincy bit her lip. "Genevieve, this is my horse."

Genevieve flipped her hair over her shoulders. "Just *deciding* that doesn't make it yours. The rules were clearly stated that ownership is claimed by the use of your *sticker.* I don't see *your* sticker on this stall. Just mine. Sorry, guess you weren't fast enough."

Quincy searched for an intelligent comeback but found none. What made the situation worse was that Genevieve slept three beds from her. What had she done to deserve such cold behavior? Her fists shook in frustration. She thought that she had left Amanda and bullies behind at Miss Heatherwood's.

Clenching her fists, Quincy walked farther and farther into the stable looking for an available horse, but each horse already had a sticker. Finally, she reached the deepest part of the stable. She looked into the last stall and met two large angry eyes. She jumped back when the horse kicked the door. Quincy looked back up the stable and grimaced when she saw that all the other stalls were taken. She reluctantly put her name next to the empty nameplate on the stall in front of her. She tried again to walk over and peek in, but the horse growled.

"Just my luck." Quincy mumbled.

"Well, looks like you got our evil incarnate."

Quincy whirled around to face the speaker. A young man in his mid-twenties, with messy brown hair and a crooked smile, greeted her.

"Sorry to startle you. My name is Aldwyn, I'm the interim stable master here until the real one comes back from sabbatical."

"I'm Quincy. Nice to meet you." She paused, then added, "Sorry, but what do you mean by 'evil incarnate'?"

Aldwyn twisted his dark hair around his finger and sighed. "He's a handful, and no one has figured out how to control him. The beast has had all the necessary training. It's just that…well, the horse refuses to use it. He's a new one this year and has all his papers, but I'm actually not exactly sure where he came from."

"Have you ridden him?"

"I haven't personally. Another stable hand tried and landed in the river. He's one of the best riders we have here, too."

Quincy grimaced again. She knew horses, but if a stable hand had difficulty staying on the horse, how was she supposed to ride it?

"So what should I do?" she asked.

"Well, I can try to help you, but most of it will be up to you as the rider. If it doesn't work out by the end of the spring, we'll look about getting another horse for you next year."

"Next *year*?" Quincy asked, horrified at the thought. She had worked with difficult horses before, but none with the title of "evil incarnate."

"Yeah, sorry about that. It's impossible to find you another one this late in the summer."

A crash came from the opposite side of the stable, and Aldwyn excused himself to investigate. "Year Ones," he sighed under his breath.

Quincy started to walk away when a thought came to her. She had grown up with horses. And she'd never met a horse that she couldn't ride. She quickly walked back and found the unnamed horse's tack and decided to ride now.

She made soothing sounds to the horse and opened the door. A powerful head met hers and knocked her away from the stall. She hit the floor with a force that momentarily stunned her. She slowly opened her eyes and saw a figure standing over her. Tears began to gather in the corner of her eyes.

Her father smiled and sat down next to her as she was instantaneously transported back in time when she had first fallen off a horse. She was six years old and recognized the smell of the rain at her first stable in Portland. How had she gotten there? Her father stroked her head and smiled at her. "It's okay to fall, Quinn. What do you want to do next?"

She closed her eyes and jolted awake when she heard the hinges of the door opening and closing to the stall. The moment had been so vivid that she had actually believed she was a child again, back at home with her family. She slowly sat up and stared at the stall. Despite the open door, the horse remained inside, snickering at her as if taunting her. She slowly stood up, and while rubbing her head, she closed the stall and went back to the changing room to grab her class uniform. At least she had hot chocolate to look forward to that evening.

***

Monty met Quincy in the family room and they walked downstairs to the Main Hall together. They found a door with the sign AQUILA'S CAFÉ located near the Lost & Found and the post office.

Inside the room, old tournament banners hung from the ceiling and polo mallets and other game equipment decorated the walls. Signatures of seemingly famous musicians, sports players, writers, and Creative Engineers who had been Oakley students, adorned another wall.

Quincy looked at the menu and saw Lomnin but decided against the odd ticklish sensation that would assault her tongue.

"I'd like a hot chocolate, please," Quincy grinned at the barista. "Oh, and do you have raspberry syrup?" To her delight, the barista held up a bottle of raspberry.

"Just plain chocolate for me, please," Monty requested.

Quincy gasped. "You're not even putting whipped cream on it?"

Monty raised an eyebrow. "Is that a requirement?"

"It should be." she grinned mischievously. "Haven't you ever had whipped cream? It's delicious."

Monty shrugged and shook his head. "My aunt and uncle do not like sweets in their home. I only have hot chocolate on excursions to town."

She immediately turned to the barista and smiled again. "He'll have whipped cream on his, too, please," Then she turned to Monty. "You'll love it.

She couldn't imagine growing up in a house where sugar wasn't allowed. She shivered at what her childhood would have been like without her mother's homemade lemon cake or whipped cream.

They grabbed their drinks at the counter and found seats near the window that overlooked the darkened sports field. Monty looked suspiciously at the fluffy white cloud atop his chocolate. He grabbed a spoon and tentatively dipped it into the whipped cream. He tasted it and quietly laughed.

"Good?"

He just nodded and tried it again. Quincy smiled and took a sip of her own hot chocolate, then sighed with contentment.

"So how was your first day?" Quincy asked.

"Uneventful, thankfully," Monty said, clearly relieved.

"Were you expecting something else?"

"Not expecting it exactly. It was more of just a hope."

"What do you mean?"

Monty kept his straight posture but switched his cup from his right hand to his left and then back to his right again. "I have been homeschooled my entire life, so I was curious to see how my first day of school would play out with professors and classmates. If my uncle could have continued with my Talent education at home I would still be there."

"The whole 'knowing things that you shouldn't?'" Quincy inquired gently.

"That would be it," Monty stiffly replied.

"Well, at least you have one," Quincy said before taking another sip of her drink.

He raised his eyebrows. "You have not discovered your Talent yet?"

“If I even have one.”

Monty made a scoffing noise from his nose. “I adhere to the school of thought that everyone has a Talent. Perhaps you already have one and just do not recognize it.”

“Maybe,” Quincy frowned. “How was your time at the library?” she asked, wanting to drop the subject.

Monty was more than happy to oblige. “Brilliant. The sheer volume of the tomes here is astonishing.”

“I haven’t visited it yet. It’s located on the fifth floor of the Learner’s Citadel, right?” she asked, recalling the map of the grounds in her memory.

Monty nodded. “The largest and newest library is, yes. The other two are located here near the Main hall.”

"We have three libraries?" Quincy said in awe. She didn't remember seeing that on her map.

Monty smiled into his cup. "There is a small library specifically for the staff in the teacher's lounge, and the third and final library is the original Oakley library. It is at the far end of the Main Hall. Only the oldest books and those not presently in circulation are housed within. The librarian in the Citadel has a list if you need a book for a project." Monty yawned politely into his hand. "Please excuse me, Quincy. I believe that I am ready to sleep. Thank you for the company."

Quincy was startled by the abrupt shift but she just said, "Goodnight, Monty." waved and watched the empty field until she drank every drop of her hot chocolate.

CHAPTER SIXTEEN

DUBLIN

Wilbright rubbed his throbbing head and frowned when he heard giggling coming from the opposite side of the eagle's compartment. He flicked a glance at the cuddling couple, and then looked quickly away. He strongly disliked public transportation—and public displays of affection. He stared outside at the morning sun and the cumulus clouds peppering the skyline. He was presently en route from Oakdale to Dublin and stuck on a public eagle since his own mode of transportation was left fifteen years in the future, in his present.

He squeezed his eyes shut trying to ease the nausea and the dizziness. It felt like his head was being pulled apart in every direction. The difference between the times played with his mind. Was it day or night? The sunny day outside told one story, but his tired head told him another.

He peered again to the two lovebirds, even as he tried to stop himself. Would they still be together in fifteen years? Would they still be in love, or united in mutual dislike? He turned away from them in disgust. His own mother had died when he was young, leaving his father a bachelor who was interested in anything and everything but his children.

How could love be both magnificent and savage?

Wilbright rubbed the locket as the eagle began to descend and sighed, grateful for the short flight. After they'd landed and he'd gotten off the eagle, he showed his counterfeit passport to the workers and walked through the streets of the Dublin of the past.

He purposefully headed for the largest bank in the center of the city. He looked at his attire, missing his tweed. He had decided on a dark-gray suit to better fit the current style and to blend in. He pulled his coat tighter as a burst of air blew past him. He smelled coffee and longed for a cup of the hot liquid. He fought against the desire, hoping to leave the past as quickly as he'd come.

As he began to walk up the bank steps, a burly man with dark skin put his hand in front of him. "My mistress would like to see you," the man murmured.

"I believe you have me confused with someone else," Wilbright muttered, trying to smile and walk away.

The man grasped Wilbright's forearm, and Wilbright looked him up and down, knowing the futility of trying to escape. "I will take you to her, Master Wilbright," he whispered while gesturing towards a café.

So this man knew who he was. Wilbright sighed. "Lead on," he answered dryly.

He followed the burly man into the café where a group of men laughed loudly and women tittered in the corners until they reached a back room. He was led by another strong redhead, who nodded at them as they passed.

In the far corner of the room, a woman was curled up at a booth next to the window, staring outside. Two steaming cups of tea had been placed on the table in front of her. She didn't look over when Wilbright approached. The strong man pointed at the seat across from the woman, and Wilbright sat down and watched her. She twirled her long blond hair around her slender fingers.

Katelyn Prendergast...

His gaze slid down to her swollen stomach, which she cradled with her other hand.

"When is the due date?" Wilbright asked.

Her trance broken, she turned to face him with hatred emanating from her cold blue eyes.

"In three months," she growled. She coughed into her handkerchief, and he caught a glimpse of red before she quickly tucked it away. The two large men jumped to her aid, and she dismissed them with a wave of her hand.

"Wait for me outside." She whispered, taking a sip of tea.

The two men nodded their heads and stepped outside.

"You're here to see if my key is locked inside the vault in my bank." It wasn't a question.

His eyes widened.

"Let me save you the trouble. It's not there, nor will it ever be again." She took another sip of her drink and motioned toward the other cup. He frowned at it.

"It's not poisoned," she said wryly.

He picked up the cup and felt the warmth bring life back into his fingertips.

"It's surprisingly cold for the time of year." she murmured, staring outside again. She sighed. "I was hoping you wouldn't come...Your being here now means you've set all the events in motion. And there isn't anything anyone can do now." She looked at her wedding band, her eyes sad, and then at her stomach.

"How did you know?" he wondered aloud.

Katelyn laughed coldly. "You think you're the only one who knows how to use their key?" She reached into her silk purse and pulled out a piece of paper. She unfolded it and placed it front of Wilbright. He stared at the drawing of the key and then looked up at her.

She narrowed her eyes at him. "I don't have it anymore. I've hidden it from you, and you'll never find it."

"Why do you hate me?" he asked, his face blank, emotionless, as he leaned toward her.

"Because I know what you're going to do." She leaned closer to him, and pitched her voice low. "And right now, you have no idea what I've sacrificed because of you." She waved him away. "Now leave me. The answers you seek aren't here. I'm afraid you've wasted one of your precious trips for nothing." She frowned. “Wasted, like these keys.” She ripped up the picture of the key and returned her gaze to the window.

“Go away,” Katelyn whispered, a tear running down her cheek.

Wilbright stumbled out of the room and ran outside into the street and the cold but sunny afternoon. The nausea finally overcame him and he puked on the street corner. What was she even talking about?

He made his escape back to the NEFS Dublin station to go back to Oakley and then home to his present-day Scotland.

Chapter Seventeen

Independent Studies

During her second day of classes, Quincy's anxiety levels grew as her Independent Study approached. By lunch, all her classmates had been claimed by a professor, except for her and Monty. She had turned in her Talent form before dinner the previous day and had left it completely blank other than writing her name. What happened to students who did not have any Talents?

After Language Arts, she looked at her schedule for seemingly the millionth time and her heart sank when she saw Independent Study was now upon her. She debated hiding in her room or the library when she heard the clearing of someone's throat behind her.

"'Scuse me. You're Miss Quincy Harris?" asked a high-heeled girl with a side ponytail.

"That's me."

"Lovely."

The young woman thrust the note into her hands and clicked back down the corridor. Quincy looked at the note and read:

> *Would Quincy Harris, please report to the Back Library located past the Main Hall to the right, at the beginning of her last class of the day. Thank you.*

Quincy flipped the note over and saw different, slightly messy handwriting with further instructions.

> *Walk inside the Back Library and down the fifth row. Turn left at the fourth shelf and grab the copy of Carolus Snekcid's* Spei Altus.

Quincy frowned at the note. *And then what?*

Shrugging, she made her way toward the Back Library, thankful that Monty had explained where the three libraries were last night. She passed the Main Hall and turned down a dark hallway. Not far down the corridor stood a large oak door with an unlit stained glass window. It was inscribed in Welsh, a language that Quincy really wished she could read, but there was also a small sign in English that informed her that this was the library entrance.

She shuddered but grasped the doorknob, despite her unease. The darkness reminded her of a reoccurring nightmare she had in which she was caught in a dark room, unable to find the door, while someone laughed at her. She slowly, tentatively, stepped inside the wraith-like library. The only light in the room was a small sliver of brightness on the floor that had escaped from the drapes.

Quincy looked around, noticing some gold lettering on each aisle of books as she drew closer to each one. Roman numerals. She quickly scanned her memory from her mathematics as a child and looked for the aisle with the symbol *V*. She cautiously walked down the fifth aisle and counted the fourth bookshelf on the left and scanned its contents for the book. She found the worn copy of *Spei Altus* and put her hand on it to pull it out. But instead of releasing from the bookshelf, it worked like a door handle and the entire shelf creaked and began to fall toward Quincy.

She squeaked and jumped away from the shelf's path just in time. Her heart pumped with adrenaline as she surveyed the area. She looked down and the shelf had vanished. She looked where it had originally stood, and in its place was a tunnel of darkness. Quincy put her hand in the black and felt around the empty space. Then she sucked in a breath and began to tiptoe into the passageway. She kept her hands along both sides of the walls as she walked down the passage until a bright flash of light appeared and temporarily blinded her. Her hands flew to her eyes, and she paused. She slowly opened them when she heard the soothing and constant sound of falling water followed by the ticking of many different clocks out of sync.

Blinking, Quincy's eyes slowly adjusted to the brightness, allowing her to scope out the room. Light continually flickered throughout the space, which seemed to be an office of some kind. She looked up and saw a thick glass ceiling that warped the sunlight. Water splashed on and fell off the roof, as if she were inside a waterfall. Papers, books, and maps covered the surfaces of the room, and mahogany bookshelves lined the walls, filled to the brim with knick knacks and books. In the center of the room, an overstuffed chair sat in front of an ornately carved desk, and a large globe slowly rotated clockwise near the doorway.

Everywhere else she looked, she saw clocks. They came in different shapes and sizes. Triangles, squares, octagons, heptagons, circles, and some original designs that Quincy could not identify. Some of them were so small they looked like children's toys next to some of the larger clocks. One of them was so tall it reached the glass ceiling. Each one ticked, but they all read different times, chiming here and there.

"Welcome, Miss Quincy. I hear that they forgot to warn you about my door. I'm delighted that you decided to come inside. I prefer that students take the initiative without the necessity of detailed instructions. I once had a student wait forty-five minutes until she decided to walk inside to come in."

Quincy whirled round to face the speaker, and she instantaneously straightened her spine when she was face-to-face with Headmaster Luther Marquam. She quickly averted her eyes from him and looked at the general direction of her shoes. She found a smudge on the left one.

The headmaster continued to speak while kindly ignoring her embarrassment. "Please, move that chair closer to my desk and take a seat," She looked up, then, and he gestured to a wooden chair in the corner of the room. "I would offer the more comfortable chair, but people tend to fall asleep in it."

She did as he requested, nervousness making her movements stiff.

"Now, you're probably wondering why I called you here instead of my…well, 'normal' office with all the other professors," he guessed.

"I *am* curious why I was told to come to the old library." Quincy admitted.

The headmaster smiled mischievously. "I do have a 'proper' office like the other staff members do, but people tend to barge in asking questions for which they usually already know the answer. Such is leadership." The headmaster's eyes twinkled. "This room is not known to the entire student body, though, because I like some privacy, and it's easier for independent studies. I strongly request that it remains this way…"

"Yes, sir." she promised. She chewed on her lip for a moment before going on. "May I ask a question?"

The headmaster nodded. "Please."

"I'm not quite sure why I'm here. You do know that I don't have a Talent, don't you? Are you sure that you're supposed to be my Independent Study professor?"

"You are here to learn are you not?" the headmaster asked, smiling.

Quincy slowly nodded but still couldn't understand why he had shown a particular interest in her.

"Excellent. Quincy, no one is without Talent. You just need to find yours. You left your paperwork completely blank, though, which isn't much help to me."

"There's not much to say."

The headmaster rubbed his chin. "Do you play any musical instruments?"

Quincy shook her head.

"Have that special touch with animals?"

Quincy thought about the talking raven, but her bruised head from her horse was the deciding factor. She shook her head again.

"Hmm." He combed a finger through his short beard, his brow furrowed. Then his eyes lit up for a moment. "There are some Talents that are passed down genetically. Do you know what your parent's Talents were, Quincy?" he asked with a smile.

"Not specifically, sir." she said, wishing she had. She'd still had so much more to learn about her mother and father before the accident took that from her.

The headmaster opened his desk and flipped through one of the drawers. "Here we go," he said with triumph. "Let's try something then, shall we? Before we begin, I would like to ask you a question. I saw you looking at the globe by the door. What did it say on the stand?"

Quincy's mouth opened in surprise. She tried to recall the wording on the base of the globe.

"I'm sorry, sir, but I really don't know."

"Oh, I believe you do. You saw it, and now it's set in your memory. You just don't have the knowledge of how to access it. Let's test my hypothesis and try a memory exercise. There are no wrong or right ways to recall moments. Some people pick a specific memory to focus on to help them recall, while others prefer to use a person. Today, I would like for you to choose an object found in this room to focus on. Look at the details, the color, the object itself."

Quincy looked around and decided on a compass that the headmaster had on his desk.

"Now go ahead and pick up the object. Look at it, touch it, turn it around, and memorize every detail about it."

She slowly reached for the compass. "Is it okay to use this?" she asked.

The headmaster nodded and smiled sadly at the compass. "My daughter gave that to me years ago." When Quincy yanked her hand away from the compass, the headmaster shook his head. "Nonsense, here." He handed her the compass. She stared at the beautiful object, surprised how heavy it was.

"Now try to remember what I said before you chose the compass, and then recall what I said even before that, all the way until you looked at the globe."

Quincy focused on the object and tried to remember their previous conversation.

"Is something supposed to happen?"

The headmaster smiled patiently. "Try repeating what I said to you. Do the best you can to repeat it word for word, but stare at the compass while you do."

Quincy looked down at the compass and intertwined her fingers. "You said, 'nonsense, here' and handed me the compass." She closed her eyes. "You told me that your daughter gave that to you years ago." An unexplainable fluttering began in her stomach. She had started the sentence from her memory of what the headmaster had said and then was suddenly hearing the last part of the sentence from his lips. It was as if she had rewound a record player.

"Now try to remember what I said before you chose the compass and then recall what I said even before that all the way until you looked at the globe."

"I know, I'm sorry. I'll try again." Quincy said, biting her lip with frustration. She looked at the headmaster and sighed.

"Did you find what you were looking for?" he asked.

"No. It didn't work. I couldn't remember, even after you repeated yourself," Quincy hated to admit her defeat. But to her surprise, the headmaster looked pleased.

"I did not repeat myself. You just remembered in exact detail what I had told you before. But it seems that you were unable to hold on for long. Try again."

Her brow furrowed, unsure if he was teasing her or not. She focused on the object again and heard the headmaster repeat himself for a third time. She stopped trying to push her mind so hard, then, and she felt a mental barrier break. The entire conversation began rewinding at an alarmingly fast pace. Quincy began to panic and suddenly found herself standing in the Back Library, staring at the dark passageway. She tried to scream but she was frozen in place. She could turn her body but could not walk away.

She looked around, seeing random black spots in the library that she hadn't noticed before. They weren't shadows, but they reminded her of inkblots on a page. She tried to focus on going back but quickly realized that she was stuck. Stuck in *the past.* She swallowed and tried to think. Inside of her head came a gentle but confident voice that commanded her to focus again and to fast-forward. She bit her bottom lip and imagined being back in the headmaster's secret office. Then wind rushed around her and the room flew past her until everything stopped suddenly, leaving her breathing heavily in the chair in front of the headmaster.

She sat back against the seat, feeling drained. "What just happened? Where did I go?"

"You never left, Quincy. Your mind was just gone for less than a minute."

"But I was. I was back there, back in the library."

The headmaster smiled. "Not exactly. You had control of some of your senses, which is why it is so important to remember each detail, so that you could *feel* like you were back in the library. You simply remember what you saw before. Did you see any black spots this time?"

Quincy nodded.

"They're pieces of the past that your brain never registered. The more you practice how to look at things properly in the present, the fewer black spots you will see in your memories. Eventually, you will even be able leave your body and walk around, but you will only remember what you have seen in the way you first saw that moment. You—and about three percent of the population— have the capability to remember something that you thought you barely glimpsed."

"I'm sorry sir, but I don't quite understand."

"When you focused on the details, you forced your mind to rewind to past memories. When most people remember past events, they just remember snippets, pieces that their minds choose to remember. The mind flushes out memories that it deems unimportant, so over time people forget the small details. The mind has to continually recall memories in order to remember them. Your mind, on the other hand, is wired differently."

The headmaster clasped his hands and looked at her intently. "Miss Quincy, you must be warned that this ability can become dangerous. As you continue to learn how to use your memories effectively, you will find that you will not have the luxury of forgetting things. There will be a point where it will be very easy for you to instantly recall small details, even without traveling back in your memory. You will remember *everything.* You will smell the same things, see what you already saw, and do the things that you've already done *again*."

"I can do all that." Quincy said in disbelief. "But *how*? It sounds complicated."

"It is at first. Just remember that you cannot change the past, no matter how much you want to. You will remember it exactly as it happened. No matter how many times you go back, and no matter how many ways you might find that could have changed the outcome, it cannot fix your present. The more you go back to the very same memory, the more things you will train yourself to see in the present. Okay?"

"Yes, sir."

"Good. "Now there are a few rules that you must follow in regard to this ability, as it can—and has been—misused before."

She nodded slowly, listening.

"Firstly, while you're beginning to learn, you must never travel back into your memories unless I authorize you to do so and you will only do it for the memories that I request. It is not easy to get out of your memories without help."

Quincy winced at the possibility of getting lost in her memory again and having to re-live her life or be stuck on pause like she was in the Back Library. She didn't know what would've happened if the headmaster hadn't told her what to do.

"Secondly, when I ask or tell you to do something that deals with your Talent you need to trust me. I will not misuse them for any reason, and I will not do anything against your wishes. Do you think you can do that?"

"Yes, but...My memory is a Talent?"

"It is."

Quincy's eyes widened. She wasn't Talentless, after all! Her quick excitement dampened suddenly, and she frowned. Perfect memory wouldn't protect her from the Amandas of the world.

"Does that make you unhappy?" the headmaster asked.

"I was kind of hoping for a Talent that would be... better? And stronger."

He smiled. "It's quite a gift, and perhaps you'll understand why later. You look tired, though. How about we keep this short today?"

Quincy stifled a yawn, thankful to be released early. "Yes, please."

"I apologize for doing this so soon, but we must move our class on Thursday to four in the afternoon in my actual office. I have a meeting that I, unfortunately, cannot miss."

The headmaster did not look excited about the meeting.

"I can do that, sir."

"Thank you. Moving class around is one of the negatives of having your Independent Study professor double as headmaster."

Quincy grinned.

"Oh, and by the way, Independent study is about learning to use your Talent. It will not happen overnight."

"Okay, thank you." Quincy said, smiling as she stood up. "Oh, and sir? May I ask one more question?"

"By all means."

"When you pulled out that folder, were my parent's information inside? Is that how you knew about testing my memory?"

The headmaster nodded. "No one could ever take advantage of your father because he could never forget anything. Perfect memory is one of the few Talents that are often inherited, so I made an assumption that you might follow in his footsteps and am delighted to be correct."

Quincy didn't know what to say, but her heart was filling with warmth. Suddenly her Talent had just become more important to her knowing that she shared the same one as her father, even if it meant she couldn't turn invisible or walk through walls. She wondered if those were actual Talents.

"So you knew my parents?"

The Headmaster smiled and nodded. "Your parents were Year Fours my first year as a language arts professor."

Quincy stared vacantly at the window behind the headmaster. She tried to imagine her parents as Year Four students. "So what's my Mom's Talent?"

The headmaster smiled. "Hospitality. She can make anyone feel loved and safe."

Quincy's throat tightened and she held her breath. That's why she remembered home so strongly and missed it so desperately.

"Thank you," she whispered.

"Enjoy your free time today, Miss Quincy. Good afternoon."

"Thank you, good afternoon to you too." Quincy paused at the doorframe and turned around.

"By the way sir, the writing on the globe stand was in another language. I'm sorry, but I didn't understand it."

The headmaster's expression showed a slight hint of surprise before he answered. "It's in Latin. It says, '*if you travel the world from start to finish, you will only end up where you began.*'"

Quincy smiled. "It's a fitting quote for a globe."

"I quite agree. One last thing, if you please...Do you know what time it is?"

She looked at all his clocks and remembered that each one told a different time. She finally looked at the headmaster and answered, "2:41 pm in this time zone, sir."

"Thank you, Quincy. That will be all for today."

She nodded and left the room.

***

He waited for the bookshelf to replace itself behind Quincy before declaring himself with a snort from his beak. "It looks like we have our work cut out for us." Talin noted.

The headmaster frowned and looked up at the raven. "Oh, Talin. I strongly dislike when you do that."

Snickering, Talin flew to the top of the chair Quincy had just vacated.

The headmaster tapped his pen against his desk. "It's going to take quite a bit of diligent work, but she has promise, especially if she is anything like her parents."

"Her parents were dedicated, and they sacrificed so much." Talin sighed. "She has a lot ahead of her."

"But do you believe she could actually find the missing keys?"

"It doesn't matter what I think, Luther. We're all out of options at this point."

The headmaster pursed his lips. "Is it truly so desperate?"

Talin whimpered. "We're past desperate. The first step in the deterioration is well underway. And I fear that others take advantage of the gaps in my foresight, which speeds up the process."

The headmaster rubbed his forehead. "Your guess was correct, though, Talin. She gave me the correct time without having to look at a clock. Quite difficult to fake in this room."

"Of course I'm right. My sight isn't completely gone, yet. When she's ready I'll test her. If she has cognition of time *and* memory, it might just save us."

"We will just have to wait and see?" the headmaster said as he clasped his fingers and leaned back into his chair.

***

Quincy walked out of the Back Library and into the Main Hall to visit the post office. She secretly hoped that there was something from her mother's institution telling her that her mother had awoken. The logical part of her brain knew it was probably too soon after her arrival to have received any mail at all, but she hoped nonetheless. She gave her name and floor number to the mail attendant. He shuffled around the mailroom, and to her surprise, he handed her a letter from Mrs. Adalin.

She opened the note and glanced at its contents as she walked back to her dormitory. Before she could walk up the stairs, the handle of an umbrella hooked her arm.

"Hiya, Quincy," Eloise said with a smile. "Just the person we were looking for! I'm dragging Monty to explore the grounds. Care to join?"

Quincy looked at her expectant face and decided that homework could wait awhile.

"So where are we going?" Quincy asked.

"If I must explore, I want to see the map room at the very least," Monty informed them.

Eloise wrinkled her nose as if hoping to visit somewhere else. "Okay, but as long as we visit the Oakley Knight's Armory."

"Fair enough." Monty quickly agreed.

They both looked at Quincy, and she gestured down the hallway. "Lead on."

The three walked away from the dormitories and past the Back Library. Once again, after a couple of turns, she stopped tracking where they were going. Finally, Monty and Eloise stopped to discuss the last corridor.

“We passed it ten minutes ago,” Monty said, his eyes rolled up at the ceiling.

“I think I would have known if we did.” Eloise shot back.

Quincy gave a soft chuckle and left them behind to fight while she visited a large room nearby. The long room had dark wood paneling on the walls with large hanging portraits spaced evenly apart. She lit some of the candles to get a closer look at the people in them. Each one had one date with a dash followed by a second date. Some contained four years, or less, while others were longer than ten years. One portrait’s date had only one year.

Behind her came a gasp and then a squeal. Quincy turned to see Eloise bouncing up and down. She dropped her umbrella and ran up to some of the pictures while reverently chanting some of their names.

Quincy gave a confused look to Monty who shrugged in reply. “I do not know why she is so excited. They are only Grand Master Creative Engineers.”

“Only? *Only* They’re *only* Grand Master Creative Engineers!” Eloise repeated in disbelief. “How are you both not more excited?”

Monty raised an eyebrow and Quincy shrugged.

“I’ve been looking for this hallway since we arrived!” Eloise went on. “Just think, all the Grand Masters in one place,” Eloise said, awestruck. “There’s no higher honor than to be elected as a Grand Master, especially since there’s only one in power at a time." Eloise turned around, and her smile widened. She skipped to the far end of the hall and stopped in front of a particular portrait. Monty and Quincy grudgingly followed her.

The portrait was of a young man with his arms crossed. He had a contagious grin on his face. In fact, it was the only toothy smile in all the portraits. He wore an immaculate pinstripe suit and had messy hair that pointed in countless directions. Underneath his picture read was a plaque that read, D. FAIRNIGHT: GRAND MASTER CREATIVE ENGINEER, followed by one date and a single dash. Eloise gazed at him dreamily.

Quincy quickly did the math in her head and realized that he had been in charge for nearly twenty-six years.

"He was the youngest Grand Master in history. Best known for his elevating box and for his multiple attempts to harness the raw power of dreams," Eloise said from memory.

"Oh, so he's the current Grand Master?" Quincy said.

Eloise widened her eyes at Quincy. "Where have you been for the last decade?"

Quincy's cheeks grew hot.

Monty squirmed before she could respond and said, "What is this Grand Master known for, Eloise?" He pointed to a portrait on the opposite side of the room.

Eloise rolled her eyes. "Absolutely nothing. See, he was only in office for a year before he resigned." She continued to walk by the portraits, sometimes giving them a small anecdote about one of the figures.

"How was your class?" Monty asked Quincy quietly.

She smiled. "It looks like memory is my Talent." A shiver rushed through her, the good kind. She couldn't believe she'd had a Talent all along.

Monty smiled. "Congratulations."

She opened her mouth to say more but the Timepiece rang, warning them of the approaching evening meal.

CHAPTER EIGHTEEN

OAKLEY AFTERNOONS

Quincy looked down at her school bag and the homework within and then up at Colin.

"Come on, Quincy," he encouraged, gesturing toward the Art Corridor. "You know you want to," he said, waving a paintbrush at her.

Quincy paused. She really did want to draw and she couldn't say no to Colin's smile and his pleading green eyes. "I'm really going to need to learn how to balance class work with a social life," she mumbled to herself.

Within the first three days, all the others had already found a pattern for their afternoons. Monty spent his time in the Main Library, Rusty usually could be found in the Band Room, and Quincy had no idea where Eloise had disappeared to for hours at a time. Whenever anyone asked, Eloise cleverly dodged the question. Mikaela, the debate team captain, often practiced and researched in the afternoons for her Debate Meets.

Quincy mocked sighed at Colin. “Fine,” she said.

Colin smiled triumphantly and led the way. “I think it’s brilliant that the arts professor Mr. A always keeps a couple of art rooms open for anybody. I hope we meet him today.”

Quincy and Colin found desk space in one of the rooms. Mr. A had left art supplies in the front with a sign instructing, USE ME. She grabbed some pencils, and Colin picked out a small canvass. Ten other students were already working on projects, and they’d sometimes talk or quietly hum. Quincy closed her eyes, enjoying the sound of pencils scratching, and peeked over to see Colin’s paper. His painting of the seemingly lifelike cat nearly jumped off the page. She stared at the depth in the feline’s eyes. “Wow, you’re amazing,” Quincy mumbled.

Colin looked up at her and grinned. “Thanks,” he laughed mischievously. “Oh, you mean this? Talent for art.” He winked.

Quincy laughed and then whispered an apology when she received a glare from a neighbor. Colin silently laughed and went back to his painting. Occasionally Quincy would look up and see a girl sneaking peeks at Colin or giggling with a friend. It made her uncomfortable, and she tried to ignore them, but apparently, she wasn't the only one who noticed his green eyes and warm smile.

She doodled on her paper until her internal clock reminded her of the time. She placed her drawing in her bag and, not wishing to interrupt Colin, stood up silently to leave.

He looked up from his work. "Where are you off to?"

"Independent Study. I'm having class late today," answered Quincy.

"Ah. Who's your Independent Study professor?"

"The headmaster."

Colin's eyes widened. "Really? I heard that he only teaches three Independent Study sessions at a time. You're very lucky."

Her own eyes widened, "Seriously?" Who were the other two students?

Colin nodded. "So what's your Talent?" he whispered.

"Memory."

"Oh, nice. Well, see you later, then." he said before refocusing on his drawing.

Quincy waved and exited the room. As she walked through the Art Corridor and downstairs, she smiled as rain drops began to splatter against the windows. It felt good to tell people what her Talent was. It made her feel like she finally belonged here at

Oakley. She briefly wondered if Amanda would continue to call her "No-Talent" before bumping into Genevieve. Her floor mate pursed her lips while tightly holding on to a box with different color paint splashes on it. The two girls icily apologized and switched places.

Quincy's neck was burning. She hadn't forgiven her classmate for taking her horse, and they both had refused to say more than five words to each other. Quincy walked across the Courtyard toward the Main Hall and to the Professor's offices. Stopping at the last door at the end of the hallway, she glimpsed the nameplate engraved with, HEADMASTER, that had been accentuated by flickering green candles. Quincy gently knocked at the door.

"Please wait outside. I will only be a minute," the headmaster said from his office.

Quincy took a seat in the hallway and waited. She tried not to eavesdrop on the conversation, but the loud female voice made it impossible.

"No. I don't believe you. My problems have always been secondary to your students and your little quest. Listen to me; they don't exist. They never have and they never will. I can't even imagine what would happen if one of your precious students happened to correspond with your obsession. I would never hear from you again."

The door swung open, and a tall woman stormed out, slamming the door behind her. Quincy didn't catch the details of her face, but the woman wore a long dark-red coat that fell almost to her ankles.

She heard the *click*, *click* of her heels as she walked down the stairs.

Quincy's mouth hung open, shocked at the woman's rude demeanor. Who was she to talk to the headmaster that way?

He opened the door and poked his head out. "I do apologize for…that. The Third hasn't been having a good week in Parliament. So, naturally she has to let everyone feel the repercussions."

It must be the same woman from that newspaper article, Quincy guessed.

The headmaster swung the door open and invited Quincy inside his shockingly clean office. She sat down in one of the open chairs in front of the empty desk. She stared at the scarcity of the office compared to his other clock-filled room. This office only had three scenic nature paintings and a handful of books on top of the plain furniture.

"Why is it such a big deal for a Third to be seen here in Wales?" Quincy asked, remembering the content of the article.

The headmaster looked outside the window and placed his hands in his pocket. "The Third who was just here has a"—he paused uncomfortably— "a difficult history. There will always be those who will watch you. Hoping to see you fail. Certain court officials believe that she will make a crucial mistake, so she's on edge. The problem is not so much that she's here in Wales, but that she's here to ask for advice. Unfortunately, I don't have the answer that she is so desperately seeking."

The headmaster sighed and then turned around to face Quincy. "Are you ready to begin?"

Quincy nodded, and Marquam looked directly in her eyes. She squirmed under his serious gaze.

"Good. I'm sorry to say this, but before we do anything fun or drastic we need to learn and master the basics. Sadly the basics are not always the most exciting, but you need to build a foundation before you build the building itself. We went a bit too fast last time in our excitement."

Quincy's cheeks burned, and she silently agreed.

"But there is no need to feel bad or embarrassed. I did say 'we' went too fast. To be quite honest, I'm surprised that you were able to go back on your first day. You first need to learn how to see in the present. What you see today will tomorrow become a part of your memories," he explained. "To begin I have a small exercise for you that will teach you how to remember objects without having to physically go back in your memories. This will help you to fill those black spots that you saw two days ago. So let's work on your short term memory." The headmaster opened one of the drawers from his desk and placed a pinecone, a cup, the compass, a fountain pen, and a pencil in front of Quincy. "Here I have six objects in front of me that I have placed in a particular order. Please look at each item briefly then, close your eyes."

After a couple of seconds of looking at each object, Quincy tightly closed her eyes.

"What was the first object on your left?"

Quincy dug around her memory desperately trying to remember. After a moment, Quincy finally admitted that she couldn't remember the first object. After being prompted, she found that not only could she not remember the first item, but she could not remember more than four of the six objects and in no particular order.

"Miss Quincy, you may open your eyes now."

She stared at the six objects with annoyance. "Maybe memory isn't my Talent?"

The headmaster smiled wryly. "You wouldn't be able to travel back like that if it wasn't. The point of this class is for you to strengthen your ability. It's already there; you just need to learn how to use it. Soon, remembering six objects will become commonplace for you. Once it is, then we will begin to work on traveling back instead of just simply remembering."

Quincy groaned.

"It does seem daunting when you look at the whole thing instead of just the first step. You will see, though." He smiled at her. "There is one thing you need to remember as your Talent develops. If you inadvertently travel back in your memories, look for a clock or something to help you fast-forward again or you could risk getting stuck."

A shiver crawled down her spine at the idea of being stuck in a moment in her past and never waking up.

“I once had a student ten years ago who swore that the Timepiece’s ticking brought him back,” the headmaster continued. “But I want you to think of possible tricks to help you.”

“How could I *accidentally* travel back?”

“Your senses of smell and taste are housed near the memories in your brain, and they can recall memories quite easily. Also, sometimes great shock or bodily pain could force you to remember, as well. I would like you to listen for the ticking of the Timepiece and practice calming your mind. By learning to keep calm, you may also be able to refocus and wake up. It’s best to be prepared. Just in case.”

Quincy nodded, and the headmaster moved the objects around. “Let’s try again, shall we?”

After half an hour, the Timepiece rang and Quincy rubbed her head.

“That will be all for today.”

“Thank you, sir.” she said, nodding to him before leaving.

She started to walk out of the Learner’s Citadel but paused and decided to go visit Monty in the library while she was there. The library was the largest room in the building and took up almost an entire level. Quincy smiled at the librarian and walked toward the end of the large room. She breathed in deeply, enjoying the smell of the books. She found Monty in a dark corner surrounded by a pile of books. He stared at the page, not registering Quincy’s entrance.

“What are you doing?” she asked.

Monty looked up from his book and to her surprise, smiled up at her. "Greetings, Quincy. I am reading a book on the theory of relativity and time."

"That sounds…slightly boring," she laughed sitting down at the desk next to him.

"To you, perhaps, but it is a part of my assignment for Independent Study. What have you been up to?" he asked, taking off his glasses.

"I had my Independent Talent Study late today, so I just got out."

"Oh?"

"Yeah, and I saw a Third."

Monty looked surprised. "Oh, indeed? I am curious as to why a Third would be at Oakley. Which of the Thirds was the visitor?"

Quincy shrugged. "I don't know her name."

"Presently, there is only one female Third, and her name is Eleanor Morrow. She was reelected last year. Ms. Morrow served her first term over fifteen years ago but resigned due to a family tragedy before she could finish out the term. Now that she has been re-elected nearly a decade later, there has been a lot of negative press regarding whether or not she is fit for the job."

Quincy remembered the angry woman and thought maybe the press was right about her not being ready to lead again. The Timepiece rang the warning for dinner, interrupting their conversation.

"Splendid, I am famished. Shall we?" Monty gestured to the door. "I wonder what we are eating this evening."

"I heard something about meatloaf," Quincy answered.

Monty turned paler than usual and wrinkled his nose.

"Not a fan of meatloaf," she teased.

"Not much of a fan of meat in general," he answered.

"Well, there is always hot chocolate," Quincy laughed.

"With whipped cream," Monty added with a grin.

Chapter Nineteen

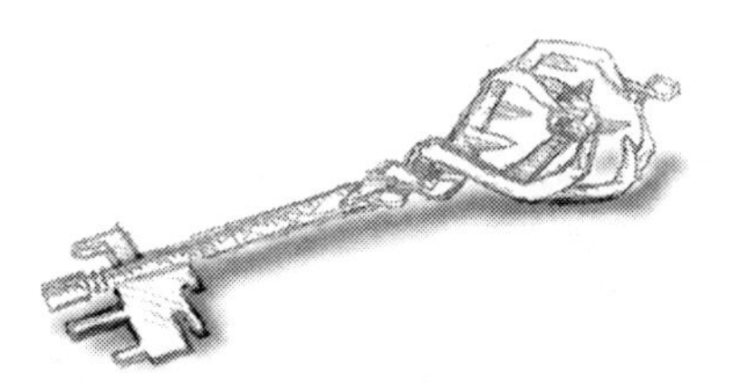

Aftereffects

Wilbright stumbled but was caught by the strong arms of his valet before he hit the ground. With Mr. Hatchet firmly grasping his arm, he hobbled toward the forest where an eagle patiently waited for their return. Wilbright closed his eyes, thankful for the dark-purple evening that successfully hid the pain etched on his face.

Damn his weak body.

The valet held on to Wilbright's elbow as he clumsily slid into the compartment and propped himself against the pillow. Once he was sitting comfortably, Mr. Hatchet left him to mount the smaller top compartment. It wasn't until then that Wilbright allowed himself to tremble in his blanket. He had never been so relieved to be going home. The woman's eyes from Dublin haunted him.

When their eagle was safely in the air, he fumbled in his vest for his pocket watch and with a shaky hand, read the date and time, and then tucked it away again. He had been gone for nearly three days, yet it had only been eight hours to him.

“How is that even possible?” he wondered out loud. How could time be so cruel?

Wilbright forced himself to breathe slowly in and out. His head felt like someone had taken a hard object to it. He painstakingly opened his eyes and looked at the dark countryside. He reached inside his breast pocket and pulled out a small key and stared at it. He wished he knew if he loved the power or hated it. A small part of him wanted to open the window and throw it out to a place where it could never found. But he needed it. He couldn’t continue without it. At least he would soon be finished and his end goal would be met. He would have his love after all these years.

He shivered against the chill. Supposedly these travels would become more and more difficult, and the aftereffects worse with each trip. And with more trips needed, the repercussions were guaranteed to worsen. Wilbright shivered. He needed to find Katelyn’s key before she had a chance to hide it fifteen years ago. And that meant traveling even further into the past.

CHAPTER TWENTY

THE MINOR KEYS

Quincy leaned forward, sucking in air. After a month of classes at Oakley, she was finding it difficult to decide which subject she liked least: Latin or Physical Education. At this moment, Physical Education was at the top of the list. She hated running from one side of the field to the other to chase a soccer ball, or a *football* as Colin kept reminding her.

Quincy tripped over a fallen student and just missed kicking the ball. Before she could further dwell on her dislike of the sport, her teammate ran up beside her to get control of it ahead of the other team.

"Stand up!" Professor Pertinax shrilly called to her. "What do you think you two are doing on the ground? Making daisy chains, are we? I'll show you daisy chains."

Quincy and the other student jumped up painfully before Professor Pertinax could walk over with her riding stick. She had never used it on any students, but it was always near their faces or legs. Quincy limped after the ball, giving the appearance of getting back in the game. She looked over and saw Monty—her opponent today—with bright-red cheeks and a heaving chest. She waved at him, but he didn't register her greeting. Then from the corner of her eye, Quincy glimpsed Monty speaking to Professor Pertinax. "Go," the professor yelled, waving Monty away.

Monty slowly walked away from the field, holding his elbows tightly. Before Quincy could ponder Monty's departure, she heard the *whoosh* of the football past her head and screams from her teammates to get the ball.

The end of class couldn't come soon enough.

***

I know where you're hiding...

Quincy woke up screaming and stopped only when she realized that no black silhouettes of men had their hands around her neck and were trying to choke her. Once again she was relieved she had closed her curtains. She took a sip of water to soothe her dry throat and lay back down. She closed her eyes, trying to hear the ticking of the Timepiece. When she only heard the nighttime silence, she opened her curtains and put on her coat. She had never been told not to leave the floor, so she grabbed a blue-flamed candle and walked outside.

She breathed in the crisp air and listened to the crickets. She shivered and tightened her coat around her. She walked toward the Timepiece and sat down in front of it, closing her eyes and listening to the ticking.

Something heavy and sharp grasped her shoulder, and she immediately tightened her shoulders and threw up her fists while simultaneously shaking her assailant off.

"Steady on. Jumpy aren't we?"

Quincy kept her shoulders tense but let out a small a sigh of relief when she heard him.

"I was beginning to wonder if you actually existed. So where have you been?" Quincy asked the bird, a note of accusation in her voice.

"Oh here and there. So what brings you outside into this particularly delicious night? Are you waiting for the Timepiece's song?"

"The what?" she frowned.

"Never mind, you'll find out."

The bird made himself comfortable on Quincy's shoulder, and she found it awkward to turn her head to talk to him. She felt odd enough having him perched there.

"Wait a second. You've lost the camouflage," Quincy said when she finally craned to look closely at the bird.

"Excuse me?"

"Last time you were brown and now you're all black. Or at least I think so in this light."

"Yes I am actually. Good memory with the brown. I got rid of it because now I'm home."

"You live here?"

"I have to live somewhere. Might as well be here."

Quincy nodded at this new piece of information. "So Talin, are you a crow or raven?"

"Excuse me! Do I look like a crow to you? Really?"

"So raven, then?" She shook her head and chuckled.

Talin snorted and didn't respond. Then he cleared his throat, and she felt him shift his weight from one foot to the other. "So, how are classes?" he asked.

"Good, mostly."

"Mostly?"

Quincy didn't feel like telling him about her last Latin quiz. She had barely passed it, and she was dreading next week's presentation. At least she and Monty were partners, so that would help her semester mark. Class work seemed to come easily to the Irish boy.

"Yeah," Quincy grimaced. "Talin, what's the point?"

"The point of what?"

"Of me being here. Taking classes. Pretending like I don't have a key around my neck?"

"Life is like math," Talin intoned. "You need to learn addition and subtraction before you can start multiplication and division."

She raised her eyebrows at him. "Meaning?"

"Meaning, you're not ready to do anything else yet. You need to learn how to use your Talent before you attempt to save humanity. And it's not your move, yet. I'm waiting to see the pieces in play."

"Did you just switch from mathematics to chess?" Quincy groaned. "Enough metaphors already."

Now Talin chuckled. "Fine. All in due time."

They sat together for a while, enjoying the silence until the Timepiece's song broke the moment. As all the dials hit the empty "zero" slots music filled the air. The different chimes reverberated in a harmonizing tune, and the whole ground trembled as if in a dance. As suddenly as it started, it stopped, leaving the world in the quiet of the night.

Quincy wiped a tear that had fallen on her cheek. "That was beautiful." she whispered. "Why haven't I heard it before?"

"You have to know about the song to take notice of it. I doubt you'll have any issues from hearing it at midnight, if you wish to."

She didn't answer, just sat in silent thought.

Time passed, and eventually, Talin gently poked Quincy's neck with his beak. "Good talk. I'll see you soon."

Before Quincy could say anything, Talin jumped off her shoulder and disappeared in the early morning. She slowly made her way back to her bed, wishing he had told her more.

***

Quincy woke up a few hours later and looked through her window at the November sky. Just watching the windy day outside caused her to shiver, despite the warm floor beneath her feet. She stretched and slowly started to get ready for the day. She had eleven minutes before she needed to meet Monty in the family room to work on their Latin presentation. Digging through her closet, she finally chose khaki pants and a thick wool sweater. After deeming herself decent enough, she walked to the family room. Inside, Rusty diligently cleaned his trumpet while simultaneously eating a sticky bun. Counter-productive, but she said nothing to that effect.

"Good morning, Rusty."

"Morning."

"I'm supposed to meet Monty here. Is he still asleep?"

Rusty finished chewing and frowned. "Now that you mention it, I haven't seen him. When I woke up, his bed was made and he'd already gone. And I got up early today to grab the best practice room. And I had it, too, until a Year Four kicked me out." He sighed.

"Thanks, Rusty. I guess I'll go look for him, then."

He nodded and returned to polishing.

Quincy walked down the stairs and toward the Main Library. Monty wasn't in his corner, though. She walked to the library, scanning the whole place for him, but he was nowhere to be found. She headed over to Miss Grastorf the head librarian, who was sitting at the circulation desk.

"Miss Grastorf, have you seen Monty yet today?"

She looked up from her newspaper and took off the glasses resting on top of her white hair. She chewed the end of her ear piece while pondering.

"No, not yet. Sorry, my sweet."

Frowning, Quincy walked back to the Main Hall, hoping to find Monty eating breakfast. The kitchen staff left a buffet table out for weekend mornings so they could eat whenever they wanted. Quincy's face fell when she only saw her advisory professor, Professor Agglebee, grabbing grapes and bacon. Where else would Monty be?

"Excuse me, sir, but I can't find Monty. We're supposed to meet up for homework. You wouldn't have happened to see him, have you?"

At first the Professor looked confused and then his eyes lit up. "Oh yes! Mr. McCalister. Glasses with the white-blond hair."

Quincy nodded eagerly.

"So many students to keep up with…You should look for him in the Infirmary."

"The Infirmary? Why would he be in there?"

The professor pursed his lips. "That would be something that you would need to ask him."

She swallowed, worry settling at the pit of her stomach. "Thank you for your help, sir," she pushed out.

"You're most welcome!"

Quincy stood at the staircase, trying to remember where the Infirmary was. She grasped the banister and closed her eyes, hoping it would help her to visualize the Oakley map. She felt her pulse quicken, and she opened her eyes. She gasped when she saw herself staring at the map of Oakley in her student handbook. But she hadn't brought it with her. How did she have it?

She jerked her head up to see her surroundings and instantaneously found herself back at the staircase. Had she accidentally just memory-traveled? She made a mental note to ask the headmaster about it. She shuddered at the thought and slowly made her way up the stairs, now clearly remembering where she needed to go.

She walked up the staircase into one of the towers. She tentatively opened the white doors and walked inside.

A nurse looked up from paperwork. "Hello, dearie. What ails you today?"

"Oh, I'm fine, thanks. I'm looking for Monty McCalister."

"Ah, Montgomery. Let me go see if he feels up to visitors." She motioned to the chairs in the waiting room.

After Quincy had sat down, the nurse walked through a second set of swinging doors. She hoped Monty was okay. And not contagious.

After a moment, the nurse's head poked through one of the doors. "You may go in and see him now. Please follow me."

Quincy stood up and followed the nurse through the doors and to a hallway connecting tiny rooms on both sides, which were separated by curtains of different colors instead of doors. And instead of bleach, she smelled pine. She caught a glimpse of an open room as they walked. It had a small window and minimal furniture, and the color of its walls matched its curtain divider.

The nurse stopped in front of a room. “He’s inside. Be mindful of the time and don’t be long.” The nurse shook her finger at Quincy.

As soon as the nurse left, Quincy opened her mouth to ask permission to enter the room when Monty himself interrupted her.”

“Come in, Quincy.”

She opened the curtain and looked at Monty. She raised her eyebrows in surprise. His usually well-combed wispy hair had been messily flattened. His sickly pale skin was camouflaged against the white pillows, emphasizing the dark shadows under his eyes. It was the first time Quincy saw him without his glasses. His icy-blue eyes pierced hers, and she saw deep exhaustion in his gaze, as if he were much older than he seemed. It caused her to involuntarily shiver. She struggled to keep her face neutral, trying not to show anymore shock and surprise.

“Don’t I look charming today?” Monty said, quietly. He started to smile but stopped to hold his head.

Quincy gasped. “What happened?”

Monty grew somber and rubbed his temples. “Oh this? This is…just a migraine.”

“Just a migraine? You look absolutely terrible! It must be more than, ‘just a migraine?’” Quincy said. He must have been sick to combine his words. He had said, *don’t* instead of *do not*. He never did that.

Monty looked slightly annoyed at Quincy's insistence, but finally he slumped his shoulders in defeat. Quincy sat down on the edge of his bed.

"You are, unfortunately, correct. It is more than just a migraine. I promise I do currently have a migraine, though. You see…" Monty paused awkwardly.

"You don't have to tell me anything if you don't want to," Quincy said gently.

"No, that's not the problem. I am trying to decide how to begin."

"From the beginning maybe?" Quincy asked, hoping to lighten the mood.

"The beginning. Yes, a good place as any I suppose," he answered looking down, clearly avoiding Quincy's eyes. "I have severe epilepsy."

Quincy widened her eyes. "Seriously?"

Monty nodded. "Sometimes the seizures are so minor that it looks like I am daydreaming for a few minutes. Other times it is so awful that I am completely and utterly spent and lose hours from blackouts. My brain shuts off. From the present, at least." he said, biting his lip. "Last night was one of the latter. It caused me to pass out in the corridor." Monty grimaced. "It's excruciatingly embarrassing."

Quincy knew excruciatingly embarrassing. Even with the heavy drapes, she still feared that her nightmares would wake up her roommates.

"What are you thinking?" Monty asked quietly.

Quincy exhaled. "I just understand embarrassing. I have frequent nightmares, and living in a group house doesn't make the mornings fun."

She looked away from Monty and blinked rapidly. She was here to support him, not to whine about Miss Heatherwood's. And what would he think about spending time with a foster kid? When she finally looked back at Monty, she saw him staring at her. He didn't look disgusted or even shocked. His eyes were gentle, and he remained silent.

"So is that why you left Physical Education early yesterday?" she asked, trying to change the subject back to him.

Monty nodded and sat up with a wince. "My body cannot take the physical…abuse, I suppose. Unlike most people our age. Occasionally, and usually without warning, I have a seizure. I have to be continually cautious in Physical Education. It does not take much for my body to collapse. Sometimes I try too hard and then pay for it afterward. I really should not play football for very long. In fact, the same goes for polo, I fear."

After the mention of polo, Monty looked down at his hands and sighed. "Both my parents were heavily involved in polo. My father, the famous Aodhan, 'The Mad Man' McCallister, dreamed of having a boy who would follow in his footsteps and become even more accomplished than he was. He wanted a son he could teach and coach. However, instead of a strong and athletic son, he got me."

She remembered the ride to school, then, and Sean's jibes about Monty's father. So that's what he was talking about.

Monty blinked his eyes quickly before continuing. "My father and I have never been close. I wonder if it is because he thought I would end up dying prematurely like my mother. In fact, many in our town believe that I still will. That I will one day have a terrible seizure and never come out of it." His eyes grew cold, and he pressed his lips together tightly.

Quincy twisted a strand of her hair around her finger. He had never mentioned his parents. She had no idea that his mom had died.

"I'm sorry, Monty," she finally said. The apology felt inadequate even to her own ears. *Sorry* couldn't make everything better.

"Thank you," he said halfheartedly.

"How do you know that you can't play polo?" she asked, trying to move the conversation away from his mother.

"Between one of my father's many short business trips, we started a simple game of football," Monty cringed from the memory. "My father quickly saw that I could not play because I tend to faint with too much exertion. Polo would be potentially dangerous for me because one has to master both one's own body and one's horse's. Also, if I were to have an attack like the one I had yesterday, I could easily be trampled. There are simply too many variables in polo. I doubt I have lived up to any of his expectations." He paused and took a sip of water. After he had replaced the cup on the table, he continued. “As I mentioned, my mother became very ill and died days after giving birth to me. After my mother passed, my father lost a piece of himself. I wonder if he secretly blames me,” he said, his voice barely a whisper.

“It’s not your fault. How could he blame you?”

Monty shrugged. “It is probably my own imagination, but when I turned five, he took a post that required a copious amount of traveling. So he gave my aunt and uncle custody of me because they cannot have children of their own. They introduced me to the only world that they know, the world of knowledge and literature. Every now and again I receive a letter from my father, but it is not often. In fact, I doubt that he even knows that I am attending the same school that he and my mother graduated from. I doubt he would care.”

“Your dad seems like jerk.” Quincy growled. “Who would want to leave you behind?”

“Thank you,” he answered, his cheeks turning a bright pink. He cleared his throat and stared at the wall behind Quincy. “It saddens me because I used to dream of playing polo one day, to be just like him. Much like everyone else, it seems that I crave what I cannot have or achieve.” Monty looked back at Quincy. “I hope I have not made you uncomfortable.”

Quincy shook her head. “No, thank you for telling me. May I ask you a question though?”

Monty nodded.

"So every time you have a seizure, even if it's a short one, you blackout?"

Monty nodded. "Something like that. I call it losing time. But for some odd reason, the seizure triggers my Talent."

Quincy narrowed her eyes at him. "What exactly is your Talent? How can you know something that you're not supposed to? I've never heard of a Talent like that."

Monty looked around the room for a moment, not meeting her eyes. "No, you would not have. For some reason, my Talent and epilepsy are tied together. There are not any known cases of this happening."

"So you're one of a kind." She laughed. She winced when he didn't join in the laughter.

"So it would seem," he answered coldly. "As a small child, everything seemed to be normal. After I turned three I had an…interesting problem that took years to diagnose."

"Problem? Which problem? The one where you sound like a grammar professor? Or the one where you refuse to eat meat?" Quincy teased.

"No, those came later," Monty answered with a grin. She smiled back at him, glad he took it as she'd intended.

He rubbed his forehead. "My uncle theorizes that my Talent stems from the Talent of planning, the one where you logically see the progression of events. Apparently my mother had it, as well."

"Planning...But I'm pretty sure I've heard about that Talent." Quincy said.

"Of course, it is not an unusually rare talent, but the one where you actually *see* what happens is."

Quincy frowned. "Wait, what?"

"You see, when I have a seizure, I lose the time *during* the seizure. But it is not time completely lost because I jump ahead."

She gasped. "So basically, when you have a seizure, you see the future?"

"Yes, a form of it. It is what *could* happen. Though it usually does." Monty took off his glasses and stared at Quincy so that his blue eyes fixed on hers. She squirmed away from his gaze and wondered how much he could see without his glasses.

"Please do not tell anyone. I do not wish for others to know that I am a freak of nature. Please," he pleaded.

Quincy's heart ached for Monty. "You're not a freak. And of course I won't say anything. As long as you don't tell anyone about my Talent for nightmares." She grinned.

He smiled and nodded. "Agreed."

They quietly sat on the bed, waiting for the other to say something. Finally, Monty broke the silence. "Quincy, have you ever felt that you were on the edge of some impending doom or something to that extent and that there was nothing that you could do to fight it?"

She narrowed her eyes. "Have you seen something? From the future?"

Monty drew the blanket up to his chin and looked down. "I'm not really sure."

"Why are you still here?" an angry voice growled at the door.

Quincy jumped up and looked, embarrassed at Monty, whose eyes widened.

"I am sorry that I missed our Latin presentation meeting. Could we reschedule the time to tomorrow afternoon?" Monty quickly asked.

Quincy nodded. "Of course. Feel better."

"Thank you."

Quincy opened the door to stare into the angry eyes of the nurse.

"I'm going, right now. I swear." She looked over one last time and caught Monty smirking.

She hurried out of the Infirmary and nearly bumped in the headmaster.

"Hello, Quincy," he greeted her.

"Oh, hello sir," she said in passing. She paused and turned to face him. "May I ask you something before you go?"

"Certainly," he answered and walked back toward her.

"I guess it's not so much a question as a statement. I think I accidentally memory-traveled. I know I'm not supposed to, but I think I did. I tried to remember the Oakley map so I could figure out how to get to the Infirmary and then I found myself staring at the exact map that I was thinking about. I was so surprised that I must have knocked myself out of it. I'm sorry."

The headmaster nodded his head. "Sometimes it happens that way. Don't be ashamed. It's a natural progression of your Talent. I would wait longer before you try to travel again, however. We'll talk more about it in class."

"Yes, sir."

"Enjoy the rest of your weekend," he said, dismissing her.

"Thanks. You too," she answered before walking toward the Main Library to hunt for an exciting afternoon read.

***

Quincy's second favorite class after Independent Study had become Language Arts with Professor Archer. It was always a welcome relief after Latin. Professor Archer encouraged independent thinking in her class and forced her students to leave their comfort zones at the door. The whole class was expected to participate in discussions, which made it easier for Quincy to speak up.

She sat in the middle of the class next to Colin. His clear and concise speech usually put him in the lead during the discussion, but he often lost points because he never took a definitive position on many of the topics of government, freedoms, and the definition of words.

"Well done today, class. For this week's homework, I want you each to write a paper on minor keys. I'm sure many of you have been told the tale of the magical keys. This paper is not meant to discuss the validity of the keys themselves but more as a creative essay. I want each of you to think about what it would do for you should you possess a minor key. What consequences could come from its ownership?"

Quincy tapped her pen on her notebook. What would she do with a minor key? So far her own key hadn't done anything for her except elicit warnings.

She thought about it all through lunch, and she wasn't the only one. Everyone at the table was discussing it.

"What would *you* do with a minor key?" Eloise asked Rusty.

Rusty shoveled a large spoonful of mashed potatoes into his mouth and chewed thoughtfully. "I would open the doors to the music rooms early in the morning so I can get the good ones first."

"That's the only thing you can think of, Rusty?" Eloise admonished.

"Well, then what would you do, Eloise?" he shot back, defensively.

"That's easy." She intertwined her fingers mischievously. "I'd find the other keys and open the door."

"Wait, which door?" Rusty asked. Quincy looked up from her plate.

Eloise rolled her eyes. "*The* door, of course."

"But you don't even know what's behind it. What if it's a sickness, or a monster?" Colin added.

Eloise shrugged. "At least then we would know for sure."

"If said door truly exists," Monty chimed in as he sat down next to Quincy. Some color had returned to his cheeks, and the darkness under his eyes had lightened.

Eloise pouted. "Just because you haven't seen one doesn't mean they don't exist. Admit it: you would love to have a special key."

Quincy rubbed the chain around her neck without revealing the key. She glanced sideways and saw that Monty's eyes were on her. When their gazes met, he broke the connection and further joined the conversation. "I would use the key to open the library after hours to have the room to myself," he said while helping himself to some salad.

"That's not at all surprising," Colin said, rolling his eyes.

Monty pursed his lips and looked down at his food.

"I would use the key to visit private museums not normally opened to the public." Colin decided. "What about you, Quincy? What would you do?"

"Not sure yet. I have to think about it," she quietly said.

Eloise looked incredulously at her. "You don't already know?"

"What I am sure she meant was that there are so many possibilities that how could she choose just one?" Monty answered for her. She smiled at him and then back at Eloise. "Exactly."

"Fair enough," Eloise conceded.

Everyone separated after lunch and left Quincy deep in thought. If she could get into any room, where would she go?

***

After her final class of the day, Quincy sat down at her desk and stared at her blank paper for over an hour. Annoyed, she closed her curtains and took the key out from under her shirt. What was so special about this key? She shivered, remembering the warning in London from the man in black about keeping it secret. Who could she trust?

She looked down at her empty page and groaned. It was time to get out of her room for a bit.

She slowly made her way downstairs and into the cold sunshine. She pulled out a list of Latin vocabulary and grimaced.

"*Ire*, to go. *Consto* to stop." She groaned and placed the list back in her pocket. Rubbing her arms, she stared at the empty courtyard watching her breath dissipate in the cold. She stayed outside until her fingers felt numb and then grudgingly went back to her room to try her paper again. But when she arrived, an argument raged in the dormitory between Lindy and Mon-Aye.

"Lindy? How can you say that Jonathan Holiday is more handsome than Gregory Hatchet?"

Were they really fighting about who was the more attractive theater actor?

"Be realistic Mon-Aye, Gregory could finish off Jonathan in a battle of good looks." Lindy shot back while gesturing to a poster above her bed.

"*Ya*!" Mon-Aye yelled in her own language. "Do you want to die?" she threatened.

Lindy rolled her eyes. "Besides, Gregory is more handsome in photos," she said, pointing to a poster above her bed. "And you said yourself that Colin was the cutest new boy, and he could be a young Gregory."

Quincy walked across the room to her space, and Mikaela came running into the room right after her. She slammed the door and pulled on the handle, holding it shut. Quincy heard a muffled, "Let me in, duffer." Eloise, probably using another British insult.

Annoyed, Quincy grabbed both sides of the drapes and closed them around her in an attempt to shut out the noise. She sighed in relief at the newfound silence and sunk into her bed. But she jumped up when a polo mallet accidentally ripped open the curtain, letting in the loud conversation. *Ugh!*

"I will never admit defeat!" Lindy howled, brandishing her own mallet.

Quincy rolled her eyes and shut her curtain again. After sharing a room for the last three years, she just wanted her own room and a quiet place to study. And then she knew what she would write her paper topic on. If she had a key that would allow her to go wherever she wanted to go, she would find a room of her own to get her homework done.

CHAPTER TWENTY-ONE

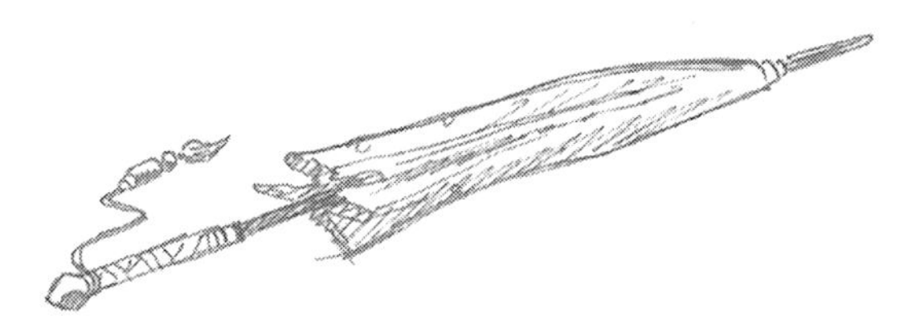

THE KNIGHT AND THE RUNAWAY HORSE

Three days later, Quincy yawned as she walked through the Learner's Citadel before lunch. She rubbed her swollen eyes, exhausted from keeping up with her studies and her new friends as November began to close. Right before she stepped outside, she realized she'd left her math book on her professor's desk after a homework check. Grumbling, she ran back inside and up the stairs, and she scooped up her book in her classroom before trudging back down the stairs. She stopped at the entrance of the Detention Hall. Rusty had mentioned a shortcut through the hall that saved minutes to get to the opposite side of the citadel, near the Main Hall.

Her stomach growled, and she entered Detention Hall hurrying at an almost jog-like pace. Her attempt failed when she tripped over something on the ground. She grumbled as she looked at the object—a purple umbrella. Eloise's purple umbrella, to be exact, but there was no Eloise attached. *Why would it be here of all places?*

The drab Detention Hall housed little rooms where students were separated from one another to write lines or to simply sit and contemplate the meaning of life. For as long as Quincy had known Eloise, she had thought that the smaller girl would be one of the last of her friends to get in trouble. She wasn't sure if she should grab the umbrella or open the door to the room that Eloise could be jailed within. Quincy knocked reluctantly at the door.

Eloise's voice was cheerful when she answered, "Come in!"

Quincy opened the door and saw Eloise on her stomach, drawing what looked like instructions or blueprints, underneath the handwritten line of, I WILL NOT DYE MY HAIR. "Oh! Hello, Quincy."

"You sound a little bit too happy to be in trouble."

"Trouble! Me? Never! I've only been in here for ten minutes and will soon be let out. Pass me my umbrella please."

"Why?"

"Because I really like my umbrella," Eloise said with a frown.

"I know *that*. Why are you *in here*?" She took a seat next to the small girl.

"Oh! Well, it's not my fault. Well, kind of," Eloise giggled.

"What do you mean?"

"Well, remember the substitute prof from Mathematics?"

Quincy nodded recalling the women with a high-pitched voice from her last class.

"Well, she saw my hair, asked me if I knew the whole, 'not allowed to dye your hair rule' and when I told her that yes, I did, she threw me in here. Apparently she thought I was being cheeky or something. Anyway, this is the fourth time I have been wrongfully put here for hair violation."

"Fourth?"

"Yup. And probably not the last."

Quincy had wanted to ask her about her hair from the moment they'd met, but she had thought better of it, not wanting to hurt a new friend's feelings. Because for as long as Quincy had known Eloise, she had never once seen her touch up the streaks in her hair back to purple. Even though she had seen Eloise's hair grow longer, the color had remained the same vibrancy.

"So the Math lady's going to tattle to the headmaster and he'll come and let me out. Again."

"Why did she put your umbrella outside?"

"She told me that umbrellas shouldn't be toted around on sunny days." Eloise rolled her eyes. "As if I were born yesterday," Eloise sighed and then burst into a fit of giggles.

"I do feel much better holding it." she added. "You never know when someone could grab me and throw me off a roof! I'm only one meter and fifty-two centimeters, don't you know? That's only five feet to you Yanks!"

It was an odd thing to fear in Quincy's opinion, but she laughed along anyway.

"Hey, Eloise," she said, growing serious. "Could I ask you a question?"

Eloise nodded. "Certainly."

"Why do you have purple in your hair if it isn't allowed?"

Eloise snickered.

"What?"

Eloise sucked in her breath, trying to keep a straight face. "Well, the streaks are actually permanent. I erm...I did an experiment on myself when I was about seven, and well, it never went away. Or something like that. Anyway, I can't fix it and neither can anyone else, for that matter."

Quincy laughed. "How did you manage that?"

"To be honest, I'm not entirely sure. I overheard a conversation on genetics. They were arguing over whether or not a person could change their genetics. You know, the practically invisible things that make your hair brown and your eyes green? Anyway, they finally decided that it would be impossible to change it so I decided to prove them wrong."

"You changed your genetics just to prove you could? How?"

Eloise gave Quincy a mischievous grin. “I haven’t the foggiest idea how I did it. I just remember finding the genetic code of this gorgeous bird with purple feathers and tied it to my own. It’s much easier to add something than to subtract it, so technically I can’t change it back. Of course, I wouldn’t change it even if could. I rather like it. It took a couple of weeks for the purple to start showing up in my hair. My parents were horrified, and even angrier when no one could figure out how to reverse the color.”

“Wait, you were seven?”

“Oh yes. I like to tinker with things. You should see what I did when I was nine. My parents—”

There was a tap at the door, and the headmaster poked his head in. “I’m sorry that I have to apologize yet again, Miss Eloise. I’ll add a note to the substitute professor papers about your hair. Hopefully that should keep you out of here.”

Eloise jumped up and followed Quincy and the headmaster out of Detention Hall.

“There’s no need to apologize, sir. I’m used to it by now.” Eloise winked and skipped with her umbrella down the hall.

“Quincy, I hope that you will not make it a habit to visit this hallway often, for yourself or your friends,” the headmaster said, laughing.

Quincy grinned. “No, sir.”

“Come on, Quincy!” Eloise hollered over her shoulder.

“Excellent. I will see you soon.” He smiled as he walked away. “Fifteen-year-olds with permanent purple hair. It’s a first,” he said, continuing to chuckle as he walked away in the opposite direction.

Quincy ran after Eloise. As they headed to lunch, a big sign met them on the notice board. Eloise squealed and jumped up and down.

"What?"

"Read it!"

Quincy stopped in the front of the sign that informed the student body that Visitation Friday was approaching in three weeks.

"What's Visitation Friday?" Quincy asked.

"You know! Parent's day…?"

Quincy furrowed her brow.

"The last day before we leave for break?" Eloise tried again. "You know? Parents come to visit the school, talk to professors, and take the eagles home with us?"

"Oh right!" Quincy pretended she knew exactly what Eloise was talking about.

"I can't wait! Come on, Quincy, or there won't be any food left!" Eloise began skipping and twirling towards the Main Hall, again spinning her umbrella as she went. By now people had learned to recognize Eloise and knew when to dodge her pointed weapon.

Quincy's throat tightened and she blinked furiously. She briefly imagined her mother walking down the Main Hall to greet her on Friday. But there wouldn't be anyone to meet her to take her home like the other students. Actually, she would not be leaving Oakley at all.

She followed a chatty Eloise toward the door of the Main Hall but paused before going inside. She suddenly didn't want to be around people.

"Hey, Eloise. I'm not feeling well. I think I'm going to lie down for half an hour before class."

"Oh, okay. Feel better then!" Eloise waved and walked off toward their lunch table.

Quincy headed back to the dormitories. Hearing a clearing of a throat, she stopped as Monty caught up to her. He smiled gently and gave her a heavy napkin. He'd made her some lunch to-go. Her cheeks warmed. Without saying a word, Monty waved and headed out the exit and toward the Learner's Citadel. When he had gone, Quincy opened the napkin to find tuna fish on a piece of baguette, her favorite sandwich.

***

After an hour of sitting on her bed, bored after classes, Quincy decided it was time to try to ride her unnamed mount again. She'd been trying twice each week to put the tack on the horse without any success. She had taken to sitting next to it and talking nonsense just so the beast would get used to her voice. It hadn't seemed to help. Ready to try again, she walked to the stables. She stepped inside and saw Colin feeding his white stallion. She tried to walk past him quietly, hoping not to interrupt him, but he turned around to face her.

"What-ho Quincy!" Colin grinned at her.

"Hello to you too." Quincy smiled back.

"So, what brings you here? Are you riding this evening?"

"That's a very good question. I will soon find out," she shrugged and gave a little laugh.

"Oh yes. I heard about that."

She gave him a hard look. "What have you heard?"

He looked embarrassed. "Oh nothing really, just that your horse is…a bit headstrong. Maybe I could help?"

Quincy placed her hands on her hips. "Oh, you think you can do better?" she teased.

Colin laughed. "Only one way to find out."

"Uh-huh, well have at it." She gestured down the stable.

The two of them walked to the end of the Year One's section and stood in front of the still-nameless plate hammered next to a second that read, QUINCY HARRIS. Colin cleared his throat, and they both heard a loud *thump* in answer. The large horse's head swung over the door showing its teeth. Both Colin and Quincy jumped back. Colin's cheeks were red and he was clearly embarrassed that he'd flinched. He walked up to the post and grabbed the tack from the hook.

"Right. Let's put this on to stop…it from biting."

Five minutes later they had managed to open the door, blockade the horse in the stall, hold the neck, and put in the bit without actually *being* bit. Colin held the bridle while Quincy threw the saddle over its back and tightened it.

The horse growled in frustration. Both Colin and Quincy tried soothing noises while attempting to gently rub the horse. In response, it began to kick the door.

"Are you sure that you want to try this?" Colin asked.

"I have to if I want to pass Physical Education."

"True, but is the grade worth more than your life?"

"Dramatic much?" Quincy said. She sat on the side of the stall and took one deep breath before jumping in the saddle. For a moment, the horse stopped and seemed to listen to her, but the moment did not last long. The horse impatiently kicked the back of the stall.

"Open the door," Quincy demanded.

"Are you sure?" Colin yelled.

"Do it!"

Colin opened the stall door, and the horse took off at full speed. She felt its powerful muscles move under her legs as she tried to hold on.

"Whoa," she hollered trying to pull the reigns, but it refused to respond to any of her commands and, instead, smashed her legs against the walls of the stable. The equipment on the wall shook and all the other horses snorted and hissed at her.

"I'm coming," she heard Colin yell behind her.

A stable hand tried to reach for her and the horse, but her mount easily dodged him.

She managed to guide the horse through one of the side doors outside. She felt the crisp rush of air against her cheek as the horse galloped around the school grounds. It stopped suddenly, and Quincy grabbed its mane to keep from falling. The horse reared and began to kick. After fifteen seconds of trying to fight it, the horse succeeded in throwing her. She hit the cold ground and felt her eyes water. She stared up at the cloudy sky and felt the blood in her head throb. The horse ran toward the forest, leaving her behind.

In the stable she heard yells of, "Hold that horse down." and "Shh, it's okay, girl." as the stable hands tried to soothe the horses inside. She turned her head and saw Aldwyn and another stable hand on their horses galloping after the black streak hurtling toward the forest. Quincy moaned. Cigfran would have been able to ride the horse. Why couldn't she?

Colin ran up to her and helped her sit up.

"Are you all right?"

Quincy felt the whole world spinning around her, and she thought she might throw up. Trying to walk it off, she attempted to get up and instead instantly sat back down. "Yeah, I'm fine," she lied.

"I'm going to go get help," Colin announced.

"No, I just need a minute."

With effort, and Colin's hand, Quincy stood up. Colin stared at her and slowly nodded his head with admiration. "That was a hard fall. I'm impressed you're standing. But we should go to the Infirmary just in case."

"No, I want to try again when they bring the horse back." She narrowed her eyes at the forest. She rubbed her head where she had hit it on the ground. Everything was spinning.

Colin frowned. "I'm not sure that's a good idea."

Aldwyn trotted up to Quincy and Colin. "I'm sorry Quincy, but your horse didn't want to be ridden today. We'll have to wait for it to decide to come back."

Quincy breathed a sigh of relief that she would not have to try again and risk the horror at being thrown off in front of Colin and the entire stable a second time. Her throbbing head made it difficult to think. She desperately wanted to lie down. She thanked Aldwyn and began walking back to the Main Hall. She stumbled and Colin grabbed her arm to steady her. He refused her claim that she felt fine and instead continued to hold on to her. They walked in the building and went toward the staircase. Quincy stared at the stairs with horror. There wasn't any way that she could make it up the flight of stairs.

"I'm going to pick you up and carry you, alright?" Colin told her.

"Ooh, he's so strong," someone giggled. Quincy looked to her right and saw three girls pointedly staring at them. She felt her cheeks grow warm and hoped that Colin hadn't noticed her blush.

"Tell the nurse we're coming," Colin growled at the girls.

Quincy heard the girls run away from them. She whimpered, and Colin slowly slunk to the floor with her still in his arms.

"Stay with me," he quietly whispered. A worried look took over his usually calm demeanor. She turned her head and saw Monty running their way from down the hall. She closed her eyes and heard, "Quincy?" before she fainted in Colin's arms.

Chapter Twenty-Two

The Oakley Winter

Quincy's heart always skipped a beat when the bookshelf fell down. She momentarily closed her eyes to regain her composure. Even after a week, she still fought dizziness and headaches from the concussion from her fall. At least now she could grasp the book without being directly in front of it. And she no longer paused before walking into the dark hallway to the headmaster's office and knocking on the already open door.

"Ah, Miss Quincy. Excellent timing as usual."

Quincy sat down on her customary seat and searched for the line of random objects that the headmaster kept on his desk for her memorization exercises. She scrunched up her nose. "Where are the objects?"

The headmaster folded his hands on the desk and stared at Quincy. "We will come back to that, but today I'd like to try something new." He pulled out a jar and handed it to Quincy. "Smell this," he requested.

Quincy took the jar and stuck her nose inside the glass. She took a whiff and smiled. "Hmm, cinnamon." She sighed, her throat tightening. Her mother used to add cinnamon in her cookie dough.

"What does it remind you of?"

"My mom," she whispered.

"Very good. Now I want you to close your eyes, smell the spice again, and recall a specific time where your mother used it." The headmaster handed her the compass. "Hold this and see if it helps."

Quincy nodded, closed her eyes, and smelled the jar again. She rubbed her thumb over the smooth glass of the compass and breathed deeply in and out, overwhelming her nose with the smell of cinnamon. She opened her eyes and found herself in a yellow kitchen with the sun streaming through the windows. She looked down at her hands for the compass, but there was a small glass shaker filled with cinnamon in its place. Without realizing what she was doing, she opened the jar and dumped the entire jar's contents inside a bowl of batter.

"Quincy Marie Katelyn Harris!"

Quincy whirled around to face her mother. She had her hair in a tight bun, and she rubbed the garden dirt from her fingers into her apron. Her eyes were narrowed at her daughter. "What do you think you're doing?" her mother demanded.

Quincy hunched her shoulders and her heart dropped with shame. "I wanted more cinnamon in my cookies." Her voice sounded wrong in her own ears. She looked down at the metal cooking bowl and saw her reflection in the surface. She was just a child—maybe six or seven years old.

She turned her gaze back to her mother, who was trying to hide a smile behind a false frown. Finally, she burst into laughter and walked over to the cooking bowl next to Quincy.

"A little bit of cinnamon goes a long way, Quinn." She smiled. "It looks like I'm going to have to remake the batter. This won't be edible."

Young Quincy giggled as her mother tried the batter and grimaced.

"Oh, you think it's funny, do you? You come over here and try this," her mother teasingly demanded as she reached for her. Quincy jumped off the chair and ran out of the kitchen, but instead of running into the hallway of her childhood home, she awoke to find herself standing in the headmaster's office.

She laughed again, expecting to find the cinnamon cookie batter on his desk. But the sudden realization hit her. There wasn't any cinnamon cookie batter and her mother couldn't be here.

Her lips trembled and she tried to blink back her tears. But the hot tears escaped, sliding down her cheeks. She hurried out of the headmaster's office without a word and back into the dark library. She curled up near a stack of books and let herself sob into her knees. After a minute, she felt someone sit next to her, and she forced herself to stop crying. Finally, she managed to stop and instead she gasped for air.

"I'm sorry," the headmaster said quietly. "It's hard to remember moments attached to those we've lost." He pulled a candy cane from his pocket and offered it to her.

"Oh that's right, it's almost Christmas," she said, staring at the candy.

The headmaster nodded. She didn't really want to take it from him. It made her feel like a little kid, having someone give her candy to make her stop crying. But the look on his face was so genuine. And maybe it would help settle her slightly woozy stomach. She thanked him and opened the wrapper before licking the peppermint stick, then wiping her eyes on her sweater sleeve. "Sir, what do people do here over break?"

"Well you don't have worry about being alone, if that's what you truly fear. There are other students who stay during the holiday. There will be activities most days, and I know the Head Porter has planned a visit to the forest. On Christmas Day there will be a wonderful dinner, and I'm sure that you will have some time to try to and ride that horse of yours." He winked at her.

Quincy grimaced, slightly horrified that the headmaster, as well as the rest of the school, had heard about her "adventures" in horseback riding.

"You might want to name your mount. It's unusual when a horse doesn't come with one, and perhaps a reoccurring word may soothe him. By the way, I promise that the week will not be too terrible. When I myself was a student here, I found it quite enjoyable."

"You were stuck here too?"

He laughed. "I don't know if *stuck* is the appropriate word, but I always thought it was much better than being *stuck* at home with a mother who didn't have the time to pay attention to the antics of a young boy."

Quincy nodded. "Thank you, sir."

He patted his knee and stood up. "Come. We have a lesson to complete."

***

Quincy heard the thump of the bookshelf fixing itself as she left Independent Study. She slowly walked toward her room and the bustle of her packing floor mates when she spotted Monty sitting on the bottom of the dormitory staircase with two cups in his hands. She sat down next to him, and he offered one to her.

She rubbed her tear-swollen eyes and took of sip of the hot chocolate. She sighed with relief. "Thanks."

He nodded and took a sip of his own drink.

"How did you know I was coming?" she asked.

He grinned and pointed to his head.

"What did you see?"

"Just that you had the appearance of being sad and that I had two drinks in my hands," he answered.

"And then you just made it happen?"

He nodded.

"Could you have chosen not to come?" she asked, wondering how much control he actually had over the future that he saw.

He nodded again. “Yes, I could have decided not to meet you here.”

“So you do have freewill?” she took a long draw drink from her cup.

Monty rolled his eyes. “You sound like Professor Archer with one of her class discussions.”

Quincy laughed. “Are you going back to Ireland for the holidays?” she asked.

“Yes,” he said, but he didn’t look happy about it. “Oh such ecstasy.” The sarcasm dripped from his voice. “Speaking of which, I probably should gather my things.” He stood up and slowly made his way up the stairs.

Colin walked down at the same time, and the two boys stared coldly at each other.

“McCallister.” Colin flatly acknowledged.

“Knight.”

Quincy narrowed her eyes as Colin took a seat next to her. She looked up and saw that Monty had already disappeared up into their floor.

“What was that about?” she asked.

Colin shrugged while fixing his shirt and didn’t look at her. “It’s a little bit silly,” he admitted. “New money verses old. I find him a little bit stuck-up.”

“Stuck-up? Monty? Have you guys even really talked?” she snapped, her defenses up.

Colin's cheeks reddened. "I told you it was silly. Anyway, I finished my packing, and I'm off to the stable to ride. Want to double up on my horse?" he asked with a hopeful expression.

She smiled. She hadn't actually enjoyed riding since before Cigfran had left, and she wanted to feel the wind on her face again. She nodded eagerly and followed him outside.

***

Just keep smiling, Quincy repeated over and over to herself. The only thing she wanted to do was find a corner and cry, but she took a sip of her lemonade and stared at her schoolmates who had all made efforts to look nice for Visitation Friday. Her friend's parents spoke with the professors about grades and class projects. They drank lemonade and nibbled on cookies around her as they mingled.

She looked over at the piles of luggage by the door. Within the hour, the carriages would take them all away to catch the eagles back to London. They'd all go home from there. She closed her eyes, trying to imagine her own parents standing nearby.

"Quincy?"

She opened her eyes and turn around to face Monty.

"May I present my aunt and uncle?"

"Pleased to meet you," Quincy offered her hand to the two adults. They slowly shook her hand before stepping back. She recognized his aunt from New York, and she stared at Monty's tall, and balding, uncle.

He gestured to Quincy, “Please meet Quincy—” he paused awkwardly “—my friend.”

They both nodded in her direction but said nothing. Her eyes widened at their cold behavior, and anger started to coil in her stomach. Monty deserved better than that. He looked at her and then stared uncomfortably at the ceiling. Since no one said anything, his aunt and uncle meandered toward the exit. Monty looked like he wanted to disappear. She couldn’t blame him. They were possibly the stuffiest people she had ever met. She quickly understood why Monty seemed so cold at first. At least both his aunt and uncle had come to pick him up.

Finally he mumbled, “Enjoy your holiday,” before uncomfortably handing her a small package. Her lips formed a small *O*, and they curled into a smile. He bowed his head and left to follow his family. She wished that she had something to give him in return.

She watched him retreat and then looked down at the small brown paper package in her hands, then across the room and her throat went dry. Colin was introducing Genevieve to his mother. Quincy wasn’t sure if she was more bothered by Colin introducing any girl to his mom or the fact that it was Genevieve, who was such a witch to her.

Quincy had spoken with Colin and had met his mom ten minutes earlier. She’d smiled at Quincy. “So pleased to have met one my dearest’s friends,” she said, laughing daintily. She was wearing a stylish dress and the fur of some creature over her shoulder.

Quincy blinked now as Genevieve giggled with Colin's mother and she resisted the urge to gag.

Everyone had been polite with Quincy, but none of them were there to see her. She knew that she should stay behind and say her final good-byes before the holiday but she could no longer watch them. Quincy looked at her enemy's pretty dress and wanted to rip it off. As kind as her friend's parents and family had been to her, they were not her parents and she was not their daughter.

After that depressing thought, Quincy decided to change and walk towards the stables to see if she could manage to stay on her horse for more than ten minutes. Aldwyn had promised to help her over the break, and she hoped that by the end of the time off, she would, at the very least, have managed to stay on longer than the last time. She sat on her bed slowly sliding into her riding boots. She stared at Monty's gift trying to decide to open it now or wait for Christmas in four days. She pursed her lips and finally decided to pull the wrapping apart.

When she opened it, a charm bracelet with a silver four-leaf clover dropped into her hand. She gasped with delight as she stared at the intricate design of the veins on the clover. After she had finished looking at her present, she opened her desk to safely store the bracelet when a piece of paper caught her attention. She opened the message and hidden underneath was the metal musical movement of her shattered music box. She grabbed the note:

Play Me. Happy Christmas. —E

Quincy stared quizzically at the broken movement and slowly twisted the dial. As the music of her childhood began to play, tears rained down her smiling face.

***

Quincy woke up with a scream, swatting away the invisible hands from her neck. She sat up, panting, and scanned the empty beds around her. She hadn't bothered to close the curtains. She still had the whole girl's dormitory to herself for one more day. She took a few deep breaths to calm her racing heart.

Quincy instinctively knew that it was too late to go back to sleep. As the Timepiece rang six times, she decided that she might as well get up. She had a lot to do today. Unfortunately, she had put off taming her horse during the holiday. The headmaster hadn't been exaggerating when he'd said there would be plenty to do. Every day there were new Christmas entertainment and activities for with the few students left behind. But she couldn't procrastinate much longer, especially if she wanted to pass Physical Education.

She grabbed her gear, got ready, and walked toward the stable. She searched the space for Aldwyn but found no one. He must have taken the day off. Quincy couldn't wait any longer, though, so she was on her own. She placed her hand on the stable door and breathed in deeply before opening it.

"I wouldn't do that if I were you."

This time, Quincy immediately looked up into the rafters. As usual, the raven looked down at her.

"Do what?"

"This. You, attempting to ride alone. You were lucky last time to have people around," chided Talin.

"Yeah. Around to see me fall."

"What is wrong with you people? Falling is not such a bad thing. It's the not trying again part that's completely unacceptable."

Quincy groaned. Cigfran had once said something similar to her when she had first arrived at Miss Heatherwood's. She narrowed her eyes at the raven. "Well, I *was* going to try again."

"Alone, yes, I know," he said with a sigh. "At least allow me to watch, just in case."

Quincy crossed her arms over her chest. "And who are you going to tell if something happens. You're a talking bird, remember?"

"I have my ways," he said, his tone haughty.

Quincy bit her lip. "Fine. But you can't say anything snarky."

"Agreed," the raven said after nodding his head.

Quincy headed to the end of the stable, and Talin flew over her and landed on the rafter above her mount. Quincy wished she had a better strategy than before but she didn't. So she slowly approached the stall. She made soothing sounds to the horse and managed to slip the bit in his mouth. Talin snickered when the horse attempted to bite her hand.

"I thought you weren't going to be snarky," she snapped.

"Oops," Talin said unapologetically. "Anyway, I had my talons crossed."

Quincy rolled her eyes and tied the reins to the post and, without too much difficulty, surprisingly got the saddle on and tightened it appropriately. Dodging kicks, she gingerly led the horse outside. She ignored the beast's protests and warily stood on the mounting block and pulled her legs over the horse. Finally, she was in the saddle and locked her knees, attempting to hold on to the best of her ability.

As before, the horse must have tasted freedom and began to gallop at such a fast pace that she feared what would happen if she fell. This time would surely be worse than a concussion. To her right, she heard a whistle and gave it a quick glimpse. Talin soared next to her, doing somersaults in the air. Somehow he managed to keep up with her charging horse.

"So what did you decide to name him? It is a him by the way."

"Maybe now is not really a good time."

Talin laughed and flew to her left side.

"*Now* is always a good time. So why haven't you named him?"

Quincy barely dodged a low branch. "I don't know. I haven't thought about it," she lied. The headmaster had suggested the same thing. She really ought to have listened.

"How would you like to not have a name?" the raven went on.

"Talin, do we really need to do this now?"

He didn't respond and landed on the horse's head. The galloping immediately stopped. The horse stayed completely still, breathing deeply as if waiting for further instructions.

"How? Why? What?" Quincy sputtered.

"Just add it to the list of my personal charms."

The horse slowly turned around and began to walk toward the stable.

"Will it—he always behave now?"

Talin snickered. "No. Just for me. You'll have to figure out what he wants."

"How do you know that he wants something?"

"I speak horse."

She let out a disbelieving chuckle. "Seriously?"

"Seriously."

"Then why can't you tell me what he wants?"

"How do you know that I haven't already?"

"Talin, why can't you just make sense?"

"Pfft. I make perfect sense. You're just not understanding me."

Quincy frowned, tired of playing word games with Talin, and instead chose not to respond. Talin snickered and stayed with Quincy until they put the horse back in the stall, and then he flew to the doorpost.

"Quincy, go back, read a book, maybe do some studying…" he told her.

She grimaced.

"Anyway, enjoy the rest of your day off."

"Thanks, Talin." she said. "I'll try."

And with that he flew away.

CHAPTER TWENTY-THREE

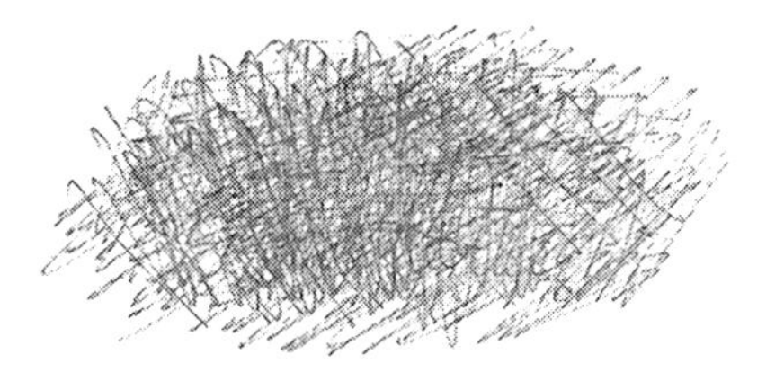

CRIME

Even though Quincy liked having the floor to herself, she was relieved to have the room filled again with her floor mates. They all swapped stories and showed off new presents. Quincy thanked Eloise for fixing her musical movement and she glowed from the compliment. Genevieve interrupted their giggling by waving a letter in their faces.

"Guess who wrote me a letter? I almost didn't have to miss him," Genevieve said, staring straight at Quincy.

Quincy pursed her lips when she saw the handwriting on the top two letters.

Another roommate saw the letters and cooed, "You're so lucky. I hear almost the entire First Year class fancies Colin."

"I know," Genevieve looked at Quincy again, as if daring her to speak.

Quincy wondered why she was singling her out and gave her a fake smile before excusing herself to brush her teeth. She did like

Colin, and she did think he was handsome, but she wasn't sure if she felt that way about him, even if the jealousy crept in whenever she saw him with Genevieve. She frowned at her reflection in the mirror. It didn't matter anyway. It seemed like he had already made his choice.

***

Classes resumed without any added excitement, but Quincy felt guilty that she hadn't studied Latin over the break and she fell, once again, behind in class. She became more and more uncomfortable when the dates for the midterms showed up on the school bulletin board for the end of February. Even with Monty's help, she still dreaded the exam. Her other classes were giving her decent marks, but for some reason Latin just didn't make sense to her.

The Sunday before the exam, Quincy and Monty planned to study Latin most of the afternoon, but once again, Monty couldn't be found in his normal places. She found him back in the Infirmary, but this time, the nurse refused to let her even see him. Apparently her patient had been up all night and had only recently fallen asleep. Worried about Monty and nervous about losing her study partner, she went to the family room to attempt to study alone. After hours of trying, the timepiece rang out in the early morning, and she dragged herself to bed.

Sleep refused to come and her nightmare of the night consisted of the Latin exam opening up to a black hole that sucked her into nothingness. She almost shrieked when Eloise opened her curtain to shake her awake. Gratefully, she managed to hold off the horror-filled scream.

"Come on Quincy-poo, wake up! Everyone is getting ready to leave for breakfast and the first exam."

Quincy rolled onto her stomach and groaned in her pillow. "Oh please no. I'm so not ready for this," she moaned piteously.

But she dutifully followed her classmates down the stairs and sat through a breakfast that she could not eat. A tired-looking Monty managed to get her to drink a glass of apple juice. Guilt crept into her gut. He's the one who was just in the Infirmary. She should be helping him, not the other way around. But she couldn't stop the panic.

When the meal was over, she followed all the Year Ones to their testing room in the Learner's Citadel. Grabbing a seat toward the back of the room, she desperately hoped that the exam would actually suck her up, just to take her away from the room and far away from the exam.

"You have one hour," the proctor announced once the tests were handed out. "You may now begin."

Fifteen minutes went by, and Quincy looked at her blank piece of paper. She couldn't answer a single question. Her heart pounded so loudly that she couldn't concentrate and couldn't remember any of her Latin lessons. She snuck a look at the other Year Ones, all writing quickly with focused expressions on their faces. Quincy pursed her lips and made a quick decision. There was no way that the headmaster would know if she used her Talent to look back, right? She would only have to go back half a day to look at her study sheets. Then she could come back and have all the answers. She had gotten out of her accidental memory travel awhile ago, so surely she could do it again. No one had to know.

She closed her eyes and let time take over. At first it didn't work. She tapped her pencil against the desk until she heard a "Shh!" coming from a neighbor. In desperation, Quincy reached under her shirt and grabbed the key. She held it in her hand and tightly closed her eyes. She released her focus and saw the room become blurry. Then she watched herself standing up and walking backward out of the room. She had done it! Quincy had a moment of delight at the realization that she had managed to use her Talent by herself. But, the moment that she allowed herself to stop focusing became a mistake. She began to move backward faster and faster until everything swirled together. She briefly saw herself shaking hands with Monty, meeting Talin for the first time, and standing in front of Miss Heatherwood's on her first day there. She began to scream when she saw the policeman talking to her about her parents. The more she panicked the more scared she became and the faster she began to go backward.

"Quinn! Focus!"

The use of her nickname and the tone of the demanding voice made her stop looking back and pause in a moment of her stirring cookie batter with her mother. The scene began to repeat herself with her mother giving her the same instructions of adding an ingredient slowly while mixing, over and over again.

"Focus!"

Quincy mentally frowned and tried to focus on her Latin midterm. She sped up, this time going forward and then hit a mental wall. She opened her eyes but couldn't see anything. Complete darkness surrounded her. She had no idea what to do. She couldn't go backward or forward. She fought down the panic, trying to remember what the headmaster told her about finding something to help her mentally move. But she couldn't see or feel anything to guide her back.

A cold breeze swept in from nowhere and blew past her cheek, and she shivered. Behind her, someone laughed coldly. A shudder traveled down her spine as the laughter began to move around her, sometimes farther away and other times right next to her. She tried to scream for help but couldn't move her lips.

Out of the nothing, she heard an exasperated sigh. It overcame the laughter and it left Quincy in silence. After a moment, Quincy could use her lips again.

"Hello?" she whimpered.

"You have no idea where you are, do you?"

"Talin?" Quincy asked, recognizing his voice with relief.

"Do you know any other obnoxious and obtrusive ravens?"

"Not that I know of. Were you the one who laughed at me?" she whispered. She trembled and tightly hugged herself.

"You heard laughing?"

"Yes," she whimpered.

The bird growled and she took two steps back.

"No, I didn't laugh at you." he said. "How long have you been hearing laughter?"

"For awhile. Who is it?"

"Believe it or not, now is actually not the best time to catch up and ask questions. Don't you think? Now, since you've gone silent, and it's pitch black here, I'm going to pretend that you nodded in agreement with me. You've reached the last moment where your memory ends or technically, where it starts. Your Talent doesn't work in the future."

"Okay, but how are you here if this is in my mind?"

"That's all you have to say? Not any thanks for the information, thanks for keeping me company…?" Talin grumbled something incoherently to himself. "I'm here because you wanted me to be here."

"I did? That doesn't make sense."

"I rarely do. Now, let's stop talking and send you back, shall we? Once again I'll pretend to see that you nodded and you just listen. First, stop squeezing your eyes shut. Yes, I know your eyes are shut. Focus and then open your eyes. I don't envy your first waking moment, but at least you're going to miss your exam, after all. You can go anytime now."

Quincy did as she was told. When she finally opened her eyes, she saw the testing room in front of her. She gasped for air as her normal beating heart suddenly pounded in her chest as if she had just been running. Her head began to throb and all the blood left her head as Quincy slumped over and fainted in her chair.

***

The smell of sterile sheets was the first thing that Quincy grasped when she awoke. She looked up and saw a focused Monty reading a book.

"What are you reading?"

He looked up, guilt written on his face. "I apologize, I became engrossed with this chapter. How are you feeling?"

"I have a little bit of a headache. How long was I out?"

"Just a few hours."

Quincy heard a knock at the door, which ruined any chance of further conversation between them.

The headmaster opened the door. "Master Montgomery, would you please excuse us for a moment? I need to speak with Quincy privately."

Monty gave Quincy an unusually worried look, and she knew that the headmaster's use of his given name signaled trouble.

Monty shrugged an apology to Quincy. "Yes, sir." He exited the small room, leaving her and the headmaster alone.

"Would you like to tell me why you are in here?" he asked, strangely calm.

"I fainted in class," she whispered.

"Yes, you did," he answered tightly. He stared at her, his gaze icy and sharp

There was a moment of awkward silence as neither one wished to go first. Finally, the headmaster reluctantly spoke. "Would you like to explain what happened during the exam?"

She knew she would be in far greater trouble if she lied than if she told the truth. And the headmaster seemed like the kind of man who would know if she was untruthful.

"I couldn't remember. So I…looked back…and got lost."

The headmaster's face dropped with disappointment, and her heart sank. She suddenly felt that she had failed him.

"Quincy, that's why I asked you to wait until you were ready. You are irreplaceable."

She resisted the urge to hide underneath the covers and disappear in them. "I'm sorry."

The headmaster sighed. "I know you are. And you must have been terrified. I'm just glad that you made it back in one piece. Talents need a chance to grow before they're used, especially yours."

He paused and Quincy wondered if he was deciding what punishment to hand out. Unfortunately, she was right.

"I hate to do this, Quincy, but every action has equal consequence. As you know, this Saturday is our annual Equospatium and you're going to excuse yourself and spend the day on your floor."

She clenched her fists and bit her lip angrily. She knew she deserved to be in trouble, but this felt like too much. Equospatium was a whole day designated for horse races, dressage, and horse jumping. Even though she couldn't compete, she wanted to see the upper classmen on their horses.

"Now I would like you to rest for your other exams and your assignment for next week is to write a five-page paper about why people of authority create rules." The headmaster walked out the door and nodded at Monty who walked back in when he had left.

"Trouble?" Monty asked.

"Yeah, something like that."

"What happened?"

"I used my Talent too soon."

"Which made you faint?"

"Yeah. I can't go to the tournament now," she grumbled.

Monty looked sorry but didn't prod and went back to reading his book until the nurse told them that Quincy had been approved to leave. Monty slowly followed her out the door toward the Main Hall. She quietly smiled, thankful for his company and relieved that he hadn't asked any more questions. Before they could walk into the hall, Sean and Monty met head on.

"Why must you always collide with people?" Monty said, raising his nose in the air.

Sean bowed mockingly. "It's the only pleasure we peasants have in this life." He turned to Quincy and gave her a nasty smile. "Did you ever find an answer to my question?"

She ignored him and tried to walk past. He quickly stepped in front of her.

"Don't you want to know the answer? He's only friends with you 'cause being friends with a poor foster kid makes him feel better about himself." He turned to Monty. "Isn't that right, *my lord*? Why else would you be 'friends'?"

Quincy looked over at Monty, hoping he would laugh and deny Sean's accusations. But he didn't say anything.

"Well?" prodded Sean.

Monty shifted his weight from one foot to the other.

"Where did you hear that?" she spat.

Sean leaned closer to her. "A little birdie told me."

She bit her lip and looked over at Monty. He stared daggers at Sean and refused to meet her eyes.

Was that how Monty saw her? A pitiful little foster kid to bolster himself?

She frowned at the two boys and fled the room, heading for the football field. She leaned against the goal and shivered in the crisp February afternoon. She felt strangely numb as she stared at the empty goalpost.

She jumped when she felt a gentle touch on her shoulder and whirled around to face Monty, holding a paper cup in his hands.

"Drink this. It will make you feel better."

Quincy frowned at him.

"It is only water."

She reluctantly took the glass and drank a sip. The cool water forced her to breathe deeply.

"Is it true?" she asked, her voice steely.

"That I befriended you because you made me feel better about my own predicament?"

She nodded.

Monty scoffed. "Do you always believe everything you are told?"

She narrowed her eyes at his rebuke, and he softened. "No, of course not," he admitted.

"Then why did we become friends?"

Monty sat down on the ground next to her and grimaced. "Probably because you did not know me already."

"What?" she blurted.

"When we met that first day, you were friendly to me without knowing me. I am used to being treated a certain way because of my title, my family, and my money. None of which inherently seem to mean anything to you."

"I don't understand—,"

"Because you simply cannot," he interrupted. "My entire genealogy can be found in the library. I do not jest. Look up the Irish families and there you will find my name, my father's name and so on."

"Seriously?" Quincy widened her eyes. "Your entire family?"

Monty nodded. "Truthfully, you make me feel normal." He slowly stood up and swatted the grass away from his pants. "When you are ready to talk more and release me from the horror that I am incapable of standing up for you or myself, you know where to find me."

He slowly walked back toward the dormitories. Quincy frowned and placed her chin on her knees. She had only told *Monty* that she was a foster kid, so how had Sean found out?

CHAPTER TWENTY-FOUR

AND PUNISHMENT

Quincy unhappily plodded toward the stables the next afternoon after attempting to study this week's Latin vocabulary. Introductory polo would be showcased in Physical Education starting next week, and she still had not managed to stay on her horse for more than five minutes without Talin's supervision.

She groaned when she overheard another excited conversation about tomorrow's Equospatium. Since she was required to stay on her floor during the tournament, it meant that she couldn't hold off riding for another day. She dreaded being locked in on the Third Floor all day while her friends would be at the tournament having fun without her. She knew that she deserved the punishment, but it didn't make her feel any better. She angrily grabbed the tack on the stable wall and, once again, managed to place it on the horse with some difficulty and a quick bite to her right hand. She licked the wound and was surprised at how much it hurt.

"Brute," she muttered.

The horse screeched and began to kick. Without thinking, Quincy pulled the first word in her head. *"Consto!"* Since she had just been studying her Latin vocabulary list she used the language's word for *stop.*

For the first time since they had unfortunately met, the large stallion remained completely still. Quincy quickly mounted the horse so he couldn't change his mind and led him out. Before she became cocky, he made a deep and guttural growl.

"Yes, yes. I understand you completely," she sarcastically told the animal.

After riding for almost an hour, her mount got bored and got rid of his rider. He followed her directions but never immediately, as if making sure she knew she was never completely in control. She took him back to the stall while rubbing her raw backside. A small victory but she had managed to ride him. She wondered if today had been lucky or if the Latin had helped. She would have to find out next week during polo. The Timepiece rang and Quincy went back to the dormitories to change for dinner.

***

Quincy awoke to Eloise's laughter as she ripped open the window to let a cascade of bitter cold air into the warm room. Not only did Quincy wake up, but so did everyone else in the room.

"Eloise!" Rachel shouted. "Shut that window, *now*!"

Eloise stuck out her bottom lip, pouting. "But it's the Equospatium!"

"Yes we know," said multiple voices with annoyance. The day's competitors jumped up to go downstairs to get breakfast before warming up. Those left over on the floor dressed up in warm clothes.

Kalleigh jumped up on her bed. "Okay ladies, line up."

The rest of the floor excitedly circled her bed and Mon-Aye yelled, "Me first!"

Kalleigh painted green streaks underneath Mon-Aye's eyes, then did everyone else's while the rest of the girls chatted loudly.

Eloise poked Quincy with her umbrella. "Come on slow coach, get out of bed and get your paint."

"You know, actually, I'm not really feeling quite well. I think I'll stay here today."

"But Quincy, it's—"

"Yeah, I know. But I think I'll stay here," she mumbled.

"All right... I suppose." Eloise gave her a concerned—and suspicious—look. "Feel better, I guess."

***

Quincy waited half an hour until everyone had left. She put on a robe and went down to the family room. Monty looked up from the couch near the fire, and she paused awkwardly at the entrance. She tapped her hand lightly on the doorframe, then finally stepped inside and sat down on the arm of his chair. He looked up at her and nodded his head, silently acknowledging her entrance.

"Monty, what are you still doing here? The Equospatium is going to start anytime now."

"I recognize that fact. I have decided that I shall install myself here today," he said.

"But haven't you been looking forward to today for months?"

"Yes, but we have three more chances to watch the tournament."

"Monty, I really appreciate the thought. I do. But it's going to be really boring here. You should go. Really. Besides, I need someone to give me in-depth details about the tournament. Rusty is playing in the pep band, Colin is terrible with important stuff, and Eloise and Mikaela are more interested in the screaming and yelling part."

He grinned. "True." He paused and rubbed his forehead. "But are you completely certain?"

She nodded. "It's okay, really."

He frowned slightly, but when she smiled and told him, *Go*! he finally smiled with relief. He waved, picked up his coat, and walked out the door.

Quincy sat curled up in front of the fire on an overstuffed chair. Alone. She didn't want to make Monty miss the Equospatium on her account, even though it would have been nice to have company. But really, she still hadn't let go of the fact that Sean knew about her "home" situation. She hadn't decided the best way to approach Monty about her breach of her trust yet.

She sighed and opened up her Latin book. She quickly grew bored of the lists of vocabulary and looked up when she caught an echo of the cheers out of her line of sight coming from the field. She sighed and yawned.

"Why so down?"

Quincy eye's darted around the room until she saw Talin, who had come seemingly from nowhere, perched on the mantelpiece.

"I'm missing the tournament."

"There are worse things in life."

"I know." She sat up and curled her knees to her chin. Talin flew to the arm of the chair.

She looked over at the perched raven who stared into the fire. "Oh, um, thank you, by the way."

Talin looked confused and raided the feathers over his left eye. "For what?"

"For last week."

"Last week?"

"Never mind," Quincy frowned. Had she imagined his voice helping her the same way she had imagined the laughter?

Talin gave her a throaty chuckle and then looked around the room. “This is a boring place to contemplate the meaning of life. Let me show you a much better locale.”

“I wish I could, but I can’t go anywhere. I’m not allowed to leave the floor.”

“Well, as long as you’re with me, I’m sure that you won’t get in trouble.”

“Too late. I’m in so much trouble already,” she said, placing her head in her hands.

“Nah, it’s not as bad as you think. Besides, if people don’t make mistakes, how can they learn. I say *people*, not *ravens*.”

Quincy groaned. “Why? Ravens don’t make mistakes?”

“Nope. But don’t feel too bad. The true numbskull is not the one who makes the mistake, but the one who makes the same mistake over and over again. So don’t be a numbskull.”

“Ugh, is this like the ‘person who doesn’t try again’ talk? This is too deep for me this early in the morning,” she groaned.

“Yes, yes it is, but enough seriousness. Are we going or not?”

“Sounds better than sitting here all day,” Quincy finally admitted.

“Excellent choice. I think we should stop by the kitchen and get some food.”

“Okay, fine.” She stood up, grabbed her schoolbag, and she walked toward the kitchen with Talin flying above her head.

In the kitchen, she grabbed some food from a tray left outside for students. Talin landed on her shoulder, making her jump in surprise. He ignored her tensed shoulders and began to give her directions as she ate her morning bun.

"Hey, save me a piece of that roll?"

Quincy offered him some of the bread, which he greedily ate.

"Grab a candle and turn here," he whispered.

Quincy stayed silent, listening to Talin's instructions. Eventually, he led her to the darkened hallway near the Back Library.

"Now take the stairs on the left," he said.

She looked around. "There aren't any stairs here."

"You've only been here for what, five and a half months? I've lived here for a long time. We're now in one of the older parts of the school. Now, please just walk here and go up the stairs."

Quincy followed his instructions and eventually found the stairs. After what seemed like ten minutes of climbing, she finally asked Talin how much longer.

"Tired already? Just keep going."

At the end of the staircase was a single door.

"Here we are, now open it up."

"Won't it be locked?"

"It's really too bad that you can't turn your head to the side to see me roll my eyes. Of course it's not locked."

Quincy looked up and saw Latin words above the door.

"*Astrum Cella*. Star Room?"

"Aw, it's so nice to see that education spilling from your mouth. See, you didn't need to cheat on the exam, after all."

"It's not like I looked at someone else's paper."

"The thing is you don't need to. Take off your shoes."

"What?"

"No shoes allowed inside. Now open up."

Quincy took off her shoes, confused by what he was making her do, and opened the door, watching the darkness escape from the Star Room.

"How do we get light in here?"

"There's already light in the room. Walk in and shut the door."

Quincy did. For a brief moment the darkness blinded her, but her eyes quickly adjusted, and she began to see details in the room. After a moment, small dots of light burst from the wall, lighting up the dome.

"These are constellations, right?"

"Yes, they are. The walls change with the time of year so you know what you're looking at. There's a dial in the center of the room that opens the ceiling up. Obviously, since it's daytime, you'll only get daylight. But at night, you get a different picture of the sky."

Talin flew off her shoulder and landed in the center of the room on the dial.

Quincy sat down on the carpeted floor and leaned up against the wall.

"Do you like the room?" Talin questioned.

"It's amazing," Quincy whispered. "It's so quiet."

"Good. If you need some alone time, it's yours."

She smiled at the raven. “Thank you for bringing me here.”

“You’re welcome. It’s rarely in use anyway, and when it is, it’s only at night.” he paused, then added, “Oh, by the way, your father had a deep affection for the night sky. He spent quite a bit of time in this room.”

Quincy stared at the bird in astonishment. Before she could ask for more information, Talin flew out the door. So she looked around and enjoyed the moment of silence. She could ask him later. After all, he had given her a quiet room in which to study, and she didn’t even need a minor key for it. She sat down and imagined her father sitting right next to her. She smiled and closed her eyes, breathing in her daydream. She had every intention of studying Latin in her new private space, but she didn’t get far before she fell asleep on the comfortable floor.

Chapter Twenty-Five

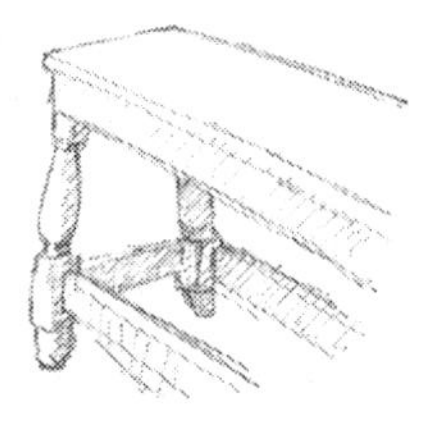

The Misplaced Forgotten

Quincy walked down the stairs and entered the family room to find a seat near the fireplace. She rubbed her swollen, sleep-deprived eyes and curled up in the overstuffed chair. Her punishment had ended after the Equospatium so she was able to attend the after celebration. Rachel had won with the most points overall, so the third floor had thrown a party in her honor.

She looked around the room, grimacing. She wasn't sure which was worse, the mess or the smell. Half-eaten food was strewn across the floor. Riding gear hung in places it shouldn't, and Savannah, Rusty's trumpet, had been left unattended beside half-drunk glasses, school bags, and books.

Throughout the day, most students trudged around or just stayed in bed. Few words were spoken until dinner when people began to perk up. Some more than others. Quincy's head started to drop off into her soup when Monty prodded her.

"Ow! What was that for?" Quincy asked, annoyed.

"Did you know that some people have two types of memory?"

"Monty, it's kind of late. Do we have to do this now?"

He frowned at her question, and Quincy gave up reluctantly. "Okay, what do you mean two types of memory?"

"Your Talent goes further than simple memory, right? You have the ability to memory-travel. Meaning you actually rewind your memories to the moment of choice."

Quincy furrowed her brow. "Yeah, so?"

"Most people's thoughts and memories can be changed, but not those of people who can actually travel to their past memories. Their present memories can be tampered with but never erased."

She looked over at Monty. "Where and why did that come about?" She pitched her voice low and leaned closer to him. "Did you see something? Something from the future?"

He slowly nodded. "Perhaps. I am not completely sure, however. The whole thing was quite blurry. I just saw you say something about how 'thirty years back should do the trick.' But I was not there." He swallowed. "This is the first time that I have had a premonition where I was not in the picture."

Quincy tried to shrug it off. "That's bizarre. Maybe it wasn't a premonition and just a weird dream?"

"Perhaps," Monty nodded. "But you were holding a book with the title, *Famous Clocks*.

"That's random." Quincy shrugged.

“I thought so as well.” He took off his glasses and rubbed his forehead. “I believe I am going to go upstairs to sleep. Perchance I will feel better tomorrow.”

She said good night and waved as Monty left, then played with her spoon, wondering what it was that he had seen.

Eloise sat down in Monty’s empty seat. “What’s bothering Monty? He didn’t even say hi back to me.”

She focused on her soup, not wanting to give anything away. “I’m not really sure,” Quincy admitted.

***

Wilbright waited for the cover of darkness before entering the school grounds. His special key opened the Oakley gates, allowing him access to his destination. Though Quincy and the McCallister boy were too well protected inside, he had finally found his “go-around.” It had taken him months of research, but it would be worth the work. He could taste victory on his lips. It wouldn’t be long now.

He had finally found Oakley’s moment of weakness, and it was time to exploit it. This moment in time would be just the chance that he needed for Katelyn Prendergast to tell him where her key was hiding.

As he came closer to his destination, loud ticking noises from the large clock drowned out everything else. He stopped at the door and placed the key into the lock, turning it counterclockwise until it released and the door opened to the dark room within.

***

The next morning, Quincy rubbed her sore head and immediately felt that something wasn't right. She sat up in bed and watched the other girls get ready.

Mikaela frowned and sat down on her bed. "Hey, why aren't you moving? Are you sick?"

"No, I'm fine actually. Thanks for asking, Mikaela." She didn't even know if she was lying or not.

At breakfast, Quincy looked to her right and saw the bench empty. Then, Colin sat down and began to talk to her. She had a hard time listening to him because Colin should be sitting across the table from her. He never sat next to her. But who usually did? She couldn't remember. Instead of the mystery person showing up, though, Genevieve came over sat down next to Colin, and he quickly turned his attention to her.

In Latin, Quincy sat next to an empty seat and frowned. A nagging feeling tugged at her mind all day, leaving her confused and unsettled. Something was wrong about this day, but she didn't know what, so she just went on to her next class.

Beginners' polo started in Physical Education and her first week with the sport had been filled with ups and downs. Any time her horse began to become flighty, she would whisper "Consto" and he would usually stop before bucking her off. She still had a difficult time staying in the saddle so she found it nearly impossible to reach the ball with her mallet. She hoped that she at least looked like she was going after it. As long as she didn't fail Physical Education, she would be fine. She just wanted this day to be over, to have hot chocolate with a friend and talk about it, but she didn't know who would want to do that with her, and she disliked sitting in the café alone.

After a full week of confusion, she even went so far as to speak with the headmaster about her problem during their lesson. In response, he gently asked her if she felt all right and that perhaps she should do fewer after-school activities. *That's not very helpful*, she thought. "It's like there's someone who should be here, but isn't. Someone who should be sitting near me, or studying with me. It feels like a there's a hole. Is that possible? For there to be a hole in my memories?"

The headmaster looked at her inquisitively and then paused as if thinking of an appropriate answer. "Yes, but only if you choose to forget or change them yourself."

"What do you mean, 'change them yourself?'"

The headmaster tapped his pen on his desk. "Meaning if you or someone else had the ability to change time.

Quincy fought back a smile. "What, like time-travel?"

"Exactly," he answered seriously.

Her eyes widened. But she guessed if talking birds and a bookstore on top of a time vortex existed, then why not time travel?

"So how would you do that?" she asked.

"There have been many theories. Some Creative Engineers have even claimed that they have accomplished such a feat. Time can be dangerous, though. It's worth it to be careful."

She just nodded.

***

When Independent Study was over, Quincy went into the Star Room to think. She sat against the dial in the center of the room and closed her eyes. Without traveling backward, she began to sort through her memories. Beginning from March through when she first arrived at school. Nothing seemed to be out of the ordinary. Annoyed with herself, Quincy decided to drop the subject and go up to her room to finish her Latin homework.

But the more she tried to ignore and forget the nagging feeling, the more intense it became. She went to bed early, hoping it would subside by morning when she needed to get up and ride her horse before breakfast.

An odd dream startled her from a deep sleep just before midnight. It hadn't been quite a nightmare. A muffled voice desperately told her that present memories could be tampered with but never erased. She sat up in her bed as the Timepiece rang its new-day song. Is that what happened to her? She jumped out of bed and grabbed her slippers and robe. The only way she could think of to know for certain was to memory-travel so she could see what she had forgotten. Even though she knew that she had to do it, she hesitated. Her actions would, once again, be breaking a rule. What if she did actually get stuck this time?

In the back of her mind, she heard her father's gentle but stern voice as he punished her for breaking a family rule.

“We made these rules because we love you, and we want to protect you,” her father had said with shaking arms as he had clung to her. She’d been seven years old, and she had walked across the street to play dolls with a neighbor. She had forgotten to tell anyone, which led her parents to panic. She had never seen her father more scared.

“You must tell one of us where you are going at all times,” he said holding on to her even more tightly. “You are not allowed to leave the house for two weeks.”

Quincy had wondered why they had been so scared, but now she understood their desire to protect their children. Eight years later, she still felt bad about it. With a pang of sadness, she felt alone and completely isolated again. If she went ahead and did this, it would mean she would be breaking the headmaster’s trust again. She didn’t want to see the disappointment in his eyes a second time. But a feeling of utter and immense dread passed through her so quickly that it evaporated her hesitation. The headmaster had created this rule to protect her, so she would just have to be more careful. She had a strong feeling that the consequences would be much greater if she didn’t go through with her new plan. She needed to know if her memories had been tampered with and in what way.

She grabbed a red-flamed candle and tiptoed down the stairs and then up the other flight to her now-customary spot in the middle of the Star Room. She pulled the key from under her nightgown, grasped it in her hand, and focused, closing her eyes until she began to go backward to her dream in bed. At first, she moved painstakingly slow, not to make any mistakes, but she gradually began to speed up. In the Star Room, nothing could pull her attention away, so she could focus completely.

She continued to rewind through her memory until she saw a whitish-blond-flash. She immediately slowed down, paused, and then backed up slowly, forcing her mind to rewind. She was drawn to his blue eyes as he stared at her.

"I just saw you say something about how 'thirty years back should do the trick.' But I was not there."

She gasped. "Monty!"

How could she have forgotten him? More importantly, why couldn't anyone else remember him?

Chapter Twenty-Six

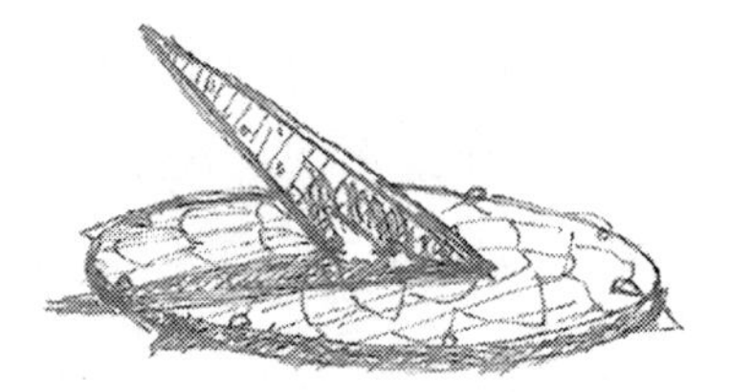

Tempus Fugit

Quincy skipped Social Studies and Physical Education to do research in the library. It had been a strange morning. At breakfast, she casually mentioned her friend Monty to Eloise, and she had teasingly wondered why Quincy had never told her about her boyfriend. Mikaela and Colin had never met him, either, and assumed he lived near Quincy. No one remembered him.

She walked down the aisles and stopped in the reference section. Monty had been right: his family really *was* in the Irish history books. She sorted through the list of McCallisters and frowned when the line ended with Aodhan, Monty's father. Monty wasn't even on his family's list. What had happened to him? She randomly flipped through the book, wishing that she knew more about his mother and her last name. Discouraged, she closed the book and placed it back on the shelf.

Miss Grastorf walked by, then, halting when she saw Quincy. "I rarely see students in this aisle. What are you looking for?"

“I don’t know,” she moaned.

“What’s the project?”

“Project?” Quincy scrunched her nose. “It’s just that I’m looking for something that should be here, but isn’t. It’s like something’s been erased.” Her eyes widened. “*Someone* has been erased.”

Monty had been erased and time had been rewritten without him. Quincy sighed, fighting back tears. She had to get him back. But how?

She thought hard about her last conversation with Monty. He’d mentioned some odd premonition about her. That she’d said something in his dream about going back thirty years. She didn’t know what it could mean, but it was a start.

“Miss Grastorf, is there a ledger here that would tell me all the major events from thirty years ago?”

“Certainly, follow me.”

Quincy walked behind the librarian as she went even deeper into the library. Miss Grastorf paused and began to slide her fingers on the spines of a shelf of large binders while mumbling years to herself. After a minute, she pulled a large black binder out and handed the heavy thing to Quincy.

“Each of the binders have newspaper clippings from the major events of each year. Go ahead and take this to the desk at the end. Just leave it there when you’re finished, and I’ll put it back tonight.”

"Thank you," Quincy smiled at the librarian. "Oh, I'm also looking for a book titled, *Famous Clocks*." she added, remembering that detail from her interaction with Monty.

"If we have it, I'll find it for you."

Quincy smiled again and began to dig through the hefty binder as the librarian headed off in search of the book. She cringed at the number of deaths that had occurred thirty years ago and stared at awe at some of the year's accomplishments. After an hour, she had only sorted through the first three months. In desperation, she turned to the present month. She began to look through March's events and stopped when she saw an article headlining Oakley.

> *Tragedy has struck at Oakley during the International Polo Tournament, which this year is being held in Wales. Eighteen-year-old academy student Katelyn Prendergast died yesterday during a freak accident involving her horse in the final round. The last heir of the Prendergast family, she is mourned by her grandmother...*

Quincy stopped reading when she saw the picture of the deceased student. She would recognize the smile anywhere. The girl was a female version of Monty.

She slammed the book shut and dashed down the center of the library.

"Miss Harris, no running in the library," Miss Grastorf hissed.

Quincy stopped and smiled apologetically.

"Oh, by the way, the book you're looking for isn't here. It's in storage in the original library in the Main Hall. I can find it and hold it for you tomorrow if you'd like."

"No, thank you," Quincy answered. "Sorry again for running."

Miss Grastorf smiled and shooed her away.

As Quincy walked out of the Main Library in the Learner's Citadel, the dinner bell rang, but she disregarded it, instead running toward the Back Library in Main Hall. Her stomach grumbled, and Quincy hated to ignore it but she kept going. She flung open the door to the library and stopped suddenly as a thought came to her. The librarian had said the book was here, but she had not told her the book's location.

"It could be anywhere," Quincy groaned.

"Looking for something?"

Quincy momentarily froze until she realized that she recognized the voice.

"Hello, Talin," she said, automatically looking up.

In a blur of feathers, Talin landed on Quincy's shoulder.

"What are you up to?" Talin inquired.

"I'm looking for a book."

"In a library? I would never have guessed." She just looked up at him. She was not in the mood for his sarcasm today. "What's the name of the book?" he asked, turning serious.

"Famous Clocks."

In the shadowy darkness, Quincy thought she saw Talin's feathery eyebrows shoot up toward the ceiling.

"Really? Indeed. Should we look in engineering? Or better yet, history?"

Quincy chose not to respond. He seemed to be having a conversation with himself.

"Oh, of course!" he said, excitedly. "Try looking by the partly closed window in the second aisle to the right."

She still felt awkward walking with Talin on her shoulder so she tensed her muscles, forcing Talin to center himself with his wings. He didn't attempt to move or fly when she hurried over to aisle two.

"I don't know why I make you nervous. I'm not going to fall off your shoulder. If I feel myself falling, I'll just do this." Talin dug one of his talons in her shirt, and it scratched across her flesh.

"Ouch!" She tried to swat him off.

"Sorry. Now look on this shelf."

She grumbled, annoyed at being given commands from the bird, as well as at the pain in her shoulder. The feeling quickly passed, though, when she saw the book his beak was pointing to. After pulling the book off the shelf, Quincy walked closer to the window to catch the last rays of the sun. She found the chapter on the Timepiece and began to skim it.

"What exactly are we looking for?" Talin asked.

"Hold on for a moment!"

He coughed and cautiously switched talons on her shoulder.

"Found it!" Quincy cried out, a smile stretching across her face.

"Well…?" Talin prompted.

"It says here that Master Creative Engineer Marcus Chenoweth specialized in clocks and had an unquenchable passion for time."

Talin nodded his head and then cleared his throat. "Okay, so?"

"Just wait. It also says that his passion for time went deeper than just theory. The author thinks that Chenoweth actually managed to create a device to travel through time. He thinks it's somewhere in the Timepiece, hidden in what he calls, 'the Heart.' He also thinks that playing with time is what made him eccentric and, ultimately, was the reason for his disappearance."

Quincy continued to skim the chapter until the excitement drained away from her face. "It also says that the Heart has never been found."

"That doesn't mean that it doesn't exist."

"True," she admitted. Then she sighed. "But what does this have to do with Monty's disappearance? Or his mother's death?" she wondered aloud, biting her lip. She stared at the drawing of the Timepiece. Finally, she slammed the book shut, and Talin's grip tightened on her shoulder.

"So what now?" Talin asked.

"I'm going to get a closer look at the Timepiece," she answered. He nodded his head in agreement and they walked outside into the twilight.

Quincy stopped in the courtyard and circled the Timepiece. She found two doors on each side.

"Well it only makes sense for the Heart to be inside." She looked around to make sure no one was watching and then climbed over the small fence.

"Mind your head, Quincy. We don't need another Linus Lewis."

"Who?"

"He's the kid who got too close to the Timepiece and—," Talin took a wing in front of his neck and made a slashing sound.

"Oh, that's just lovely," Quincy grimaced while Talin sniggered.

She watched the swinging dial and ran toward the side of the clock. She tried both sides and found that all the doors were locked. She sat down behind the clock, figuring out how to get inside.

"Well, what do you want to do next?" Talin asked.

"I don't know. Both doors are locked."

"No, really?"

There he was being sarcastic again "If you're so smart, you tell me how we can open them," Quincy snapped.

"Well, obviously, we need a key," Talin answered, rolling his eyes.

"So we just need to waltz up to The Head Porter and request the key?"

"We could do that, but he doesn't have the key to the base of the clock."

"Then who does?"

"Hmm, who has it...?" There was a minute of silence before Talin rolled his eyes and pointed his wing at her neck.

Quincy looked around to make sure they were alone before pulling it from under her shirt. "Is my key like a minor key? Will it actually open the door?"

"As you well know, that key is not ordinary."

She stared at the old key that shimmered in the evening light, despite its age and tarnish.

"Yes, that key will open this door. But this particular entrance goes up to the clockface, or rather the 'brain' of the clock. You want the other door to go down to the base and its heart."

She narrowed her eyes at him. "Wait a second. The book said that 'the Heart has never been found.' How do you know all about this?"

"Because I'm not just anybody, clearly. Now please, try the other door."

Quincy walked to the other side, leaned toward the door, and placed the key into the lock. She gasped when the key slid easily inside. She tried to turn it clockwise, but it refused to budge. She turned it counterclockwise, and the lock released.

"But why don't the porters have the key to this door?"

"As it happens, this door was made especially for a specific set of keys and yours happens to be one of them," he paused. "This clock can do more than you could ever imagine. Now walk inside."

Quincy did as instructed and jumped when the door slammed shut behind her, leaving them in darkness. She shuddered and placed her arms out in front of her until she found a railing.

"Mind your feet," Talin warned.

She nodded and slowly took another footstep, feeling for the edge of the floor. She waited for further directions from the raven, but he remained silent, so she inched forward and took the first step. She clung to the rail as she went, fighting against the panic of being blind. She took a few more steps, and suddenly the rail ended. She slid against the wall until she ran into something at chest level. She glided her hand over the flat surface of the object and her hand found a cold glass orb. It grew warm from her touch and began to glow until the whole room became visible.

When Quincy's eyes adjusted to the light, she gasped. The chamber had been delicately built, filled with countless pieces of small machines that looked like an intricate puzzle. The room beat and whirred, reminding her of a real heart. She finally understood how engineering could be considered creative. Chenoweth must have been a great artist in his own way.

She searched the room—for what, she wasn't quite sure—pausing at the far corner in front of a podium. On the top was a large metal face with intricately engraved lines and numbers, similar to a clock without hands. On the front, there was a keyhole.

She stared at Talin, who shrugged. Quincy placed her key inside the lock and turned counterclockwise again. As she turned, she heard a *click* as the lock gave way and a metal needle popped out of the face, turning the device into a sundial.

She frowned, confused. "Why would you put a sundial underground?"

She touched the needle and startled when it moved. Metal gears inside the podium clicked as if re-winding a clock.

"Is this the heart?" she asked, staring at Talin.

Talin slowly nodded. "Yes, this will take you where you want to go. Or rather *when*. Speaking of which, when do you want to go?"

"Monty told me that I said something like 'thirty years back should do the trick.' I'm pretty sure I need to get to Oakley during the International Polo Tournament exactly thirty years ago today. How do I do that?"

"You need to go three clicks. One full turn of the dial is a hundred years, while each click is ten. A click is that winding sound you heard, by the way. To go back a year, you would need to just gently tap the gnomon. When you've chosen the date, push down."

"Gnomon?" Quincy asked.

"Technical term for the metal needle."

Quincy turned the gnomon back to zero to start over and then turned it until she heard three clicks.

“Remember, the Timepiece doesn’t turn like a normal clock,” Talin said, poking her in the neck.

She had turned the dial counterclockwise as she would a normal clock, to get it back to zero. Instead, she should have turned it clockwise.

“So to go back in time, you have to move the gnomon forward?” she confirmed. The bird nodded. “So if wanted to go to the future, I would have to move the gnomon counterclockwise? That’s really confusing,” she groaned.

“That was his point. He liked confusing things,” he said quietly.

She looked over at Talin. “You knew Chenoweth?”

“I did...”

“But isn’t Chenoweth supposed to have lived over two hundred years ago?”

The raven cleared his throat. “Something like that.”

Quincy gasped. “How old *are* you?”

“Older than you! And you should respect your elders,” he snapped.

Quincy narrowed her eyes at his rebuke. “Okay so I’ve forwarded the gears three times. So thirty years ago from today.” She pushed on the gnomon and felt the hair on her arms stand up, goose bumps rising across her body.

“Want to see something incredible?” he asked, his eyes dancing mischievously.

Quincy nodded and grinned.

"Good. Let's go outside because, believe me, you won't want to miss this."

She shrugged and walked back up the stairs. She paused before stepping out. "Can we still time travel if we're not in the heart?"

"Yes, technically we're already traveling. So us walking out won't change that. Only those inside of the Heart's chamber were affected."

"So everyone is okay in the present?"

"Think of it as a kind of limbo or frozen time. Everything is safe as long as you don't do anything drastic to the past."

Quincy bit her lip. "So no pressure, huh?"

"Just the disappearance of your friend and the change in your timeline. So no. No pressure."

She frowned at the bird and paused in front of the moving clock face. The darkening sky was the only change that Quincy could see. "Nothing's happening."

"Just wait. It takes a minute. Oh, and don't be too shocked if you suddenly feel wet."

Quincy crossed her arms and focused on the clock faces again. After another second, it moved clockwise. Then it began to turn quicker and quicker until it became a blur. Around her, the seasons changed faster than a second of time. Large trees that she had never seen before suddenly showed up out of nowhere and began to shrink until they were the same size of the Timepiece. She became wet, dry, hot, and immediately cold, and then everything stopped.

She let out a sigh of relief as she felt her dry sweater. She looked at the magnificent trees in beautiful formation near the Timepiece. "Talin, why aren't these trees by the Timepiece now?"

"There was a nasty windstorm about three years before you came to the school. By some miracle, they barely missed the Timepiece. The courtyard right around here was only built ten years before this time, so it's still relatively new now."

"How long have you lived here?"

Talin snickered. "Awhile."

Quincy recognized him dodging the question, but she didn't have the time to push. She would have to bother him about it later. Now, she needed to know why Monty had seen her come here. And how to get him back in the present.

"By the way, how do you feel, Quinn?" Talin asked.

"What do you mean? I feel fine."

Talin looked intently at her.

"What?" she asked the abnormally silent raven.

"Can you tell me what time it is without looking at the Timepiece?"

Quincy thought about it, surprised again that she knew two different times. "From our time or right now?"

"Do you know both?"

"6:40 in our present at home, but here it's only 10:18 in the morning. Why do you ask?"

"How's your head? Do you need to sit down a moment?"

She sighed impatiently. "I'm *fine*, Talin. Just hungry from skipping dinner."

"Curious."

Quincy started to shiver from the cold morning and just wanted to go inside. "So, what do we do now?"

"This is your adventure. Someone had to keep an eye on you, with you being a minor and all," Talin retorted.

She bit her tongue before replying. "Well...I think Monty's mom is going to die today, but she's not supposed to. Somehow we need to stop her from having that accident with her horse." She groaned at the sky. "This whole thing is ridiculous! I have all these memories of my friend who seemingly no longer exists. It's like he's been erased but not from my head."

"Confusing isn't it?"

She ignored his snickering. "So we're thirty years in the past. We need to find Katelyn."

In a gentle voice, possibly the gentlest Quincy had ever heard from Talin, he explained the fallacy of the plan. "Please remember that the lady is just a young student who probably doesn't know the future and will have no idea what you're talking about."

She cringed. She hadn't thought that far.

"Let's walk inside and find seats for the tournament, okay?" Talin nudged. Quincy nodded. "Yeah, everyone will be there. Maybe we can find her somewhere in the crowd." She walked toward the Main Hall, but stopped before walking in. “One problem.”

Talin groaned. “What, Quincy?”

Quincy noted the use of her full name. “I have a black bird on my shoulder. Walking around Oakley during the day is going to be a little conspicuous.”

“We’ll be fine.”

“But how—”

“Just trust me. Please. Keep walking.”

She pursed her lips but went along with his plan. As she walked into the Main Hall, she felt a sense of relief at the familiarity of the building. Even the school uniform hadn’t changed. Students dawdled in groups laughing, and she walked past them, trying to act as normal as possible. She was struck by how little the place had changed. It felt like home. Talin laughed, interrupting her reverie.

“What?” she asked.

“Let’s hit the lost and found.”

Quincy frowned. “Why?”

“Remember my brown feathers at Miss Heatherwood’s?”

Quincy nodded. “Why? Are you going to paint me brown?”

“Red.”

Quincy watched a student wearing a dark red sweater with matching ear muffs walk past.

Huh? She shook her head in confusion but followed the raven's request and turned toward the Post Office. She walked in the Lost and Found next door.

"Grab that red one—it's a Whistler's sweater. Oh, and better ditch the Oakley tie and switch with this one." Talin directed her toward a black and red tie.

"Why a Whistler's sweater and tie? Shouldn't my own Oakley clothing be okay?"

"This will actually make our lives much easier. Less chance of you getting caught by an Oakley student who doesn't know you and calling you out. It's all about the camouflage."

Quincy nodded and rolled up her tie and shoved it in her pocket. She refused to leave her school clothes thirty years in the past. She touched the dark-red Whistlers sweater and rubbed the stitching of a detailed grizzly bear. She put it on over her Oakley sweater and looked down at herself.

"This is too big."

Talin rolled his eyes as she put on the striped tie. After completing the uniform, the two of them walked back outside. She felt awkward walking around wearing clothes from a school that was not her own. She wondered if at any moment, she could get kicked out of the school for pretending to be a visiting student. She watched the students with purple, orange, and teal sweaters, wondering which schools they represented.

Talin motioned to a large poster on the bulletin board that had numbers and a list of schools, names, and rank.

"So if this is a multi-school tournament, am I going to need something like a tournament ticket or badge to get around?" Quincy asked.

"Nah, you're with me so you're fine. Oh, it's an even better thing you don't look like an Oakley student now. Especially from floor three."

"My floor? But who—"

"Shh. Let me do the talking."

Quincy breathed slowly through her nostrils, both nervous and irritated. She expected the two girls—a blond and a brunette—to walk past them, but instead they stopped in front of Quincy and Talin.

Quincy stared at the blond girl and blinked, not able to believe her luck.

She had found Monty's mother.

The brunette giggled. "Hello, Talin!"

"Oh, hello, Katelyn—Chelsea," he responded politely.

At the sound of her mother's name, Quincy's gaze darted to Chelsea. It was like someone had punched her in the stomach. Her mother, who couldn't be older than eighteen, was staring back in her direction.

"So Talin, who's your friend?" Quincy's mother asked.

"Uh, this is Quinn, um, Holding from uh Whistler," Talin mumbled.

Chelsea looked interested. "I didn't know that you knew students from Whistler?" She turned back to Quincy. "It's lovely to meet you, Quinn. Your name is really unique."

"Th-thank you," Quincy stuttered, looking into her mother's hazel eyes.

"It's been lovely chatting with you both," Katelyn chimed in, "but please excuse us, we're due at the field for a meeting in five minutes."

As they began to walk quickly by them, Katelyn stopped and yelled back at them. "I thought you were visiting Scotland," she said with a mischievous Irish accent.

"I, uh, changed my mind and delayed it until tomorrow."

"Well then, you must come and watch us in the tournament," Chelsea begged.

"Oh, yes, of course. I wouldn't miss it," Talin promised.

Quincy watched them leave for the field. The two girls giggled again as they walked away, shooting glances back over their shoulders.

Her mom and Monty's mom had known each other? After they had left Quincy looked accusingly at Talin. "You knew them both?"

"Well, excuse me if I don't tell you my life story. Besides, I just took care of the details. It will now look normal for me to be around."

"Normal? First of all, you're a *talking bird.* How do you keep forgetting that?" "Think of me as the unofficial school mascot. I'm basically an Oakley secret, which is why I'm supposed to be in Scotland. Students here won't be surprised to see me around and everyone else will just think you're an eccentric Welsh kid who had a black bird for a *pet*." Talin rolled his eyes. "It happens."

"Why aren't you still the unofficial mascot?"

Talin ground his beak together. "It was easier this decade. Fewer people wanted me dead."

"What!"

Talin hissed. "Keep your voice down."

Quincy frowned but kept walking. "So what would've happened if you hadn't been out of town? What if you had come face-to-face with yourself? Aren't there rules against stuff like that?"

"Yes, and I can tell you that it's not a pleasant experience meeting oneself."

"You've done it before! What if—"

Talin dug his talons into her thick sweater. "Look, I'm still here, all right? The universes and Time itself have not imploded, yet. Okay?"

Quincy wondered if she imagined it or if Talin really did look a little smug at his comment.

"So just breathe and let's figure things out. We know that today is the International Polo Championship, so let's play this out. Why today of all days?" Talin frowned.

"Apparently Katelyn is supposed to die in this tournament. Obviously she didn't originally, because she had Monty. So the cause of his disappearance is his mother's early death."

"That makes sense. So you're saying that someone wanted to change the outcome of what happened—or rather happens— today so that Katelyn has her accident."

"Who could do that? And why? Why Monty? Why Katelyn? Why—,"

Talin growled. "One question at a time. As to the *who,* remember what I said about your key?"

"Which part?"

"The part where I said that your key is only one in a set."

"Yes..." She paused. "So someone with another key did it...but I thought none of the other keys were accounted for?" Quincy argued.

"Oh please. Like you would announce to the whole world that you owned a minor key. *You're* not going around talking about having the Master Key...Right?" he narrowed his eyes at her.

"True...Okay, so someone is here who potentially shouldn't be."

"Just like us."

"So not only do we need to find out what happened to Monty but we need to find the person who is messing with time?"

Talin nodded. "You work on finding out what happened to your friend, I'll work on finding the other time trespasser."

"Fine," agreed Quincy.

They walked together back to the bulletin board, and she glanced down at the list of names that were competing over the course of the weekend. Today, only the women teams were listed. Quincy scanned the list and stopped when she saw Katelyn's and her mother's names.

"So according to the newspaper article, the accident will happen in the finals. Katelyn and my mom are still only in the first round."

Talin nodded.

"Okay," she said, still pondering aloud. "Let's find seats to watch their first round, see if there is anyone suspicious around. Then we'll plan what to do next."

She turned and walked toward the crowd surrounding the main field.

"There's no way that we'll be able to find seats in this mess," Quincy groaned as she surveyed the crowd and the packed arena.

"Actually, there might be a way. I know a guy. Walk to that tall young man with the dark hair over there."

Quincy walked over to him, and Talin jumped right in.

"Hello, Julian," Talin greeted him.

She looked over at Julian and began to uncontrollably shake.

"Are you alright?" Julian asked, gently placing his hand on her elbow.

Quincy nodded silently, wide-eyed, as she looked at a younger version of her father.

"She's fine. By chance, are there any extra seats close to the front for my friend and myself?"

Julian smiled at both of them and waved for them to follow him. "For you, Talin, of course."

After motioning for someone to take his place, Julian began to walk through the hundreds of people from all the different schools around the world.

"Here you go," he said, pointing to the two empty spots in front of them.

"Thank you, Julian. I knew I could count on you," Talin said.

Julian smiled. "See you later, mate." He bowed slightly, and then disappeared into the crowd.

Quincy wiped her eyes on her sleeve and bit her lip to keep it from quavering. "Is he gone?"

"Yes."

Quincy slumped in her seat, and Talin dug his talons into the sweater again to steady himself. "That was my dad," she said longingly.

"I know."

She quickly sat up straight her hands clenching the seat handles. A grin spread across her face. "I don't know why I didn't think of it before! I can save him. I could stop him from dying!"

Talin growled in her ear. "You would be risking *everything*. There's no guarantee that he won't die another way, anyhow. Maybe he doesn't go to the United States and *you* are caught and killed as a little girl. Maybe he doesn't marry your mother and you don't even exist. You cannot do anything."

A tear ran down her cheek as she stared at the polo field.

"I'm sorry," he whispered.

***

Wilbright drew his coat closer to his thin body and leaned against one of the ancient trees in the Oakley forest. He closed his eyes and willed his body to get used to the time difference before he walked toward the Oakley grounds. He breathed slowly in and out, concentrating on not losing his last meal. He reached into his pocket to make sure that everything he'd brought with him was still safely tucked away. His key clinked against the sharp scissors, and he took care not to stab himself. He pulled out the third item and looked at it in his palm. A small white pill lay cradled in his hand. Not one of his creations but the manufacturer promised that it would do the job to his full satisfaction. The horse would fall, taking its rider to the ground with it. If it did not work, he would have to enforce the threat he had made to the Creative Engineer.

Wilbright E. Fairnight did not make idle threats.

He placed the items back in his pocket, careful not to poke himself with the fourth item. The needle, combined with his special serum, would guarantee that a recently injured girl would offer any information that he desired.

His brown eyes narrowed at the growing noise from the polo field. The tournament had already started. Not to worry, though.

He had arrived with plenty of time to spare. So far his plan was coming together quite nicely.

CHAPTER TWENTY-SEVEN

DAYS OF OAKLEY PAST

Katelyn and Chelsea's match wasn't for another forty-five minutes, so Quincy anxiously watched the tournament below, skimming the crowd here and there for any unsavory characters. She moved her knee up and down, her anxiety high, shaking the chair where the raven had perched.

"Talin, how do you get into this tournament?"

"The top three men's and women's teams from across the world compete," he started. "And—,"

Their conversation was interrupted when someone yelled near her ear. Quincy jumped up and clenched her knuckles when she saw her mother behind her.

"Oi, June!" Chelsea waved her arms. "Katelyn wants her lucky eagle back. We're up next."

A girl in the row in front looked up sheepishly and unhooked a chain from around her neck. She tossed it back to Chelsea, who looked down apologetically at Quincy.

"Sorry for screaming in your ear." A look of recognition crossed over her features then, and she smiled at Quincy. "Hi! Having fun, Quinn?"

"Yes, thank you."

"Talin's not bothering you too much, is he?" She winked at the raven.

"Not at the moment, no."

Chelsea laughed with Quincy while Talin pointedly ignored them.

"Forgive me for asking, but isn't Quinn a boy's name? Is it a nickname?"

"It could go either way." Quincy paused and quietly added, "My parents called me Quinn. It's short for Quincy."

"It's a wonderful name! I'll have to remember it. So sorry, I can't doddle, I'm in the next match. Bye!" Chelsea hurried off and Quincy felt the air leave her body, leaving her lightheaded.

Quincy turned to Talin, worry on her face. "Did I just change something by giving her my name?"

He gave a throaty chuckle. "There's no need to get excited. You just insured that you will get your own name."

"So if I didn't come here, maybe my name wouldn't be Quincy?"

"Something like that," he sniggered.

"Hmm," is all she said in response. Instead, she stood up to watch her mother. She had stopped to quickly talk to Quincy's young father. Chelsea's confident exterior weakened visibly, and she suddenly seemed shy. She shifted her weight to her toes and then quickly back to her heels. She waved at him before dashing toward the locker rooms. Julian waved back, staring at her retreating figure with a dreamy expression.

Quincy sat back down and felt a tear run down her cheek. She looked away from Talin, not wanting him to see her heart aching. She wanted to talk to her mother more and ask her questions. Logically, she knew it would be a mistake, but that didn't stop the desire. It had been so long since they had been able to talk to each other. Quincy remembered her mother's laugh and dancing on her mother's toes while her sister had held on to her back. Her father would play his fiddle and laugh at his girl's antics.

She looked back at the tall, young man who would become her father as he pointed to things on a map for a student wearing a purple sweater. His clothes were well kept, and his smile obviously enthralled every woman who walked by, including herself. No wonder her mother had been shy around him. She could barely stop herself from running up to him and burying her face in his chest to smell his aftershave. She coughed, trying to hold back the tears.

Talin respectfully cleared his throat. "Heads up, Quinn, Oakley's second-tier team has been called to the field."

Her focus snapped back to the field. She would have time to mourn them again later. Right now she needed to save Katelyn.

Eight horses, four on each side, met in the center of the field. An additional two riders—a man and a woman—wearing white-

and-black uniforms, rode up between the two teams. Her mother and Katelyn fell into their individual places, and after a moment of instruction from the referees, inaudible from Quincy's vantage point, the two teams separated. One designated player from each team—Katelyn being one of them—stood on opposite sides of the referees as one of them whistled.

The players nodded respectfully as they all seemed to size one another up, holding tightly to their individual mallets. The referee dropped the ball in the center and backed off. Quincy could actually feel the anxiety of the two girls and their horses. The large field bell rang, and the two girls were off. Katelyn's horse responded quickly, but her opponent's reacted even faster. Suddenly the Oakley girls jumped into action as the ball began to soar toward their own goalpost.

One of the Oakley opponents bumped her horse directly into Katelyn's with such force that it unseated Katelyn, and she landed hard on the ground. Six of the other seven horses waited patiently for Katelyn, but across the field, the seventh player galloped toward Katelyn. She took possession of the now-unguarded ball and began to hit it closer to the Oakley goalpost. One of the other opposing players rode up behind her and scored a goal against the goalkeeper, who was still distracted by her fallen teammate.

Katelyn made a rude gesture at her retreating opponent, and after looking around, found her mallet across the field. She shifted her gaze from the unattended mallet to the goalpost. She had a large welt around the eyebrow from her fall, and it began to bruise.

She put two fingers to her mouth and gave a piercing whistle. Her horse instantaneously responded, trotting toward her. Effortlessly, she grabbed the reins and took her place on her mount again.

Quincy watched, impressed at how well Katelyn's horse obeyed. What would happen to make the same horse do something later that would kill her?

The same opponent who had bumped her now rode toward Katelyn's unguarded mallet. The audience gasped in simultaneous horror and shock.

"Katelyn, mind your mallet!"

Quincy recognized her mother's voice as soon as Katelyn galloped toward her mallet. But just before the opponent's horse's hoof could snap the mallet, a large crash echoed through the field. The audience jumped up from their seats with mixed expressions of surprise and confusion. The huge bell that cued the start and finish of every match had fallen from its perch, just missing some of the spectators. The Oakley opponent's horse reared in surprise and knocked off her own rider, much harder than Katelyn's had.

Play stopped and they all stared at the large bell that had fallen across the field. A couple of the players trotted over to investigate. Quincy hoped that no one had been hurt. Then she saw a dark blur running away from the field. Before she could direct Talin's attention to it, the culprit had disappeared into the forest so quickly that she wondered if she had imagined it. She looked over at the raven, who was rubbing his head with a wing and mumbling nonsense to himself.

"What's the matter Talin?"

"My memory must be skewed. That bell has never fallen in its history, or at least this particular history," he answered thoughtfully.

"Unfortunately, due to the loss of the field bell," a voice echoed across the field, interrupting Talin, "we'll be taking an hour break to repair and re-hang it. We apologize for this inconvenience and thank you for your cooperation."

After the announcement, everyone in the stands began talking or getting up to stretch.

"Should we go see what happened?" Quincy whispered to Talin.

"We know what happened. A bell fell that wasn't supposed to. A hole in time," he growled.

"Hole in time...Wait! Talin, what if she wasn't supposed to go past the first match. What if she lost the first match in my timeline and the bell now forces her to a rematch? And I'm pretty sure I saw someone running away from the bell tower and into the forest."

"You think someone is deliberately playing with today to keep her in the next couple of rounds, ultimately killing her?" he mumbled.

He closed his eyes and became so still that Quincy wondered if he had fallen asleep.

"Talin?"

"Shh."

Finally, he opened his eyes and sighed. "It's not working at all here. I can't see anything, so I don't know what's going to happen or what's connected to this event."

"What do you mean?" Quincy asked, narrowing her eyes at him.

"I can do something similar to your memory travel. Except that when it's working, it doesn't go just backward and forward, it also goes sideways," he smirked and then frowned. "When it's working." He sniffed. "So we're going to have to do it the old-fashioned way and do some sleuthing."

Quincy nodded and furrowed her brow. She wanted to scold Talin for not telling her about his Talent from the start, but it would do no good. Especially if it wasn't working. Katelyn's and Monty's lives rested on her figuring out what to do.

"This is so frustrating," she moaned. "I know we need to change things back to the way they were, but, if we make a mistake and end up changing something else?" She held her head in her hands. "What if I change the wrong thing? What if my future no longer exists?"

Talin flew to the now-empty chair in front of her and perched on the top. "I can't answer that. It really depends on what you change, how you change it, and when you make the change."

"So what if we just tell Katelyn what happens? Then she wouldn't even think of playing."

"What are you thinking exactly?"

"I'm not saying that we tell her *everything* or anything drastic for that matter."

"Drastic as in 'If you don't disqualify yourself from the tournament, you're going to die?'"

Quincy pouted. "Well, when you say it like that, it sounds like a terrible idea."

"Quinn, there are so many loopholes and too many what-ifs to your suggestion."

She sighed. "Could we go back in time again and catch the person who cut the bell?"

"The Timepiece won't allow travelers to come back more than once on any given day." he said, shaking his head. "Besides, even if it would, time is fragile. For all we know, there could have been more than one accomplice, or if you jumped the person, you might have been taken in for questioning. I can see it now, 'Yes, that's right, I'm from the future.' Brilliant! And, that's not even taking into account the possibility of bumping into ourselves, looping time more than we are already. To make things even worse, there is the minor fact that there are multiple realities. There is another girl similar to you who is not you and who lives in a world completely different than yours."

She blinked at him. "Thanks, Talin. My brain is now completely numb. If I wasn't confused before, I sure am now."

He snorted, a habit that was starting to annoy Quincy.

"You're welcome."

And his sarcasm.

"Hang on, Talin, you said that you bumped into yourself before?"

"Not a lovely experience that I want to mirror anytime soon." Talin mumbled.

She decided to drop the question. "Fine, all right, I understand. I think. But do you have any better suggestions?"

Neither of them spoke for a moment.

"You know, come to think of it, I liked your first suggestion the best," Talin finally admitted. "And it's probably the least risky."

Quincy felt a short shiver of triumph. Very short. Especially when Talin told her that, "In fact, I like it so much, that you're going to do it."

"Me, as in just me? As in *alone*?"

"Now you're getting it."

"But...I have to go alone?" Quincy asked, horrified at warning Katelyn by herself.

"Think of this as…character building. While you're doing that, I'm going to hunt down bell cutters."

She took a deep breath. She knew she had to do this. "Okay."

"Oh, and Quinn? Please be exceptionally careful about what you do and do not say."

"No pressure again, huh?"

Talin softened his tone. "This could become more significant than you or even your friend. The person doing all this must be connected to the keys in some way or another, and is clearly intent on changing time. I just don't know why yet. Otherwise, why Monty? Why Katelyn? There are bigger things at work here, both and at this very moment in *this* present and in your present."

Quincy gulped, and after another minute of silence, she looked at Talin. "I don't know if I can do this."

"You're going to need to believe in yourself anyway, because you're the only one who *can* do it."

She crossed her arms over her stomach, put her head to her knees, and quietly rocked back and forth for a few moments while trying to find an extra dose of courage. Her fingers tingled, and she looked up in surprise. She had accidentally-memory traveled and was back at Miss Heatherwood's and the cruel woman was glaring at her. "You are simply a child, and practically an orphan," she said. "That means you have no say in anything. You have rights to nothing. I tell you how to live and think."

Quincy clenched her fists and repeated her own answer. "No, you don't."

She blinked and found herself staring back at Talin again, anger still bubbling inside her. "Okay, let's do this."

Talin nodded his head. "Good. Trust your instincts." He paused, and they locked eyes. "You're a smart girl."

"What, a compliment? From you?" she asked with mock surprise.

"Yeah, well don't get used to it."

She grinned and stood up. "I'm going to go and find Katelyn. Wish me luck."

CHAPTER TWENTY-EIGHT

FAMILY GENETICS

Quincy paused outside the girl's locker rooms in the hope that Katelyn would be waiting there. A large sign had been nailed to the door that read, POLO PLAYERS AND OAKLEY MEMBERS ONLY. She looked down at the large, red sweater she was wearing and delightedly got rid of it. She straightened her Oakley sweater and smoothed her coat over her patch.

The student security guard let her pass when she saw the Oakley sweater. Quincy caught the woman's confused look, though. The guard clearly didn't recognize her. Quincy waved and pretended that she knew the security guard well. Luckily, she wasn't stopped from going inside.

When she arrived at the door to the locker room, she tentatively knocked. When no one answered, she opened it a crack and met a wave of hot and sweaty air. The only sounds in the room came from the nervous breathing of the occupants. Within a moment, all eyes were on her. She laughed uncomfortably.

"Sorry to bother, but I'm uh looking for Katelyn." Quincy asked loudly.

Katelyn stood up from the end of the room and walked toward Quincy.

"What might I do for you?"

"We met in the Main Hall, by the bulletin board...I'm—"

"Quinn Holding," she finished.

Quincy felt a moment of déjà vu, and Katelyn in response to Quincy's surprised look, smiled and said, "I'm quite good with names. How might I help you?"

"Could we talk somewhere else?"

Katelyn looked at Quincy's attire and saw the Oakley sweater and frowned. "Not really from Whistler, are you?"

Quincy gave her sheepish look. "No, not exactly. I've never even been to Colorado."

Katelyn looked deep into Quincy's eyes, reading her. Quincy shifted from one foot to the other uncomfortably. Finally, Katelyn nodded. "I thought not. Follow me, I know somewhere that's a little more private."

Quincy followed Katelyn as she led them into the forest. She stared at the greenery and listened to the distant trickle of a creek, making a mental note to visit the forest more often when she got back to her present.

If she got back.

She gulped and focused on walking after Katelyn. They stopped later, and Quincy glimpse a sign that read, THE TEMPLUM.

Behind the sign, a wrought iron gazebo encased in glass, sat nested between tree branches and vines from the surrounding forest.

Katelyn caught her looking at the seemingly dead plants. “The vines will be full of roses soon.”

“Where are we?”

“This marks the boundary of the school grounds that students can visit without supervision. Very few people visit in the early spring, though. I like it because I think more coherently outdoors.”

Quincy held back a smile. Outdoors—a place Monty preferred not to venture. Actually, if given the chance, Monty would probably never go outside.

“I didn’t even know this was here,” she said in awe as she stepped into the Templum.

“Forgive me, but have you actually been to Oakley before?”

“Yes, I have. Though, technically, not yet.”

Katelyn gave her a confused look. Quincy felt glad that for once she wasn’t the confused individual in the conversation.

Quincy stepped into the gazebo. It was warmer than outside the walls, as if something kept the interior warm. Vine seats stretched from the ceiling, and she looked at them, wary.

“You can sit on those. You don’t have to worry. There aren’t any thorns so nothing will prick you.”

Quincy nodded and sat down across from Katelyn, who folded her arms and looked at Quincy pensively. “Now, what was it that you wanted? I had a feeling it was rather important.”

Quincy looked over at the intense stare that felt so familiar to her, and sadness filled her at the sudden realization that Monty would never have a conversation like this with his own mother.

"I'm sorry, but you need to drop out of the tournament," she finally just said.

Katelyn looked confused and then angry. "Excuse me? Who did you say you were?"

Now or never, Quincy decided. She could always pass as crazy if worse came to worst.

"Something happened today that shouldn't have and it's important that we make it right."

Katelyn frowned at her, and Quincy breathed deeply in mental preparation for the cascade of questions that were guaranteed to come.

"Who are you really?"

Quincy quickly transitioned from Plan A, which was to sound smart and tell the least number of damaging truths possible, hoping that Katelyn would follow her lead to Plan B; do whatever it took to save everyone.

"Me? I'm nobody, really. At least, not yet," she grimaced. "I'm just here to save your life."

"Save my life? Do I die today?"

Quincy bit her lip. "You're not supposed to, but for some reason, you do."

Katelyn raised an eyebrow, exactly as Monty would have done. Under different circumstances, Quincy would have found it hilarious.

"You might not—actually, no you won't, understand exactly what I'm trying to say."

Katelyn crossed her arms and leaned in toward Quincy. "Try me."

Quincy sucked in the air through her nose and slowly released it from her mouth. "Let me tell you a story. You can either believe me and drop out of the tournament, or you can ignore me, but if you do the latter, I can't promise that you'll live past today."

Katelyn nodded, agreed, and motioned for her to continue.

"Someone in the future wants you dead. I don't know why, but it ends your line." Quincy winced at how ridiculous the whole thing sounded, even to her. "I don't know why you or your...offspring is so important, but for some reason, someone is willing to let you die to stop your line from continuing."

Katelyn's face turned white, and she clung to her seat. "With all due respect, you should stick to reality. Your depressing storytelling leaves much to be desired. Any idea on how they plan to 'get rid' of me, since this has supposedly already happened?" she asked stiffly, crossing her arms.

"Yes! I mean, no. This whole thing wasn't supposed to happen, originally. The only thing that I know is there's an accident involving your horse in the final round of the tournament."

"My horse?" Katelyn snorted disdainfully. "She's my own horse that I brought with me from home. There isn't any way that she could kill me. Besides, why?" Katelyn growled. Quincy squirmed in her seat. "I told you, I'm not really sure."

Katelyn looked unconvinced. "How do I know that you're not actually from Whistler just trying to get me to leave the tournament?"

Quincy looked around desperately trying to recall something that only an Oakley student would know. Then it came to her. "You live on floor three, right?"

"Yes…?"

"On the doorway to the girl's dormitory are there carved roses with only one red one in the cluster of flowers on the right side? Near the corner?"

Katelyn looked at her in surprise. "You're from floor three, too? Only a student of Oakley would know that."

Quincy nodded excitedly, delighted that she and Katelyn had found common ground.

"Wow," she said, shaking her head in disbelief. "So time travel really does exist."

"Yes. And I need you to help me make sure that no one messes with the future. Now, the question is, what do you have that someone could possibly want?"

Katelyn's lips tightened.

"So for the story's sake, let's say that you are actually from the future. Why are you doing this? Why come here?"

"I..." Quincy paused, not sure what to say.

Katelyn looked unsure at her unwillingness to share. "You need to be more direct with me, Quinn. Hypothetically, what is your best guess as to what I have in the future that would be worth killing me now? Either tell me that or tell me exactly what has happened in your future that was caused by what happens today."

"I'm not supposed to give you details, though. I don't want to change anything."

"Do the best that you can."

Quincy met Katelyn's eyes and decided to take a leap. She pulled out the key from under her shirt. She slowly showed it to Katelyn whose eyes widened.

"I've seen that key before," Katelyn said numbly.

"Wait, you've seen this *exact* key before or one like it?"

Katelyn grinned at Quincy. "Both, actually."

Quincy started to wonder how she could have seen her key before, but then it clicked. Her mother was wearing this very same key at the very same moment.

"Well now I know how you got here, but I really want to know the why. Why do *you* care if I live or die?"

Quincy shifted uncomfortably on the vine seat and wiped sweat from her forehead. "I'm doing this for my best friend."

"The last of my "line'?"

Quincy nodded, and Katelyn grinned. "Boy or girl?"

Quincy had already told her practically everything and the answer to that question wouldn't do any more damage than she had already done. She couldn't change the gender by knowing, anyway.

"Boy," Quincy muttered.

Katelyn laughed delightedly and then grew somber.

"You should hide your key. Don't show it to anyone else, yeah? That would make things even worse than they currently are."

Quincy nodded.

"I need some time to think about this," Katelyn said. "And I want to visit my horse, the one that somehow is supposed to kill me."

Quincy nodded again, and together, they walked back towards the academy. As they approached the stable, June ran to meet Katelyn.

"Hey, Kate!" June panted. "There's something wrong with your horse."

Katelyn took off, running inside the stable. She paused outside a stall and the friendly horse nickered a hello. She leaned against her mount and sighed with relief.

"What happened?" she growled at the stable master as he walked up.

"Not sure, but if there's a substantial gash on her back leg. It's not fatal, but it will stop you from riding her this afternoon. I'm hunting down a decent replacement."

Katelyn spat out a phrase in Gaelic and turned her head to Quincy. "I'll take it from here."

“But, what are you going to do?” Quincy sputtered.

“I’ll take care of it. Go back to the stands,” demanded Katelyn.

Quincy clenched her fists but nodded before walking away. She held back the desire to kick the wall out of frustration. Then, from the corner of her eye, she saw a stable hand staring at her. Her eyes widened, and she swung around. “Cigfran?” she called.

But the figure had turned around and didn’t turn again to face her. Even if it had been Cigfran, he wouldn’t have known her in this time, she realized. Quincy’s cheeks burned, and her body tensed up angrily as she stormed out of the stable.

***

Quincy found her spot and sat down, fuming.

“Well?” Talin nudged.

“Katelyn said that she’s going to take care of it,” She glared at the polo players.

“And you believe her?”

Quincy slouched in her chair from sudden fatigue. She looked up and saw the darkening horizon turning red and orange. People around her had started to light candles around the area. There was even a bonfire burning. She shrugged. “I can’t do anything more.” She suppressed a yawn, realizing that she had been awake for over twenty-four hours straight.

Her stomach growled, and she sighed. “So I guess Katelyn’s team is scheduled to compete after the next two teams,” she said, stretching.

“What!? I thought you went to talk her out of competing?”

"I did! I'm just not really sure what she's going to do."

"She had better not play."

She ignored the raven and attempted to keep her breathing even. Exhaustion and anxiety were not a good combination.

"I'm sure you did the best you could have," Talin said softly, his mood shifting.

She nodded and rubbed her eyes. "So what did you find out while I was talking with Katelyn?"

"Well, I have an idea." Talin informed her while looking around at the crowd. Quincy's mouth pinched shut, and her eyes widened in astonishment when he suddenly hissed. "What's wrong?"

"Nothing. Quincy, put your hand out."

She frowned at the intensity of his voice and obediently held out her hand as Talin dropped a coin into it.

"Go to the Main Hall and buy some soup and cocoa."

She paused and titled her head at him.

"Go now," he growled.

She nodded. "Uh, thank you?"

"You're most welcome," he said, not seeming to register her confusion. "Bring me back some crackers, please," he added, his voice sounding light again.

But Quincy still heard the urgency laced in his words, so she just nodded again. "Done."

***

Talin watched Quincy leave and breathed a sigh of relief when she went inside the Main Hall. He didn't want these two people to meet. At least not yet. He focused on the man lurking in the shadows and couldn't repress another growl. "Wilbright."

He flexed his wings and narrowed his eyes. He looked one more time just to make sure that the girl had disappeared from sight. Inside Oakley would be the safest place for her while he decided what to do. He needed to wait for the right moment and place to confront him. Now wasn't that time.

After some quick thinking, Talin moved over to a security guard that he knew fairly well, a large, muscular Year Four named Mattie.

"Talin!" the boy greeted him.

"Hello, Mattie. Will you do me a favor? Do you see that gentleman over there?"

"That one?" Mattie asked, pointing.

"Yes. Would you please see if he's supposed to be here."

Mattie didn't even ask why. "Of course!"

He called over two other guards and walked over to Wilbright. Talin didn't hear the words but found it easy to guess the conversation. It ended with the three security guards escorting Wilbright away from the fields.

Talin sighed and went back to his seat. Oh, Wilbright. Ever still the bitter but brilliant moron.

***

Wilbright growled and dusted off his tweed jacket while kicking at the recently-closed gate behind him. He might not have good seats in the arena, but he knew the Oakley grounds well. He remembered a fantastic climbing tree that would give him a fairly decent view of the field. His job had already been done anyway. All he had to do was wait. Katelyn would not last beyond the next match anyway. She just needed to make it to the second set. The pill and the drugged horse would take care of rest.

He breathed deeply and rubbed his forehead from his seat in the tree. Afterward, the only thing left to do would be to slip into the Infirmary during the pandemonium and grab the hidden medical uniform behind a portrait in the waiting room. With the force in which Katelyn would hit the ground, she would certainly need pain medicine, and with his own special elixir added, she wouldn't have any problem informing him of her key's location.

He placed the empty pill bag into his pocket.

***

Quincy left Talin and navigated through the crowd to the Main Hall to get something to eat. She walked up to a table covered with self-serve breads and steaming chili that had been placed at the edge of the room. She grabbed a seat on her customary bench and out of habit looked up to talk to her friends. Sadly, no one around her was familiar, and from the many different colors of sweaters, few knew each other, either. She dipped a piece of cornbread into a bowl of the chili and took a bite. She felt her blood sugar rise, waking her up. After finishing her food, she smiled at the dining room's resident fox, who then winked at her and dived into his hole in the painting. Finally, she walked outside to find Talin and gave him his requested crackers.

"When's Katelyn's match?" she asked as she approached him. She handed him the crackers and he tore into them.

"She should be next," he mumbled with a beak full of crackers. Quincy's shoulder was already covered in crumbs.

"Do we know her opponents?"

"Four wee bairns from Scotland."

Quincy groaned at Talin's attempt at a Scottish accent.

"I'll have you know, you urchin, that my Scottish accent is flawless. You just have to be Scottish to understand," he told her.

She just shook her head at him and then looked over at the current match confused when one of the competitors—who was built like a bear—took her polo mallet and began to twirl it like a windmill. There must have been a powerful wind current released with the motion, because another competitor's horse balked and its rider completely missed the ball. The other girl whacked the ball, and it soared across the field. Quincy remembered Colin telling her about playing polo, "Talents style" and wondered how much of that was involved in the tournament.

"How much longer is the match?" she asked.

"It's nearly—"

The Irish announcer's voice interrupted ringing out and echoing around the field. "Acadia wins! Next match will begin momentarily."

"—finished," Talin said with a small chuckle.

But Quincy was hardly listening to the bird. As soon as she heard the Irish accent over the speakers, she wondered if it was Monty's father. She hadn't yet seen him around the school, since his match wasn't until much later in tomorrow's tournament. She looked up at the darkening sky and rubbed her arms as a chill swept in. Hopefully the weather would hold.

The first player trotted across the field. In this morning's match, it had been Katelyn, but she couldn't tell who it was now. Quincy bit her lip until she tasted blood. It was impossible to tell.

She sat on the edge of her seat, a pit of dread in her stomach, and Talin flew to her other shoulder in anticipation. The bell, which had been re-hung, rang across the field. The two front riders nodded at each other and held tightly to their horses' reins. The bell rang again, and immediately both girls ran at full force with their polo mallets poised for action. At the last second, just before they crashed, Katelyn had managed to bump into her opponent and take possession of the ball.

Overhead, a crack of thunder caused people and horses alike to startle. Except for Katelyn's new mount. It seemed to stare at the horizon, bored. A second bolt of lightning struck, and everyone rode off the field. Katelyn nudged her horse to follow, but it tripped, bringing down its rider.

Quincy, as well as most of the audience, stood up. Raindrops began to fall from the sky, and land on the motionless horse and rider. People all around began to run down toward the two. She stared down in horror as nurses, doctors, and stable hands swarmed the girl and her horse.

The Irish announcer's voice echoed in response. "Please carefully—and safely—make your way inside."

From the corner of her eye, she caught a flash of burgundy and she whirled around. Ten feet away, the man in red stared at her. She quickly blinked and looked again, but he had disappeared into the hurried crowd.

Quincy felt a hand on her shoulder, and she whirled around, shoulders and fists tensed and poised for action.

She nearly cried with relief when Katelyn grasped her shoulders and faced her.

"You need to go. Thank you, Quincy, for caring enough to do this. I hope all the best for you and…my son. One of my friends was the school alternate, and I need to go see how she's doing."

Talin hissed at Katelyn. "No. You need to stay away from the Infirmary. The one who perpetrated today's events is still here. Go to your room and stay there for the rest of the day."

Katelyn's eyes widened and she nodded.

"He will never stop coming for you." Talin added. "We'll talk more later. Now go." Katelyn bit her lip and ran inside the Main Hall. "She's right, though. It's time for us to leave," he growled.

Quincy didn't argue even though she yearned to see her mother and father one last time. They ran to the Timepiece, the rain dripping from their hair and feathers.

"Congratulations, you've changed the future again, hopefully back to its original course."

"Hopefully? Have I still changed the future?"

"Possibly and probably. The real question is how drastically."

She nodded. "Only one way to find out, I guess."

As they stood at the base of the Timepiece, she turned to watch the bustle of people running in and out of the Oakley buildings, and she hoped that Katelyn's friend was going to be okay after that fall. She sent her a silent thank-you. No matter what happened to the girl, she just saved someone's life. Quincy hoped.

***

Wilbright grabbed his lab coat and took the stairs two at time to the Infirmary. As he walked inside, he dodged the head nurse and paused next to Katelyn. He grasped the needle that would force the Irish girl to tell him where she kept her key. Two of the nurses pulled off the girl's helmet, and he gave a quiet gasp.

It wasn't Katelyn.

His breathing became shallow and uneven. How could this be possible? He had run every likely scenario. This hadn't been one of them. He wanted to scream. He couldn't have been wrong. What had happened to Katelyn?

His heart pounded from the fear of his failure. His fault. His responsibility. He would be blamed.

And this was the last time Katelyn Prendergast had been publically seen until her death, he reminded himself. There would never be an open day like this at Oakley again. And with

Montgomery so well protected in the present, how was he supposed to get Katelyn's family key?

Wilbright forced himself toward the Timepiece. He needed to get out of here, and quickly. He needed to run the numbers and figure out why he failed. He grabbed the key from his pocket and stopped just before walking into the clock. There he saw his problem. A girl with a black bird on her shoulder.

"Talin," Wilbright spat.

He slammed his fist against the clock's marble. Now he knew why he had failed.

***

Quincy thought that she saw someone standing near the Timepiece, but as she grew closer, no one was around. She shrugged and grasped the door handle. Then she froze. The door was already open.

"Talin, I promise I made sure the door was shut. And I am certain it was locked. I—"

"Shh, shh. I know. It's not your fault."

"It's not?"

"No. Let's go."

They silently walked down the stairs and Quincy stared at the lit large glass orb.

"Ah, so he's been here and gone already?" Talin sighed.

"Who?"

Talin remained silent and flew over to the heart.

"Who, Talin?" she pressed.

"Just an annoyance."

"Just an annoyance?" Quincy yelled. "An annoyance who tried to kill Katelyn. Who rewrote Monty. Who—"

"My dear Quinn, I cannot play question-and-answer with you now. I have nothing to offer you and much to think about."

She frowned angrily but nodded as she twisted the dial to go back home.

Chapter Twenty-Nine

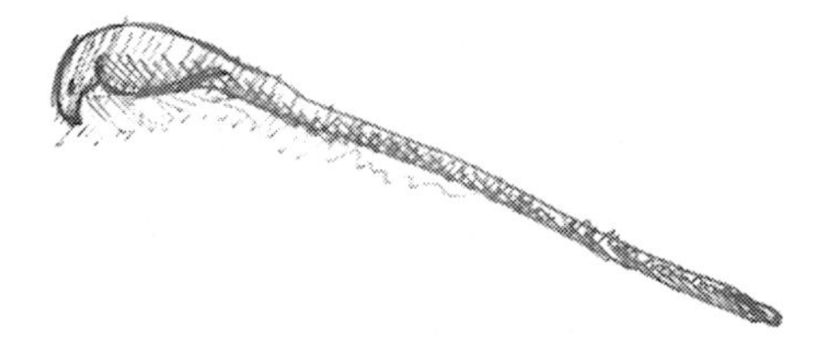

Confrontations

Talin and Quincy walked out of the Timepiece, and Quincy unsuccessfully hid a yawn.

"How are you feeling?" he asked quietly but anxiously.

"You mean other than being awake for over twenty-four hours?" She rubbed her swollen eyes, and her brow furrowed when she realized that Talin was waiting for a serious answer. "I'm fine, just tired." Her anger had lessened, leaving her even more exhausted.

"Really?" he asked, frowning. "Interesting."

"Why do you keep saying that? You asked me the same thing when we first left and I answered the same way. Why do you keep wondering?"

"Most people feel really disoriented after the time difference from traveling. The human brain is not meant to travel like this. It plays games with humanity's internal clock. But you seem to be all right." Talin clicked his beak and stared at Quincy.

"So what does that mean?"

"That perhaps you were born to time travel."

The Timepiece rang behind them—the dinner bell—and Quincy frowned. "How is this possible. We were in the past for almost a whole day, but here we've been gone less than a minute?"

"I don't use the Timepiece often, but one of the perks of traveling with me is that we come back exactly when I wish. It's a talking-bird thing. Actually it's a *me* thing. Anyway, there have been cases of others using the Timepiece alone and some of those people have lost *days*. The Timepiece is not an exact science. Which is why you shouldn't *ever* travel without me, all right?"

Quincy nodded. "Okay."

"Good."

She touched her damp sweater. "And I'm wet. Great." Completely exhausted, she burst into giggles. Talin quickly grasped her shoulder before he fell off. Finally, she stopped and straightened up.

"Hey, Talin?"

"Uh-huh?"

Quincy paused and turned her head to look at the raven. "Thank you...for coming with me."

"You're welcome. It's certainly been an adventure. One that I hope we don't have to redo anytime soon. Now I have to go and tidy things up," he added.

"What things?"

"None-of-your business things." Talin smirked. "Oh, and Quinn?"

"Yeah?"

"You should get some sleep. You look terrible."

"Thanks. You look great yourself, you know," she shot back while crossing her arms and trying not to laugh.

"I know. My curse to bear," Talin winked and flew away. She waved at the retreating bird and ran into the Main Hall. Before she did anything, she needed to find Monty, to make sure it worked.

She raced through the Main Hall and into the dining hall. Her heart dropped when she saw his empty seat.

She held back the tears as she turned around to run back to the dormitories. She had failed. Monty still no longer existed in her timeline. He had been rewritten. She wiped her eyes on her sleeve and bumped into someone. She looked to apologize and then saw who it was. Without thinking, she threw her arms around him and hugged him tightly. His cheeks burned against her skin, and after an uncomfortable moment, he awkwardly hugged her back.

"Monty! Are you okay?" she whispered. The relief made her legs feel like jelly.

He nodded. "I am fine." He slowly smiled and gestured back to their seats. "You look like you need something to eat."

She released her hold on him, and the two of them walked to the floor-three table. Eloise looked up and waved at the two of them. "Did you find the book that you were looking for, Monty?"

"I did, thank you," he said as he sat down in his customary spot next to Quincy. It was as if nothing had happened. She closed her eyes and sighed with contentment.

Eloise looked at Quincy and frowned. "Quincy, where have you been for the last half hour? And why are you all wet?"

Quincy looked down and saw her reflection in the silverware. Her sweater was soggy, and she had dark circles under eyes as if she hadn't had much sleep recently, which of course, she had not. She tried to smooth down her rumpled clothes, and quickly re-tucked her shirt. She had stains on her khaki pants and one shoe was untied. Quincy held back a smirk. She would have been in so much trouble for arriving to dinner at Miss Heatherwoods in such a state.

"Oh come now, Eloise. She obviously went on an, erm, run in her, erm, uniform, and almost…tripped into the pond?" Monty tried to answer matter-of-factly.

Quincy laughed at seeing her friend completely flustered. His furrowed brows reminded her of his mom. She wished that the two of them could have met.

"Fine, I'll admit it. I'm secretly taking up polo." She winked. "But don't tell anybody or I could get into serious trouble."

Eloise, Monty, and Quincy laughed and began to eat.

***

Wilbright staggered into his room and leaned against the cold fireplace. He knew he should go upstairs straightaway and admit his defeat, but his legs refused to comply. He jumped when he heard a rap on the door.

"What is it?"

"Do you care for some tea, milord?"

“No, I don’t want anything. Leave me,” he sputtered to his valet.

“As milord wishes.”

Wilbright waited until he heard the man’s retreating footsteps before he sighed in relief. At least he was home and alone. He probably should start to work on another plan, but it could wait one day at the very least. He needed rest.

Wilbright looked in the mirror, and the hairs on his arms and legs stood straight up as he stared into a pair of eyes not his own in the reflection. He whirled around.

A hooded figure sat in his chair in the corner of the room, one hand clenching the armrest and the other clutching a mahogany cane with a hand-carved bird on the handle. The figure seemed to be looking directly at him. Wilbright involuntarily gasped and then held his hand over his beating heart. After taking a moment to catch his breath, he addressed the hooded figure.

“Hello again, Uncle Cigfran. I really shouldn’t be surprised. I wondered how long it was going to take you before you paid me a visit.”

“So you were expecting me then after your time-traveling fiasco?” Cigfran asked.

Wilbright nodded.

“Please have a seat.” His uncle gestured at the floor next to him.

“Isn’t that what I’m supposed to say? I’m no longer a boy that you can simply invite to sit on the floor by your knees.”

"Aren't you, though, Wil?"

"Perhaps to *you* maybe."

"When you do things like you did today, I do tend to think that way." His voice sounded disappointed, and for a brief moment—very brief—embarrassment washed through Wilbright.

"Am I supposed to apologize or explain myself to you?" Wilbright surprised even himself by sounding so juvenile. He sighed. "You don't seem to bring out the best in people."

His uncle chuckled and then grew somber. "Wilbright, I've chosen until now to let you prance around time, unguarded, with your key. As long as you followed the rules, who was I to stop you? Today, however, you broke the cardinal one."

"What does it matter to you? It fixed itself in the end," Wilbright spat out.

Cigfran sucked in his breath and let it out in a growl. "Not without repercussions. I now have two children who have to live with two timelines in their heads. They shouldn't have to be shadowed by those memories for the rest of their lives. And what's even worse is that if your plan had succeeded, you would have killed the young Prendergast girl. Are you a murderer now, Wil?"

"Not possible. I ran every scenario."

"And yet it happened. You cannot account for everyone." His uncle paused. "Not even I can do that."

"Well, obviously, I didn't mean for her to die," Wilbright whispered. "She would have been collateral damage."

"Collateral damage! You truly believe that?" He roared angrily at his nephew. "Maybe you're right. I can no longer punish you as I would a child, but so help me, Wilbright, if you continue down this road I will have to step in and punish you as I would *an adult*. We both know what your Talent is, and it is certainly not the cognition of time. You of all people know what time traveling does to a human mind that can't bend around it."

"So why step in now?" Wilbright asked.

"I will not have you creating more time loops and alternate realities than the extra one you already created. Though, to be quite honest, with the way you're holding your head, I might not have to step in, after all."

Wilbright quickly took his hand off his forehead and looked out the window.

"How many times have you time traveled now, Wilbright? You're already seeing the effects of it. Is it nighttime or daytime right now, Wilbright?"

"It's dark outside. Does it matter?"

Cigfran slammed a fist down on the armrest. "Enough. I'm tired of your petulance. By all means, keep time traveling. Because in the end I won't have to stop you. You'll have done the deed yourself when they place you in the madhouse. I wash my hands of you." He walked toward the fireplace. "Besides Wilbright, in every timeline and in every reality, you lose."

"That's not what I saw."

Before he could say anything else, another knock interrupted their conversation, and Wilbright looked over at the door.

“I told you not to bother me,” he shouted through the wood.

“Apologies,” his valet whispered. “I heard yelling...”

Wilbright whirled around to glare at his uncle, but Cigfran had disappeared into the darkness.

CHAPTER THIRTY

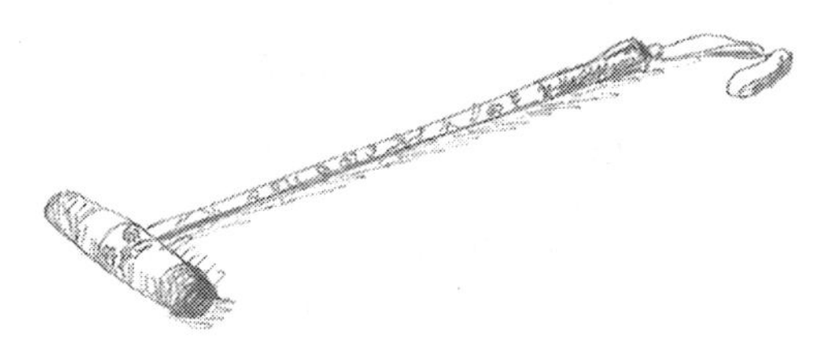

PRESENT FROM THE PAST

Two months had passed since Quincy had traveled back in time, and everything was thankfully back to normal. She sat in the library and stared down at her Latin homework, groaning.

"Still having difficulties?" Monty asked without looking up from his book.

"Yeah," she answered reluctantly. "I think I'm going to go to the Art Corridor. Go clear my head. Want to come?"

He rolled his eyes. "No, thank you."

"Are you sure? It could be fun?" she pleaded. Even though nothing drastic had happened since she came back to the future, she still worried about Monty.

He quietly shut his book and looked up at Quincy. "I am not disappearing again. At least not in the foreseeable future." He grinned. "Go and paint. I will meet you at dinner."

Quincy nodded and walked away from Monty toward the door. She peeked over her shoulder at him one last time. He was already hard at work on his own homework.

“Still here,” he mumbled, not looking up.

“Okay, I’m leaving,” Quincy forced a laughed. Neither of them had actually spoken about what had transpired. She kept telling herself that she was just waiting for the right time to talk to him.

***

She found a seat by herself in one of the rooms along the Art Corridor. She looked around, disappointed that Colin wasn’t there. They often sat together while they worked, and made sure never to mention Genevieve. Quincy grimaced at the thought of Genevieve and Colin. She pulled out her tattered notebook and stared longingly at it. She hadn’t had much of a chance to draw recently. She opened it to an empty page and without realizing it, had begun to sketch a raven. She looked up when she heard a whistle.

“Not bad,” Talin gestured towards the picture. He flew down and landed on her shoulders.

Quincy jumped. “You really should warn me before you land,” she said with a pout.

“And lose the element of surprise and that little leap of yours? Now where’s the fun in that?”

“There are people across the room,” she whispered. “What if they see you?”

“Ah. Not to worry. People see what they want. Or they have to know what they’re looking at to see it.”

“In other words, they can’t see you?” Quincy rolled her eyes. “There’s always something with you.”

Talin grinned. "Something like that. But they *can* see you talking to yourself."

One of the older students gave her an odd look. Quincy smiled at the student and waved.

"Let's walk shall we. Don't say anything. It makes you look even more…odd."

"Um, thanks?" She stood up and followed Talin's directions.

"Where are we going?"

"Just keep walking."

"It's pretty convenient that people can't see you." she started. "I could use something like that."

"Maybe if you're good, I'll teach you someday," Talin snickered.

"So where have you been the last two months?" She hadn't seen him since the night they used the Timepiece.

"I've been busy."

"Oh." Quincy did not want to admit, even to herself, that she had actually missed his company. She groaned when she saw yet another unrecognizable staircase. "Hey, Talin…"

The bird sighed, "What?"

"I know that you said more people are after you, but why are you mostly invisible now? Back in time, everybody knew you. Everybody saw you."

"What's your point?"

"Why doesn't anyone know you now? Don't you miss it?"

"What makes you think they don't know me? You see me, right? We're having a conversation now, aren't we? I've just decided to be more choosy with whom I decide to be friends with."

Surprisingly, she liked the idea of Talin being a friend, despite the fact that he was generally irritating. "So then why me? Is this about the..." Quincy mumbled. "The key?"

"What is it with you and the never ending questions?" Talin rolled his eyes.

"I'm sorry," she said, exaggerating a frown.

Talin glared at her and then chuckled. "No, you're not." He paused for a moment. "Glad to know someone has picked up a sense of humor through all of this, though. It is true that I know you through your blasted key, but that's not to say that I don't occasionally actually enjoy your company."

"Only occasionally?" she asked, trying to shake him off her shoulder.

"No respect, that's your problem," the raven growled.

Quincy smiled and stopped wiggling.

"The true answer to your question," he continued, "is that times have sadly changed. I wish they hadn't but they have. And in times of need one must change one's strategy and ideas."

"Talin, you're an odd bird."

"Met a lot of talking birds, have you? Anyway, thanks a lot. I'll choose to take that as a compliment." He sniffed.

"You're welcome. Where are we, by the way?" Quincy frowned again—genuinely this time—and looked at the unfamiliar staircase in front of her.

"In an older part of the school. Classes used to be held here before they built the Learner's Citadel."

Her eyes widened. "The Learner's Citadel is new?"

"Depends on your definition of *new*. So, no, not really."

"Oh," Quincy nodded. "It's that age-old question I'm not supposed to ask again, huh?"

Talin gave her a throaty chuckle. "Last flight of stairs." He pointed a wing at the winding staircase.

She walked up until she reached a completely round room with an open door.

"I trust you enough to show you where I live, but I don't do company."

She turned around so that Talin could fly into his home alone. She heard a grunt coming from the doorway. It sounded like he was moving something around. She leaned against the wall and shut her eyes until she heard a crash echo in the room, followed by an "A-ha!"

"Everything okay in there?" Quincy called out.

"You may turn around and pick this up," he grumbled, dragging a large box with his beak.

She grabbed the box and stared at it. "What's in this?"

Talin winked and flew to the banister in front of her. "It's a none-of-your-business box. It's between Katelyn and her son."

“What?”

“Katelyn asked me to give this box to you to give to her son when he turned sixteen. Which is today, by the way,” he explained.

Quincy gasped. “Today’s his birthday? But he never told me...”

“Some people don’t like to tell people their birthdays or their ages.” Talin deadpanned.

“Rewind. So you’ve had this box before you met me?”

Talin nodded. “Don’t try. You’ll only hurt your brain.”

“Do you know what’s inside?”

“I have an idea, but Monty needs to be the one to open it.”

“So exactly how long have you had this?”

“Like you said, long before we ever met.”

“Really? But this means that I had already visited her in the past and that I, in actuality, didn’t change anything?”

“I know. Confusing isn’t it?”

“Yeah, it is.” She rubbed her head. “Talin?”

He groaned, which she decided to take as a, “Please, by all means, ask your question.”

“I’m really confused. I have memories that no one else has.”

“Ah.” Talin responded, not sounding surprised.

“I still remember the week when Monty disappeared but no one else does. They have memories of that week that I don’t. Is that because we fixed our timeline? If we did, why don’t I have the fixed memories everyone else has, then?”

“Because you were the one who went back in time. The memories will never be fixed for you.”

"What about for Monty?"

"Monty is a special case. You remember an alternate timeline, but with his mutated Talent, he remembers the original timeline and yet is completely aware that there is mistake timeline in which he was never born. Ask him to tell you about it."

She sat down on the floor and put her head in her hands.

"Don't worry," Talin told her. "He'll live. Just another personality quirk."

"This is all so confusing,"

"I'm sorry to say that with regard to time, you will forever be confused in some way or another. I've known some intelligent people who went slightly mad trying to find and understand the implications. Well, not exactly *slightly*."

Quincy nodded at Talin and picked up the package. They stared at each other uncomfortably, not sure what to say next. Finally, Talin cleared his throat. "So are you ready for exams?"

She grimaced. "Mostly."

"Mostly?"

"I'll be ready." She paused. "I hope."

"Good."

"Will I see you again before I leave for the summer?"

"Maybe. Probably not," Talin hastily answered.

He had said it so quickly that Quincy felt as if she had been dismissed. "Oh, okay."

"I'm sure the holiday will go by quickly," he added lightly.

"I seriously doubt that." She frowned. "Well, thanks for this." She gestured to the box and Talin bowed his head slightly. "And thanks for, well, everything." She slowly smiled and began to walk down the flights of stairs.

"I'll see you soon." she heard the raven call after her.

She walked down to the Main Hall and grumbled when she learned she had missed dinner. Grudgingly, she made her way back to the dormitories. Her eyes widened when she saw Monty waiting on the bottom step of the dormitory staircase.

"Greetings, Quincy," he said, looking up.

"Hey, Monty," She grinned and sat down next to him. "Happy birthday."

Monty grimaced. "Thank you, I suppose. How did you find out?"

"An annoyingly expressive bird told me."

Monty grinned, thinking she was making a joke. *If only*, Quincy inwardly groaned.

"That is an irregular type box," Monty stared at the package in her hand.

"It's a present. For you, actually."

Monty didn't look surprised. "I hope this isn't a birthday present. Is it from you?"

"Not from me."

Monty frowned. "Then from whom?"

"Open it."

Quincy sat down next to him and handed him the box. He raised one eyebrow and untied the ribbon that held the box together. He peered at the contents and reverently pulled out a medium-sized polo mallet. Roses and vines carved into the wood curving gracefully around the mallet's handle. He held it and quickly rubbed his eyes. Quincy thought she saw a tear escape.

"It is hers, is it not?"

She gaped at her friend. "How did you know?"

A slight smile appeared at the corner of Monty's mouth. "Just a premonition. Which is how I know to do this."

He brandished the mallet—much like Katelyn had done—and was about to swish it when they both heard a metal object thunked against the ground. Monty bent down and picked it up. When he opened his hand, he revealed a key. The eye of the key was in the shape of a clover, and he brushed over it with his finger.

He frowned and informed her, “That’s where the premonition ended.”

For a moment they were both silent while looking at the key and the polo mallet.

“Quincy, do you know the meaning of this key?” he asked.

“I’m not sure,” she lied, placing her hand over the key hidden under her shirt. She wasn’t sure how much to tell him, but surely he’d figure it out without her help.

“I wonder...,” Monty looked at the key, pensively. “Let us put this key to the test. Follow me.”

He put the mallet back in the box and began running with it over his shoulder. She jumped up and chased after him. He ran outside and toward the library, which would be certainly locked this late at night. He gave Quincy a mischievous look and placed the key in the lock. The library door opened.

Instead of walking inside, Monty closed the door and turned around. He looked down at the key, his eyes darting over each and every curve. He walked across the hallway and used the key a second time to open a locked classroom.

“How is this possible?” he murmured.

“Monty, what is it” she nudged.

“How could she have acquired one of the keys?” he asked himself, ignoring Quincy.

“I thought you didn’t believe in the keys” she teased.

Monty grimaced. “Even I have been known to be erroneous on occasion. If I am correct, this key should open any lock, save one door. Which requires five keys to open it.”

She choked at a memory that flashed in her mind—a door with five locks in the attic of Miss Heatherwood’s. “Like the door in the Main Hall.”

He stopped walking and looked at her. “What do you mean? Have you seen the door? According to the legend, only the Master-Key Bearer can call the door. As you well know, I thought it to be a tale...”

Monty looked expectantly at Quincy who could only shrug in response. But inside she was panicking.

“I’m sorry, Monty, really.” she said, shifting the subject back to his mother. “But I don’t know why your mom had one of the keys.”

He sighed and dug through the rest of the box, smiling as he pulled out two letters. He stared at both of them before meeting Quincy’s eyes. His gaze was confused but awed. “This one is addressed to ‘Quinn...’ Is that you?” He handed her one of the envelopes.

She swallowed. “Yeah, um that’s strange...Thanks.” she said as she placed it in her pocket.

Monty stared at his own letter and furrowed his brows. “What was she like, my mum?”

"She was amazing." Quincy said quietly. "She reminded me a lot of you." She paused and laughed. "She has the same look you do when you're frustrated. Same eyes, same laugh..."

She couldn't have given him a better compliment. He smiled and simply said 'Brilliant', and then became quiet again.

"Our moms were actually friends," Quincy said, breaking the silence.

Monty nodded, not looking surprised.

She narrowed her eyes at him. "You knew?"

He turned pink and pulled out a plaid wallet. He opened it up and smiled, then handed a picture to Quincy. Her jaw dropped when she was the photograph. It was Chelsea and Katelyn leaning against each other and grinning.

"Why didn't you say anything?" she asked softly.

"I wanted to be friends with you because we chose to be, not because our mothers were friends. I was hoping that you would want to be." He stared down at his hands and Quincy awkwardly looked over at the window.

She ended the awkward silence again when she looked over at him. "Could I ask you a question?"

He blinked and stared at her. "By all means."

"What do you remember about that week?"

"That week? You still remember a week without me?"

Quincy nodded.

"I recall warning you before your adventure, and I also remember my state of nonexistence. It was what I imagined being dead was like. I could see what was happening but was incapable of doing anything. It was not altogether a bad feeling, just slightly frustrating. Yet I also have the memories of a week that you do not have, but you were there. Astonishing, is it not?"

Astonishing was not the word she would have chosen. He had two different timelines in his head. At least she only remembered a week without Monty.

He fingered the key and frowned again. "So my disappearance was about this key."

She cleared her throat. "Yeah, kind of... Let's say this isn't just a story. Do you think people are after what's behind the door for power"

"That would be my best conjecture. Their hard work is all worthless anyway. The other minor keys, like this one, have not been heard from or seen in years. No one knows what became of the Master Key. It is almost a pity that it has not been found," added Monty sadly. He looked down at the key in his hand. "I believe that this is one of the minor keys. You know, minor keys can be given, stolen, lost, and then found," he explained. "They will work on any door in the hands of anyone. The Master Key, however, is believed to bind itself to a specific person of its choice and can only be used by same holder."

"I actually knew that." She laughed.

He widened his eyes. "Indeed? So what else are you hiding," he teased.

Quincy paused and slowly smiled before pulling out the key from under her shirt. "Just the Master Key."

His eyebrows shot up and his glasses slid down his nose. His mouth hung wide open, and he almost dropped the box in his hands.

He looked intently at the key. "Are you sure that it is, in fact, the Master Key?"

"Well since it won't come off, I assume it is."

He shook his head in disbelief. "How did I not see that? I never saw that." Monty pushed his glasses up his nose and rubbed his head, clearly in shock.

"Never saw what?"

"I see a lot of things and usually they're quite random. I knew that you had some importance..."

Quincy frowned at the term "some importance" and Monty quickly backtracked on his statement.

"Other than to be a friend, that is. But I had no idea."

She quickly forgave his comment.

"Quincy, I believe that you are the Master Key Bearer."

At this point, Quincy doubted that anything could surprise her anymore, and she slowly nodded in agreement with Monty's statement.

"Do you comprehend the full meaning of all of this?"

She rolled her eyes, a nasty habit that she had picked up from Talin. "Condescending much? Yes, Monty. For once in life, I'm ahead of you."

“We have, right here, two of the five keys! Have you told the headmaster, or anyone.”

Quincy shook her head. “Honestly, I don’t know what he knows. I met someone who scared me enough not to tell too many people about this,” she said, rubbing the goose bumps on her arms.

“As you should be,” Monty said seriously. “It is truly better to be safe than sorry.”

“I’m not sure what to do next though,” Quincy admitted.

“I am not entirely sure, either. I will have to do some research this summer and see what information I can discover on the key’s creator and any known inventions.” Monty paused and played with his glasses. He frowned as he began to make a mental checklist for himself.

“So we have two keys, where are the other three?” Quincy wondered.

“I do not know. I wonder if anyone knows. If we could find the other three keys, you could find out what is behind the door.”

“The same door that houses something that could potentially cause world destruction?”

“Or great peace.” Monty added. “I will look into that as well. If all the stories are based on truth, I will also look into Master Creative Engineer Chenoweth. If I recall they were close contemporaries. Chenoweth is the same man who built the clock in the courtyard. Do you know the one that I am thinking of?”

Quincy nodded, not sure how much to tell him about her knowledge of the Timepiece. Talin seemed very protective about it, and she decided to wait and ask him about what she could say or could not.

Monty hadn't waited for her answer about the Timepiece and had continued talking without her full attention. Quincy felt numb. How could she find three other missing keys and open a door that had refused to open up for her earlier?

"What if it shouldn't be opened?" She felt the blood rush from her head and leaned against the wall.

"Then we do not open it." Monty answered.

Quincy breathed slowly. "I think I need hot chocolate."

Monty nodded and followed her to the café, where they ordered two cups and sat on the steps outside. The café stayed open until midnight the three weeks before, during, and after exams. She sipped her hot chocolate, thankful to have something warm to fill her up.

"Forgive me for inquiring, but how did you manage to time travel back to the past? I only saw snippets of the whole event. I saw you looking for the book in the Back Library and then saw you in the past."

Quincy paused unsure what to say. Slowly, she said, "I found the device from the book, but I'm not really supposed to talk about it."

"From the *Famous Clocks* book?"

She nodded. "But I've been sworn to secrecy. For now at least. I'm sorry."

His face fell, but he nodded his understanding. "Hopefully one day you can tell me the story in its entirety," he said. "You know, it is odd, but almost every time I see you in the future, you have a something or someone next to you. But it, or they, seems to have been sloppily erased."

Quincy pondered his question and pictured a cranky raven.

When she did not respond, he continued, "So? What is your next plan of action, Quinn?" Monty turned white. "Is it okay to call you that? I saw the name on your letter, and I quite like it."

She shook her head. "No I don't mind," she smiled. "And to answer your first question, I have no idea."

"Well, you will have some time to think. It is almost the summer holiday after all."

Quincy groaned.

"What? Is that a problem?"

"Seven words, Monty; Miss Heatherwood's Home for Boys and Girls."

He cringed. "For that I do not envy you."

"I wouldn't envy myself, either."

"My best advice is to think cheerful thoughts."

"Thanks a lot." She rolled her eyes, but then her face broke out into a grin.

Monty laughed. "Delighted to be of service."

He abruptly stopped laughing and stared soberly into his empty hot chocolate cup. "By the way, I swear that I did not speak of your group house to anyone," he said. "I wish I knew how someone had found out. I am sorry that you were embarrassed."

Quincy looked into his earnest eyes and nodded. "Thank you for saying that." He smiled and stood up. "Shall we?"

She returned the look. "Yeah, it's getting pretty late, I guess."

They left the café and made their way to floor three. They stopped in the hallway before leaving for their designated rooms.

"Good night, Monty."

He wiped his glasses without looking. "Thank you, Quinn." He smiled. "For saving me."

Quincy grinned. "Anytime. But please, not again anytime soon."

He laughed and walked way.

"Oh, and happy birthday," she called after him.

She slowly made her way to her bed, her hand brushing against the painted flowers along the wall. Her heart felt heavy, each beat counting down to the end of the school year. She closed her curtains and curled up in bed before pulling out the envelope from Monty's box. She broke the wax seal and pulled out the letter.

Dear Quinn,

It was a pleasure meeting you and getting to know you briefly. Time is an odd thing. You will probably read this less than a year after we first met, but for me, it has been just over ten years since we last spoke. I'm ill now and will not live much longer after writing this letter. I'm looking at my son, who now is only five days old, and even though I'm miserable about leaving him behind, I know he has good things and friends ahead of him. Please continue to keep an eye on him.

You came at an interesting crossroad in my life. You see, my grandmother wanted me to inherit the same key that was in this box, and we had argued viciously about it over the winter holidays before you showed up at Oakley. My great-great-grandfather was the man who built the molds for the four minor keys and was asked to keep ahold of one until a willing Master Key Bearer was ready to assemble the set. I'm sorry, but the secret behind the door died with him, and I have no idea what is hidden within.

I don't know what your plans are with my key, but I hope that Montgomery will be a more willing caretaker for it than I was originally. At eighteen years old, I didn't want to be in charge of something so potentially powerful. But when I saw you coming from the future because of my son being threatened, I realized that I needed to overcome my fears and grow up.

I have some difficult news for you now, but I fear that if you don't hear it from me, you may not be told in time. If you remember, I mentioned the fact that I had seen your key before. As I'm sure you have figured out by now, the key cannot be removed from the neck of a living Master Key Bearer. This means that the person that held the key during my youth has probably now died. I don't know how the key is passed down, but the last person to bear it was your mother, whom I loved dearly. I hope that you had a chance to spend more time with her than I was allowed to with my own son.

When I saw your key that first day, I understood the implications. I never told your mother that I had seen her key on your neck, and I'm sure that she lived life fully without that knowledge. This key business is ruthless, and I'm terribly sorry for all the pain that it has caused your family.

Be careful moving forward, Quinn, for you are not the only one who hunts the keys. I wish you the best of luck in finding the others.

I have helped you the best that I can before I die, and I know we will meet again in your future or my past.

Good luck with your quest, and I hope that you are prepared for what you will find behind the door.

Thank you,
Katelyn Prendergast-McCallister

Quincy read through the letter twice before folding it and placing it in her desk. She crawled into bed and shivered under the covers before falling fitfully asleep.

***

The raven perched on the edge of a grandfather clock and was feeling a desire to smack something, or rather *someone*. "Okay, okay. I admit it, you were right. So far," Talin growled.

The headmaster's lips curled into a smirking smile.

Talin harrumphed and fluffed his feathers. "You were right okay? How many times must I say it?"

"I'm not sure but I could get used to the idea that I'm in the right and you're in the—"

"Are you done yet? I admit that…I wasn't right."

The headmaster's whole body shook with laughter. "That will do Master Talin," he replied, still laughing.

Talin finally joined him with that throaty chuckle of his but he quickly grew somber. "Luther, we need to open that door," he said reluctantly.

"Are you absolutely sure," Marquam asked, sitting up straight.

Talin nodded slowly, his heart sinking. “Yes. Time deterioration is speeding up, and I’m losing my capability to...time jump, which is starting to leave gaps in my memory.”

“How can you be sure those two things are related?”

“I know it.” Talin growled. “I should have ended this centuries ago.”

“You told me yourself that you were incapable of dismantling whatever is behind that door.” The headmaster clasped his hands together. “Are you sure that I cannot know what is being kept there?”

Talin narrowed his eyes at the headmaster. “Positive.”

The headmaster nodded and bowed his head.

The raven shifted his weight. “So we have two of the five keys. It’s a good start. But it will only get more difficult for her. And honestly, I don’t know how much more help I can be to her if I can’t see what’s going to happen.” Talin breathed deeply through his beak. “And I don’t know if it’s because I’m failing or if there simply isn’t anything to see.”

Marquam clenched his fists. “As to the other keys, will Chenoweth keep his promise? Will he give his up?”

“The loon,” grumbled Talin. “He’d better.”

“We’ll just have to trust that he took care of things before he disappeared, I suppose,” the headmaster sputtered.

Talin looked at the window and stared at his reflection. “I can’t keep bumping into Wilbright,” he whimpered. “I have an emotional blind-spot for that boy.”

The headmaster looked at the window sadly. “I’m sorry. I take it he’s using the family key?”

Talin nodded.

“To what end?” the headmaster wondered.

“He wants something he cannot have,” Talin said with a sigh.

Marquam held his head in his hands. “Is it only Wilbright doing this?”

Talin snorted disdainfully. “He’s smart, but not that smart. He has help. The question is, whose help?” Talin added as he flew down to the headmaster’s desk and sighed. “During that midterm fiasco, Quinn told me about hearing laughter. In the fifteen years I’ve followed her, I’ve rarely seen her so scared. I don’t think it was the first time she heard it either,” he whispered.

“Do you think it could be—” the headmaster paused. “—him?”

Talin hissed. “For all of our sakes, we’d better hope not.”

The headmaster sat dejectedly in his chair. “Let’s focus on what we know and take things one step at a time. Perhaps you could talk to Wilbright’s—”

“Already ahead of you my old friend. For as much good as that will do. We’ll see,” Talin groaned.

“Good. So I’ll see you in the fall?”

Talin nodded. “After Miss Heatherwood’s, oh joy of joys,” he said sarcastically.

Luther Marquam stood up to look outside, and the raven flew to perch on his chair so that they could both watch the waterfall in silence.

CHAPTER THIRTY-ONE

AT YEAR'S END

Quincy walked into the hallway toward the headmaster's office in the Back Library. She stifled a yawn, the product of having stayed up too late during finals weeks. She couldn't believe that today was her last Independent Talent Study class for the school year.

The headmaster smiled as she walked in and gestured to her seat. "Welcome, are you ready for your final?"

Quincy nodded, and the headmaster began to find objects around the room and leave them on his desk. Her eyes widened when she counted fifteen, the compass among them.

"Are you ready?" he asked again.

"Yes, I think so," Quincy pushed out a smile still biting her lip. She closed her eyes and breathed deeply. In her mind, she caught the snapshot of the memory of the fifteen objects. She kept her eyes closed and recited them by memory.

"Acorn, teacup, candle, compass, pocket watch, spoon, shell, pinecone, feather, fountain pen, spectacles, whistle, hand bell, book, and flower."

"And for bonus points, what's the title of the book?"

Quincy frowned, keeping her eyes closed. "May I memory travel?"

"If you must."

Quincy breathed in deeply and released her mind to rewind until she watched the headmaster pull the book out from his desk. She smiled and looked up at the headmaster back in the present.

She grinned. "Famous Clocks."

The headmaster laughed and clapped his hands. "Excellent! Perfect score."

"Why did you choose that book?" Quincy asked.

The headmaster clasped his hands. "Because of its meaning to you. Now that you've finished with your exam, I've asked Montgomery to join us. Our mutual raven has asked not to be included in any way this afternoon." the headmaster said, staring seriously at Quincy.

"Wait. Has Talin told you everything?"

"Just what he thought I needed to know." the headmaster's eyes danced mischievously.

Their conversation was interrupted by a knock on the door.

"Ahh, Monty...Come in Mr. McCallister."

Monty walked into the office, not a speck of surprise registering on his face. He pulled a chair from the corner and sat down next to Quincy.

"Have you been here before?" she whispered.

Monty nodded.

"Montgomery is one of my other three Independent Talent Study students."

"My head thing is a difficult...Talent," Monty explained.

"Let's finish quickly so that you may join your classmates out in the sunshine," the headmaster requested. "May I please see both of your keys?"

Quincy and Monty looked at each other before pulling out their individual keys and showing them to the headmaster. Monty gave up his, and the headmaster studied it.

"Montgomery, I trust that you understand the importance of this key?"

"Yes, sir."

"Excellent. Since it was your mother's key, you should be the one to hold on to it." The headmaster handed the key back, and Monty placed it back in his pocket.

"Sir, do you know where the other keys are?" Quincy asked.

"Yes, and no. We know of a Scottish family who has one of the keys. And the gentleman seems to be using the key for his own benefit. Quincy, I don't think he'll simply give it up to you."

"So what do we need to do?" Quincy frowned.

"We will work on finding the other two keys first. One was lost during a break-in at a Swiss Bank two hundred years ago, and it hasn't been heard of since. Another was given to Marcus Chenoweth, a prominent Master Creative Engineer." The headmaster grimaced. "Unfortunately, we don't have any idea what he did with his key, either."

“I apologize for stating the obvious,” Monty said while wiping his glasses, “but it seems quite hopeless.”

The headmaster nodded. “It seems that way, yes. But we have help, and I’m sure together, we will be able to find some answers.”

Quincy worried her lower lip. There was still one question she really needed to know the answer to before they kept searching. “Do you know what’s behind the door, sir?”

The headmaster pursed his lips and frowned. “The only thing I know for sure is that we need to find out before others do. According to a friend,” —the headmaster looked over at Quincy— “it’s imperative that we do.”

The headmaster stood up, and Monty and Quincy followed suit.

“Keep yourselves safe, and let’s not mention any of this to anyone, all right?”

Quincy and Monty nodded simultaneously.

“Excellent. You are both dismissed.”

The two thanked him and walked out of the Back Library in silence.

“It does seem hopeless, doesn’t it?” Quincy groaned when they stepped out into the fresh air. She blinked in the sunshine.

Monty shrugged just as they were interrupted by a trumpet blast and a giggle from Eloise.

Quincy and Monty joined with Colin, Rusty, and Eloise on the front lawn. They had all just completed their last exams and were finished for the school year.

"Where are you all off to?" Quincy asked.

"I dug up some of the older blueprints in the library yesterday, and I found something called "the Templum" in the forest. We're going to explore." Eloise answered. "Want to come?"

Quincy and Monty locked eyes and smiled. "Lead on," Quincy laughed.

The five of them walked toward the forest and past the stable. When they arrived at the Templum, they all sat around the space in various vine seats. Rusty pulled a rose off a nearby bush and peeled off its petals one by one to find out if he had passed or failed Mathematics. Colin sketched the Templum while Monty quietly sat on a bench with a dreamy and empty expression on his face. Quincy and Eloise discussed the dresses they were planning to wear to dinner. The last night would be formal in honor of the end of exams and the semester.

"Can you believe that it's been a whole year already?" Eloise said as she flopped over on her stomach. They heard the Timepiece's echoes, and Eloise perked up. "Oooh, it's almost dinnertime!" She sat up and squealed. "We should be getting back to our floor now to get ready for tonight."

Rusty and Colin got up with Eloise, but Monty made no move to go anywhere.

"Sounds good," Quincy said. "I'll catch up with you guys in a minute."

Colin looked reluctant to leave but followed the other two toward the dormitories. After another minute, Monty sat up, rubbing his head.

"Seizure?" she asked.

He slowly nodded. "A minor one."

"Are you—"

"Ah, Colin wanted to speak with you about this evening," Monty rushed on, stopping her from asking about his seizure.

"Did he? I'm sure he'll find me later."

Monty nodded and stood up carefully. He rubbed his eyes and yawned.

"Anything else I should know?" Quincy teased.

"Not entirely. Though, I do appreciate the green dress." He grinned, his cheeks turning a bright pink. He quickly looked down and took off his glasses to clean them. Again.

Quincy frowned. "What green dress?"

"The one that you are going to wear tonight." Monty answered, pretending to cough.

"I'm wearing a blue dress." She narrowed her eyes at him.

"Oh?" He looked up. "All right, then," he answered, clearly not believing her. Quincy laughed and then pursed her lips, staring at Monty.

Without looking at her, he grinned at the sky. "You may ask," he permitted with a smile.

"Do you think you'll ever be able to control the …?" Quincy pointed to her head. "Knowing-what's-going-to-happen thing?"

"I hope so. Hence my excellent reason for staying in school."

Quincy's eyes widened, and before she could say anything, he laughed again and stood up next to her. He offered his hand. He helped her up, and they slowly made their way toward the dormitories.

At the family room door, Monty waved and walked off to the boy's room. Quincy walked into the girl's dormitory and saw Lindy eyeing the blue dress on her bed.

"Quincy, Quincy, Quincy! I *love* this blue, and we just happen to be about the same size! Would you be willing to trade dresses tonight?"

"What do you have?"

Lindy pulled out an emerald-colored dress, and Quincy laughed. "Yes, I'd be happy to trade."

Lindy squealed and began dancing around the room with the blue dress. Quincy put on the green dress and ended up liking it more than her own. She linked arms with Eloise, who of course, wore purple, and they walked down the stairs together. When they met up with the boys at the bottom of the staircase, Rusty, ever the southern gentleman, offered his arm to Eloise, who gladly took it as they began to talk about other things. Eloise gave Quincy an apologetic look, but Quincy smiled encouragingly back.

Both Colin and Monty came up from behind her. She turned to look at them. Had they been in a fight? Their eyes were narrowed and hands were clenched.

She put her hands on her hips. "What's up with you two?"

"Nothing," both boys said at the same time.

"Uh-huh," she answered, not believing either one of them. "Well then, if you'll both excuse me." She tried to walk past them, but Colin and Monty blocked her passage.

"Seriously?"

"You shouldn't be walking to the banquet without an escort." Colin said.

Monty shot him a frosty glare, and Quincy looked back and forth between her friends, her cheeks turning bright red.

"I have two arms," she muttered, her stomach in a tight knot.

Both of them looked unhappy at the suggestion but both also offered their arms. She couldn't get over the embarrassing sensation of people arguing over her attention. Too bad Genevieve had the flu. Genevieve's loss was her gain for the evening.

The dining hall sparkled for the occasion. Tapestries of their school mascot were hung from the walls, and a lifelike eagle hung from the ceiling. Everyone, including the professors and staff members, was dressed up for the night. The magnificent banquet had multiple courses of breads and cheeses, meats and soups, and finally countless small desserts. Everyone enjoyed it until no one could eat another bite.

The headmaster stood up to speak, and the room became instantly silent. "First of all, I would like to congratulate those of you who are leaving us next year to go on to other things. We all wish you the very best and look forward to seeing what you choose to do with your future. You will be missed."

Everyone clapped and whistled for their favorite Fourth Years. Quincy's friends high-fived Rachel, the only girl leaving from floor three.

"It has been a wonderful year in academics, sports, and the arts. We all"—the headmaster paused and motioned towards the staff—look forward to next year and the return of the rest of you all in the fall. "The headmaster's eyes twinkled at his rhyme while some students cheered and others groaned. "We hope that you have a fun, but safe, summer holiday. Be well."

***

Quincy shined an apple on her sleeve as she walked into the stable. She had pocketed the treat at dinner as a thank-you for Consto. Yesterday, she had actually enjoyed the polo match for Physical Education and Consto had only tried to throw her off once.

Consto took the apple and munched the fruit with ecstasy, spraying Quincy with the juice.

"Gross," she giggled.

Consto suddenly became eerily quiet and shrieked in Quincy's ear. Startled, she jumped back and caught the reflection of a flash of dark-red from a mirror behind her. She swung around, shaking. Consto continued to kick at the door and Quincy made soothing noises until the horse gradually slowed down. She frowned and closed her eyes until she felt the tips of her fingers tingle. She slowly replayed the moment of Consto's panic until she paused on the mirror's reflection.

It was unmistakably the man in burgundy from her worst nightmares. He had been here, at Oakley, and in the flesh.

If Consto had seen him, it meant that the man in burgundy wasn't a product of her imagination. This man actually existed.

She stared at the jet black horse, who had gone back to munching oats, and wondered how many times Consto had seen the man and reacted in fear.

She gently patted the velvety nose until the horse tried to nip her fingers. She slowly walked through the stable and back up toward the dormitory, checking each hallway and corridor as she passed.

***

The next morning, after final promises of letters from Eloise, Monty, and Mikaela, Quincy waved good-bye and walked towards the eagles. She had left most of her possessions behind in her room. She did not want her things to conveniently "disappear" at Miss Heatherwood's or to break like her music box. Her trunk felt much lighter now and more manageable. Even so, Colin helped her to get it down the stairs.

"I look forward to seeing you at the start of the next year, Quincy," he said. "Hope you have a good holiday."

"If I make it through the summer," Quincy mumbled under her breath. But she looked up at Colin and smiled. "Thanks. You too. I'll see you soon."

Colin waved and ran to catch up with Rusty as she dejectedly followed the crowd toward the horses. She looked back one last time to see if she could spot the raven. She had secretly hoped that he would find her, or that she would bump into him, before she left. He seemed to be impossible to find if he did not wish to be found.

Quincy found her friends waiting for her at the field for the trip back. She smiled stiffly, pretending to be excited when hearing her friend's plans for the summer. Even Monty would be taking a trip to Switzerland with his aunt and uncle.

When they asked her what she would be doing, though, she simply replied that she would do some horseback riding and maybe some studying. She felt almost relieved when the eagle finally landed. Mrs. Adalin stepped out the carriage at the end of the field and waved. Quincy was about to walk toward her when she felt a tap to her shoulder. She turned around and was face-to-face with Monty.

"Quincy, in case something goes terribly wrong and you need help, here is my address. My aunt and uncle will come to your aid. I will do some research on my own with regard to..." He looked around and made sure that no one was watching them, then pointed to the key around Quincy's neck.

"I will tell you whatever I manage to uncover when we meet back in the fall," he promised. "I think it would be best not to put anything secret in the post."

She agreed and imagined another student at Miss Heatherwood's getting ahold of her mail.

"Everything will turn out as it is meant to be," he added. "Just keep your head down and count the days until school resumes."

Quincy gave him a hug, which at first he tensed to, but then he hugged her back.

"Americans," he teased.

"Thank you, Monty."

He began walking in the direction of his aunt and uncle when he stopped suddenly.

"Oh, and Quinn? Thank *you*…for everything." He bowed his head and then disappeared into the crowd.

Quincy closed her eyes and took one last breath of freedom before returning to Miss Heatherwood's.

***

Wilbright shivered in the unnaturally dark room and waited for his partner to speak. He tried to stand in what little light had been left in the chamber. He usually enjoyed the nighttime, but he could not trust the shadows in this room. He wondered if these particular shadows were the ones that moved. Those scared him to the depths of his soul. He wanted desperately to leave and go back downstairs, but the other man had chosen to let him sweat by leaving him in silence. He looked over at the red hawk perched on the chair and chills ran down his arms when he saw it looking directly at him.

"So what do you wish to do now?" a shadowy man finally asked.

“I have a number of other ideas that I’m working on. I will let you know when I have chosen the best way to proceed.” Wilbright answered, fighting to keep his voice neutral.

Prieler nodded. “You may leave me now if that’s all you have to say.”

“I’ll keep you informed.” Wilbright said as he slowly backed away toward the fireplace door.

“You do that,” Prieler answered evenly.

Wilbright retreated as fast as he could. He hated that he had put himself in this position. Prieler made him nervous with how emotionless he had become. He had showed neither anger nor any other emotional outburst when Wilbright had brought the news. This lack of emotion scared him more than anything he could have said or done to him. It had all started with his experiment and the resulting silhouetted shadows—the stuff of nightmares, but he knew that it was none of his business. That was part of Prieler’s job, not his.

Shaking, Wilbright walked away.

***

Prieler waited for Wilbright to leave the room before moving to the window and gazing at his own reflection in the glass. He had dark circles under his eyes that stared back at him.

“Tell me, Iblis, does this mirror image represent the person for who they are or the mask we all wear?”

Prieler grasped his dark cloak closer to his body, and the hawk-like bird that had been perched on a seat nearby looked up at the shadowy form at the window. The bird launched off the chair and landed on two feet. The hawk disappeared, revealing a tall man with fiery-red hair and a three-piece burgundy suit to match. His physique put him at no more than forty years of age, yet the dark depth in eyes hinted that he must be considerably older than he looked.

"You do not doubt yourself now?" he asked quietly in his deep and honeyed voice.

"Of course not. We've come too far."

"Good."

"What do you wish to do about Talin?"

Iblis hissed, and for a brief moment, he lost his gentlemanly facade. He clenched his fists, and his dark eyes turned blood red, and bright sparks of fire seemed to emanate from his body. He quickly regained his composure and looked over at Prieler. "I'll take care of him. Talin is mine."

Prieler agreed. "And the girl?"

"As for the girl, we'll simply wait for Wilbright's next plan. He'll find her. The rest will follow in due course."

Acknowledgments

This page was difficult to write. Looking back at the twelve years it took me to write this novel, I remember the friends, family, classmates, and coworkers who had a hand in its creation and development. There simply wasn't enough space to list you all. If you're not here, I'm sorry, but I'm so thankful for your help.

First and foremost, thank you, parents for your love, encouragement, and for believing in me. And Titi, too!

Thank you, Auntie Norma Grastorf and my dear friends Nancy Clausen and Helen Gilbert. I wish I could have shared this book with you.

Thank you to my second family: Kate, Jon, and the terrific trio, Grace, Orion and Pirate. Thanks for being my guinea pigs, make-up artist, and photographer.

To the ones who've had to hear all about QH over and over again: Cassie, Kaley, Miki, Kate, Stephen, Monica, Chelsea, and Paul...you guys are the best. And to the customers and coworkers throughout the years who have been kind enough to ask me about the progress. And the Turnbulls, my Canadian fam.

And for Helen. I would have given up long ago without your help and encouragement. Also to Alex for his help with all of the design work and proving that the Timepiece faces could theoretically work.

To Dan. (Have you all seen the amazing cover/illustrations in this book?) I'm overwhelmed by your generosity and Talent.

To Danielle, editor extraordinaire. I cannot thank you enough for your time and guidance.

To my writers group: Sarah, Jean, Kassie, and especially to Jordan for getting me to the finish line. I look forward to reading all of your stories.

To all the teachers throughout my life. I would not be where I am without you. I wish I had space to thank you all by name. Mr. Hottman, thank you for being the first editor. That first draft was pretty awful...

To my test readers: Geoffroy, Allen, Katie, Kurt, Lanie, Christopher, Perry, Erin, Kelsey, Soojin, Nikki, and Megan, and the others that didn't make this list, your help, thoughts, and ideas made this book what it is..

And finally, thank you to Brian Jacques, C.S Lewis, J.R.R Tolkien, JK Rowling, Eoin Colfer, Lemony Snicket, Rick Riordan, Sarah Maas, Kiera Cass, Maggie Stiefvater, and the countless other authors who have transported me to another world. Waiting for your next book (or a ride to the library) forced me to create a world of my own. Thank you.

CPSIA information can be obtained
at www.ICGtesting.com
Printed in the USA
FSOW02n1006100317
31769FS